The Sea Pearl

The Sea Pearl

By

Eileen Thennis

ISBN: 978-0-6151-8132-5

Produced in the United States of America
by
Eileen Thennis
in affiliation with
EZT Books and Specialties
11222 Cedar Drive
Mabank, Texas 75156-8929

The Sea Pearl

CHAPTER ONE
1692

Mr. Silvas, a prominent English trader, paced the floor of the library within his stately mansion. His step lingered alongside the oak desk. A note, delivered earlier by courier, lay open on the green felt blotter. The elderly man's eyes rested on the scrawled words: *Sea Pearl anchored off shore in darkness, sails furled, awaits your arrival. Co-captain comes to escort you to the pier.* The message ended with the specific time to expect the clandestine visitor.

Fists clenched, Mr. Silvas tapped lightly against the paper with whitened knuckles. His eyes shifted to the clock on the wall. Almost time. He reached an unsteady hand into a lacquered box atop the fireplace mantel and drew forth a lucifer. A quick scratch of the tip against a fireplace brick and the lucifer burst into flame. With this he ignited the paper in his other hand and tossed the message onto the blazing logs of the fireplace. Again his eyes lifted to the clock.

"Why isn't he here?" he quietly spoke, breath constrained. "Captain Andrew Leyden, my former partner and friend, like myself, has seen his day. With a price on his head, he dares not step on English soil. Therefore, it's understandable why his reliable young co-captain should be sent---why then has he not arrived?"

The worn face tightened. "I'll give him three more minutes. If not here by then---" Lean fingers raked through his hair, grayed by time and distress. Aware of the action, he jerked his arms down. "I must remain calm. We knew this was a hazardous venture from the onset."

Thoughts crashed about in his mind. Have the port authorities spotted The Sea Pearl? If so, Andrew is in dire danger. Its fame as a pirate ship was a complete misconception.

"Buccaneers, indeed!" he sneered. "There's no such thing as a buccaneer. It's a misnomer created by those ignorant of the vast difference between a bucaner and a privateer. What do these English people know about the goings on along the *Spanish Main* operations in the *Caribbean Sea* area? They've mistakenly combined the two factions to coin the word buccaneer. The crew of *The Sea Pearl is* composed of honest hard working bucaners, not a pack of thieving privateers in search of adventure and riches." What if, the aged man wondered, Andrew's man, Captain Brett, has been waylaid enroute by the King's Guards? Without him all hope is lost. *The Sea Pearl* is our only escape."

Music, laughter and voices, produced by the lavish party underway elsewhere in the mansion, drifted to his ears. He had deliberately planned every element to the last detail. Trays, laden with delicacies to please the most discerning palates, lured guests to indulge themselves. Heady spirits flowed like honey from the gods.

Beyond the library walls he could hear tongues, loosened by intoxication, now bold with flagrant language. Promiscuous advances were being made toward the opposite sex in the spacious parlor and along the dimly lighted verandah. Musicians, on his orders, played louder than usual to camouflage other sounds within the house that may arouse suspicion.

All this preparation was important. To error meant disaster. Mr. Silvas' step hesitated beside the desk as he mentally went over the carefully prepared guest list. It included, he assured himself, everyone of prestigious status in England. Earlier in the evening he made a brief appearance among them and spoke to each in turn. In case of failure verification of his presence may be needed. He had then unobtrusively retreated at the first opportunity to the privacy of the library down the hall. Actions taken within the immediate hours ahead must be carried out with utmost discretion. His guests must not know of his departure from the premises. "The revelry will soon reach its peak," he speculated aloud. "Timing is important if my escape plan is to succeed."

He slammed a fist into a hand. "Where is he!" The thin shoulders beneath the expensive suit sagged. The clock began to chime the hour. With each measured drop of the mechanism's hammer, the shoulders sank lower. England's grisly Debtors Prison waited, where the condemned were left to suffer a slow and miserable death. His only alternative was an attempt to escape to a new land. If he chose the latter, and was caught, he risked sudden death by the Royal Guards. To his mind, death was preferable to chains.

The clock, loud on his ears, neared the end of its hourly chime cycle. Young Captain Brett had not arrived. The plan failed. He drew a ragged breath, resigned to the fate before him.

Meanwhile, under cover of darkness Niles Brett, together with his black companion, Toro, had set out for shore in a landing boat. They glided in without a sound, Toro at the oars, to broadside a wharf in the harbor. The hour was late; the dock, for the most part, was deserted. He vaulted from the craft with ease onto the thick heavy planks of the time-weathered wharf. His nostrils immediately rebelled against the repulsive stench of rotted fish and decay. He signaled with a light tap of a boot heel; the black silently slipped the small boat into the shadows of the wharf. Toro would wait, hidden, until his captain returned with the rescued party.

A cold winter fog swirled through the garbage laden streets and alleyways. Before Niles entered within the dim glow of light he paused, adjusted his tricorne to partially conceal his face, and drew the fine leather gauntlets tighter on his hands. Should any trouble emerge from the shadows, it paid to be prepared. With the dexterity of a phantom, he wove undetected through the maze of dark streets and alleys. Familiar with harbor activities and piracy operations of the *Spanish Main,* he was in his element. Within a very short time he reached the elite section of the port city.

A faint whistle, and a horse drawn carriage approached an appointed corner of the cobblestone road. He leaped inside as it came abreast. The carriage rolled on, gradually increasing in speed, its pace slowing several blocks later behind the carriage house of the stately Silvas mansion.

Niles Brett lowered himself to the soft ground and paused a moment to straighten his clothes. With a cloth drawn from an inside pocket of his coat, he wiped the harbor dust from polished leather boots. Satisfied with his appearance, he began a stealthy advance through the well trimmed formal gardens behind the estate.

Amid the noisy debauchery Mr. Silvas, caught up in his own profound sense of defeat, had failed to hear the arrival of his awaited guest. The library door opened as the last chime completed its reverberation. Mr. Silvas whirled about and stepped forward to grasp the young man's hand. The two faced each other, both fully aware of the serious risks they were about to take.

Niles saw before him a once successful importer of the late 1600's. His scrutiny instantaneously took in the proud shoulders of the slight of build older man, now bent under the weight of recent disastrous business ventures. Tired eyes from within a haggard face reached out to him in a desperate plea for help.

In turn, he watched Mr. Silvas appraise his unlikely guest. A thin smile of approval tugged at the lined face. "Ah, Captain, I see you have chosen to appear the epitome of a suave, distinguished, English gentleman of the day. Andrew has told me of your exceptional talents of disguise. I must agree, no one would suspect your true profession." The eyes brightened. "If any man possesses the expertise to make this flight possible, I fully believe you are the one. I have the utmost faith in Andrew's judgment."

Aware of the urgency of timing, Niles asked in lowered tones, "Everything ready?"

"All except one subject that is more important than my own life." He moved toward the drape obscured window, and closed a hand around the thick silk bell cord alongside. "I shall signal my servant to bring Victoria immediately. She knows nothing of our plans."

Niles stiffened. His eyes darted toward the elderly gentleman. "Victoria?"

The hand hesitated a moment on the cord. "Yes, Victoria. Didn't Andrew mention her?"

Niles quelled the reaction of disapproval that threatened to flash across his island tanned face. One curled end of his smartly waxed mustache twitched on his otherwise shaven face. "He made no mention of a woman. I understood this dangerous undertaking involved only the two of us."

"Surely he did not presume I would leave her behind while I fled to safety. I could never abandon her to suffer mistreatment in the hands of the Royal Guards as a result of my own misjudgments.

Niles forced himself to appear relaxed. "Likely only an oversight." However, this sudden revelation, he calculated, presented more than a few serious problems. To pirate Mr. Silvas out of England was one thing; an aged wife could prove complicated. En-route from the harbor he had the opportunity to see first hand the difficulties they faced. To transport a tottering old woman through those streets may, indeed, prove disastrous. Alone, he managed to arrive without detection. Two men on the return would be doubly difficult. A woman? Preposterous! If we are to evade the guards speed is essential. Even if we reach the wharf, how can I possibly transfer a senile woman from the unsteady landing craft to the *Pearl's* deck?

My beloved mentor, Captain Leyden, occasionally plays the trickster but this is downright ridiculous. To take risks with another person's life is not something one jests about. His thoughts on the matter, however, were interrupted as a soft rustle entered the room.

A vision of unexpected loveliness floated toward them. Niles involuntarily caught his breath. Accustomed to island women, he stared speechless at this regally poised young lady. He felt hot fire begin to course through his veins. This goddess possessed the delicate facial features and slender form of a finely sculpted figurine. Engrossed, he drank of her rare beauty. Mr. Silvas quickly stepped to close the door, took her hand, and presented her to Niles.

"This is my daughter, Victoria."

Niles stood entranced, immobilized by the shock of this revelation. He watched her sapphire eyes take in the thick blue-black waves that cascaded onto his strong shoulders. They moved to the firm jaw line above the ruffled silk lace at his throat. Interest aroused, her attention slid to the brocade waistcoat; the rich fabric shimmered with each rise and fall of his broad chest. The fitted black topcoat, adorned with ornate gold buttons, did not escape her appraisal. Nor did the strong sinewy legs within tight trousers and polished high boots. He watched one shapely eyebrow lift in approval. It clearly indicated, ah, here is a real man worthy of my considerations!

When their eyes again met, he glimpsed a heightened glow of excitement equal to his own. Her gracious smile held a hint of flirtation; hypnotic perfume tantalized his senses. The whisper of the elegant gown was as distant music, gentle as the kiss of a soft breeze on his ears. She offered her hand with the smooth grace of a swan. A profusion of tiny jewels, sprinkled like stars among the folds of her evening gown, responded to her every movement. Abruptly he recovered his manners. Bowing with a sweep of his ostrich plumed tricorne hat, he took the extended hand and touched his lips to the scented fingertips.

Returning to an erect stance, his attention was drawn to the sheen of the dark brunette hair piled high upon her head. Moreso, his experienced eye recognized the string of natural pearls twined among the curls was of exceptional quality.

Mr. Silvas eyed the two before him and chose to intercept. "Victoria, my dear, this gentleman is Mr. Brett." Niles remained transfixed in the moment. Again Mr. Silvas broke the silence, voice crisp, "Formalities dispensed, I shall get right to the point. Time is short." Her rapt absorption with this stranger disturbed him. Brows drawn together with a father's concern for the protection of a daughter, his tone took on an edge. "Victoria?"

Niles, meanwhile, remained preoccupied with an appreciation of her fair skin, proud tilt of head, and flash of a flawless diamond and ruby choker. Nor did he fail to appraise the socially acceptable bosom cleavage visible above a trim, tightly corseted waist---a waist so tiny he longed to partake the pleasure of his hands around it.

"Victoria!" her father insisted.

With obvious regret, her eyes shifted from this adventurous newcomer; yet she made no effort to remove her hand. "Yes, Father?"

"First, Daughter, a word of caution. Contrary to appearance, you must not mistake Mr. Brett for a typical young Englishmen to tease with your charms. This is none other than the renown Captain Niles Brett of *The Sea Pearl.*"

The hand quickly withdrew as if it touched something contaminated. She whirled away with a superior air. "What is a vile pirate of his reputation doing in our house?"

Apparently, Niles calculated, she has already painted a gruesome picture in her mind of the two reputedly notorious captains. No surprise. Vastly exaggerated tales sweep the ports about our operations on the *Pearl.*

Normally, the erroneous judgments of others did not bother him. However, he found himself very disturbed by what this lady thought of him. He wanted to reach out, make her understand he was not the heartless, bloodthirsty privateer those overblown stories implied. "Victoria," Mr. Silvas groped for the right words, "time is of an essence. There's no gentle way to say what must be said. I deliberately withheld information from you about our financial situation until now. It was imperative I carry out my plan for this night with the utmost secrecy."

Deaf to his words, she pointed a finger of accusation at Niles. "Father, this villainous-"

"Patience, my Child," he raised a hand for silence. "I shall try to explain. You see, several business deals did not go well for me the past few years. In short, I gambled deeply on shiploads of merchandise. Those ships, sorry to say, were overtaken. All my investments were lost to gluttonous privateers. I tried to protect you, but the time for truth has arrived. We are penniless. My debts have forced me to take action tonight."

She turned on Niles, face distorted with contemptuous disdain. "I'm sorry, Father, but as I see it, you can blame the likes of this Captain Brett, and all the other scum of his breed!"

With a haughty toss of head, her lips curled into an ugly snarl. "As for you, Captain Brett, it takes insidious gall to come here after your kind stole from us! I shall ring to have you immediately put out of this house. The Royal Guards shall slap you in irons before the night is out." She spun about and reached for the bell cord. Her father's firm hand closed upon her wrist.

Her temperamental display filled Niles with disappointment and revulsion. Gone was the feminine grace, the flirtatious smile, the musical voice. Instead, he saw a woman---proud, haughty, spoiled, and yes, downright obnoxious. He felt an uncontrollable anger rise to the cords of his throat; not in response for the accusations she made, no, it was because she destroyed the beautiful illusion of moments ago. Lessons learned as a lad along the *Spanish Main* ran through his mind and now took precedence over personal emotions. When he again spoke, his voice was calm, yet emphatic.

"Miss Victoria, we never consciously attacked, nor robbed from your father. To set the record straight, it's not the practice of the *Pearl* to attack other ships."

"Ha!" her head threw back with a contemptuous sniff. "You pirates attack anything you can lay your greedy hands on.

You're nothing more than a pack of thieves and murderers!"

"No, my Child, you are wrong," Mr. Silvas interceded. "I have the utmost confidence in Captain Brett."

"Confidence! You would believe a bloodthirsty pirate?"

"Not only do I believe him, but I also believe in my friend, Andrew Leyden. They never knowingly fired on, nor confiscated anything of mine. *The Pearl* got cargo through when no one else could. If that were not so, we would have come to this---"

"Father!" she feinted disgust. "Andrew Leyden is a criminal. He carries a price on his head throughout England."

"I know Andrew is an honorable man," he asserted. "He killed a member of the Royal Guard who attempted to molest his wife. That doesn't make him bad."

Victoria cast aside her father's statement of justification. "Think what you like. I've heard much about the notorious indiscretions of *The Sea Pearl*, none of it good."

"Victoria, enough. While we stand and quibble, valuable time is wasted. Captain Brett came for us at great risk to his own safety. We should be grateful."

Victoria forced a twisted sneer to the corner of her delicately rouged mouth. "I'm sure the King's Guards will thank us if we turn him over to them. Think of the sizable reward we can collect, Father."

"I'm shocked, Victoria!" Mr. Silvas pounded a fist into the palm of his hand. "Be a Judas to Andrew? Never! We'll owe much to him before this night is out. Now be silent while I explain our plan."

"Please do, Father. I'm just dying to hear your explanation for this despicable man's presence in our respectable home."

"He came to help us slip out of the country."

Her breath caught in shocked disbelief. "Leave England? You can't be serious. Surely there is be a better alternative."

"Not this time, my dear. I'm deeply in debt to creditors, and without funds to supply their demands. I considered every possibility, and arrived at an undeniable conclusion. Only three avenues remain open to us."

"And of the three you choose to trust our lives to the likes of Captains Brett and Leyden?"

"To flee the country with them is not the most serious thing that can happen to us, my daughter. The captains propose to take us to a colony in America. There we can start a new life away from all this."

"America? Our roots and home are here in England."

"I said there were three choices. Now for the second. Any moment the Guards may arrive at our door to lock us in Debtors Prison."

"No!" a delicate hand flew to her rosy mouth. Tears misted her eyes.

"Don't interrupt until I finish. There is so little time," he cautioned. "The third option is to hide from the authorities. Many others have tried, and failed. We could live, for a time, in fear and shame among the rats and other vermin down among the decrepit lodging houses of the waterfront scum. Eventually though, we would be discovered and hauled off to the dungeons, you included, my dear.

"Now I ask, what shall it be? Debtors Prison, hide in the squalor and stench of the slums, or---" he offered a hand toward Niles, "escape with what honor and respectability we have left?"

Victoria had listened, stunned and

speechless, to the cold, factual alternatives. Watching her face Niles recalled the slum area he observed when he slipped ashore. It was not, by any standards, a pleasant place for a lady of refinement.

Added to the foulness of the waterfront, carousing voices drifted from crowded taverns and bawdyhouses, where the cast offs of England's society intermingled. He saw them as no different than the down and outers in the many other ports he chanced to visit in the past. Ochre yellow lights, filtered through dirty windows, rested upon rubbish littered streets. The narrow thoroughfares crawled with all nature of vermin.

The raucous alehouses and doors of ill repute that lured the wayward were all very similar to other dens of lust found in any port of the seventeenth century---with one exception, that is. Nicole's ladies, he was quick to admit, sported far more gifts of promise than these impersonators of delight. Nicole, after all, operated the most refined establishment of its kind in his homeport of Jamaica.

Vaguely through his preoccupation, he heard Mr. Silvas' urgent pleas. "It is far too late for tears, Victoria. We must hurry. The Guards, thank God, were busy with other upsets the past few days; else they would have already arrived to arrest us."

Victoria whimpered. "If we went into hiding, don't you think it would be poss---"

"No!" he slammed a fist on the desktop. "Damned if I will see you there! Have you any idea what becomes of women amid that discreditable area?"

"I need time," she wailed. "Time to pack all my lovely things."

"Your satchel waits in the carriage."
"One satchel? Surely, Father, you jest!"
"One satchel. That is final."

Precious minutes slipped away; Niles became more anxious. If they were to clear the harbor undetected the timing of fog, wind, and tide must be perfect. One spit polished boot shifted on the thick carpet. The movement attracted the eye of the older man.

Mr. Silvas looked from Niles to Victoria. "We shall leave by the back door. Go directly to the carriage house in the rear. My driver already waits to take us to the ship."

"I must change into clothes appropriate for travel," Victoria demurred.

"You will go as you are," her father ordered. "Captain Brett, do you wish to add anything at this point?"

"Only that we must move with utmost haste. From the time we leave this room, we face grave danger. Let's hope the fog will provide a screen for us until we are safely aboard the *Pearl*. Once there, pray for sufficient wind and tide to slip her out to sea."

"Then so be it, and may the Saints travel with us," Mr. Silvas declared. He took his daughter's elbow, and urged her to the pathway that led to the carriage house.

Niles, unaccustomed to the damp chill of English winters, shivered beneath the tailored coat. Ahead, Victoria's taffetas whispered, and her perfume drifted to tantalize his nostrils. The scent brought pleasant memories of warm nights on subtropical islands, where the fragrance of exotic blooms permeated gentle breezes. With an effort he checked himself and recalled her display of temperament while in the library. He darted through the open carriage house door, and again adjusted the tricorne solidly upon his head. The driver, hand outstretched, hastened to assist the lady. The horses stamped in readiness. Harnesses jangled. To Niles' cautious ears, the sound seemed amplified amid the night.

"Easy there boys, easy," the groom softly crooned in an effort to quiet them in the traces.

Mr. Silvas' butler rushed forward to cry an alarm. "Hurry Master! Guards approach."

A smart snap of reins---the team bolted---the carriage wheels spun onto the curved drive. The handsome steeds emerged from the shadows of the mansion at a full gallop.

Niles caught a glimpse of brightly colored uniforms. A shout rose from the leader. "After them! They attempt an escape!"

The carriage careened onto the cobblestone street, rounded a corner, precariously tilting on only two wheels. Mr. Silvas cried out, "Someone alerted the Guards!"

The fugitives sped through the roadways and alleys leading to the waterfront district. Niles, within the darkness of the coach, nodded with satisfaction. I should have guessed Mr. Silvas would possess the finest horseflesh to make this run. Fortunate for us, for time is now at a premium. Our very lives are at stake. Even if we succeed to rendezvous with Toro, it can prove a hazardous distance before we reach *The Sea Pearl* anchored offshore.

Luck and time, however, did not ride with them this night. The hoof beats of the Guards' horses drew closer in pursuit as the escapees veered around another sharp corner.

"Faster!" Mr. Silvas shouted to the driver, voice scarcely heard above the jangle of harness chains and rattle of wheels over the cobblestones. "Victoria, hold on tight!"

The leather whip cracked over the heads of the team. The carriage lurched toward the shabby lodging house district. To Niles' surprise, Victoria bore the tooth jarring discomforts without complaint. There was little time, however, to waste on the distraction of her composure, or lack of it. His attention was focused on the blackness and fog to their rear. How much edge did they have on the Guards?

They sped ever deeper into the decrepit waterfront district. The pair of bays plunged headlong down the refuse strewn streets; the pound of their hooves sent emaciated dogs and derelicts scurrying to safety. The top-heavy carriage whipped around another sharp turn. Again it threatened to overturn. The coachman drew the horses to a sudden halt. Their nostrils flared noisily; white lathered sides heaved with the exertion. Directly ahead lay the shoreline and wharf of the waterfront.

Niles leaped off before the wheels ceased to turn. He reached to swing the lady down. "Quickly, Victoria, out!" her father shouted. "Run, girl, run! Follow Captain Brett!"

She clutched her skirts and attempted obedience. The toe of one satin slipper caught on the uneven planks and sent her sprawling headlong onto the foul pier. In answer to her cry, Niles, without a break in stride, quickly scooped her upright.

The end of the dock lay directly ahead.

He gave a low whistle. A dark shadow slipped noiselessly from the shadows beneath. Toro at the oars, it drew parallel to receive its passengers. Niles leaped downward and turned to assist the hesitant lady.

"Fall forward. I'll catch you."

Overcome by fear the Guards would close in, she obeyed. The elegant gown billowed in midair above his extended arms. Strong hands about her waist, he swung her down to the craft. Mr. Silvas jumped next, steadied by the powerful Toro.

The small boat surged forward.

"Hurry, Toro!" Niles urged. "They're directly on our aft!" The black laid his muscular arms to the oars with the dexterity of expert seamanship. The light craft shot forward through the water.

"Seen any other ships that may give

chase after we reach the *Pearl*?"

"No Suh, Cap'n Brett. Fog be so thick you no see the devil, himself, if he stare you right in eye."

"Good. At least that much is in our favor. If we can't see them, it means they can't see us. However, now that the wind has begun to rise it will quickly dissipate this fog cover."

Muscles across Toro's broad chest bulged. The craft lunged with each rhythmic dip of the oars toward a scarcely discernible yellow glow that penetrated the damp mists. Cold seawater sprayed their faces. A quick glance over his shoulder told Niles the Guards were at the pier. Dull thuds of wood against wood indicated preparations were underway for them to follow.

A few random shots rang out into the night. The projectiles, as yet out of range, fell ineffectually into the water. The escapees continued their flight. The yellow glow grew brighter. Toro laid all his strength onto the oars. The dark form of *The Sea Pearl* loomed into sight, lantern slung at her bowsprit; like a beacon, it glowed to guide the swiftly approaching craft.

They were almost there.

The Royal Guards closed in fast.

Shots splashed ever nearer their target.

The fugitives dared not fire back; to do so, would reveal their precise location in the fog curtain. Nor could the ship's firepower come to their rescue. Niles had left orders to remain silent until his charges were safely on deck. To fire earlier opened the possibility they may hit the wrong target. Defenseless, Toro pressed hard for the shelter of the ship. Voice low, Niles turned to Victoria and Mr. Silvas huddled together in the rear.

"There will be a ratline---a rope ladder---alongside the hull. The moment we strike her side, Mr. Silvas, grab the ropes and climb. When you reach the top the crew will help you over the side. Victoria, you follow immediately below your father. Toro and I will steady the ropes and give assistance from below."

Victoria, in defense of her dignity as a woman, began to object. Niles could see his suggestion she mount a rope ladder in skirts with a stranger below, to her mind, was unthinkable.

Her father came to his rescue. "Child! This is no time to question Captain Brett's orders." The man cringed when more projectiles whined overhead. "Do as he says. Any moment, one of those balls may find its mark!"

The craft scraped and bumped against the *Pearl's* broadside. Niles' hand felt the familiar thickness of the coarse, tar coated rope. "Quickly, Mr. Silvas! Grab hold and climb. Fast!" Rocked and swayed by the craft, the older man, satchel in hand, scrambled forward on unsteady legs. He groped for the rope in the darkness. Niles shoved it into his hand, and urged him upward.

He soon saw the man was in distress. It would be a challenge in itself for an amateur to scale the unfamiliar flexible ropes with both hands. Mr. Silvas, heavy leather satchel in one hand, was left with only one hand to master the ladder---a difficult undertaking even for an experienced seaman. "Damned!" Niles cursed aloud. He knew there was nothing anyone could do at this point to assist the man in his struggle.

Musket balls struck the hull with sharp, splat sounds. Each hit sent a shower of wood slivers down upon the landing boat and into the water. Victoria's cumbersome skirts, timidity, and vanity were not what Niles would have chosen for a fast escape. To manipulate those skirts in a manner to free her feet on the rope rungs posed a problem. With half the king's army about to bear down, the situation became even more complex. He steadied, half carried, her into position at the base of the ladder, and placed her hands on the ropes.

"I can't do it!" she screamed, and struggled to break free.

"Yes, you can! Put your foot on the first rope sling," he instructed. "Now climb!"

Another burst from the pursuit boats struck the hull directly beside the pair. The impact forced them to turn aside to protect their faces from flying wood.

"I can't!" she cried in terror. "I can't see the ropes!"

"Never mind. Here, close your hands around these ropes. I'll guide your feet into place from below. When you feel your foot on the rope, slide your hands along the ropes and pull yourself upward."

"I shall never make it!"

"You must! Now climb, unless you want to die," he ordered. Trembling violently she began a slow ascent. It did not require an expert to see the Silvas' were inexperienced to the sea, ropes, roll of ship, and flying balls. "Faster!" he urged. Amid the confusion the petite, high heeled, satin slippers made him acutely conscious of the slender, trim ankles, warm and feminine under his hands. He cursed himself for the distraction.

Overhead a volley of shot peppered the hull. Mr. Silvas gave a cry of dismay. The satchel he had so carefully guarded plummeted downward. Toro, in a vain attempt at recovery, extended an arm. Alas, the cumbersome leather bag passed beyond his reach, splashed and sank from sight into the watery depths of the harbor. Niles, vision obscured by Victoria's skirts, could not see what was happening above. His concentration was centered on how much longer it would take to get Victoria aboard.

Increased shots, splashes and shouts told him his crew had begun to return fire. They struck their marks with whatever firepower each man drew from his thick leather belt. Voices on deck indicated Mr. Silvas reached the top. Behind, the Guard leader shouted his men forward. With a wild splash of oars, they tried to close the distance before the last of the fugitives succeeded to ascend to safety. Any moment Niles expected to feel the hot flame of a ball strike his back.

He struggled for patience, teeth tightly clenched. Victoria's skirts brushed against the plumed tricorne. Dislodged from his head, it floated down to bob on the water surface below. Just as well, he thought to himself. If the Guards discover the hat they may assume one of their shots struck its mark. Let them think my body joined Mr. Silvas' satchel at the bottom of the harbor; deception never hurt at time like this. Quickly he placed another slippered foot. His sensitive hands detected the frightened tremble of the ankle.

Directly overhead the first mate called out. "We got her!" Victoria's weight shifted; the crew lifted her to safety. In an instant, Niles vaulted over the rail with Toro directly behind. Before their boots struck the deck the crew sprang into action.

"Full sail!" the first mate cried. Men ran to their posts and began to work the heavy ropes. Others dashed to the capstan to weigh anchor.

"Douse that lantern!" Niles pointed. Toro ran to comply. A light breeze rippled and caught at the fast unfurling canvases. A familiar quiver underfoot told Niles the *Pearl* was underway.

The Silvas' were momentarily forgotten amid the crucial work at hand. Every man labored at his appointed post. Each knew, without orders from their two captains, precisely what must be done to accomplish flight. The sails caught the wind, billowed, and *The Sea Pearl* slipped toward the open sea. None too soon; the fog screen had broken.

Victorious, Niles threw up his arms in a signal of triumph. The white lace fluttered at his throat as, boots planted apart on the fore of the poop deck, the breeze played through the waves of his long dark hair. The Guards, left behind in the ship's wake, shook their fists in anger. A single cannon on the *Pearl's* stern roared a jubilant farewell over the heads of the losers.

For the captains and crew this part of the operation was little different from many other times in the past. Often they entered a port and, upon discovering their safety threatened, made a quick retreat. Everyone worked together to fine tune the *Pearl* into a smoothly operated ship: a ship both Niles and Captain Leyden were proud to command.

Niles allowed a smile of satisfaction to break across his face, as always, when a mission proved successful. He turned, signaled an all is well, and watched the crew relax. Only then did he descend from his vantage point and return his attention to their passengers.

The quarterdeck was shrouded in darkness. The pastel color of Victoria's gown guided him to where a group gathered. When he drew near he saw Kleet engaged in an attempt to restrain Victoria's arms that flailed against him. Niles approached to where Captain Leyden, aged eyes misted with tears, looked up from where he knelt beside a dark form. A widening pool of fresh blood beside the body gave silent testimony there was no further help for Mr. Silvas. He had escaped Debtors Prison at the cost of his life.

"Toro," Niles said quietly, "take Mr. Silvas away."

"No!" a cry of protest arose from the daughter.

The powerful arms of the muscular black, upon a nod from Niles, lifted the limp body as easily as if it were a child in sleep and bore it silently away to the dim recesses of the ship. Victoria struggled to follow, but found herself held by Kleet's iron grip.

"No use, Miss. There's nothing you can do," he soothed. "He caught a ball 'tween the shoulders as he cleared the rail."

She glared in open hostility at those who tried to help. Clearly she opted to unjustly blame the crew for this tragedy. She refused to accept that her father, who knew the risks in advance, chose to take his chances. Niles deemed it best to ignore her verbal accusations in consideration for her present state of mind. Perhaps, come morning, after the initial shock passed, she would view the misfortune differently and understand.

"Kleet, take the lady to my quarters for the night," he directed, then turned and strode away with the composure of one in command.

Captain Leyden joined him shortly later

at the rail. "I've instructed Toro to prepare the body for burial," he said, voice cracked with sadness.

Niles nodded. "Best we put it over the side before dawn. With plenty ballast it will quickly sink. We dare not take a chance that another ship in the area may pick it up." After a moment of silence, he sighed. Mr. Silvas, he knew, meant a great deal to the aged man beside him. "If it sinks fast sharks are less apt to get it." Captain Leyden nodded agreement and took his leave, shoulders bent in grief. Niles proceeded the length of the quarterdeck and instructed Kleet to post an extra watch. Two other questions yet remained on his mind that must be resolved.

The original plan was to trade their Caribbean cargo before the preordained time of the rescue. However, their arrival was delayed by unfavorable winds over the Atlantic. Trade negotiations, of necessity, were therefore put off to keep their appointment with Mr. Silvas. This now presented a problem. Word would spread fast of the escape. Under the circumstances, to drop anchor in any prominent harbor along the English coastline would be extremely risky.

Victoria Silvas presented the other complex issue. When and where could they put a pampered young lady of refinement safely ashore? The funds her father carried, to establish their new life, sank with the satchel in the harbor. She was penniless. As if that were not enough, the lady's satchel likewise fell overboard in the haste to raise the landing craft onto the deck. He stared across the black, moonless water, and pondered the situation.

The damp winter wind increased and grew colder. Discomfort forced him to seek the warmth of his quarters. Before he could enter, however, Captain Leyden stepped out and quietly closed the door. "I wouldn't advise you to go in there, Niles. She's resting on your bunk." In an appeal for understanding, Captain Leyden added, "It's been a hard day for all of us---and a close one, I might add. For my dear friend, too close."

With consideration for the somberness of death that hung over the ship, Niles made no comment. He could excuse Captain Leyden for being overly excited by the prospect of a reunion with his old friend. Inwardly he still resented the fact that he had neglected to mention there would be a lady involved in this dangerous venture. *The Sea Pearl* carried an all male crew. No private quarters were available to accommodate a woman.

Though irritated by this inconvenience, Niles refused to be upset by the omission. Nor did he question the older man's oversight. Whys were not important now; the solution took precedence. "If you will slip in and bring my cloak and some coverings, I shall bunk with hands tonight."

"Aye," the old man turned with a mirthful chuckle. "Glad she chose your bunk. I don't care to swing in a cussed hammock at my age, much less try to get some sleep among the crew."

Niles peered at him with suspicious good humor. "Sure you had nothing to do with her choice of bunks?" Captain Leyden only sniggered in response.

Niles, unaccustomed to loud snores, curses and the odorous air of the crowded crew quarters, emerged in the predawn. He stopped to stretch his stiff limbs. Spoiled by the use of a sturdy bunk, they ached miserably after a night in a hammock. A cold wind blew across the dark sea and jarred his senses. He shivered beneath the folds of his heavy woolen cloak. The warm climate and familiar waters of their home port in the Caribbean would feel good on their return.

Beads of water coated the decks and every thing around him. He saw Toro bent over the canvas wrapped body on the quarterdeck. The shadowy form of Kleet approached, stopped to utter a few low words to the black, then proceeded, as ordered, to the Captains' Quarters to alert Victoria and Captain Leyden.

"Plenty ballast at feet like ordered, Cap'n," Toro confirmed in his broken English. "Cut like knife to bottom."

Niles, engrossed in thought, looked down on the rumpled bundle at his feet. So little time to become acquainted. He would have considered it an honor to regard the courageous man a friend. As for the daughter-

The sound of a door brought him around to the sad duty before him. Miss Silvas and Captain Leyden emerged. Niles hoped she would not choose to make a scene. After a sleepless, uncomfortable night, he was not in a mood to contend with the complexities of a temperamental, pampered female. Her situation and grief was understandable, but he doubted she carried any thoughts beyond the present. Nor did she have any knowledge of the many complications her presence created on board. Yet strangely, he felt a twinge of guilt for his feelings of resentment as she drew near on the sympathetic arm of Captain Leyden.

"Miss Silvas," he addressed her, with a slight, chivalrous bow of courtesy.

An icy glare and a face that shifted seaward met him. The implications were clear. She wanted nothing to do with him. Her attitude did not escape Captain Leyden, who glanced imploringly at Niles for patience.

"I'm sorry, Miss, it is time," Niles ventured, as he noted the classic beauty of her profile under its mask of hostility. "Dawn will soon break."

She remained stoic, delicate hands on the cold wet rail. Captain Leyden nodded a signal to ignore her actions and proceed with the gristly task ahead. Before Niles completed the brief eulogy, he motioned to Toro and Kleet. The pair lifted onto the rail the plank on which the body rested, poised for the proper moment. "---and now we entrust his body to the sea," he concluded. The canvas wrapped body slid from the raised plank and cut the water surface below. Immediately, it sank downward into the dark depths below.

Niles stepped forward to offer his condolences for the sake of courtesy, and nothing more. The firm set of her averted jaw line gave him cause to hesitate. Two can play the standoff game, he told himself. With that, he abruptly turned away and went forward to the galley. Cleve, the cook, rushed over with a pewter tankard of black coffee. As usual, it was hot enough to curl the feathers on a duck's back. Brewed of aromatic beans taken on before they left Port Royal, Jamaica, the dark beverage served to smooth Niles' temperament. "Time," he said, in answer to the question behind the cook's quizzical expression. "She won't think she's so high and mighty after little time on board."

CHAPTER TWO

The two captains held a private conference while they leaned on the rail to allow the weak sun to chase the chill from their bodies. Captain Leyden, in particular, could well use warmth and sunlight. The deep-seated cough he contracted on the voyage had become more persistent as each day passed. Niles could detect the tightness in the man's chest was intensifying. His system, after living the past years amid the warm climate of the Caribbean Sea and Greater Antilles region, was no longer accustomed to this unfamiliar dampness. Gravely concerned, he secretly watched the old man's physical condition with misgivings.

It was a rule each crewman on the *Pearl* had a voice in its operation so they decided it was time to call the men together for an open discussion. Eyes averted, Captain Leyden spoke. "She blames you for her father's death."

"I gathered as much. Her father knew full well the risks before he made his decision. Naturally, we all hoped it wouldn't end this way. Sometimes, try as we may, things go awry. Believe me, there was no way I could save him."

"It wasn't your fault, Son. No need to carry a load of guilt on your shoulders. We're only sea captains; we cannot change the fates. Right now your hands are full with the operation of this ship. Meanwhile, let me try my hand with her. Her present frame of mind won't accept anything you say anyway."

"I'll gladly handle the ship, if you'll handle her. While you're at it, give some thought on how and where we can unload our cargo. Besides food and supplies, Kleet tells me our ammunition is dangerously low."

"Aye. If we can't slip into a port to take on staples, our little lady best develop a likin' for fish!" A raspy spasm of coughing cut short the older man's chuckle. Recovered, he gasped, "She's got spunk to spare, I'll say that much. From the attitude she's shown toward you I'm sure you've already gotten the message. Ah, but it will mellow after a taste of boredom at sea. It's too bad she's so danged spoiled, or else---" his voice trailed off. Niles was left to wonder how much conversation passed between the two throughout the night---and on what subject?

The crew began to gather amidships with an abundance of muttering and a scuff of tall boots. Grouped together in a huddle, their low voices spoke of dissension and objectionable speculation.

"Well," Niles straightened, "I guess it's time to face the storm clustered over there by the mainmast. As for me, I don't have a single idea to propose as a solution to our dilemmas."

"Aye," the older man shifted his feet with another jovial chuckle. "If they glare any longer we'll be sportin' holes bored clean through our backsides."

Together, they advanced toward the sea hardened crew. A few in the fore, shoulders hunched in heavy coats, squatted on their heels. Dark eyes glared from hostile faces discernable within the protection of upturned collars. Others, leaned against lines, or sat atop cannon carriages on the far side with a staunch air of opposition. All waited, faces set, ready to contest any suggestion the two captains may offer. Kleet, Niles noticed, had made a point of centering himself among the men on the cannons. The first mate, he had learned from experience, possessed a highly unpredictable streak. Superb to call on to settle differences among the crew, yet with the ability to influence their minds in the opposite direction, if he chose to do so. As such, he could be one's greatest ally or--- without warning, their most treacherous foe.

Niles took his place before them, and began to recap the events that led to the present. He braced himself when the first mate vaulted with the grace of a dancer upon his perch, and let his crafty eyes slide over the group. The mate's head, tilted at a familiar self-assured angle, was the signal a charge was primed for detonation and he held the torch ready to set it off.

"Wait up there, Cap'n Niles," he challenged. The sinewy body twisted into a sardonic stance. "Don't try chinin' us, Cap'n. I'd say it was your boots stepped us into this fix. Now your boots gotta do the steppin' out. There's not a man aboard who'll back you on this one. Furthermore, this meeting concerns our passenger. It now appears she, by pure coincidence, is the latest member to join the crew. As such, the lady should be included to voice her views, same as any one of us. We wouldn't want her to miss what our wise and gallant captains have to say for themselves."

Before Niles could open his mouth to object, Kleet checked him with an upheld hand for silence. The derisive grin turned to receive confirmation from the other men. How well Niles recognized the strategy. It meant their troubles were about to double. The first mate wielded power with the men. His smooth ways and speech, when he chose to exercise them, could easily sway the majority to follow his diabolical tricks. Today, as so often in the past, his tongue strove to lead them like blind sheep---only this time he meant to slaughter the captains. The collar of the woolen cape suddenly felt uncomfortable and scratchy against Niles' neck.

"Now Cap'n," his antagonist pressed, one eyebrow lifted in challenge, while the cleft deepened in the prominent chin, "you know the rules. All crewmembers have a say on important decisions and," he turned to the crew for verification, "I believe we have some important matters before us on the table. Therefore, we demand her presence."

The seeds of deviltry satisfactorily planted, he again dropped lightly to his former perch, and waited to see the fireworks that would result from his disruption. Grunts and nods of assent told Niles he had no option but to submit to majority rule and produce the lady in question. He motioned for Captain Leyden to bring Miss Silvas. Within himself, he felt it was an invitation to her own hanging.

Silence awaited her arrival. Only the wind in the sails and the creak of taut lines was heard. He stood before the group of aroused men and knew he must somehow regain command. How many more tricks was Kleet prepared to toss into his already kindled fire?

The man thrived on instigating trouble, even when there was nothing to gain from the outcome; he loved the excitement of the game. To watch another man squirm served to fuel his insatiable ego. Easy to hate with a vengeance, he made enemies throughout the Caribbean and Gulf of Mexico. He would meet his Maker one day at the very hand, most likely, of one of those enemies. Life came cheap along the pirate infested *Spanish Main.*

Miss Silvas arrived, attired in the elegant ball gown, tattered from the rigors of flight. Kleet sprang from the cannon with a gallant wave of his hand. "Come, come, you sea dogs, let's have a seat for our lady of honor." Woolen skullcap in hand, he bent in a pretentious bow to the lady. "We can't expect a queen to squat like a common deck hand."

A crewman, aptly called Weasel for his small dark eyes closely set in a thin weathered face, skittered off to the galley. Momentarily he returned, a heavy wooden crate in tow. Miss Silvas accepted the crude seat with grace, and primly smoothed the remains of the jeweled gown.

Kleet, with a jaunty air and a last smirk, returned to his vantage point. "Proceed, Captain. I'm sure the lady will be most interested in what everyone has to say about a lady on board." Niles cleared his throat and resumed, relieved to see the mate back off. He stepped forward to call their attention to the dire need to find a port where they could sell their cargo and dispense of their passenger. "As I see it, we can sail for the Colonies and put our passenger ashore at Boston harbor. There we can sell our cargo and proceed down the American coast to the Caribbean."

Now came the crucial point. "I am open to hear everyone's opinion on whether we choose Boston, or return directly to our home port in the islands." The clustered men scowled their displeasure at his suggestions. Primly seated on the crate, his passenger's expressionless eyes watched and waited. A discomfiting silence followed. Niles knew he must go on, if he was to maintain a position of control.

"Also, since we're not prepared to carry passengers, I am open to ideas on how we can provide proper quarters for the lady."

Weasel sprang up, face reddened in opposition. "I say dump her overboard where we picked 'er up!"

Miss Silvas' face remained unchanged, except for the slight drop of her eyes.

"Weasel, you know that's impossible," Niles discounted the statement. "Unless, that is, you want to go back and face the Royal Guards again." Weasel slunked back into the group with a sullen snarl.

Kleet uncurled from his slouched position, a fresh gleam in his wily eyes. "I'm sure the little lady has a simple answer. Let's hear what she has to say." Unruffled, her gaze fixed steadily on his.

Voice calm and controlled, she answered, "I have no knowledge of the sea, nor am I experienced in life on board a ship. You have me at a disadvantage. Therefore, I suggest you weigh the alternatives, present them to me, and I shall take them under consideration."

"Ha!" he mocked. "Hear that? She'll take them under consideration!"

"Captain," she turned to Niles, "this manner of attitude will accomplish nothing. Perhaps if each man spoke openly instead of moping, we could come up with something constructive."

"Lady, if we sea scum spoke openly," the mate laughed, "it would sear a lady's tender ears to a crisp!" A chorus of loud guffaws rose in agreement from the men. Niles thought he detected a slight flush creep across Miss Silvas' face, checked immediately by pride.

A large, burly form unfolded with a grunt from where it leaned against a cannon carriage near Kleet's perch. Brog was a man of few words. His muscular strength usually spoke for him. Heavy brows knitted in concentration, his bass voice rumbled. "Everyone knows a female on board is downright bad luck---which we don't need none of. *The Sea Pearl* never carried a woman before, an' I'm not for goin' back on that. I say the sooner she's off this ship the better. Don't much matter to me how we do it, long as we rid our decks of her."

"Now men," Captain Leyden, fearful the situation might very easily get out of hand, interceded. "That's only crazy superstition. We all agree she should be placed on land. The problem is, where and how?"

A voice yelled from the rear. "Any pirate ship would throw her overboard. I say we do the same." Shouts of assent rose from the agitated men. The hostile group began to push forward on the two captains.

Niles raised a hand and called out above the uproar. "Hold it!"

"Why, pray tell?" another voice spat in response. "There's not a man among us who's ready to risk his neck over any stray female!"

They surged forward, faces twisted with animosity, to encircle the captains. Niles and Captain Leyden took up positions in an attempt to protect Miss Silvas. The throng closed in, intent on their self-preservation and driven by age-old omens. Miss Silvas remained seated, chin resolutely set. Either a very courageous woman, Niles observed, or petrified into immobility by fear. Quickly he spread-eagled himself as a shield. Vastly outnumbered, he felt himself torn aside, while hands clawed to reach the doomed Victoria Silvas.

A deafening thunder split the air overhead!

All action stopped. Niles whirled to the direction of the explosion.

Kleet, cuffed boots widespread, stood atop the cannon, a heavy pistol gripped in each hand. With his long blond hair streaming in the wind, eyes narrowed to slits, he held the menacing barrels leveled directly into the mass of enraged men.

The voice grated cutlass sharp and cold. "Next one 'at moves gets his buckle blown right through his backbone!" Gone was the careless abandon, the egotistical deviltry. In their stead towered a man intent on his word, a wild animal that would kill without neither second thoughts nor regrets. The entire crew, in respect for the mate's deadly personality, froze before the ugly black bores of the pistols within the grip of his deft hands. One barrel gave a jerk to the side as he growled, "Back off, you scum, and settle your haunches. Captain, get on with the meetin'. There's other things on the Pearl need tendin'."

The men slowly eased away, eyes riveted with distrust upon the dangerous figure silhouetted against the sky. Not until they shuffled back from the captains, did the mate jab the barrels under his wide leather belt. Nevertheless, he continued to stand guard, arms akimbo.

Quite unexpected, it was Victoria who broke the silent tension. "Captain, may I say something?"

Niles nodded assent against his better judgment. "Certainly, Madam. Kleet has expressed you should be regarded as one of the crew and, as such, that means you have a right to express an opinion along with the others."

"My aunt and uncle live in a small village down the coastline along St. Brides Bay," she began. "If you can put me ashore there, the problem of my presence will be solved."

The suggestion caught Niles' interest. "What is their exact location?"

Her eyes lowered. "I'm sorry, Captain.

I was but a child when my father and I last visited them. We traveled by land, but I recall water and large ships in a harbor." Abruptly her head lifted, face bright. "My father's map! I remember the spot he on it. Do you have a map of the area?"

Kleet gave a jubilant shout from his perch. "Aha! Escort the lady to the charts, Captain. If we're lucky, we can unload her, trade cargo, and take on supplies in one drop of anchor." The crew bellowed in accord and began to stomp their boots against the deck.

Niles offered an arm to steady her balance. She stared in contempt at the offer of assistance as if repulsed to touch the sleeve. She took a step to move forward, only to stagger with the ship's motion underfoot. Her arm flew out to grab his in an attempt to break her fall. Niles stifled a laugh. The lady was about to learn her first lesson on putting wisdom ahead of stubborn independence.

They presented a strange pair as they proceeded to the Captains Quarters. Although silk lace still rippled at his throat, the fine clothes were disheveled after a night in a hammock; she walked alongside in the lavish gown, now crumpled and torn. Her expertly coifed hair blew in loose wisps upon the wind, costly pearl tiara, perhaps lost somewhere in the night. The hollow sound of her heeled slippers against the wooden deck stirred in him the memory of trim ankles in his hands a few short hours ago.

A shiver traveled from her hand to his sleeve. She had sat without complaint throughout the meeting, while the cold damp wind whistled about her bare white shoulders and penetrated the sheer folds of the tattered gown. Without a wrap for warmth, she was undoubtedly chilled to the bone.

Niles drew up short, ashamed by his inconsiderateness. "Wait." Gently he draped his own woolen cloak about her. Gentleman that he was, he declined to take the liberty to fasten it at her throat. Her eyes lifted to his, and he thought he recognized a hint of gratitude.

They entered the Captain's Quarters and he was immediately struck dumb by the total state of disarray. How, he wondered, could one woman, in the space of one night, so completely upset its customary neatness? He knew some women were untidy but, meticulous himself, he saw this as downright ridiculous and inexcusable.

Captain Leyden, who followed the pair, spoke from behind. "Son, you handled the men out there just fine."

"I ran aground!" Niles, already agitated, slammed his cuffed gauntlets down alongside the discarded coat with its rows of gold buttons. "Kleet had control, not me!"

"Sh-h-h," the older man's eyes twinkled. "True. Nonetheless, don't say it so loud the crew hears you."

"What difference? They all know it. If he hadn't reversed the tide---"

"So? Everything worked out. Therein lies the value of a few choice men among the crew. Kleet, cursed though he is, backed you in the end, didn't he? Now," he motioned with urgency toward their small desk, "lay out the charts. Let's see what our lady can show us."

Victoria stared, brow creased in concentration, at the long rolls of parchment colored leather Niles placed before her. At length she backed away. "I'm sorry, I can't identify a thing."

"You have to!" he shouted in anger. "Out there on deck you asked to see a map. Here's a chart of England's coastline." He repeatedly jabbed a finger on the leather chart. "Where is the village?"

"I was only a child!" Her eyes misted before his display of rage. "Besides, I can't understand these marks on your map."

Captain Leyden interceded. "There,

there, Miss," he patted her shoulder sympathetically. "Maybe I can help. Take your time. Perhaps all is not lost." With a glance at Niles, he added, "These nautical charts confuse a landlubber. What we need is a little patience."

He began to trace the shoreline with a gnarled forefinger. "Here is where we picked you up. Now let's follow the coast south from that point. You say Brides Bay? That would be---just about here. Look closely, Child. Do you see anything that resembles the marks on your father's map? The lay of the coastline, perhaps an inlet, or---" He squinted his aging eyes and turned to Niles. "Bring a little more light over here."

A hush came over the room. Slowly she moved a slender finger, hesitated, stopped, then moved it back a short distance. "There! I'm sure of it."

Niles looked to Captain Leyden for an opinion. Once England was Andrew Leyden's homeland, whereas Niles grew up along the *Spanish Main*. The older man smiled with satisfaction. Jolly crinkles spread across the leathered face. He lifted a hand to pat her shoulder. "Little Lady, I commend you. Indeed, this may solve all our problems."

Before Niles could open his mouth to express his appreciation to the lady her air of prim hostility froze the words on his tongue. Faced by this frigid woman he felt completely asea on what to say. It was not, he told himself, that he neither expected nor wished her to act like island women. However, their associations would definitely be more tolerable if she lowered her barriers, was less aloof and more sociable. As things stood, he would be glad to reach the port she indicated.

Despite this, he remained confused. No other woman in his past possessed the quality to make him feel so uncomfortable, and at the same time, so drawn to her. To evade her antagonistic stance, he turned back to the chart to calculate their day of arrival with a strange, unexplainable, sense of regret. Why do I always feel so disconcerted in her presence? he wondered, upset by the unfamiliar quandary within himself.

Miss Silvas clutched the woolen cloak closer about her shoulders and began to pace the room. "How can you men stand to live in here? I'm freezing to death!"

Niles left the charts to check the tiny wood burner along the wall. "I'm sorry, while we were at the meeting it seems the fire died down. Captain Leyden will build it up for you. Our ship is not equipped for northern waters in winter."

He returned to chart their new course.

When finished, he restored everything neatly to its proper place. Surprised to find she watched with open curiosity while he worked, he asked, "Are you interested in how this is done?"

"Not in the least," she sniffed.

All right, he told himself, it's time someone brought you down from your lofty perch. He strolled across the room toward his bunk with casual abandon. "The *Pearl* is a small merchant ship built for speed. As such, we do not have accommodations for passengers. These are my quarters, Madam, and I must warn you I intend to retain them." He began to work the buttons of his elaborate attire, then added boldly, "And the first thing I must do is change into my customary seafaring garments."

"Do whatever you like," she snapped.

"You make it plain I am an unwelcome passenger. Let me remind you this silly escapade was no idea of mine."

Out on the quarterdeck, he inhaled deeply while he surveyed the ship. The *Pearl* he could understand, the woman in his quarters he could not. To divert her from his mind he strolled over to where Kleet stood by the mainmast.

"We'll set to a new course. If the winds are with us, the charts suggest two, maybe three days, to arrive at the port she spoke of. Once there, we'll see her off in a carriage. That will eliminate the female headache from our minds and free us to deal our cargo and take on supplies."

Kleet, always anxious for activity, broke into a wide grin. Gains from the sale of cargo were customarily shared by all crewmembers. And he, as usual, was eager to pocket his cut. He turned and shouted to the steerage with a swing of an uplifted arm. "Take her so' by so'east. One dock and we'll be headin' home!"

The crew leaped into action. Sails were set to best catch the wind, and the helmsman swung the tiller to bring the ship around to the new course. Niles watched with satisfaction. As Captain Leyden so often stated, they were a reliable crew, and pulled well together. He relished the feel as the vessel reacted under his feet, the repetitious sound of the sea in his ears. Spirits restored, he called after the mate. "Tell the galley all the men need something hot for their innards." Then, in reference to the meeting incident, added, "Thanks. That's one I owe you."

"Do you mean for, or agin'?" He looked Niles over with amusement. "Good thing you got out of those fancy frills before the men mistook you for a foreigner sneakin' passage.

That coat wouldn't look so fine with a slit down the back. By the way, how's the old man this morning?"

"He won't admit it, but the cough is quite bad."

"Aye," Kleet nodded, "he's an ornery salt. Won't give even when down. Tell him to stay where it's warm. No need freezin' his backside out here. We'll handle the ship."

Niles remained, one hand on a thick oil and tar coated ratline, while he debated his next move. "Why couldn't Mr. Silvas' offspring been a son!" he cursed under his breath. A female, unexpectedly thrown among a crew of immoral men to whom integrity meant nothing, presented some serious problems. Billet arrangements, for instance. As captain, it was his duty to protect her, but how? Every inch of the *Pearl* was already in use. Private quarters were out of the question. Dilemma unresolved, he returned to his quarters, forgetting she had not seen him after he changed clothes.

An audible gasp of shocked surprise escaped from her lips as he entered. She drew back in fear and stared open mouthed at the transfiguration. Now she understood what her father meant when he warned her this was definitely not the breed of man to which she was accustomed. Gone was the finery, the cultured gentleman. Instead, before her stood a hardened, virile man of the *Spanish Main*. He watched her eyes dart to the blood chilling cutlass and brace of deadly Spanish *pistola*s that jutted from his wide leather belt. She stared at the open shirtfront that revealed a broad, island-tanned chest and the heavy gold medalion that lay against it. The flawless jewels reflected slivers of rainbow colors with each breath he took: deep green emeralds, blood red rubies, midnight blue sapphires, iridescent opals, and ice clear diamonds held her transfixed. She gaped in awe at the magnificence of the goldsmith's art.

"You like it?"

"It---it is absolutely beautiful," she breathed, overwhelmed by the multicolored fires that flashed from the many facets in contrast to the crude, rugged attire of the wearer. "I'm amazed you wear such a valuable item on the ship---unless," she gave a haughty toss of her head, "you try to impress me. If so, Captain Brett, it's a waste of your time."

"Impress you?" he lifted one dark eyebrow. "Not at all, Miss. What makes you think I would bother to impress you? You're only a passenger who will be gone shortly." Her mouth pressed into a thin line in response to the rebuke.

"I came to escort you to breakfast. You

must be famished." She drew away from his extended arm, and attempted to proceed unaided. Before she reached the door he saw her lose her balance. Quickly he caught her about the waist and restored her upright. "Now will you accept a little help, Madam?"

Two red spots appeared on her cheeks although the eyes remained adamant as she timidly conceded. He placed one of her hands on the coarse fabric of his gathered sleeve and felt her grip tighten as they progressed against the roll of the deck.

"The crew has already eaten. We have the galley to ourselves. Normally, we captains take our meals in our quarters."

"Isn't that a bit uppity of you?"

"Not at all. There are reasons I shall not go into at the moment."

As predicted, the last stragglers of the crew had left, wiping mouths on sleeves. The hefty cook, swathed in an oversized apron, looked up in surprise when Miss Silvas entered. "Galley 'taint much of a place for a lady," he apologized, and hurried to set the meal for his new arrivals.

"It's nearly midday," Niles explained, " so I saw no reason for you to bring it to the quarters. Besides, our guest needed a lesson on how to walk with the roll of a deck." Victoria attempted to hide the flush that crept up her neck. Her attention turned to the hot bowl of unappetizing, bland *burgoo;* a gruel made of oatmeal thinned with water. Niles tried to mend her spirits, thinking she had perhaps suffered sufficient humiliation. "If it's any consolation, Madam, you are not the first person to lose their balance on a deck."

The cook returned to set two pewter mugs filled with freshly brewed hot island coffee before them. Niles looked up from his *burgoo*. "Captain Leyden eaten?"

"Yes Sir. He ate with the crew."

Concern deepened the lines of the perspiration-wet forehead. "I don't think he felt so good. Rhumatiz joints got him done in, I'd say. And that croup," the jowls of his face, reddened by heat from the enormous stove, shook sadly. "It's gettin' worse by the day. Should never chanced comin' up into this dampness and northern chill."

"I agree," Niles answered, in a tone of deep trepidation. Then, with a grin, he returned his focus to their guest. "Cleve, it appears the lady likes your cooking. I do believe she can stand another bowlful."

"I must admit, I am accustomed to more tasty fare. However, I suppose this watery soup, whatever you call it, will serve to kill my hunger for a time." She took a careful sip from her mug. "Oh my, coffee of this quality must be terribly expensive! How can you afford it?

"Compared to prices in England, along the Main it costs a mere pittance. Fact is, a great percentage of our cargo in the hold is coffee we brought to trade in England. Although most English people prefer tea, some of your countrymen appreciate good coffee."

"What else do you carry, Captain?"

"Various island commodities: salt meat, sugar cane, citrus fruits, cotton, cacao, tobacco and assorted spices."

"How very interesting. I had the impression ships like yours dealt with a different type of cargo---jewels and gold, for instance?"

Niles held his gaze steady. Her amateurish attempts to pry secretly amused him. "There are some things a captain, out of discretion, does not reveal."

"I see. Aren't you afraid the crew will steal them?" she whispered, and cast a wary glance toward the cook.

"That is true, Madam, for most pirate ships, but the *Pearl* is not a ship of privateers.

You see, it would be useless to steal from their own pockets. Now," he rose, "it's time we tackled the problem of what you shall wear. That gown is much too cold. I can't afford another sick member on board."

Captain Leyden, reclining on his bunk, raised on one elbow when the pair reentered the cabin. "Lad, I'm sure glad you're old enough to take over for me on deck. I'm plumb tuckered out after all that activity last night."

"Rest is the best thing for your cough." Seeing an opportunity to assure the old man of his usefulness, he added, "However, I need your suggestions on a problem before you take a nap."

"Certainly, certainly," the wizened eyes lighted with interest. "I'm only a crippled up old bucaner, but nothing makes a man feel younger than a sense of being useful."

"Our lady is in need of something else to wear. This gown is a bad idea on board."

The old captain gave a knowing nod. "If I were a might younger sprite, I'd take a long look myself," he chuckled with a merry wink. The grayed brows drew together in thought while he stroked his short trimmed beard. "The only clothes on board are those our men wear." A long pause followed before the lined face brightened. "Toro! Tell Toro to go down in the hold and bring a roll of fabric from the cargo we are carrying---and mind, Niles," he raised a finger of caution, "he selects one that's subdued in color and warm."

Niles caught the old man's thoughts and hurried out. While he waited for Toro to return from the hold, he checked on the helm, then located Kleet hard at work on a faulty pulley.

"Figured you'd want the damages taken care of. Never know when we might encounter one flyin' the colors of England that's gotten the word." He eyed Niles with a brazen grin and one eyebrow suggestively lifted. "Must be somethin' mighty good goin' on in your cabin, Cap'n. You've kept yourself in there most of the day. Kind of hard to leave the pretty little skirt?"

"Best keep your imagination under control, before it gets you in trouble," Niles admonished casually, yet with serious undertones.

Toro returned, a roll of fabric under one muscular arm. Together the pair entered the cabin. "The lady needs a dress," Niles motioned toward their passenger. "Fix her up in one of those long wrap around affairs like your island women wear when they are cold." The Negroid responded with a wide grin, white teeth gleaming behind the dark pigmented face. Without a word, he unrolled several yards of the woolen fabric.

"Ah, a soft, warm shade of gray," Captain Leyden expressed approval. "A fine choice."

The black took one quick swipe across the fabric with a razor sharp knife from his leather belt. The required yardage fell from the roll. Victoria shrank back in fear as he approached with the length of cloth.

"It's all right, Miss," Niles assured. "I realize it's not likely you've ever seen a black man before, but I can vouch he won't hurt you. You'll find he can be a very handy man to have around when needed."

She trembled under the man's gentle touch and looked to Captain Leyden for assurance. Toro, in one deft motion, swirled the cloth with experienced ease about her body and secured it firmly around the slim corseted waist. The formerly seductive lady, although beautiful, was instantly transformed into the appearance of a commoner, well draped and covered neck to floor.

"Very good, Toro," Niles said, and turned his attention to Victoria. "This is what you will wear until we reach a port. To allow privacy while you replace your party clothes with this new manner of dress the rest of us will vacate the quarters."

Outside, he addressed Captain Leyden. "You came through on that one. Tell me, does that grizzled head hold any ideas on how to solve the billet question? It's not my intention to freeze my backsides another night in the crew quarters. Besides, they snore so bad it's a wonder anyone gets any sleep."

The elder scrubbed his knuckles against his bristly whiskers and chuckled. "Can't understand why you complain. I rather enjoyed myself last night." Niles peered at him sideways. "No Lad, I don't reckon it was very pleasant over there. Can't change places, either. That would leave you and the girl---wha---what I mean is, I trust you---b---but---you are a grown man now. And---and there's her reputation to think of. Danged it, Son---you know what I mean," he squirmed, embarrassed to speak of intimacy. "Besides, word gets around, even if not true. We could end up with a real problem---with the men, I mean." Niles grinned at the older man's discomfort.

He gave a pat of reassurance on the oldster's shoulder. "For me to sleep in the cabin alone with her is definitely out. With the attitude that exists between that woman and me, you can be sure there's not a thing to worry about. She's got far too much starch in her little ol' backbone, if you want my opinion. Her insolence has already given me a bellyful."

"Don't judge too harshly, Lad. This has been rough for her, too, remember? We shall try Toro again. His people are geniuses at making do in any situation."

Niles reentered the Captain's Quarters shortly before nightfall. Within he saw the table already prepared for his arrival. Captain Leyden, across the room, washed his face, reached for a towel, and turned, bared chest visible behind his open shirtfront. Miss Silvas looked up and uttered a shudder of revulsion. A small, intricately etched, gold earring lay suspended from two fine holes in the exposed flesh of the old man's chest. Niles did not consider it necessary to reveal details of their private lives to their passenger. He chose to ignore the reaction and proceeded without explanation to the small basin, where he casually remarked on an alteration made in the room while he was absent.

"I see Toro erected a fabric curtain to insure your privacy, Madam."

She stiffened. "Does this mean you plan to sleep in here?"

"It will be crowded with the three of us, but thankfully it's only temporary."

"I'd sooner retire with the crew!"

"You don't realize what you say, Miss," he reached for the towel. "For any lady to associate with a crew of this breed would be neither wise, nor safe."

"And who says I can trust you, Captain Brett?"

He delivered a polite bow, and noticed her eyes turned a deeper, vibrant blue with the onset of anger. "Let me assure you, Madam, my only interest is *The Sea Pearl*, her crew, and her cargo. Anything else is immaterial. Now I suggest we enjoy our meal," he motioned a hand in invitation.

She accepted the chair he held for her and stared with open wonder. Silver gleamed, polished candleholders reflected the light and, laid out in proper order, fine china waited at each place. She fingered the texture of an expensive linen napkin where it lay against the starched white tablecloth. Before she could pick it up, Niles touched a hand to her arm and nodded in the direction of Captain Leyden. The grayed head bowed. What followed was not a verse recited in haste, but an expression from the heart.

"---and bless *The Sea Pearl* and our people upon her decks wherever we may sail. Humbly we give thanks to thee for all thy goodness. Amen."

"I imagine we present a strange contrast, Miss," Niles said, as the food was passed. "I mean, to partake a spread like this in our present mode of dress."

"An elaborate show for my benefit was quite unnecessary." "Your benefit? Is that what you think?"

"What else?"

"On the *Pearl* we don't strive to impress anyone. We always dine in this manner when circumstances allow."

"You expect me to believe such lies?"
"In your England, Miss Silvas, I hear beautiful things are kept for special occasions. On the *Pearl* we believe one should enjoy beauty each day. There may not be a tomorrow."

"What a ghastly attitude!"

"Because I speak of death? It's a fact men of our profession accept. Death may be difficult for a landlubber to face, but we live to promote a cause. If that cause demands we die it's worth the price."

"There's only one cause you pirates know: that cause being to prey on honest merchant ships and kill innocent people for sport. Hardly admirable reasons, I would say."

Niles smiled at her misconception and held his patience. "There you go again, Madam. You draw conclusions before you know the facts, same as so many other land dwellers. True, nowadays there are ships afloat that meet your description. They are adventure seekers. We, and several others like us, dislike their presence as much as anyone does. Together we form an alliance to the cause."

"All your talk about alliances and causes sounds like nonsense to me."

Captain Leyden raised a hand. "Now, now, you two stop bickering for a few minutes. You've been cannon to cannon ever since you laid eyes on each other. Let's not make our situation any worse. It shouldn't be hard to at least be sociable until Miss Silvas is again on dry land."

CHAPTER THREE

Niles checked the lookouts for the night, and returned to his Quarters. He found the sleeping older man, knees drawn up by another coughing spell. Niles soon discovered concentration on his part was impossible between the captain's restlessness and his own awareness of their passenger's presence behind the fabric curtain. Was she awake? Perhaps she, even now, listened to his movements? Watched his shadow flit across the surface of the curtain? He tried to convince himself it was only the alteration of the orderly arrangements of the room. Or perhaps his sense of danger nearby made him feel uneasy. His ears picked up no sound except the rise and fall of the wind outside their small glassed porthole. Only the persistent cough of the old man disturbed the quietude within the cabin.

He stopped before his reflected image that stared back from the small mirror over their wash stand. It confirmed his appearance really was one of a freebooter. Any wonder she feared to spend the night in the same room? Perhaps, as the cook implied, he had came down a bit hard on her. He rubbed a hand across his jaw, and admitted he needed a shave. Then again, he questioned, why should I be concerned? Surely not because she is here. The lamp's glow touched the necklace jewels and little fingers of fire danced about the room.

The memory of her shocked expression when she first saw him as Niles Brett, renown pirate of the high seas, and captain of *The Sea Pearl,* brought a rueful smile. Many falsified stories circulated in the ports. By now the magnified Captain Brett of whom they spoke bore no similarity to the Captain Brett of reality. How can I make her understand the tales are nothing more than misconceptions? he wondered. Then again, what difference which man she believes I am?---the looting, brutal, murderous Brett---or the Captain Brett who runs an honest a ship? Or at least as honest as possible amid English and Spanish feuds along the Main. He could not perceive why her cold sarcasm disturbed him---yet it very much did.

His silent self-examination was interrupted by the muffled voice of the aged man. "Better snuff the light, Boy, so's the lady and I can get some sleep."

"Sorry," Niles answered, and

extinguished the lamp. "I was only thinking."

"Uh-huh. I reckon whatever it was, and mind I'm not too old to have a good idea, it will keep."

The sage remark brought a grin to Niles. He could picture a devilish smirk on the old man's lined face as he enjoyed his little pun in the darkened room.

The second day passed uneventful. Niles occupied himself with the operation of the ship. Each time he found it necessary to enter the cabin his passenger wordlessly retreated behind her curtain. Weasel's dire prophecies in regard to a woman on board seemed not to have any affect among the crew on deck. Regrettably, on the third day the winds stilled. Their progress slowed.

Mid-day he was forced to enter his quarters to retrieve a tool. Victoria, when he entered, fled into the seclusion of her draped area. Not, however, before he noticed one of his many books in her hand. To discover she could read came as a surprise. English people, to his knowledge, did not consider education important for young ladies. Instead, they were trained to fulfill the role of proper wives and mothers. What other talents did she possess, he wondered, as he returned to work.

She emerged from the Quarters and

onto the deck in an extremely disheveled and unkempt state late in the day. Frightened by the moving surface beneath her feet, her hands made a grab for the nearest rope. There she clung tightly while her body swayed unsteadily with the rise and fall of the deck. Niles, not busy at the time, decided to be gentlemanly. Besides, he had something to say to this uninitiated passenger. She shrank on his approach as if faced by a fearsome, villainous, woman beater.

"I'm not going to bite, Miss. I came to help you over to the rail. You may find the view across the ocean very interesting."

The prominently displayed brace of Spanish *pistolas* and well honed blade of cutlass at his leather belt riveted her panic stricken eyes. "M---Must you wear those horrible things?" she uttered, as yet retaining her critical defensive stance where he was concerned.

"Without them I would feel quite undressed. It is never wise, I have learned, to be without one's arms, particularly while underway in questionable waters."

She motioned a hand of disdain across the empty expanse. "I see nothing out there to fear. You only try to frighten me with your wild imagination."

"Perhaps you're right. We shall see." He had no desire to

disagree with her naive remark and call forth her temper.

With his assistance, they made hesitant progress across the quarterdeck. Her slim willowy figure, accented by the closely fitted island dress, did not escape his masculine appreciation. In a strange way, he felt proud to walk beside her. He placed her hands upon the safety of the rail. A tremor of relief passed through her as she clutched the solid support. Beyond the ship, the ever present gulls noisily dipped and rose over the water surface. Fascinated, she watched the graceful ballet. He hated himself for the necessity to intrude upon this new found interest. Yet sooner or later it must be said.

"There are certain rules, Miss Silvas," he began, "that everyone on board must strictly follow. As your captain, it falls upon me to inform you of one of these. Contrary to what you may have heard, we run a clean, well groomed crew on the *Pearl*. This rule is not a matter of vanity. Sanitation must be maintained to avoid illness among us. Nothing can cripple a ship more. There can be no exceptions." She stared in bewilderment. "I suggest, Madam, you comb your hair and wash. Evidently you have done neither since we left port. Look around," he motioned. "As you see, all of the men comply. True, they may appear disheveled due to winds and type of work, but they are clean and groomed. Our men, with the exception of Captain Leyden, don't wear beards. Even he keeps his clean, well trimmed, and neatly combed. That again, is for sanitation reasons."

"Are you insinuating you don't approve of my appearance?"

"Hair, beards, body dirt, and soiled clothing transmit diseases. It takes only one person to start an infestation of lice, fleas, or other serious health disorders."

"Infestation, indeed!"

"Yes, infestation. Fleas and lice are the scourges of men who live in close quarters at sea. I doubt you want your pretty tresses inhabited by the dastardly little creatures." Strongly in need to see his orders followed, he added, "And they bite, Madam."

The lady shuddered. "I see," she brushed a hand daintily against the wispy strands. "I didn't know such a hazard existed."

Successful on the first count, he decided to be even more specific. "In the Captains Quarters, as you may notice, we make it a rule to replace personal items when they are not in use. We abhor disorder of any kind, there again, for very practical reasons." Instead of the reaction he expected, she lifted a guilty smile. Could it be the lady was beginning to mellow? He wondered if that were possible after what he had witnessed up to this point.

At dinner that evening her hair glistened in the lamplight. After many licks of the brush it now formed a thick braid arranged in a tiara about her head. She flushed with embarrassment under his nod of approval. The trio ate in silence until Captain Leyden spoke.

"Will you sleep tonight, Niles?"

Miss Silvas, a puzzled expression upon her face, looked up from her plate. To her it seemed an odd question. "It's been quiet---almost too quiet," Niles tilted his head as if listening for a sound. "We've changed course to veer in a wide arc toward our destination. The closer we draw in the touchier it will be." He paused for a sip of wine, then added, "Let's say I shall go to bed but, just in case, be ready for an alert."

The elder nodded. "I was thinking along the same line."

Protective of the man's physical condition, Niles quickly interposed. "You may as well retire like usual. If anything comes up the rest of us can handle the situation."

"Sometimes every hand counts."

"If you insist on being in on the action," Niles chided, "I'll make sure you don't miss anything."

"You sound almost as if you want to get rid of me," the old man commented with serious undertones.

"You know better than that."

Miss Silvas looked anxiously from one to the other. "Do you expect trouble?"

"Not necessarily," Niles tried to sound casual. "However, as the good captain here so diligently taught me, it's always better to take precautions than be careless." He rose, stretched, and drew an island cigar from his pocket. "Care to make a deck check with me tonight, Captain?"

"No," the gray head gave a negative shake. "I'm smart enough to stay put where it's warm. It's enough if one of us goes out there and freezes his *trasero*." He had reverted to Spanish in respect for the presence of a lady. Growing up along the Main, Niles understood.

Later, when he returned, he found Victoria curled up near the dim glow of the oil lamp. Her hands held the well-worn book he saw earlier. Homey as this scene was, his eyes instantly went to the small porthole. The glow of light might perchance be seen by another ship in the area. Quickly he moved to jerk the heavy curtain across the glass. Victoria, engrossed in the book, paid no heed to his actions.

Exhausted, he stretched out on his bunk completely dressed, weapons included. His hand reached for a nearby volume and he, too, began to read in silence. Captain Leyden taught him long ago that rather than pace the floor it was far wiser to keep one calm and occupied. Tonight was one of those nights. Only this time he found it more difficult to concentrate on the printed pages. Was it that a sixth sense of another ship somewhere out there in the darkness tugged at his nerves? When he last checked with the lookouts all was clear. Perhaps, he shrugged, it was because he felt he was being watched. A discreet glance in her direction, however, revealed her eyes were fixed upon the open page before her. Often he sat for hours in the same room with Nicole and did not feel this disturbed. Was it Miss Silvas' rather mystic personality? He dismissed the idea. Nicole was sometimes very withdrawn when behind the privacy of her doors. Why then, did he sense this lady's presence any moreso than Nicole? Both were equally attractive women. And after all, he rationalized, Miss Silvas was nothing more than a passenger.

The soundless touch of Toro's hand on his arm in the deep of night brought him instantly awake. He sprang upright, instantly alert from long experience on the seas. With a finger to his lips for silence, he motioned to where the captain slept and Victoria's curtained area. Then he bolted quietly out the door, the big black at his heels. "Britisher?"

"Can't say, Suh, fog too thick," his partner murmured in low tones. "Whatever, it be mighty big!" The crew, already alerted and rolled from their warm hammocks by Kleet, were gathered along the rail. Niles dashed across the deck to join them. His eyes darted in the direction their mute fingers pointed. Through the darkness he could make out the dark silhouette of another ship, the Pearl a dwarf by comparison.

It was close, too close, the side of its bow glided directly toward the *Pearl*. He could almost hear the dull scrape of wood against wood; feel the impact of two hulls about to collide. For a brief instant, he tore his attention from the ominous hulk. His head turned with a quick irritated glance in response to the insistent elbow that shoved for space beside him.

"Get back where you belong!"

Eyes wide, she turned to him. "What is

it?"

"Kleet, get her inside!"

"No!" she declared, defiant to hold her ground. "I have a right to stay if I choose."

Niles cursed under his breath. This was no time to argue with a stubborn female, he said to himself. Apparently she lacked the good sense to retreat to safety. All right, if that's the way she feels, let her get a real taste of danger. It's her decision, not mine. At least she can't say I didn't warn her.

He waved an arm to the men. "Spread out! You know better than to bunch up like a school of fish. Man your posts!" The men leaped to their stations, where each waited ready, silent, deadly intent. Like crouched tigers, they watched, as the threat approached.

Slowly, ever so slowly, the distance narrowed. One heave of either vessel at the right moment and the two hulls would come together in a mighty, crushing, catastrophe. As the opponent's bow broke through the night all hands on the *Pearl* held their breaths.

Kleet sucked air through his clenched teeth, and hissed, "Whoever she is, Cap'n, she's bloody big!"

"What puzzles me," Niles breathed, "is why their lookouts don't sound an alarm?

Surely they have seen us. Christ, they can almost reach out to shake our hands! Either they are asleep, passed out on Dill Devil, or---"

"Or dead," Kleet finished. "I'll get the cannons ready."

"That's suicide! We'd only blow ourselves right with them. Look---would you look at that?" Niles pointed in open-mouthed disbelief.

The mate leaned into the blackness. "Why, she's a bloody galleon! What are Spaniards doin' up in these waters? A body would think they'd have their hands full makin' trouble down on the Main. Are we going to sit here and do nothing, Captain?"

"Exactly," Niles confirmed through tight lips.

Kleet whirled on him. "You mean to say we wait and let 'em blow us clean out of the water?"

"Calm down. At this range our only chance is to sit tight. Just hope they glide by before their lookouts send up a shout.

Kleet's feet shifted in anticipation, hungry for action. "At least let me put a hole or two in her side!" he begged.

"Quiet! Here she comes alongside."

They waited. White knuckles gripped the rail.

Only the slap, slap of water, and sound of each other's heightened breathing was heard.

Added to the ghostly foreboding quality of the suspense, was the creak and moan of two ships instead of one. A gasp escaped from Victoria. She reached to clutch his arm, fingernails digging into the flesh.

It was too late to enforce his order that she return to the cabin. Together they stared into the deep black threatening barrel of the first giant cannon as it passed directly before them. To a man, everyone's blood ran cold. He felt the hand on his arm tremble.

The deadly weapon inched by.

They expected a mighty, earsplitting roar to belch forth in their faces at any moment.

More of the same was to follow. The unbearable suspense tore at every nerve.

Kleet's impatience for adventure and excitement reached a feverish pitch after the third gaping barrel. How he would love to signal his cannoneers to blow the blasted proud galleon to smithereens! It took all of the restraint he could muster to obey his captain. Niles, meanwhile, silently prayed for the mate to contain his rash impulsiveness.

Every man counted under his breath. Each waited---five

---ten---twenty cannons on her broadside passed in review. The huge galleon continued to creep eerily past. All eyes followed as the stern slowly disappeared in the blackness off the *Pearl's* aft. The men collectively drew a ragged sigh. Tensed shoulders sagged in relief.

Niles broke the silence in whispered awe and admiration.

“Did you ever see anything like it?"

"No, Suh!" Toro stepped up alongside the three. "A've seen 'em carry twenty-two---ten a'side, two rear. She be forty-four, countin' twenty a'side, two bow, two astern."

"Aye, that was close!" Kleet drew a tattered rag from a rear pocket to mop his face and neck. "Could'a counted the pegs in her hull. Hope her lookouts stay blind 'till we are clean out in the middle of that ol' ocean ag'in. I'm for puttin' a heap of water 'tween us!"

"That goes double," Nile wholeheartedly agreed.

"Better we take precautions in case there's another one. Tell our watch to keep their eyes doubly peeled. Like some breeds of snakes, they like to travel together. Another encounter like this and the saints may not be with us." Then with an afterthought added, "Break out some of my private Madeira wine stock. One drink per man, mind you, no more. This isn't a time for anyone to get soused. None for the lookouts though. Instead, Cleve can brew a supply of strong coffee to help keep their eyes open."

"Aye, Sir," the mate broke into a wide grin and licked his lips in anticipation. The opportunity to indulge in the pleasure of an expensive wine did not often come his way. This meant a taste of pure luxury compared to the cheap, sometimes deadly Dill Devil, or common grog the crew usually drank. Common seamen, tossed amid the many temptations found in the ports, seldom hung on to their purses for long. Higher grade liquors produced along the *Spanish Main* of the *Caribbean Sea* were too expensive to slake the desires of their gullets.

"That means you in particular," Niles warned, well aware of Kleet's propensity for liquor. "Miss Silvas," he offered an arm, "I invite you to join me for a glass in my cabin. We all can use a little bracer right about now."

In his quarters he withdrew two long stemmed crystal goblets edged with gold and a bottle of the choicest Madeira from his private locked closet. He laced the potent liquor with the appropriate measure of water and offered a goblet to his guest. With hesitation, she held the stem gingerly between her slender fingers. In the symbolic gesture of a toast, he raised his glass.

"Go ahead, taste it. You'll find no finer wine in all England."

She looked at him with uncertain reservation. Could she trust this inexplicable man before her? Slowly she tipped the golden rim to her lips and tested a small sip.

"Although I hate admit it, you are quite right," she smiled, and her eyes held a glow when they met his. "This amazes me."

"Because I am right? Or the quality of wine?"

"Both," she laughed with an upward tilt of her delicately formed chin.

Their laughter, only the nervous aftermath of tension release, returned to its former restraint. Niles, attracted to the sound, wished they could always be this congenial when together. Her past behavior had given no indication a mischievous trait lay hidden beneath her cloak of frosty dignity. He liked that in a woman. "I must say, it's a mystery to me how you managed to dress so fast. You were at the rail almost as soon as I."

She flushed under her secret. "When you thought it best not to undress in case of an emergency, I decided to do the same."

Amused, he shook his head. Which is she more afraid of? Me, or danger from the outside? he wondered. "If something did happen, what do you think you would do?"

The flush deepened to scarlet. "At least," she hedged, "I would not be caught in my nightclothes. Especially since, without my satchel, I have none."

Shocked to hear her speak so forwardly, he couldn't resist the opportunity to quip, "I agree, that could arouse one's curiosity." With a light chuckle he looked away rather than increase her embarrassment.

"You can be very cruel, Captain!" she retorted, and turned her back. The cords of her neck swelled in anger.

Captain Leyden raised from his bunk on one elbow and rubbed the sleep from his eyes. "Wine, this time of night?" Before they could answer, he suspiciously peered at the pair through the dim light. "Something going on here I don't know about?"

"All clear," Niles assured, and moved to sit on the edge of the elder's bunk. He tried to make light of the incident as he described the galleon. When it came to the part about the cannons the old man's eyes widened in a mixture of excitement and concern.

"Why didn't you wake me?" he shouted.

"Wasn't time. It was already about to come alongside when Toro and I arrived on deck." The older man's face registered disappointment. "Come," Niles invited. "Join us. All's well that ends well, no matter how accomplished, aye?"

The three sipped the cold wine in the mellow light of the lamp, saying little. Victoria and Niles felt drained after the nerve wrenching experience. Captain Leyden nodded his head, and declared, "You done right, Boy, you done right when you ordered Kleet to sit tight and hold fire. Those Spaniards would have blown both us, and this fine wine, clean into infinity."

The lady shivered. "I expected one of those cannon balls to go off in our faces any minute."

"Don't worry," Niles gave a nervous laugh. "At that close range you would neither have seen, nor known it."

The two captains, Miss Silvas, Kleet and Toro met in conference early the next morning. It was important for everyone to synchronize their activities once they hit port. Every man must know the alternatives should anyone be recognized, and what to do if any other emergencies arose. They must plan every movement to take place in the shortest possible time, yet achieve their three main objectives: transportation to deliver their passenger to her relatives, find a buyer for their cargo, and take on trade goods, food, supplies and fresh water.

Another consideration was Miss Silvas. Her light skin would most surely draw attention if they brought her ashore under the pretext of an island slave woman. They must think of a way to darken her color.

"How about passing her off as a crewmember?" Kleet proposed.

"Sounds good," Niles nodded.

Appalled by the suggestion, she sputtered, "Me, dressed as a deck hand?"

"Right," Niles replied. "If the alarm went out, Guards will look for a lone lady on board. It's ideal for our purpose." He sized her up from head to toe. "Our men are larger built. Their clothes are much too big for her."

"How about Weasel?" Kleet asked. "He's about the same height and weight."

"You know how he hates to do laundry. It would be pure luck to find any clean ones." Niles replied. A trickle of laughter passed between the assembled group. "She'll need boots, too. Those fancy slippers need to go--- and gloves. No deck hand walks around with uncaloused hands. We can stuff her hair from sight under a knit skullcap. Kleet, see what you can chase up." The mate hurried out to procure the necessary items. Niles turned to Captain Leyden. "Can you think of anything we haven't covered?"

"No---," the older man stroked his beard, "but let's go over everything one more time. Kleet will be in charge of the crew to unload and load. Toro, Miss Silvas, you and I go ashore. We hire a carriage for the lady. Once she's off our hands, you and I find a trader, deal our cargo, and bargain for exchange merchandise and supplies. Toro will oversee the transfer of our trade goods."

"No!" the black stubbornly shook his woolly head. "Toro stay wi' Cap'n Brett."

"Not this time, Toro. We need you as a dependable overseer to get the new cargo transported to the ship. Do as I say and consider it an order." The Negroid reluctantly subsided into morose submission.

"Next," Captain Leyden resumed, "we hit a place where we can stock up on ammunition. Cargo and ammunition handled, we go after a stock of food staples---especially fruit and fresh vegetables. We don't want any of our men to come down with scurvy for lack of them. Garden produce will be in short supply this time of year. Likely means settle for apples, dried fruits, and vegetables wintered in cellars. If there are any available, street venders will have them." He raised a finger of caution, "And make sure Kleet adds paint, tar, oil, and rope to the supplies. Our lines show wear. The Royal Guards encounter didn't do them any good either. To play around with worn rigging can be downright dangerous if we get caught in a whoppin' storm."

Kleet reappeared with a bundle of clothes under one arm. "One thing, if I may say---" he looked at Niles with hesitation.

"Yes, what is it?"

The mate's feet shifted. "It's just that---with regard to the danger of recognition, this may be a time to take exception."

"Come, come, man. Spit it out."

The words rushed forth. "I think it wise if the Captain removed the earring." He turned to the older man and added apologetically, "Sorry Sir, I know how you feel, but it's for your own safety."

"I'll leave it up to him," Niles conceded, then changed the subject. "Now, Lady, get into these clothes, and come out looking like a man---or at least a passable cabin boy." Flushed with embarrassment, she retreated to return shortly later.

The men appraised the transformed figure top to toe. They scrutinized the disguise, each in search of defects. Miss Silvas awaited their comments, head lowered, extremely self-conscious in this strange, unladylike attire. Niles gave a negative wave of hand.

"Face too pale for a seaman. She lacks the tanned, weathered look of salt air and sun."

"Cacao," Toro blurted.

"What's that you say?"

"Cacao in hold. Cleve press, dry, grind, oil, rub on," he gestured, and rubbed his hands on his face. "Not too much, or be black like Toro." His grin widened to display an even row of white teeth. The others laughed at the implication.

"Stop funnin', this is serious business," Captain Leyden reprimanded. Victoria, meanwhile, unaccustomed to boots, chose to stroll awkwardly across the room to a chair.

"Wait!" Niles jerked around. "Come back here." She complied, Weasel's boots clumping heavily upon the wooden floor. "Those boots are much too big, aren't they?" She nodded. "Some heavy socks will fill the excess space. Here," he said, and drew a couple pairs from a trunk. "Put these on. Then walk around the decks this morning until you can master the rolling mannerism of a seaman."

Captain Leyden shook a warning finger, accompanied by a playful wink. "Means forget all about being a lady until inside the door of your kinsfolk. For the present you must play the part of a man to the letter. Niles, what about her voice?"

"You're right. If anyone hears her talk it will mean a rope for all our necks." Toro's hands began to make suggestive motions about his mouth. Irritated by the distraction, Niles asked, "What now, Toro, speak man." The black only continued the motions as if using sign language. Niles failed to understand and frowned. "Can't you speak?"

Toro enthusiastically bobbed his head. "No talk," he said, and motioned to his mouth. "How you say---" he fumbled for the right words within his limited English.

"You mean a mute? A man who can't

talk?"

He vigorously nodded, "Mute, yes Suh, mute."

"Good idea!" Captain Leyden slapped his knee. "Wouldn't be the first mute on a ship. One of us can talk for her." He looked at Victoria as a twinkle rose to his eyes. "Think you can keep quiet that long?" The lady's flush returned. "Just funnin' Child. Watch the men. Learn to walk and act like us, and you will do all right."

Meeting concluded, Niles left to circulate the decks to inform each man on precisely what would be his job while in port. Next he checked the supply of ammunition concealed at strategic locations should the need arise. Mid-way he paused the inspections. His attention settled on Miss Silvas. He watched her stagger about among the rigging, clutching at anything within reach for balance and shook his head. "How can she possibly emulate the stride of a seaman," he muttered, "if she can't even master her sea legs?"

Other than the walk, he marveled at how well she seemed to adapt to her new masculine role. It was hard to believe this dark skinned, shoddy, unrefined pawn was once a vision of loveliness in a jeweled gown. It unnerved him to find his initial attraction to her still remained. A twinge of guilt swept over him. Was it really necessary, he questioned, to disgrace her to this degree to insure their safety? Or was it only a derisive need, on his part, to degrade this haughty social butterfly to one step above the gutter?

Consumed with shame, he tried to sort his frustrated mind; decide between necessity and revenge. It was not too late to change the disguise he personally imposed upon her. He closed his eyes, but could not blot out the contrived mute before him. He wanted the sloven creature to go away, disappear. Wanted it replaced by the lady in the elegant gown, complete with jeweled flowers, pearls laced among dark curls. Alas, when he opened them again the ugly cracked boots erased the memory of heeled slippers in his hands. Captain Leyden stepped to his side, invading his reverie.

"My suggestion may not be as attractive as the scenery over there, Lad, but I brought our glasses. Time we looked at the lay of the shoreline. Need to calculate the best place to bring her in." Niles tore his attention away from the mute. Together they climbed to the forecastle. From there they had a clear view.

Niles lifted his spyglass and scanned the area. "Quite a traffic of ships over to starboard. Must be the main harbor."

Captain Leyden shifted his glass for a

look. "They could be an uncomfortable pack to mix with, I'd say. Too many, too close together. Best we stay clear if we can possibly spot an alternative." His gnarled fingers fumbled to adjust his glass. "These old eyes of mine aren't as sharp as they once were. Tell me, do you see a little bay over to their port? May not have depth for those larger ships, whereas the *Pearl* might be able to handle it."

"Not too far from that main harbor either," Niles mused. "Let's try for it."

Captain Leyden's eyes strayed to the wind-billowed sails overhead. "You go below and change into trader clothes, while I call instructions to the helm. If all goes well, we'll soon be ready to dock. It won't do for anyone to see you as you are now."

Clothing changed, he returned to join the older man. The two centered their experienced eyes on the water. Any change of color or currents could be an indication of jagged rocks or shoals below the surface. One thing the *Pearl* did not need was a hole torn in her hull. To sink now would mean certain disaster.

"How does it look to you?" Niles asked, as he continued to scan the busy secluded bay. Totally unexpected his glass riveted on a miniature harbor nestled farther along the shore. Even at this distance he could already make out a few buildings partially hidden among winter's leafless trees. The village Miss Silvas spoke of? He motioned to his partner toward this new discovery.

A slow grin spread across the wizened face of Captain Leyden. "I jolly well believe it's the answer to what we need at a time like this."

The most crucial area lay dead ahead. They must make a swift entrance into the smaller bay without being seen by any ships that lay at anchor in the larger harbor. They drew nearer the shore; the depth became dangerously shallow. It became understandable why larger ships had abandoned this bay for the port farther up the coast. Niles motioned to the helmsman, whom swung the tiller. Their course shifted into a wide smooth arc.

Kleet, former egotistical antagonism cast aside, now faced the serious business at hand. In obedience to his barked orders the sails were adjusted to slow the vessel's approach. All hands stood by, and anxiously hoped for sufficient depth to accommodate the *Pearl's b*ottom. Under Kleet's expertise, the ship glided slowly, ever so slowly to broadside an ancient wharf. Its decayed condition gave silent witness of once better days, long since gone. A line snaked through the air, followed by more of the same. Hands quickly lashed them fast to the dock. So far, Niles thought, everything went almost too easy. He waited, eyes narrowed, every nerve tensed in anticipation of what they may meet when they stepped ashore.

CHAPTER FOUR

Niles made a careful analysis of each detail of the weathered buildings that stood near the wharf. It appeared, on the surface at least, peaceful.

Local inhabitants, curious of their new arrivals, began to gather in small groups to speculate on this unexpected event. Their faces registered surprise at sight a ship the size of the *Pearl*, or any other ship for that matter, tying up at their impoverished wharf. If Niles could trust himself to read their expressions correctly, they appeared pleased and excited.

He stepped onto the pier and found it even more dilapidated than he had anticipated. The once thick planks showed advanced signs of rot; many hung raggedly downward from the structure, and horizontal gaps appeared where others had long since disappeared. Several weathered buildings, long abandoned by their owners, waited nearby: deserted, decayed, sad leftovers from another time. Their stark empty windows stared blankly seaward. Wooden pilings jutted from the water at tired angles, stark relics of a forgotten era.

Niles turned to Captain Leyden, who had joined him. "What do you think? Should we bring our passenger ashore now, or test the air first?"

"I'd say now. The sooner we hire a hack and get her out of sight the better. Our hands and minds will be free then to get on with the other things we need to do."

Niles motioned her onto the wharf and warned, "You better put on a bloody good performance, or we'll all be turning in our sea legs for the discomforts of a cell in the tower."

She ignored his statement, and fumed, "First you give me a lecture on cleanliness, then turn around and insist I wear these awful clothes. As if that's not enough I have this smelly guk smeared all over me."

"Stop complaining. This is no time to get vanity conscious with strangers around. After you're out of sight, and we're safely back at sea, you can do and say as you please."

"Gladly! These heavy boots kill my feet."

"Forget your feet. Instead, loosen that shirtfront and draw the jacket more forward. You need to appear flat chested to pass as a man."

"If that's what it takes to keep my feet on dry land consider it done! I swear never to step foot on a ship again."

"Quiet! You can't talk, remember?"

The entourage moved forward the length of the pier and advanced toward the inhabitants. Niles, with the air of a professional merchant sea captain, strode confident and tall, the mute cabin boy in castoffs, Captain Leyden and Toro followed. More villagers gathered about in inquisitive clusters. Their eyes stared in bewilderment: some amazed, others openly curious. Niles carefully analyzed the assemblage. His attention focused on a man past middle age, neither rural, nor too distinctive. Ah, Niles thought, now there was a man whom might possess the financial means to serve one of the Pearl's most important needs.

Without hesitation, he boldly stepped forward and extended a hand. "I am Captain Brett." Deliberately, he avoided to mention the name of his ship. "Would there be a carriage for hire in your village, Sir?"

The man in the expensively tailored suit removed his matching gray felt hat. He turned, one gray brow lifted in question, to the others grouped about him. Blank stares, a few pursed lips and a negative shake of heads met the inquiry. The stately gentleman, taking on the role of spokesperson, answered, "No, Captain. It's been a long time since we've had a call for such here. May I suggest you try the main harbor area." With a motion of one arm he indicated toward the crowded harbor down shore. "Hacks nowadays work over there where there is more demand for their services." Unable to longer contain his interest, the man posed the question foremost on the minds of all those clustered nearby. "Would you mind, my good Captain, if I ask---I mean, it is highly unusual these days to see a ship such as yours dock in our little harbor. True, once this was a busy port," he nodded in affirmation. "But now all the ships choose the deeper waters. No one has tied up here for many years." Nods and vocal assents rose from the townspeople.

Niles turned to insure the attention of the entire assemblage. "The answer to why we chose your harbor is both simple and practical. First, to deliver this lad closer to his destination. Second, we thought your people would like the chance to make considerable profit from top grade Caribbean cargo. Why let the big dealers over there make all the money, right?" He paused to allow comments of agreement ripple through the throng. "In addition, I must admit to a selfish reason of my own. We are short on time. My men have been at sea for months. They are anxious to return to their families on the island of Jamaica. Large ports are very busy. That always makes a long delay before we can bargain with a buyer. Each day means one day longer before we can return to the *Spanish Main*. My tired men long to go home."

The man in gray rubbed the back of his neck, stared at the cracked planks at his feet, and pondered the matter. "What you say makes good sense, my man, but you must understand," he held up a hand, "we are no longer prepared to receive ships here. There are things that must be taken under consideration. We need dock workers to unload the goods, suitable places to store merchandise, money and trade goods to handle such a transaction."

"Perhaps we can be of help," Niles pressed. "My crew will lower the cargo right onto your wharf. Then they will help transport it to one of these nearby storage houses. As for the last requirement, I assume," he pried cagily, "someone here is, or was once, a very successful trader?" The man nodded. Aha! Niles thought, my initial judgment was correct. He is a retired trader of the first rank.

To further nudge the man's interest, he

added, "I can assist your decision by providing a complete cargo list. As for trade goods and money, our needs are quite ordinary. We need ammunition to protect ourselves against the bloody troublesome pirates encountered on the high seas these days, the usual food staples for our return voyage, and a limited quantity of clothing. Beyond those items, we are ready to consider any goods suitable for trade in say---the American Colonies?"

Captain Leyden, who up to now had remained silent, interrupted. "Don't forget fruits and vegetables. We need plenty of both. And some repair and upkeep stores for the ship."

The expression on the elderly trader's face clearly revealed their unexpected arrival baffled his aged mind. His retired brain slowly began to reactivate while mentally he returned to memories of more prosperous days. At one time past he was the most successful trader in the now abandoned port. Captain Leyden lowered his eyes and shifted one foot. Niles caught the restless signal. The elder felt Niles pressed his man too fast, albeit they must move quickly and risks must be taken.

"Surely, there is a merchant among you financially able to take the entire load."

"Perhaps, perhaps," the man continued to nod, in deep concentration.

"Good." Niles whipped the cargo list from his inside coat pocket and shoved it into the man's hand. "While you look this over, perhaps these other men have remembered a conveyance for hire." He deliberately turned away to allow the man time to think, appraise, and become desirous of the wares. Meantime, as he expected, among those gathered, he found no answer to his transportation question.

"Mighty good assortment of cargo, Captain," the man regained Niles' attention. "How do I know if it's top quality?"

"You are most welcome to personally come aboard for an inspection, my good man. You'll find no finer products from the *Main* on any ship afloat." Now Niles was certain his practiced eye chose wisely. This was a professional buyer, albeit perhaps retired from the trade. To add fuel to fire the interest of his objective, he tantalized, "Island commodities this early in the season should bring a fine price, sir. An excellent return on your investment, don't you agree?"

"Yes, yes," the gentleman quickly responded and assumed a proud stance. "I still have my connections, Captain, although in recent years I've not been extremely active in the business."

"It's easy to see you are highly respected among traders," Niles said, with an eye to capitalize on the man's pride by the use of a bit of flattery. The pleased man drew to his full height. Age aside, he struggled to resume a semblance of former prestige, dust off his old skills and experience a revival of crafty techniques plied by him in his prime. "I never bargain sight unseen, young man. Only after I take a look for myself will I make a judgment and consider talking business "

The change of character did not deceive Niles. He motioned a hand toward *The Sea Pearl*. "Welcome aboard, Sir. I invite you to take a tour through a feast for your eyes!" The opportunity was more than the retired trader could resist.

At the conclusion of the inspection the man, no longer able to conceal his pleasure, revealed a definite reluctance to return topside. As Niles expected, his senses longed to remain to drink in the wares appreciatively. His nostrils reveled over the scent of fragrant spices and teas that promised pleasurable brews. The age stiffened fingers lingered over the luxurious feel of fine silks, items of gold, carved ivory and priceless jewels. It became a second chance for him to relive, if only for a few precious moments, the profession of his former years.

Niles, by habit, was about to invite the

prospective client into his quarters to discuss prices when at the last moment he remembered the draped curtain. Undoubtedly this man had entered many a captain's cabin in the past. He would immediately recognize something was amiss. Quickly, he changed course. "Let us go to the galley to talk," he proposed. "There you will not only see the fine teas and South American coffees, but can taste a mug for yourself."

"Well now, I can't say anyone presented a more perfect suggestion in all my trading years."

Niles had to restrain his sense of relief when, after a lengthy discussion and compilation of figures over steaming pewter mugs, the man at last extended his hand. "It is a deal."

The two captains, transactions with the trader completed at the money house, headed toward the road that led to the main port. Suddenly Niles remembered Miss Silvas. If left alone among the townspeople her disguise would most certainly be discovered. It would mean disaster. He spun around, raced back to the dock, and grabbed her arm. They rejoined Captain Leyden on the road, who was standing beside a wagon loaded with potatoes. "Those for sale?" Captain Leyden asked.

The driver nodded. "An' a few carrots an' turnips we been storin'."

"How much do you want for them?"

The man pondered the question before answering.

"Too much," Niles shook his head.

"They be scarce come this time o' year. Ships be wantin'. They pay good."

Niles offered up a tidy sum in his outstretched hand. "We will give you this much for the entire load."

The driver leisurely tapped his pipe on the wagon side to empty its cold ashes, glanced briefly at the hand, and shook his head. "Not enough."

With an eye to the useful potential of the horse and wagon, Niles increased the gold coins. "Tell you what I'll do. I will give you all this if you agree to throw in the rental of your wagon for the day."

Unhurried, the farmer tamped fresh tobacco to his satisfaction into the pipe with his thumb. Finally, with a dubious shake of his head, he answered, "You might not bring it back. Buy load, wagon, and horse."

Niles could see his opponent's mind was set. "You pack a hard bargain, Sir, but I accept."

The driver climbed down and pocketed the agreed price. The trio mounted the wagon, Niles at the reins. Captain Leyden nudged him from behind as they entered the narrow streets of the larger harbor. Rows of cannon stood guard along the shoreline, their ominous barrels pointed seaward.

"Good thing we decided not to enter the main harbor!" Niles responded out of the corner of is mouth.

They watched as an English ship entered from the same direction as the *Pearl*. Could it bear news of their escape? Niles cursed under his breath. "We lost too much time convincing that old gent on our cargo!"

"Couldn't be helped, Son. We were lucky to swing the deal at all."

This seaport was a drastic contrast to the sleepy village they had left behind. Here the narrow wooden walks teemed with activity. Traders, peddlers, sea captains and deck hands jostled shoulder to shoulder with the usual waterfront riffraff. Dusty streets were crowded with all form of conveyances, mounted riders and pedestrians. Each pushed in search of an opening they could squeeze through. Music, noise and boisterous yells emanated from a profusion of grog houses to mingle with the sounds of the busy thoroughfare. Niles guided their horse and wagon deftly through the maze toward a peddler's stand where he reined to a stop.

"We shall make better time if we work our way on foot," he explained. Then added quietly, "If, perchance, we need to leave in a hurry, we'd never get this rig out of that mess up ahead. From here, if need be, we can hoist anchor and make a run for it."

Nearby a ragged street urchin loitered against a building. He reached up to deftly catch the coin tossed in payment to watch their wagon. Niles took Miss Silvas' arm, began to steer her toward a peddler's stand and motioned for Captain Leyden to follow. Only small quantities of dried prunes were found, nothing else. They purchased, to the vendor's delight his entire supply, and rejoined the throng. Inquires of other vendors along the way, met with little success.

"Appears the only way we shall accumulate enough is to buy all the small batches we come across," Captain Leyden observed. "I sure don't relish the thought of a sick crew on the return trip."

Miss Silvas pointed to the far side of the street to where a poorly dressed man carried two large, sadly worn, reed baskets. The apples within were not of the best quality, but at this point the trio could not be choosy. They bargained for the lot and induced the vender to also sell his baskets. They would be handy to carry further purchases. They emptied the apples into the wagon, covered their purchases from sight, and resumed their search.

"Paying a boy to watch our wagon was a good idea," Miss Silvas remarked.

"Maybe. He will, like as not, fill his pockets with our fruit and run when we are out of sight."

"Why did you pay him if you knew he could not be trusted?"

With no desire to admit he was a soft touch for unfortunates, he snapped, "You're a mute, remember? Stop talking." He turned to the older man. "Captain Leyden, we'll save time if you take one side of the street while Miss Sil---" he glanced around at the ears that may have overheard his error.

Quick to correct himself, he continued, "---the dummy and I comb the other side. Best try to keep each other in sight though; one never knows what we might come across in a port such as this."

"I agree. It's taking too much time this way."

They hastened off in the two directions to bargain for everything edible in their paths. Purchasing in such small lots proved slow and frustrating; each return to the wagon, however, increased the bulge under the cover.

Niles cut through a side street and suddenly drew Miss Silvas up short before a shop window. She gasped, "It's the most beautiful gown I have ever seen!" There it stood: vibrant red, tantalizingly low cut bosom accented by snowy white lace frill, bouffant sleeves of fine lace tapered down to slender wristlets closed by rows of tiny fabric covered buttons. Niles recognized the shimmering brocade as imported. None so fine was produced in all England. The wasp waist, trim bustles at either hip, graceful flow of draped skirt, all bespoke an unsurpassed air of elegance. Breathless with anticipation, Victoria needed no encouragement as he led her inside the shop. He motioned for a clerk, inquired of the size and whether a matching hat was obtainable. The sallow faced clerk, with an energetic nod, rushed off to the rear of the shop. Victoria used this moment of opportunity to urgently tug at Niles' sleeve. Head shaking vigorously, she attempted to tell him it was a size too large for her petite body. No sooner than she done so, than the clerk returned to present the perfect complement for the gorgeous gown. The wide brimmed feminine hat matched the fabric, bore identical lace, and in addition, an airy ostrich plume accented it. Niles inspected it critically, yet made no inquiry on the price of either item. Instead, he asked, "And would you also have a sun parasol to match?"

The clerk smiled broadly at his prospective patron. The opportunity to make such a profitable transaction did not come his way every day. He scurried off to produce the requested item and presented it as if it were a jewel. "Ah, a true complement to any lovely lady, wouldn't you say, Sir?"

"Yes, quite distinctive," Niles agreed. "Wrap it up."

“The parasol, Sir?”

"Everything," Niles corrected, amused by the shocked expression upon the clerk's face.

"B---but my good sir, I don't believe you---that is---the price of these---"

"Price is not important. Wrap them up, if you please. I’m in a hurry."

"Y---yes, Sir! As you wish, Sir."

While the man fumbled nervously amid the rustle of paper and string, Niles discreetly slipped a leather pouch from a concealed pocket inside his coat and emptied the contents onto the counter.

"Will this cover it?"

"Very definitely! Thank you kindly, Sir."

Out in the street again, Miss Silvas sputtered, "B---but my size---"

A quick jab in the ribs called for silence. "Remember, you can't talk, so stop making noises before you get us all killed."

Taverns and grog shops where men from ships and local riffraff converged for drunken revelry butted together on both sides of the crowded street ahead. Niles hesitated in his stride. The chances were too great of being recognized by someone who Captain Leyden, or he, had met before. Friend or foe, honor meant nothing when tempted by rewards from the Crown. The Judas could be almost any face among this shifty crowd. Before he could turn around among the crowd to take a different route he was suddenly struck from the side.

An off balance drunk reeled and jostled hard against him. He stepped to catch his own balance only to hurled against yet another man. He whirled, feet planted solidly in preparation for an encounter. One hand instantly gripped the sharp pointed dagger within his coat front. His actions froze mid-way. He was face to face with a Royal Guard!

"Excuse me, Sir," he quickly recovered, and stepped aside. If they were extremely lucky, perhaps the Guard would continue on his way. To his dismay, the uniformed man's eyes locked suspiciously on Miss Silvas.

He grabbed her arm with a shake rough enough to rattle any man's teeth, and demanded, "Who are you?"

Niles intercepted. "A mute, Sir. He's from a ship in port."

"Let the lad answer for himself," the Guard angrily growled, unconvinced.

"Sorry, Sir, I fear you did not understand. He's a mute." In a deliberate effort to draw the Guard's attention away from his subject Niles asked, "Haven't you seen a mute before? A dummy---one who cannot talk? I will need to speak for him if you have any questions.

The Guard delivered a dubious glare at the pair. "What ship do you sail on?"

Niles had to think fast. "The *Sea Spray*."
"Never heard of it. Where's she from?"
"Norway, Sir."
"Your captain?"

"Svenson," Niles snapped back, grateful

for the dim light lest the Guard detect the false coloring on her face.

The Guard relaxed. "Orders to watch all strangers. We've a report *The Sea Pearl* may be in the area. She may carry a lady, and possibly a man we be after."

"Is that so?" Niles feigned interest.

The Guard, once he began to talk, warmed to mix a bit of social conversation with his more serious duties. "Word is, one or both men tried to escape and were killed in the fray, but they aren't certain. We have orders to arrest either one on sight. I hear the two captains of that ship are right tricky. Even if they are dead the crew may try to smuggle the lady back ashore. If so, they'll find us Guards aren't easy to fool."

"I am sure you aren't," Niles readily agreed.

"Wish I could nab her. Better yet, the older captain, if he still be alive. With the reward that's on his head, I could retire and rest my bones." He looked again at the dummy. "This boy doesn't begin to resemble the lady, he be too dark. We've been told the woman is very fair skinned, long dark hair---one of those fancy society ladies."

Niles kept his eyes averted from the

skullcap lest the Guard get an idea to remove it. If so, her disguise would come to an abrupt end when the hair tumbled down about her shoulders.

"Have you seen that *Sea Pearl* anywhere in the harbor?"

"Not only have I not seen, but also I've never heard of her," Niles lied.

"Then you are a rare one. She's manned by a crew of the bloodiest pirates afloat, they tell. All plain kill crazy, I hear. Need to be strung up, drawn and quartered, same as they do to their captives!" He bobbed his head for emphasis. "If that lady were still alive she'd be better off dead, that's what she'd be. As for the captain, they say he wears a fancy golden earring punched right through the flesh of his chest. That gives you a purty good picture of his bloody barbaric character. Well, I must be on my way. Best teach your dummy how to take a bath!" He laughed, and moved rigidly off through the mass of shoving humanity.

Miss Silvas went limp under Niles' hand. He gripped her arm more tightly, and began to advance past one of the more popular grog houses. A loud voice that could be heard out into the street rose above the music and revelers. "Hear she's a right ravin' beauty." The words instantly caught Niles' attention, although the voice itself was not familiar.

"Was," someone corrected. "You can bet she ain't no more; that perverted crew will have seen to that by now."

"If they do put her ashore, only place that'll have 'er is a ratty waterfront parlor house. Even then, nobody'd want her wares---wot's left of 'em!" Uproarious laughter drowned out any further statements. Although Niles refused to admit any interest in the lady himself, he shoved her toward the center of the street. No need to expose her to embarrassment and humiliation expressed by the idle talk of such gutter trash.

Close by he caught sight of Captain Leyden attempting to strike a deal with an old woman. Niles, seeing she was being extremely uncooperative, pushed in their direction. Her age and appearance said she had frequented the waterfront enough years to be expert on how to drive a hard bargain. He elbowed his way through the crowd with the dummy firmly in tow. Almost there, his attention was drawn to a commotion that erupted ahead. Two liquor enraged men tumbled from a tavern doorway. Fists swung, as the pair threw their weight into a drunken brawl. Several others soon joined the fray. A throng, hungry for blood and excitement, soon gathered. They shouted encouragement and pressed in closer around the combatants.

A powerful swing, a crack of jaw, and one man sprawled backwards.

His bulk crashed into Captain Leyden, knocking him off balance.

The wrinkled, hag, unwilling to lose her prize customer, darted forward. Her bony fingers clawed at his shirt. As he went down the fabric ripped and exposed his bare chest. For an instant the shriveled woman stared open mouthed at the now exposed telltale earring.

Niles sprang forward.
He shoved her roughly aside, scooped the captain up from the street and attempted as he did so to conceal the golden ring.

The riotous street brawl was sure to draw the nearby Guards. Before them the crone screamed in excited anticipation, one bony finger raised to shake accusingly at Captain Leyden.

"I know you! Tha' earring---I've heerd about tha' golden ring!" The deep set piercing eyes glinted of greed and evil. "The name---my old mind can't recollect the name---" she stamped angrily and tore at her stringy hair. "Aye, I was aworkin' the waterfront the night you and tha' wife o' yourn ran off wi' the Royal Guards at your heels. Ah, the reward on your head will take care o' me for the rest of me days! No more freezin' me bones sellin' in the street." She began to wave her arms wildly and shout. "Guard! Someone get the Guards!"

Niles spun the captain around and called out to Miss Silvas. "Run for the wagon!"

They ran.

Shoving and jostling everyone from their path, they reached the conveyance. Victoria and Captain Leyden climbed on. Niles grabbed the reins. A snap of whip, the horse lunged forward and the wagon nearly overturned as it careened sharply around. The trio dashed straightway for the small village, horse at a dead gallop, harnesses jangling. Carriages and people afoot, alarmed by the fast approaching travelers, scurried to a place of safety. The wheels of the wagon jolted over the profusion of ruts along the roadway. Miss Silvas and Captain Leyden clutched the wagon's sides to avoid being thrown off. Dislodged apples and potatoes began to spill from the rear. They bounced and rolled like red and brown balls along the road.

"Grab the corners of that cover," Niles shouted over his shoulder. "Or they'll leave a trail right to the *Pearl*!" The pair threw themselves across the load and pinned the cover with their bodies.

Nearing the ship he made an upward motion

with one arm to Kleet, who watched their approach from the rail. At sight of the emergency signal the mate barked to the crew. Men sprang into action, prepared to unfurl sails and release mooring lines. The lathered horse whipped the wagon onto the decadent pier and jerked to a standstill alongside the hull.

"Heave down ropes," Niles yelled. "We'll take her up, wagon and all!"

"Horse, too?" Kleet shouted back in disbelief.

"No, you fool!" he answered, already at work to unhitch the traces. "Miss Silvas, climb for the deck! Captain, give me a hand with these ropes. We'll make a sling."

Within seconds he ran to release the last moor line to free the straining ship. As he did so, he motioned to Kleet. "Heave to and take her up." The wagon wheels began to lift from the pier. "Hop aboard, Captain!" he yelled, and vaulted atop the load.

The crew above hauled at the ropes. The wagon groaned, and slowly scraped and bumped its way up the side of the hull.

"How we gonna' land it on deck?" Kleet called down.

"Dump it over the rail! Captain, jump on the deck before they roll it!"

The wagon tipped onto its side, and crashed onto the quarterdeck. Wintered fruits and vegetables spilled from under the released cover.

Their pursuers began to close in. A clamor that rose from the throng brought another yell from Niles. "Full sail! Heave to!"

Canvases caught the wind, and with a shudder underfoot, *The Sea Pearl* was under way. None too soon, Niles thought, as he watched townspeople, accompanied by a force of Guards, storm onto the wharf. The *Pearl* rapidly gained speed. Since there were no cannon in the small bay, she would soon be out of range of any firepower they possessed. One more possibility, however, remained: an interception as they passed through the bay entrance to open sea.

The deck rolled sharply as they veered to point her bow directly toward the narrow entrance channel. Niles caught sight of a movement over at the rail. He whirled around, fearful someone from shore had succeeded in climbing aboard. His hands flashed to the grips of his *pistolas*. A dark head appeared over the side.

"'Bout lef' us behind, Cap'n," a wet Toro

grinned broadly. Several other crewmen, who had been at work on shore, began to climb onto the deck. "She done cleared port when we got there. We swim hard. Good you forget line hang over side when you lef' in hurry."

Niles gripped the wet shoulder, "I'm glad you all made it. Can't afford to lose a single one of you."

"You glad? How you think we feel? If'n mob catch hold us they'd already drawn an' quartered for sure. Ain't nobody mo' happy than Toro be right here," he pointed with emphasis to the deck.

"Pray your luck holds. We haven't escaped the king's gallows yet. Enemy ships may lie in wait for us when we pass through the channel."

They approached the narrow entrance, all hands alert. Trees blocked the view on either side. The helmsman swung the tiller to veer around the end of the sandbar. The open sea came into sight. Niles quickly swung his glass from left to right and back again. If English ships waited beyond, a couple cannon balls to the *Pearl's* broadside would send her down before her crew got off a single shot. Did they lurk behind the dense cover of the trees? Perhaps the Pearl would at least have a chance to fight back if not taken by surprise. His eye strained to catch sight of a patch of sail or a mast hidden beyond the maze of twisted branches. The gray winter forest blended with the gray of sea made it hard to distinguish anything.

Bow aimed straight for the safety of the ocean, his glass suddenly revealed a splash of color. Yes, there it was, crouched, ready to spring. Out of range, but closing fast! He pointed toward their assailant. Captain Leyden shouted an alarm. The first mate bellowed orders, and the decks came alive. Niles swung his glass back and forth in an anxious search for additional vessels. To be caught in a crossfire trap was a deadly game. He drew a deep breath when the shoreline dropped off their wake and the Pearl gained access to the open sea. A little farther, only a little farther. Now they had a running chance. Free from the shelter of the cove, the winds grew stronger; the *Pearl* picked up speed.

The pursuit ship set off an explosive barrage of deadly cannon fire. The lethal missals fell short of target, sending geysers of water erupting high into the air.

Larger, more cumbersome, heavily armed vessels began to close in. If it came to a contest of speed and maneuverability, the *Pearl* surpassed all but the smaller lead ship. Niles needed but one look to see its load line indicated she traveled nearly empty. The Pearl carried a full cargo. He knew the situation called for tacking; it would be more difficult for the cannon to strike a zigzagging target. The evasive tactic may help them survive until their opponent gave up---or *The Sea Pearl* became too crippled to remain afloat.

Kleet would play it cool, save ammunition until they came into range, not foolish as they, firing their port cannons in unison. Instead, when the time came, the first mate would shrewdly set theirs off in a series. Thus when the last barrel fired, the first would be ready to resume. In that manner they could keep up a constant barrage. The *Pearl's* barrels, as for now, remained silent. With the aid of superior speed the crew hoped to out run their pursuer until it gave up the chase.

On orders, the helm sharply swung the tiller. The deck rolled under the sharp turn. A large object struck hard against the steerage with a loud crash and splitting of wood. Niles and the helmsman, thrown off balance on the impact, were sent sprawling onto the deck. Niles, whom's spyglass faced directly at their opponent's cannons before the impact, saw no flash of fire immediately preceding the strike. They most surely had been hit, of that there was no doubt. Leaping to his feet, he spun around to make a quick check on damages. At the shattered doorway he stopped short, released his breath, and gave a nervous laugh.

The splintered remains of the

demolished farm wagon lay heaped against the steerage. Spilled fruits, vegetables, and potatoes bounced and rolled all about the deck. Apparently, with the lean of the ship, the wheels began to turn and gained momentum until it slammed against the solid wall. Niles wiped beads of perspiration from his forehead with the back of a hand. The foodstuffs and steerage repairs must wait. He dashed back to his observation post, again adjusted his glass, surprised to discover an unexpected transformation taking place.

The lead ship, and its followers, had turned around. Could it be they had abandoned the chase so easily? If so, why? Baffled by this startling change, his mind raced to calculate this reversal. A warning shout rose from Captain Leyden. Niles wheeled the spyglass to starboard, his jaw went lax, a cold chill raced down his spine!

A monstrous ship, prepared and ready to intercept, loomed before him against the gray evening sky. One needed only a glance to know the *Pearl* did not stand a chance against this newcomer's firepower. Escape route most assuredly cut off, there remained no place to run except toward the English shore; an alternative that presented no feasible respite with English warships laying in wait. The entire situation spelled certain death to *The Sea Pearl*.

Awestricken, Niles slowly slid his scope along the enemy's broadside. He began to count under his breath, dread crushing in on his chest. A long row of cannon jutted ominously from the ports along her side. Two---six---ten---Wait!

He whipped the glass along the ship's length to take in the elaborate structure and detailed craftsmanship. Quickly he lifted it skyward. Up, up, to the very top of the main mast. There before his eyes fluttered the dreaded banner of Spain!

Could---yes, indeed---the giant galleon they nearly collided with in the fog. What did her captain have in mind? The *Pearl* bore the colors of England. That made her as much an enemy of Spain as those skittering for the safety of the harbor. Body tensed, he waited.

Kleet, in the belief one enemy was equal to the other, did not alter sail. Instead, he opted to continue full speed toward the hull that loomed ever larger in their path. Niles braced himself in preparation for the impact.

Unless one or the other in the immediate minutes ahead changed course they would most surely ram the galleon dead center. If so, against so formidable an adversary, the *Pearl* would disintegrate on impact. She would remain only a legend in the ports.

Even at this precarious appointment with fate, Niles admired the superior construction of the brilliantly painted majestic giant. He had never seen one so magnificent as the one that towered before them. As his eyes roved appreciatively over the lavish ornamentation he detected a slight change of movement.

He stared, mouth agape. The floating palace slowly, ever so slowly, eased away from their suicidal path. Through the wake of her stern the *Pearl,* a mere dwarf, passed unscathed.

High above on the deck of the superior vessel stood the captain. Resplendent in gold trimmed uniform, he waved a friendly all clear sign. Niles returned the signal, legs gone weak beneath him. Puzzled and downright dumbfounded, he failed to phantom the opposing captain's strange act of charity. Captain Leyden descended from the forecastle and came to stand beside him.

"Now what do you make of that?" Niles breathed in a mystified whisper.

"To tell the truth, Son, I'm not fussy if I understand or not. I'm only thankful it ended the way it did."

The first mate hastened to join them. "Did you see that? He could've blown us to Judas Priest!" he sputtered.

"You can say that again," Niles nodded,

as he watched the powerful galleon glide smoothly toward the horizon. In his heart he wished its captain could know how grateful they were for sparing their lives. As it was, the most he could do was let his eyes send a humble hand of indebtedness across the expanse of water. Never before had he thought he would meet a Spaniard he did not hate for the many atrocities their countrymen had done. Yet his mind could not help but wonder what prompted the other captain's benevolent actions.

Kleet picked up one of the spilled apples, turned it over to check for wormholes, then chomped into its side. "Here's one less to collect up later---not bad either. Captain Brett, how about you?"

Niles declined. Apples held no interest for him at the moment. However, his eyes narrowed when he detected a decided limp when Captain Leyden moved to retrieve one.

"Captain, what's with your leg?"

Apple in hand, the man feigned nonchalance. "Nothing, only a little bruise, I reckon."

"If your limp is any indication, I'd say more than a bruise. What happened to it?"

"I tell you it's nothing. Be all right in a

couple hours."

"That's not what I asked. How did it get hurt?"

"I'm not as spry anymore as you are, Boy. Didn't quite clear the wagon when she rolled onto the deck. Got myself caught under the edge."

Niles motioned to Miss Silvas. "Help him to our quarters. I'll be in to check him over after I've given our new course to the helm."

"B-But---I can't keep my balance on this deck myself, much-less help someone else."

"Then time you learned," he countered. "It appears you will be with us a long time." She stared, open mouthed in response to the statement. "To the quarters---now!" he pointed with emphasis. "I'll explain later. Make him lie down to get off that leg. There may be broken bones." Before she could object further, he wheeled to enter the steerage with a motion for Kleet to follow. "Put a double watch on again tonight and spread the word for a meeting of the crew after morning gruel. I shall be in my quarters checking the captain if you need me."

He entered the Captain's Quarters and scowled. "Why aren't you lying down with that leg elevated?"

"Couldn't lift 'em," the older answered, with eyes that conveyed a sense of embarrassed helplessness.

"If you let them dangle over the side it will swell."

Captain Leyden gritted his teeth in pain while Niles raised the legs and helped him to lie flat on the quilts. Gently he removed the boot and noticed how the captain's weathered face flinched. The reaction proved the man was in more pain than he was ready to admit. With faith in his sense of touch, Niles slid deft hands slowly down the leg to check the bones. Satisfied, he moved on to inspect the ankle, already blue-black, skin stretched taut and shiny over the progressive enlargement. Silent examination completed, he turned.

"Miss Silvas, fetch a bucket of cold seawater. Then keep wet packs around this ankle to control the swelling."

Captain Leyden began to cough uncontrollably. Convinced his lungs suffered from the damp chill, Niles added, "And keep him warm with lots of blankets. You'll find several stored under the bunks. Let's see if we can sweat that cough out before it gets any worse. It needed attention long before this, but as usual, the stubborn goat wouldn't listen. Thinks he's tough as an old rooster. He forgets even old roosters get sick if they freeze their tail feathers. I'll have the cook mix up something for the cough and be right back."

Waves whispered and slid along the hull, accented by the familiar creak of the ship. A light breeze billowed the sails and whistled among the rigging. Darkness lowered its hand and shadows crept silently along the decks. Steam rose from the concoction Niles carried in his hand when he reentered his Quarters. A quick surveillance revealed his orders were explicitly being carried out. Captain Leyden formed a bulky bundle of well tucked quilts and blankets, candles had been lighted and the wick of the brass oil lamp touched aglow. Miss Silvas patiently attended the cold packs on the injured ankle that extended from the pile of bedcovers.

"I think you can quit now, Miss. Cover it up and we'll see how it looks in the morning. Instead, let's try to get some of this liquid medicinal down his throat."

"He's asleep now. Should I awaken him?"

Niles looked down at the relaxed face. "No, let him be. Sleep is the best thing for him. We'll give it to him if he starts to cough in the night." Shoulders limp, he sank into a nearby chair and released the air heavily from his lungs.

"You're tired," Miss Silvas said, careful not to arouse the sleeping man. "One question, if I may ask. What did you mean when you said I would be on the ship a long time?"

He contemplated the best words to use in response. "Miss Silvas, you saw for yourself we made every effort, and at great risk I might add, to put you ashore in your England. The mission failed."

She nodded agreement. "Wasn't any fault of yours. As you say, you tried."

He smoothed his neatly trimmed mustache and debated in silence on how to broach his next question before he spoke. "I'm sure you heard the disrespectful comments made by the men at the tavern. After such degrading rumors on your honor; do you really think you can create a new life there?"

"I suppose not," she sighed in resignation. "But if not England, then where?"

"I expect the crew shall vote to proceed with our original plans at the meeting tomorrow. In the Colonies, an ocean away from cruel rumors, you can start over." Her face showed no enthusiasm. "You'll have plenty of time to make plans. It will be two months, maybe more, depending on the winds, before we tie up there. Meanwhile, you will be on board with us."

"Ugh! And am I supposed to twiddle my thumbs and pretend I'm enjoying myself all that time? I'm accustomed to action, parties---not going crazy with idleness!"

"Make no mistake," his eyebrow lifted in admonition, "everyone on board has a job. For the present, yours lies right over there on that bed. I make his care your responsibility. We've a very sick man on our hands, whether he admits it or not. He was already ailing when we hit England. This accident complicates his condition even more. Unlike the rest of us, he's not young anymore. As I see it, you shall be kept very busy for a long while. I assure you it won't be easy. He can be a stubborn old bull to handle."

She looked upon the aged face and her eyes softened. "I doubt that. He appears gentle as a lamb."

"Ha!" Niles tossed his head. "Don't let his innocent sleeping image fool you. He can be soft as pudding one minute, angry as a disturbed hornet the next. You'll see."

He glanced at the cabin boy disguise and cacao darkened face. "I know you're as tired as the rest of us, but one favor, please?" Her face lifted to meet him and he grimaced with distaste. "Wash that mess off your skin and get rid of Weasel's clothes. Cleve shall be over soon with our dinner. I refuse to look at such a sight across the table."

Her fingers slid down one cacao stained cheek. She had forgotten her appearance while involved with the urgency of Captain Leyden's emergency. A soft laugh escaped from her.

"You should do that more often," he grinned.

Aghast, she answered, "Dress like this?"

"No, I mean laugh. Now get over to the basin and wash!"

CHAPTER FIVE

Niles spent a restless night. The agonized moans of the older captain consistently drew his attention. He gave up on further sleep and rose from his bunk in the gray darkness of predawn. A dense blanket of fog waited outside the small cabin porthole. Softly he crossed to the captain's bunk, candle in hand, and bent over the rumpled quilts. The lined face, illuminated by the soft light, was twisted with intense pain. Their passenger, swathed in a quilt for warmth against the cold chill of the room, came to stand beside Niles. Her eyes mirrored the same deep concern. He motioned her to follow him to the other side of the room. Certain the old man would not hear, he whispered, "Doesn't look good, does he?"

"It's the pain. Isn't there something we can do to bring relief?"

"A bad sprain often causes more misery than a break. Likely twisted and pulled the tendons on impact."

"Are you absolutely positive there are no broken bones?"

"I'm sure," he nodded. "It's the combination of sprain and bruises."

"How can you stand to watch him suffer like that?" she lashed out. "You *must* send one of your men to bring a doctor!"

With a sneer, Niles delivered an empty laugh. "Physician? Miss Silvas, may I remind you we are at sea."

"What difference does that make? He needs a man of medicine to look after him."

He waved an arm toward the porthole. "My lady, if you see a physician out there riding on a wave to solicit patients you are welcome to invite him aboard. However, I wouldn't put much stock in that, if I were you."

"Are you a captain, or not?" she angrily stamped a bare foot. "A good captain is supposed to know what to do when emergencies arise."

"Captain I am, physician I am not. Yes, there are things we can and will do. If he were a common crewman I would have already given the order. And if you knew this man better you'd understand why I hesitate."

She flashed an icy glare. "Does that

mean, Captain, you will not do as much for this poor man as for one of your crew?"

"Quite the contrary, Miss. What I say is, I will not take the captain's physical concerns into my hands while he can yet state his own wishes."

"Ridiculous! A person could die while he waited for you to take action. That man," she pointed a slender finger for emphasis, dark sapphire eyes afire, "is in pain!"

"I'm well aware of that, Madam. I also know he's the closest thing to a doctor on this ship. He taught me everything I know. Therefore, if you don't mind, I prefer him to decide what should be done. He'll likely say the same as I. I will not step in to rob him of his rights, particularly when it concerns his own physical body. Besides, he's slept little enough the past hours. I do not intend to wake him."

Miss Silvas shivered beneath the quilt; his eyes went to her bare feet on the cold floor. "For the present I suggest you quietly get dressed before you catch your death. We don't need two sick patients on board. The cook shall be in shortly with our morning meal. I question the wisdom of any crewman, even one as moralistically trustworthy as Cleve, to see you in this manner. Meanwhile, I shall see if I can convince the burner to give out more heat. It's so cold in here we can see our frosty breaths."

She stepped back and glared up at him. "There you go again, ordering people around like a captain. While we talked last night I began to get the impression you were almost human. I was wrong."

"Madam, may I remind you I *am* the captain. As such, you will do as I say. Whether you regard me as human is no concern of mine." She whirled about and retreated to the draped area.

The cook, who ordinarily tapped a boot toe against the door bottom to announce his arrival, now waited for an answer from within before he entered. Niles welcomed the more discreet approach insomuch as there was a lady present. To insure her privacy against a morally disreputable crew would be a difficult task to master.

The rotund cook stepped inside, food baskets in hand. Round face twisted in genuine concern, he immediately glanced toward the sleeping man. "How is he this morning?"

"Not good. He put in a very restless night. Keep your voice down."

Cleve gave a nod and began to scoop

steaming hot gruel into bowls on the small table. A homey scent wafted from warm biscuits wrapped in their spotless linen towel on a china plate. A pewter pot filled with freshly brewed South American coffee, heated to scald the tongue, waited in the center of the table. He always took pride in how he laid the captains' table. Every item from linen to silver was double checked to insure he had forgotten nothing. This was one responsibility in which for a few moments each day he could pretend he was an accomplished professional, not a nondescript galley cook.

The other hardened seamen on board appreciated none of the refinements of an elegant repast. Their only demand was an abundance of food hot enough to sear their innards. The Captain's Quarters, however, were different. Here he liked to spread a table equal to renown eateries frequented by patrons of the elite class. His chubby hands caressed the delicate chinaware, engraved silver pieces and fine linens with reverence as he laid them out to perfection. Lastly, it was a ritual to touch a lucifer to the wicks of candles set in engraved silver holders. The wee orange flames rose and lent a mellow restful atmosphere to the room.

"You'd best coax some hot food into his innards," he advised, as he gripped the basket handles and turned to leave.

Miss Silvas reappeared clad in the draped sarong Toro fashioned for her. She rubbed her cold hands together and huddled close to the small burner. Across the room Niles placed a hand on the old man's shoulder. The captain, attuned to respond at the slightest signal of danger, immediately jerked awake. The face winced in pain with the sudden movement. He struggled to break free of the entanglement of heavy quilts. Niles restrained him with a hand on his arm.

"Stay put while I bring you some biscuits and hot gruel."

"In bed? Don't talk foolishness, Boy. I'm not a cripple." With a stubborn set to his jaw he squirmed from the mound of coverlets. His legs swung to gingerly make contact with the cold floor. Hidden flinches of the creased face did not go unnoticed by his comrades.

"Hand me my clothes," he motioned. "And you, Young Lady, either go into your section, or turn your back while I dress." Miss Silvas flushed behind a weak smile of amusement and turned her chair. She preferred to remain near the feeble warmth of the burner if at all possible. "There," he exclaimed as he pulled on his pants. "Now hand me my socks and boots."

"I seriously doubt a boot can be pulled over that enlarged ankle," Niles cautioned.

The old man leaned forward to inspect the severely bruised limb. His eyes went indecisively toward the boots then back to the swollen leg. "I'll pull a sock over it. No need for boots anyway this morning." He looked up and hastily added, "Unless, that is, you have a chore in mind for me to handle on deck?"

"I've called a meeting of the crew, but it's not important that you be there."

"Yes, it is," the gray head bobbed emphatically. "Every man needs to show his face at a meeting to have his say. This leg only tightened up while I slept. Once I move around a bit my boots---" Seized by another violent cough seizure he was unable to speak further.

"You won't be able to get around for a few days," Niles reasoned.

"Let me be the judge," the old captain declared, and made an adamant attempt to stand upright. He eased a bit of weight onto the injured limb; the face twisted in agony. Niles and Miss Silvas quickly stepped to his side and helped him onto a chair at the table. "Bit touchier than I expected, I must admit. Could have made it by myself though. You two act like I'm an invalid."

"You're the doctor on board. What do you suggest?" Niles asked.

"The usual; bind it up. No use to make all this fuss. I've been hurt lot worse before. You best be careful or I may get spoiled with all this pampering." He chuckled a bit and the familiar twinkle again returned to the aged eyes.

"Toro runs second to you as a doctor, I'll call him in---"

"You'll do no such thing!" he sputtered. "True, Toro is good when it comes to tropical things learned from his people. A sprained ankle is nothing tropical. Witch doctor mumble-jumble or island witchery medicine is the last thing I need!"

"All right, we hear you," Niles said, and produced a narrow roll of cloth. He knelt on one knee before the man and began to wrap the injured limb.

Captain Leyden's eyes squinted to watch Niles' movements. "Tighter, make it tighter," he insisted.

"Wrapped any tighter you know very well will cut off the blood circulation. Furthermore, I better not come back and find you have tightened it more after I leave."

"All right, all right," he grudgingly agreed before he doubled over in another coughing spell.

Cleve returned to clear the table and shook a worried head. "Chest sounds right bad. Think I should brew a stronger concoction?"

Before Niles could answer Captain Leyden rasped, "Those poisons you mix are worse than any ailment they mean to cure! If a man ain't dead when he drinks the stuff, he wishes he were before it's all the way down his gullet."

"Cleve is right," Niles interceded. "Your chest is worse. It's time we put a plaster on it."

Captain Leyden slammed a fist on the table. "Not on your life! There'll be no stinky plasters slapped on me."

"Don't let yourself get all upset. Come, Victoria and I will help you back to your bunk."

He sank onto the pillows with an exhausted sigh. They left him to rest and retreated into the room.

"At the meeting I shall bring up the subject of your accommodations, Miss Silvas."

She answered coolly without so much as a glance in his direction, "Whatever you say, Captain. I wouldn't want to inconvenience anybody."

"It's not a matter of inconvenience, it's---" She waited, one neatly shaped eyebrow raised in question. "It's---for instance---there may come a time when both Captain Leyden and I are out of the quarters. A crewmember may decide to---invade your privacy, shall we say."

"They appear quite trustworthy to me."

"Madam, there is one thing you must remember and take my word on. Those men, as I cautioned before, are not of the same breed as you have associated with in your past. They are men of the sea. As such, they are not above displaying behavior to match the crude tales you've undoubtedly heard about pirates.

"Captain, I do believe you exaggerate."

His eyes met hers, voice deadly serious. "Believe me, Miss, I do not. I know my crew."

"There you go, trying to sound like a stern captain again." Head at a tilt in challenge, she asked, "Whom are you most worried will stray? Yourself, your crew or, are you so stupid as to think," she motioned toward the man asleep, "he might step over the line of proper conduct?"

"Don't be absurd. His morals are above

question."

"Yourself, then?"
He did not answer.

Later, seated at a long plank table in the galley, he analyzed the moods reflected on the faces of the men as they filed in. Somehow he must convert their adverse opinions into a unified endeavor. On trade ships the captains expected their men to follow orders without question. *The Sea Pearl*, although a trade ship, by choice operated more like a crew of privateers. This meant each man had an equal voice in its operation and shared profits. They could replace their captain at any time by majority vote or, if necessary, overpower him physically. This morning he could feel the air was heavy with opposition.

Kleet, true to his flair for drama, unfolded from among the men seated on the benches. With a sound rap of his tankard on the thick tabletop before them, he growled, "All right you sea scums, pipe it down!" The characteristic smirk spread across his face and he waved an arm. "Our honorable captain wishes to speak. Captain, suppose you lay out why you called this meeting."

Irked by the mate's exaggerated mannerism, Niles began. "The main concern is our destination. Our last mission went aground. As a result we have a passenger---"

Weasel sprang to his feet with an angry shake of a fist. "I say the sooner we rid ourselves of that female the better!"

"Quiet down, Weasel," Kleet snarled. "We all know your opinion. Personally," the secretive smirk reappeared, "I sort'a like the idea. Who knows, she just might arouse our interest before we git wherever we are going!"

Several speculative chuckles rose from the assemblage. Someone chided, "Speak for yourself, Kleet?"

From another rose the comment, "If anyone tries to slip around the corner for a peek you can bet it will be ol' Kleet!"

Niles waited until the guffaws subsided then proceeded. "It's useless to consider further attempts to return her onto English soil. Captain Leyden and I have concluded our best option is to sail for the Colonies."

Again Weasel leaped to his feet and shouted. "You're crazy in the head, Captain!" Thoroughly enraged, his arms wildly flailed the air as he screeched to the men, "You all know a woman on board spells bad luck. Liable to git us all killed. If not that, captured and hauled off to the Spanish Inquisition!" With a bang of his fist upon the table, he pressed, "You saw the proof in tha' last port.

Got out by the skin o' our teeth, we did. Wha' about the run in with the English Guards---and that big galleon that near scraped the paint off our side? What more proof you want 'at she's a hex?"

Niles knew such talk could become infectious to superstitious minds if not brought under control. He interrupted. "We warned all of you in advance before we set sail on this voyage that there could be trouble. One could say she's brought good luck, not bad. Thus far everything has turned out well." To change the subject until tempers cooled, he proceeded to explain Captain Leyden's condition. The men listened intently.

"As I see it," he continued, "we can set a course for the Colonies and deposit our passenger there among the settlers. That handled, we barter our cargo and proceed southward along the coastline. We cross by the Bahama Islands and catch the Windward Passage over to Jamaica. Not too different from our original plans."

Yet again Weasel came to his feet. "Except those original plans did not include any woman on board!"

"Batten down your hatch!" Kleet snarled with an impatient shove. "What's done is done. Captain, I'd say we all agree unanimously and that includes Weaselface here." He snapped the phosphorus tip of a lucifer with a thumbnail, and touched the ignited flame to the end of a foul smelling cigar. "Will that be all, Captain?"

Niles, relieved to have the session over said, "Everyone go back to work, except Toro and you." The crew filed out and the two men turned expectantly to Niles. "Toro and Kleet, take an inventory of the island and European cargo we carry and---"

"Right here, Captain," Kleet responded, as he withdrew the pages of manifest from a coat pocket. "Knew you'd want. I tallied all cargo as it left ship, and what came on board in that last port. Anything else?"

"Yes. Bring some lumber up from the hold; it appears our passenger will be with us all the way across the Atlantic. She needs, shall we say, a more private billet."

"Afraid you might succumb to invade that curtain, Cap'n?" Kleet needled.

"I'm in no mood for crude jest," Niles snapped, irritated by the insinuation on his character. "We need a solid structure. One easy to remove after she is put ashore. One more thing. On the wagon, Toro, were two crates. I scratched an X on them for identification. Take them to my cabin."

Cleve approached with a tankard; its hot odoriferous steam rose into the air. "Here's the medicinal you ordered. Have 'im sip it slow so's it scalds all the way down."

Kleet and Toro, about to take their leave, grimaced and averted their noses from the fumes. "If smell is any indication, it should cure Satan in Hades."

Niles crossed the deck, tankard in hand. The fog overhead was slow to lift. Behind the mists the sun failed to penetrate the icy fingers of winter, although it was time to herald the spring season. Or, Niles wondered, was it an omen of treacherous weather ahead?

He entered the quarters and abruptly froze. Before him Miss Silvas danced and whirled rapturously about the room. The voluminous skirt of the red gown he had purchased flared out from her slim body. Overhead the lacy parasol twirled daintily above the hat's airy ostrich plumes that bobbed with each movement of her head. He went rigid.

Rage crept up the cords of his neck and along his jaw. His words, sharp as the edge of his cutlass, cut the air. "Take it off!"

"Captain, it is positively gorgeous!" She turned, eyes aglow with excitement.

"However, as I tried to tell you in the shop, it is too large a size. Perhaps if I take in---" Her words faded when her eyes met his slitted lids.

"Take it off. Now!"

Captain Leyden, awakened by the sharp command, stirred on his bunk. "What's going on?" Victoria spun around in hopes he would intercede in her favor against this beast. The captain glanced at Niles and back to the flame red dress. "Put it back, Child," he calmly nodded.

"If he bought it for me, why can't I wear it?"

"You misunderstood, my dear," the older answered. "It's red."

"Of course it's red, any idiot can see that," she retorted. "So? What's wrong with red?"

"You don't understand. It wasn't bought for you. Do as he says."

"If not for me, then---" her words ceased, choked by the dark smolder behind Niles' narrowed eyes. "I---I see. It never occurred to me---" the voice died to a whisper. "I mean---I think I understand."

"You do not understand," Niles snapped. "Nor is it any of your business to know."

"What else is there to understand? Evidently there is another woman in your life. I should have guessed as much. After all---" she turned aside, gently closed the ruffled parasol and removed the plumed hat. Replaced in their wrappings, she stepped behind the draped area in submission to remove the gown.

A boot sounded against the door. Niles, face still flushed with rage, barked loudly at the intrusion. "You're not helpless, open it and come in!"

A series of loud thuds were heard as planks of lumber dropped onto the deck. A heavy wooden crate pushed its way through the door followed by Kleet. "Had I known you were in a bad mood I'd have thought twice before I brought this stuff you ordered. Where do you want it?"

Captain Leyden spanned the tension. "Right there will do nicely for now."

Kleet turned to the older man. "How's the gimpy leg, Sir?"

"Right painful, a sprain always is. I'll be about again in a few days."

"Sure you will," the mate agreed as he

reached for the drape. "I'll get this curtain out of the way so we can work."

"Wait!" Niles halted the movement. "The lady is dressing."

Kleet feigned an amazed gasp. "This time of the mornin'?" He flopped into the nearest chair and threw back his head. "I declare, Captain Leyden, I never imagined you'd stand for such behavior. Right in your own quarters, at that!"

"Enough, Kleet," Niles growled, anger rekindled. "We can do without snide insinuations where the lady's honor is concerned."

The mate's hands went up in defense. "I only go by what I see, and it's not hard to see what's been---"

"You see nothing. Because you play around in the gutter, don't judge others to act the same."

"Come, come, you two. Break it off," Captain Leyden cut in. "Next you'll be at one another's throats. There'll be trouble aplenty before this run is over, without foolish squabbles ---particularly over a woman."

He was cut short by a coughing spasm before he could say more. It shook his bent shoulders and left him gasping for air. Niles rushed over, propped him up, and attempted to spoon a bit of Cleve's vile mixture down his throat while the patient sputtered and cursed.

Niles turned when Victoria, dressed in the garment wrap, emerged. "Miss Silvas, take over the captain's care while I help the builders."

The marked crates remained untouched in the middle of the floor. Each time Miss Silvas crossed the room throughout the day she was forced to step around them. She frowned yet asked no questions, nor did Niles volunteer any information on the contents.

It was late that evening before the men ceased their work. She tucked the quilts snugly about Captain Leyden and retired into her newly constructed cubical.

Niles felt too exhausted to dive overboard at this hour of the night although his skin itched from dust and wood particles. No sounds could be heard from the new cubicle. Satisfied she was asleep, he went to the galley for a bucket of hot water. Having returned to his quarters he found it extremely unnerving to perform so personal an act as bathing with the lady only a short distance away. A female on board, he concluded, promised to present several unforeseen complications before this voyage ended. Refreshed, albeit disturbed, he drew the quilts halfway over his head for warmth and instantly relaxed into a deep sleep.

The next day, with the exception that Captain Leyden's condition worsened, things went smoothly. The men completed the final details of the temporary structure. Victoria, with an impatient frown, adjusted the contrary sash of her wraparound garment and conceded to help clean the quarters. With respect for the aged man's breathing difficulty, she took care not to raise any construction particles into the air. Niles, meanwhile, polished dust from the carved woodwork with an oiled cloth. He hesitated in his work to glance toward Captain Leyden. "What do you think of our new cabin arrangement?"

"Appears a fine job, Son, right down to the lock on her door. Can't be too careful about some things."

Victoria straightened. "I didn't expect this much attention to my comforts."

"It wasn't done solely with your comforts in mind, Madam. It was a necessity," Niles answered without further explanation. His bath experience of the previous night had proven the captains, too, needed privacy. The new walls provided a reasonable solution, yet he knew they were not the total answer.

The knowledge of her nearness in the quarters, he discovered, confused his thoughts and concentration. He could not shut her out of his mind. The way she moved, the flame that ignited when they perchanced to touch, and the effect of her sapphire eyes when they met his. In short, her aura churned undesired yet pleasurable sensations deep within his being. Woodwork cleaned, he lighted a fresh island cigar over the nearby candle flame, aware her eyes followed his movements.

Toro gingerly entered after first giving a light rap on the door. "Come boots an' clothes, Cap'n," he said, while he remained respectfully beside the door.

"Come back later after I've changed. Then you can also take these I'm have on."

"Ya Suh, Cap'n." The black man flashed his white teeth as his eyes roved over the room. "I see all's shined and back in order." With a bow of woolly head, he retreated and was gone.

Captain Leyden expressed tiredness and took to his bed early. Satisfied the old man rested peacefully against his pillows, Niles stepped outside. Along the quarterdeck he stopped to watch skyward. Small dark clouds, like heavy eyelids, moved to obscure the frigid moon. Dusk deepened. The night stirred only sufficient wind to hold the sails taut. He tossed over the side the loose end of a rope secured to a cannon carriage and removed his clothing. Braced against the shock of contact with icy waters, he dove over the side in a perfect arc.

He did not emerge until the day's cleaning dirt was thoroughly rinsed from his body. Hand to hand, he quickly scaled the rope to topside and clean garments. They felt warm against his flesh chilled by frigid water.

The soiled clothing he deposited atop the pile that waited beside the door in the quarters and added his boots alongside. He drew a freshly oiled pair from his closet and noticed a scowl of disapproval cross Victoria's face.

"How did your hair get so wet in this weather? You will catch your death!"

"I went for a swim."

"Nobody in their right mind would swim in this cold."

"I just did." Amused by her shocked reaction he added, "How else do you think men of the sea get clean? Really quite a refresher. You ought to try it sometime." Their testy verbal exchange was interrupted by Toro's wordless entry.

The black gathered the boots and pile of discarded clothes into his thick arms. As soon as he left Niles closed a hand around a nearby iron crowbar. The claw end glistened menacingly in the candlelight as he advanced toward their passenger.

"The time has come to take care of you, Miss Silvas. The captain is asleep and we are at last alone." With an audible gasp, she visibly shrank backward, eyes wide with fear. Bar lowered to hang limply at his side he asked, "What are you afraid of?"

She retreated in terror to flatten her back against the wall. With lips that quivered she tried to speak. "I---I've heard about pirates---and---what they---"

"Forget those wild tales. I already told you we are bucaners, not buccaneers. I hope, My Lady, you will never have the misfortune to learn the difference first hand. Believe me, boucaners and so-called buccaneers are not of the same breed. If you will kindly step aside, we shall see what's inside that crate beside you."

He jabbed the bar under the wooden lid and pried it off. She watched his actions in silent curiosity. To her consternation, he handed her a pair of woolen trousers, shirt, cloak, heavy socks, and a tall pair of shiny leather boots. "Try those to see how they fit."

"Trousers for me, a lady?" she exclaimed, shocked by the suggestion.

"They'll be much warmer; definitely less cantankerous to manage than any silly island garb."

"B---but ladies don't wear pants!"

"Who said? Put them on," he ordered with a jerk of a thumb toward her new room. While she changed he studied his charts to check their present course. All appeared well.

Face flushed with embarrassment yet eyes aglow, she reappeared. "The hose are so cozy! My feet have felt like two blocks of ice from the moment I stepped on board."

"Forgive my negligence. A captain is responsible for the welfare of his passengers. I should have opened the crates earlier." He pried the second lid free. Since it contained intimate apparel a lady would prefer to inspect in privacy, he stepped back. "While you were checking some venders back there in the village, I stopped in a shop. The owner's wife was very helpful. She selected everything you need, not only to keep you warm in this cold climate, but fair weather as well. Unpack the crates at your leisure tomorrow."

She hugged herself in blissful pleasure totally preoccupied with the new woolen clothes. "It seems ages since I felt this comfy!"

"Leave the wrap for island women. When you arrive in the Colonies you will dress like a colonist anyway." He nipped the end from a fragrant cigar and bent to light it over the candle flame. Satisfied, he leaned back in his chair to watch the smoke curl lazily up into the air. The silence, however, was short lived.

"I shudder to think what I shall do if by accident I come upon one of those horrendously painted Indians in the Colonies!" Victoria's eyes clouded with anxiety. "It's said they lurk behind every rock and tree to kill, capture, or torture any unfortunate victim who comes by!"

"Don't believe every tale you hear. I seriously doubt you will encounter any bloodthirsty savages in a city."

"City?" She turned to him, eyes puzzled.

"Certainly," he nodded. "Boston harbor is quite populous." She leaned forward with interest from where she was seated nearby. "You make it sound very adventuresome," her eyes lighted. "As for me, the social activities in England became a bore."

Her remark provided him with the perfect opportunity to learn more about the private life of this complex guest. To satisfy his own curiosity, he decided to pry a bit into her past. "Do you mean to say, among all the available gentlemen friends you left behind there's no one in particular you love? None you wished to marry?"

"Love?" she tossed the question aside. "Among English social circles love and marriage are two separate things. Not one and the same. A lady doesn't marry for love; she marries a man who shows potential for success. This insures he will possess the means to provide for her and her children. And, of course, it helps if his name carries public prestige."

"I'm sorry," he shook his head. "I can't comprehend how two people, even for a moment, consider marriage unless a profound love exists between them. It's incomprehensible to marry without ever experiencing the depth and pleasure of real love."

"I mean they seldom love their mates," she corrected, as a secretive smile crossed her face. A face, Niles noticed, made even more beautiful by soft candlelight. "Please, Captain Brett, I find it an embarrassment to discuss this subject. Why---we are almost strangers. What I tried to say is they find satisfaction for their desires in the arms of other lovers."

"You approve of such infidelity?"

"I'm not sure. Life would be wonderful and much simpler, I suppose, if one loved their spouse. Then again---"

Each absorbed with their own thoughts on

the matter they sat in silence while the slow sifting sand in the hourglass on the shelf heightened her discomfort. In search of an excuse to escape the conversation she murmured, "It's late. If you will excuse me I shall retire. Goodnight, Captain."

He watched with masculine appreciation the sway of her body as she moved toward her small cubicle. The new attire distinctly outlined the well-rounded curves and graceful legs. It stirred an awareness unlike any he experienced around island women in the past.

She paused at her door, turned, and added, "Miss Silvas is so very formal. You may call me Victoria, Captain."

"Thank you, Victoria. With respect for ship discipline, I am sorry I cannot dispense with formality as easily. I must insist you continue to address me as Captain Brett."

"Yes, Captain, I understand."

CHAPTER SIX

Days dragged into weeks. The sun became but a memory of fairer skies to those aboard *The Sea Pearl.* She continued to sail encompassed within a gray vacuum. Cold sleet set in, driven by gale force northern winds. A layer of slippery ice soon coated the rigging and decks. Yards creaked and groaned under the weight of innumerable icicles that thickened and grew day by day. The giant translucent points, aimed downward, presented ever present threats to the men who struggled below. Intermittently, grown too heavy to cling any longer to its mooring, a frozen missile crashed downward. The impact shook the deck under the boots of those whom labored at their tasks. Each incident sent fearful shudders through every soul on board.

The angry sea continued to howl and rage. Its frothy fists clawed and beat the small merchant ship in an attempt to conquer and draw it captive into the watery depths.

Victoria concentrated her efforts on Captain Leyden. Under her attentive care his injury improved. Against her admonishments, he refused to remain quiet and rest. Instead, to her dismay, he constantly hobbled restlessly about the quarters on his crutch. The chest cold, however, continued to present deep concern.

Niles, meanwhile, became increasingly conscious of the shapely figure moving about in masculine garb. When they first met her graceful form secreted beneath the jeweled gown attracted his natural male instincts. That instinct now slowly increased into desire. He could imagine the pleasure of placing his arm around the slim waist to draw this beautiful spirit close.

Lately the elderly captain's perceptive eyes penetrated his reveries. On these occasions he forced himself to tear his attentions from the lithe body. As an excuse to leave, he used the pretext Kleet needed his assistance on deck.

Often he debated whether he erred. Perhaps when he purchased her clothes it may have been wiser to choose a larger size. Her shapely endowments would not then have been so obvious to an all male crew when the time came for her to venture on deck. If his own reactions were any proof, her visible curvaceousness may prove too suggestive in close proximity with the men.

Victoria, her patient no longer in need of constant attention, became bored by idleness. She begged Niles' permission to help Cleve in the galley. He submitted to her request, although he doubted she possessed any culinary abilities. Cleve, struggling to feed a crew against the adverse weather conditions, could use any help available.

Wave after wave perpetually pounded across the decks. The vessel shifted and tossed in the deep swells. The layers of ice, already thick upon her decks, increased with each successive deluge. The waves, powered by the constant surge of the roiling angry sea, returned with a ferocious snarl again and again without respite.

To walk, muchless work, on the frozen surface became ever more perilous with each new dawn. Several crewmen had already narrowly escaped being washed overboard. Jagged nerves became as sharp as the edges of frozen chunks of broken icicles awaiting a victim at every turn. Victoria's safety when she crossed from cabin to galley became of deep concern to Niles. To lessen the danger he insisted she remain in their quarters; an order she staunchly refused to obey.

The solution, he decided, was to order taut guide ropes lashed station to station. This precaution was taken not only for her sake, but the men as well. A firm grasp on these lines and one could avert being washed into the frothy sea.

Niles and his first mate, swathed in heavy coats covered by oilskins, woolen caps drawn low, followed these lifelines each morning and evening. In defiance of the icy onslaught, they toured the entire ship, feet firmly planted, shoulders hunched into the wind.

Faces coated with hoarfrost, they peered through ice coated lashes and eyebrows at the massive ice formations overhead. The strong yards, emitting ominous, crackling sounds, bent in submission under the increased stress of the suspended ice bayonets.

To send men up to break the formations free was too risky a venture to ask. If the yards snapped under the strain, men would be thrown to their deaths onto the hazardous deck below, or into the hungry waiting sea. Yet, if not relieved and the yards broke, the results could be equally disastrous. Upon their collapse the deck would become a maze of tangled ratlines and severely frayed and cut rigging lines. Planks that split under the initial impact would give way to gaping holes, allowing flooding within the hold.

Rather than hazard a remedy, the ship lived day to day in hope the weather would break.

Meanwhile, Niles and Kleet pushed on with their daily inspections. Collars upturned, gloved fingers numb with cold, they made a check of shredded lines and splintered wood. They moved about making mental notes of the many repairs needed if the lines were to hold.

Each night Niles forced himself to personally examine all injuries his men sustained through the day. Although exhausted, he refused to rest until each man received proper care.

Temperaments flared, verbal arguments erupted that quickly resulted in unjustified rages. Niles could identify with their frustrations. He too, felt the intense pressure and discomforts. They were fighting a futile battle against the mighty ocean.

Unlike them, however, he also suffered under the burden of command. As their captain, therefore leader, it rested on his shoulders to make correct decisions and be accountable. They at least, could argue among themselves to gain some degree of release from tension and fear. For him, no such outlet existed to expel pent up emotional strain. He dared not reveal the secret deep within his breast---the evidence his charts and compass confirmed as dire fact. Their efforts were in vain.

He suffered alone. The knowledge he

privately carried began to take its toll, both mentally and physically. A crew may suspect all is not well---as captain he knew the fateful truth: *The Sea Pearl* would meet its sisters at the bottom of the sea before this voyage was accomplished.

Each night he returned to his quarters wet, shivering with cold and bone tired from the day's strenuous labors. Lest he worry Captain Leyden and Victoria, he retreated within himself. It would only serve to upset the lady if he voiced an honest assessment of their situation. Ignorant of the sea and its eminent dangers, he hoped she could be fooled into complacency. Whether the sea wise Captain Leyden was really deceived by his silence was another question. Often Niles glanced up to find the old man's knowledgeable eyes resting on him without comment.

Surprisingly, Victoria adapted quickly to life at sea. She had by now assumed most of the chores within the quarters formerly performed by Toro. She instilled a warm, pleasant aura Niles could not define in words, yet found most gratifying. Each evening, after he changed into dry clothes, he collapsed into his chair, thoroughly spent. It had at these times, by her own volition, become her practice to approach and massage his sore shoulders and painful muscles. His shivers ceased, chilled body relaxed and troubled mind tranquilized in response to the touch of her hands and attentions. He could not fathom, however, why he always felt disturbed during these moments of closeness. Was it brought on by his trepidations about their survival? The captain's failing health? Or did he detect dissension from the pair about his capabilities as captain of the ship?

It's not fair! he silently declared. How can they blame me for the unexpected tempest that even now tosses them about? I didn't ask such a violent storm to descend and destroy us at its own leisure! Don't they realize that if there were any means to pilot the ship to safety I most definitely would do so?

He longed to reach out, take her hands in his and plead she understand he was doing his very best. More than anything, he longed to hear soft words in response; sympathy, as balm for the intense guilt that tore at his insides. The sense of failure made him want to scream, to shake his fists in defiance at the blackened sky. But, judging it a sign of weakness to reach out to a woman for strength, he refrained. Instead, he elected to remain silent, head back, eyes closed, while he absorbed encouragement from her nearness.

CHAPTER SEVEN

Battered by hurricane force unceasing winds, sleet and rough sea, *the Sea Pearl* held on; her sails and rigging now torn, frayed and tangled. The decks were precarious mazes of fallen ice, frozen solidly onto the surface where it plummeted.

Splintered and broken rails were visible everywhere. White mounds of ice concealed the ineffectual cannons ranged along her sides. The valiant men who toiled doggedly in the frigid temperature suffered severe frostbite along with their injuries. They could no longer keep up with the constant onslaught of destruction.

The last grain of sand dropped in the hourglass and the man in the steerage rang the bell to announce the hour of another dark morning. Overhead the weather promised no hope to lift their hearts. Niles stared at the unrolled charts before him. Depression threatened to overcome sound reason. The weight of command had become too heavy a burden for him to bear.

Within the soul of every man on board there lived the memory of another clime and place. But for now, their entire world had become a vacuum of unbearable cold, gales, sleet and ice. Helpless, they were being pitched and churned, with no means to break free of its grip.

Niles' tormented mind refused to focus anymore. Benumbed, he stared vacantly, seeing nothing. He felt a light touch as a hand came to rest on his shoulder. Buoyed by the strength of her presence, he slowly turned.

She leaned closer to better see the marks on the chart in the dim light. Voice calm, she asked, "Where are we?"

"Somewhere in this area," he motioned a finger vaguely over a broad scope.

"Somewhere? Am I correct if I assume we are lost, Captain?"

Her eyes spoke traces of fear behind the dark lashes. "No, Victoria, we're not lost," he lied. In a feeble attempt to dispel her anxieties, he fought to make his voice sound casual. "It's hard to say we are right on this spot or that when at sea."

He felt, more than saw, her eyes drop. A tense silence followed; the sounds outside the cabin walls louder on their ears than usual. When she again spoke, it was soft as a sigh. "Do you really believe we will make it, Niles?"

"Of course. This cussed weather can't last forever."

"We've said that for a long---" Her words trailed off with the arrival of their morning meal.

Niles welcomed the interruption. The days at sea had proven the lady far more intelligent than he first surmised. He had found her pointed questions increasingly difficult to evade. She would most certainly draw the truth from him, given time and opportunity to press further.

Seated at the table, head bent, he felt extremely discomfited. Captain Leyden mutely watched and waited for him to speak. Niles pushed his bowl of gruel aside, unable to force himself to eat. By his calculations their lives may soon end. Did they not, therefore, have a right to know?

He opened his mouth to speak, resigned to the inevitable. Before the words had a chance to leave his lips the door to their quarters suddenly burst open. A rush of icy wind and sleet swirled across the floor, accompanied by a massive bundle of windblown oilskins. The figure turned to shove the door shut against the gale. A panting Cleve braced himself against it and gasped for breath.

"Captain Brett---you best get---over to the galley quick!" he jerked a thumb. "Kleet and Brog---they's at it!"

Niles sprang to his feet before the excited cook finished. He dashed out without benefit of coat or oilskin.

It had to happen.

Taut nerves, suppressed for days, had waited like coiled springs within every man aboard. There only lacked the identity of whom the first testy combatants may be. In the end it proved the two most dangerous assailants of the entire crew. Each highly adept, one deadly as the other. Kleet, fiery tempered and fast; Brog silent, slow, yet fatally accurate when he made a move.

Victoria grabbed for a heavy coat. "Wait! I'll go with you. Someone may be hurt."

"Stay where you are," he shouted over a shoulder. Hunched forward against the force of the blow, he ran to grasp hold of the guide rope. Displeased, he knew by the feel of the rope that she followed directly behind.

He burst into the galley and jerked sideways in a half crouch. Through a sixth sense born of experience he felt, more than saw, the sleek pointed stiletto slice the air. He shoved Victoria down onto the deck with a sweep of a protective arm. Kleet dropped from his perch atop a table at that precise instant. The well aimed knife passed harmlessly over the first mate to thunk into the wood only inches from Nile's head.

Kleet rose with the resiliency of a jungle cat and whipped a pair of *pistolas* from his wide leather belt. Equally swift, another razor sharp dagger flashed into Brog's powerful fist, poised for the pitch.

The first blade was as yet a quivering menace overhead when Niles spoke. His voice firm, controlled, bore a keen edge of its own. "Break it! Both of you. Drop it!"

The combatants remained crouched: motionless savage beasts consumed by primeval animal instincts anxious to move in for the kill. Niles measured the situation through narrowed lids; his own brace of Spanish *pistolas* were primed and ready. He waited, tensed, muscles taut along his jaw line.

Inch by inch the weapons were cautiously lowered and returned to belts. Niles, with forced calm, took a firm grip on the hilt of the embedded knife and yanked the blade free. "Brog, I believe this trinket belongs to you." Then he sent it across the room swift and true as a lightning flash. The bear of a man caught the hilt in midair with the dexterity of the best. With one smooth motion he twirled it into place at his belt.

Niles stood to face the two. "Listen up. You both know the *Pearl* is bad off. We can't afford to lose a single man. Kleet, you're too valuable on board to risk being cut, drawn, and quartered. Brog's the man who can do the job if you slip up just one time. As for you, Brog, Kleet doesn't play games with those deadly *pistolas* he carries. From now on, if either insists on a fight, come to my quarters and I'll oblige. Don't tangle between yourselves, do you hear? If the *Pearl* is to make it through, we must all hang together."

The first mate's eyes darted to meet his. "You agree then, Captain, we won't make it?"

They waited for an answer. Niles slumped against the wall in tired submission. "I'll be honest. The *Pearl* is in bad shape. Truth is, I'm amazed she's still afloat. Everyone's nerves are on edge, mine included. All I ask is for you to keep the faith and direct your energies to save her. We can't do that if we destroy each other. Understand?"

They nodded assent, anger replaced by

sober facts. The pair turned away, retrieved their coats and without another word returned to the crew's quarters.

Niles heaved and strained alongside the men throughout the day that followed. Their battle, pitted against the conquering onslaught, was hopeless from the very start. The disabled ship, gone completely out of control, rose and plunged upon the turbulent sea. Cargo broke loose within the hold. Crates shattered crates, barrels smashed into barrels. The valiant crew fought to a man. Oilskins ripped, torn gloves exposed frozen fingers and the jagged ice slashed their boots. Mid-afternoon found Niles hauling at lines beside Kleet.

"Brog and you settled your differences?"

"Forget it. We got the *Pearl* to worry about. 'Sides, not much I can do about him now." His head tilted back to peer high up the foremast.

Niles' eyes followed, astounded by what they saw. He shouted at the top of his lungs through cupped hands. "Brog!" A dark figure swayed high above. "Brog!" he ordered, and frantically motioned a signal for the man to descend.

Brog, a length of rope clenched between his teeth, only waved recognition. He rocked precariously back and forth on his hazardous perch, but made no move to comply. Niles saw the problem the man strove to rectify. Meanwhile, the tall mast, caught in hurricane force winds, rocked back and forth in a wide arc. Any man who conceived a hope of advancing along the yard would find it nearly impossible. The men below scarcely dared breathe. All eyes followed Brog as he inched his way out upon the ice-laden yard. He came dangerously close to being flung into the blackened sea with each pitch of the decks.

Suddenly the ship listed steeply to one side. Brog slipped on the ice and lost his hold. A loud moan rose from below. The figure slid downward toward the end of the yard. Gloved hands clawed in desperation at the icy surface. A black trench in the sea, like a savage hungry beast, waited to swallow him up.

The brawny hands, stiff with cold, at the last instant regained their grip. Muscular arms closed the distance slowly, ever so slowly, in what seemed hours to those who stared with open mouths below. Brog, with one final desperate heave, hoisted his bulk back into position. Once there, he set to work with the rope.

"Jeez," Kleet exclaimed, and released the breath from his lungs. "How can anyone fight a man like that?"

Task completed, Brog eased his way toward the foremast, grabbed onto a shredded ratline and swung downward onto the deck.

Niles took a step forward, then felt the first mate's hand on his arm. "Let be, Captain. He doesn't expect any compliments. Only tried to bandage the *Pearl's* wounds to keep her alive."

The men dispersed in silence to drift about the decks like ghostly shadows in a fantasy world of ice. Their grotesque white forms became one with the storm itself.

Darkness closed in. Niles and Kleet, heads swathed in several woolen knit skull caps pulled low over their ears, tugged at their upturned frost coated collars. Together, they analyzed their plight, hunched against the force of the blow, clothing frozen stiff against their flesh.

Niles voiced his decision through immobile lips, face stiffened by ice, hands blistered and pain throughout his body. He could not bring himself to ask the men to give more of themselves. It was pointless to continue the battle. They had tried with every ounce of strength within them. God, how they tried! And lost.

Wind pushed against him with a giant hand. It was an effort to draw each frost-laden breath. He forced his heavy feet to make the rounds of the decks at a sloth's pace, motioning each human white-coated mound he encountered to retreat to the galley. Tankards of strong island coffee waited to thaw their nearly frozen bodies. Meanwhile, he took a mental count, own brain succumbing to confusion from exposure.

One man short---which one? His dulled mind tried to concentrate, recall each white form. Then he remembered---he had seen no small mound. Overboard?

The first mate appeared out of a swirl of white.

"Where's Weasel?" Niles yelled, to be heard above the howl of the storm.

"Weasel?" Kleet wiped the frozen drips from his nose with the back of a frozen glove. "Oh, Weasel," he motioned. "Don't worry. I sent him down in the hold a long time ago. He's tryin' to lash some of the shifting cargo."

"He'll be crushed to death!"

"Not Weasel. He's cousin to a rat when comes to skittering out of the way. 'Sides, I already gave 'im a holler to come up."

Men accounted for Niles, weak with exhaustion, clutched the guide rope for support. His eyes, almost frozen shut, were mere slits behind their ice coated lashes. Ahead, through the snow and sleet, he made out the faint yellow glimmer of Victoria's candles in his quarters. He staggered blindly, their glow as a guide, until he fell against the door.

"Thank God!" she cried. "Here, let me help you." She struggled with the frozen buttons of his coat.

"He'll be needin' dry clothes," Captain Leyden said. With an angry curse, he turned. "Danged this gimpy leg! I should have been out there to help."

"Not a thing you could do that wasn't done."

"All the same, every pair of hands counts. These may be old, but they can still work along with the rest."

Niles sank onto his bunk, head in hands, fingers laced through his damp frozen hair. "Those men out there---they were really something today, Captain."

"I know, believe me, I know," the older nodded, as he returned with an armload of dry clothing. "Best crew a man could ask for. Now shed those wet duds. Your ice has started to melt all over this place."

Comforted by the warm dry clothes Niles, with hands that shook, lighted a cigar over the lick of a candle flame. Then he retreated to lean back in the leather chair close to the open charts. The smoke drifted lazily upward. The thunderous roar of the storm outside provided the only sounds in the otherwise silent room.

He knew he should comb his hair and wash. It was not like him to ignore his appearance, particularly with a guest present. As things stood, he no longer cared. Nothing mattered anymore---not him, not Captain Leyden, nor their passenger. He was powerless to change or control fate; it alone held the balance. A cloud of depression wrapped itself about him. He stared absently, aware of nothing, cigar forgotten and his mind adrift in a void of emptiness.

In the dim recesses of consciousness he heard the old man speak from behind. "If you don't put that blamed thing down, Son, it's liable to burn your hand off." Slowly Niles stirred from abstraction. The elder advanced to lean forward over the charts. Everything considered, Niles concluded, it was wasted effort for the man to look. Everything was useless now.

"Where would you say we are, Niles?"

"Way off course," he evaded.

Captain Leyden, with a quick glance toward their guest, lowered his voice to an almost indistinguishable whisper. "I knew a long time ago she was adrift by the feel of her. The storm has blown us wherever it pleases---"

"We did all we could. There was no way to hold her."

"No need to tell me that either. What worries me is how you secretly blame yourself." He laid a work worn hand on the younger's shoulder and their eyes met. "Let me assure you, no captain done better. I'm right proud how you handled her, Boy."

"You won't be by morning," Niles gave a heavy sigh. His fingers gripped the desk edge, knuckles white, an ear to the wind. "Storm's whipped up even worse, if that's possible, and---"

"I can hear it too, you know," the old man's head nodded in somber agreement. "But if it's time, it's time. Nothing further you or I can do about it. Providence is no longer in our hands. Not so bad for me; I'm an old man. You are young and that is my sad regret. If *The Sea Pearl* were one of those big galleons, she might ride it out. As it is, she's not.

"All I ask now is for you to grant an old man one wish. Before she goes down kindly show me the approximate area where I can expect to take my last breath."

Niles laid a finger on the charts.

"Somewhere in this region, I'd say."

"Can't be---weather isn't this cold around those islands."

Niles turned palms upward in a helpless gesture.

"A freak storm maybe? Who knows."

"That's the region of the islands named after that Spaniard, Bermudez. So close, yet so far," the captain shrugged. "Too bad we didn't make it to one of those."

Victoria brushed softly against Niles' side and lifted her eyes in question. "Tell her, Niles," Captain Leyden turned away. "We've never chosen to lie on the *Pearl*. It's her right to know if we are to meet our Maker."

Her face lowered to the abandoned charts. When she spoke, it was in soft resignation. "Then I gather we will not make it, Captain Brett?"

Gently he placed an arm of consolation about her shoulders. "Victoria, our chances have run out. Not a glimmer of hope remains." He thought he felt a shiver passed through her shoulders. "Don't be afraid. They say to drown is the easiest way to go---like going to sleep."

"The wait will be hardest." Face clouded with fear, she turned to him. "How long?"

"I'd venture late into the night."

Captain Leyden's soft gentle voice across the room brought the pair around. He stood quietly before the porthole, its thick cloth cover drawn back. His face gazed into the wild teeth of the storm with an aura of serenity. His words were not directed to anyone within the room. "If I must go, Lord, I'd have preferred to rest beside my love. But I reckon it doesn't really make much difference, 'cause I know her spirit is somewhere up there with you. One last request I ask of thee: I pray you see fit to reunite us when you call me home. Amen."

Victoria moved to offer comfort. Niles laid a hand of restraint on her arm. The captain continued to stand before the night darkened porthole, his weather lined face relaxed in tranquil peace. Comforted by sincere faith, his heart was at rest. Prepared to meet the inevitable, he slowly limped to his bunk.

"I don't know about you two," he said, "but I can think of nothing better than go to bed as usual. However, I'll make one exception---keep my clothes on. Don't relish being washed up on some strange shore in my nightshirt." He managed a mirthful chuckle even in the light of the catastrophic event they were about to face. Niles and Victoria crept noiselessly to his bedside a short time later. "If only I could look out there and fall asleep as relaxed and assured as he," she voiced in a nervous whisper.

"I'm sure he would be pleased to share his porthole with you. If you can find solace somewhere out there in the blackness, so much the better. You'll need all the help you can get for the hours ahead."

"How can you be so sacrilegious as to jest about such matters?"

"Who's jesting? The captain is a very religious man in his own way."

"And you, Captain Brett?"
"Mine went with his."

"Are you saying that while he stood there---"

"What difference the form an altar takes?"

Victoria, exhausted by the struggle to keep her balance against the pitch of the floor beneath her feet, curled her slender body into a chair. "You people are a strange lot, I must say. Without conscience you loot, kill, and take slaves one day, then turn to God the next."

"Slaves? There has never been a slave on *The Sea Pearl*."

"What about Toro?" she countered. "If not a slave, then suppose you explain why he waits on you hand and foot. He cleans your cabin, does your laundry, towers like a shadow ready to serve when you whistle. If that isn't a slave, then---"

"Toro acts as he does by choice, not on orders. If he feels indebted, I cannot deny him the right to show gratitude in his own way."

"Gratitude!" she sneered. "Gratitude for what?"

"His rescue from the post," he answered and turned away.

"Post? What post?" she asked, critical accusations replaced by confusion.

He took a seat nearby before he volunteered an answer. "They have a thing commonly called the post on many islands of the Caribbean region and that includes Jamaica. It's a method they use to punish prisoners, errant slaves or sometimes only for sport. Believe me, it's not a pretty sight to see. Are you sure you really want to know the more lurid details?"

"Yes, Captain, do continue."

"When a prisoner is sentenced, guards tie their feet and hands to an upright post located in the town square. The unfortunate soul is then left without food or water throughout the day, sometimes longer. A slow and tortuous dehydration begins under the fiery tropical sun. His sunburned skin becomes covered with painful blisters." Explanation of the sordid facts completed, he lifted a brow of assurance. "Toro has been worth every gold piece I laid out for him that day."

"Aha! Then you do admit you own a slave?"

"Bought a slave, yes, own? No. I bought him freedom. Toro has the same rights as any other man on board. He carries a paper that attests to the fact, should anyone ever accuse him of being an escapee."

"No wonder he's so devoted. I had no idea---"

The floor pitched sharply. Frantic, she clutched the arms of the chair, eyes wide in fearful expectation.

Niles could relate to her inner terror. Although he had adjusted to face death at any moment either by attack or storms, his own throat was dry, emotions difficult to constrain. The fight for survival is a natural instinct of all life. Never is man more aware of his vulnerability than when forced to experience mortal helplessness before the powerful hands of the Almighty.

Rudder broken, *The Sea Pearl* now lurched, tossed and turned like an inconsequential cork aimlessly afloat in a world of endless fury. The turbulent sea seethed, hissed, and writhed. Incessant waves vehemently crashed, and crashed over her decks. Portholes and walls of the Captains Quarters creaked and strained under the pounding force of the powerful deluge.

Any moment the wooden structure threatened to disintegrate and allow a hungry flood of seawater to claim the hapless occupants within. The ship's heavy timbers moaned a funeral dirge. Shrill whistles and wails of the squall's tongues howled through the mass of tangled rigging.

Niles' jaws ached from the firm set of his teeth. Clenched fists revealed whitened knuckles. If he reacted this strongly, surely she suffered even more. He ached to ease her fears, but felt she may not wish him to reach out in comfort. After her attitudes of the past, would she reject an extended hand?

More than a hand, he yearned to take her

into his arms. He had disciplined himself to maintain a stoic resistance to her charisma throughout the voyage. Now his greatest desire was to hold her close while there was yet time: touch her smooth flesh, smell the clean scent of her, run his fingers through the silkiness of her long dark hair. His lips waited ready to murmur words of comfort to ease her agony. But, he reminded himself, she is an English lady, while I only a man of the sea. She is untouchable royalty by comparison. Instead, he offered a suggestion.

"Perhaps if you do as the captain the wait will be easier." He motioned a hand toward the man asleep across the room. "Then you won't know when it happens."

"No," she shook her head. "I cannot sleep. What about you, Captain?"

He averted his eyes. "I wouldn't sleep either."

"In that case, let's talk. It may ease our tensions until the end comes."

"Sounds all right by me. What shall we talk about?"

"To begin with, as you know there are many things about people of your existence I don't understand. I would like to learn more about your lives, pirates, Port Royal---and

Nicole. What happened to the captain's wife and son? If you are not that son, why does he call you Son? I understand *The Sea Pearl* belongs to Captain Leyden. How then, can you both be captain on the same ship? All this talk about the *Main,* Spaniards, and why they are
hated---"

"Wait!" Niles smiled and raised a hand of protest. "Before I can begin to answer all those questions we will all be at the bottom of the sea. Besides, I doubt the details of our lives would interest you."

The blue of her eyes, he noticed with admiration, deepened their intensity as she leaned closer. "How else can I understand why you are as you are?"

"How am I?" he teased, amused by the flush of embarrassed color that rose to her cheeks.

"I know what I would like to think you are. Your explanations may alleviate my present confusion."

"Hm-m-, sounds reasonable," he agreed. "Then first I shall give you a brief lesson in the geography of the *Spanish Main* and throw in a bit of history for good measure. Next I will explain the distinction between buccaneers and boucaners."

He settled himself more comfortably and began. "England and Spain have not been on good terms since the *Spanish Armada* attempted to attack England. At present, ships directed by the Spanish throne are bent on a ruthless scheme to dominate an area we know as *The Spanish Main*. This takes in an enormous expanse. It stretches roughly along the eastern and northern coasts of South America---"

"Those places are foreign to me," she cut in. "Can you show me their location on your charts?"

"If you like." He reached to the pile stacked neatly near the desk, retrieved a particular one and unrolled it across his knees. She shifted her chair closer to peer intently at the marks. Her eyes followed his finger with genuine interest.

"Spaniards raid, loot, and kill all along there and over here in Central America. Wherever they go they steal shiploads of gold, silver, and gems. They take whatever valuables they can lay their glutinous hands on to add to the coffers of Spain." The finger traced a wide circle. "This area is known as the *Caribbean Sea;* so named after the savage, cannibalistic Caribe Indians who once inhabited the region. Spanish ships control it now by sheer force of numbers and firepower. Thereby, it became known as *The Spanish Main*.

“There are many islands scattered throughout *The Main*. The English, Dutch etc. colonized some. Others came under the control of Spain. The Spanish endeavor to conquer as many lands as they can. Their ships continually attack other settlements. People dread the appearance of Spaniards everywhere along *The Main* for very good reasons.

"They arrive in big heavily armed galleons to invade the shores and kill off the natives. Those taken prisoner are locked in stockades. Many die in the vermin infested pens. Those who survive are either taken to Spain, or sold as captured slaves to large plantation owners on any number of these islands.

"Spanish merchant ships and galleons arrive in the fall. Throughout the winter they gather riches, invade, or indulge their greed by any other means that strike their fancy. Come spring, their ships, heavily laden with bloodstained cargo, wallow back across the Atlantic to vomit their sinful gains into the King's Treasury. Any remaining tortured prisoners are left to rot in Spanish dungeons. So much for the history and geographic part of your questions."

"How deplorable," she breathed. "Is there sufficient wealth among these places to justify Spain's actions?"

"Wealth? Victoria, there are riches the like of which you have never dreamed---gold bars, silver ingots, jewels, pearls by the bushels. All of it passes over counters and thence onto ships."

"Like the jewels in the necklace you wear?"

"It's a sampling," he nodded. "The finest gold, silver, and artworks in the world can be found there."

"You fly the English flag---so why does England regard you as pirates?"

"Like you, they believe the stories. The truth is, island people band together for protection against the Spaniards and piracy. They do this mainly in an attempt to settle grievances. However, men in search of power and adventure hear exaggerated stories. Excited, they think this is their opportunity to obtain fast riches so they jump into the fray. Ships, innocent victims on the seas, are being attacked solely for lust. The actions of these privateers give honest boucaners a bad name. Captain Leyden was, and still is at heart, a true boucaner, not a pirate."

"Boucaner, buccaneer---are they not the same?"

"Not at all. There again, we have a misconception. England pronounces it buccaneer, and assume that means pirate. Correctly, it is boucaner. True boucaners were men who survived by capturing and killing wild cattle and hogs on the islands with their bare hands. They preserved and tanned the hides by smoking them over what they called boucan fires. Those who worked at the fires became known as boucaners. Smoke tanned hides, called boucans, and smoked meat, sold well to ships that passed their island. It was a peaceful operation until the armed Spaniards arrived. When Captain Leyden first went to the islands he worked as a boucaner."

The quarters jerked convulsively. Niles went silent. The pair clung tightly to their seats. The floor heaved. Victoria went white with terror.

“Wha---what time is it?“ she asked.

Niles turned his palms upward and shrugged. “Our clock has fallen and broken and there's no one in the steerage to watch the sand timer or sound the bell on the hour tonight.” In an effort to alleviate her fears he forced himself to continue on their subject, voice lifting to compensate for the din that pressed against their ears.

"The Spaniards destroyed the herds of wild cattle and hogs. The captain, left without a livelihood, moved to the English ruled island of Jamaica."

Victoria pressed close against him, eyes riveted on the small porthole. To coax her concentration he asked, "Shall I continue?"

"Y---yes, yes," she quickly responded. One quivery hand clutched his arm even tighter while the other gripped her chair. "Please, talk about anything. Only don't stop!"

Niles forced himself to resume. "Jamaicans welcome boucaners, adventurers, fortune seekers and full-blown pirates in their port. Although a rowdy lot, the island tolerates them as a deterrent against invasion by the French."

"What about the captain's wife?"

"She was taken prisoner by the Spaniards during one of their invasions of their island. The boucaners in retaliation struck out against the Spanish ships and rescued the prisoners. She never recovered from the injuries sustained at the hands of her captors, nor the fever contracted while imprisoned in their filthy hold. The earring in his chest belonged to her."

"How sad," she breathed in a whisper, compassionate eyes on the bundle of quilts.

"He's never forgiven the Spanish for---" his voice trailed off. "I ask you, would you consider the man over there a bloodthirsty pirate?"

"Don't be ridiculous," she scoffed. "I now understand what you meant when you said, 'There are pirates, and there are blameless pirates. The latter are only peaceful hunters trying to protect their families."

"Exactly," he nodded. "All this talk about loot, theft and murder---we leave that for the adventure seekers. As for us, we have neither thirst, nor stomach for such gains."

"Has *The Sea Pearl* ever been involved in a sea battle?"

"When forced to protect what is rightfully ours, yes."

"After what you say, I view your lives from a different perspective. And tell me, are you his son?"

"No," he replied, his countenance a mirror of consummate fondness for the aged man. "His son, born with a crippled mind, was taken captive with his mother. The Spaniards knew he wouldn't bring money on the slave market. Therefore, while his mother screamed and pleaded, they threw him over the side. She watched him drown while they laughed at her anguish."

"How terrible! Such sad, sad memories the captain carries. And you?"

"My parents were killed in an attack on another island. Found by boucaners, I was set ashore at Port Royal. There I was, a young lad, miserable, alone in a strange harbor, with no people of my own, no place to go."

"How then, did you meet Captain Leyden?"

"He came across me, pathetic, lost and homeless on the beach. His extended hand is a sight I shall never forget, nor how wonderful it felt when it touched mine."

Long minutes passed before he cleared the emotional swelling in his throat to resume. "He took me home to his wife. Thought I might ease the pain of her loss. Three days later she died. He's done for me ever since like I am his own. To me, he's more than a father. He bore no obligation to take me in. Could have turned his back there on the beach. At the time, I've heard it said, he needed me as greatly as I needed him."

"If, as you say, he was a boucaner, how did you become captains on *The Sea Pearl*?"

"Your father, Captain Leyden and---

another party purchased it a few years ago. Later, your father became in dire need of money to cover his losses. The captain, in an effort to be of assistance, bought out his share of the ship. Captain Leyden, out of camaraderie, continued to favor your father with the choicest products available in the Caribbean region. As I grew to learn and handle the ship he gave me command alongside himself."

"Must be quite an honor."

"Indeed it is. I've tried my best to live up to his trust. We've experienced a lot together, both good and bad. Now that our last night has come, it's very hard to express my sentiments of finality in words."

The candle flame continued to flicker and sputter wildly with each mighty pitch and roll of the doomed vessel. He released a heavy sigh. The stirred recollections presented a visitation into a past; a past of which the two captains seldom spoke. Odd, he thought to himself, to share those intimate memories now with a stranger.

Visions, sounds, and emotions began to flow in rapid succession behind his closed eyelids. The cry of a young lad caught in the stench of a dark hold---roar of cannon---screams of terror---hunger. An outstretched hand---the touch---the warmth---the immediate bond.

A mighty surge from beneath brought the present violently back into focus. Again, as when a small boy, his world was being torn asunder. Helpless to stand against an enemy larger than himself, with no hope of survival he, as before, faced the unknown.

The old man slept peacefully across the room like rocked in a cradle, oblivious to the savage pound of the storm against the walls.

Suddenly, the floor beneath gave a mighty convulsive pitch. A loud **CRACK** of wood! An earsplitting crash of timbers!

"Niles!" came Victoria's shrill scream. She clung tightly to him, face buried into the hollow of his shoulder. He braced his boots to avoid being thrown across the room. Mouth open, he tried to say something, anything to allay her terror---but what could be said now that the end was eminent?

Out of instinct he wrapped his arms protectively around her trembling body, cheek pressed against the clean scent of her long dark hair and waited. Waited for the final moment of annihilation. The intense roar of the storm, in those dark moments, bore down upon their bent heads.

A thunderous **WHUMP!**

The Sea Pearl gave a mighty groan. And then . . stillness.

Niles braced---expectant to hear their door rip from its iron hinges, wood explode before the force of a wall of water. He flung himself as a bodily shield over Victoria and crushed her within his arms. His heart prayed for power to transmit courage to her as they faced death together.

CHAPTER EIGHT

The heavy iron latch grated.

The door burst open, accompanied by a flood of frothy seawater.

Two ice coated figures staggered from within the deluge.

One, released from the arm that sustained it, collapsed in a limp heap onto the wet floor. The other laid his weight against the door and threw the latch bolt into place. Niles leaped forward, dropped to a knee and turned the collapsed body over to make identification. Kleet's face twisted in a moan.

"Careful, Captain," Brog panted, as he leaned against the door to catch his breath. "He's hurt bad in the back."

With stiff fingers he tugged at his frozen gloves

and clawed at the buttons of his coat. At his feet Kleet's body writhed in agony. A long slash: saturated with blood, ice, and seawater, gaped the length of the injured man's coat. Niles whipped a razor sharp knife from his belt and with a quick swipe cut away the clothing.

A long jagged laceration came into view. It extended from shoulder blade, across the spine, and came to an end at the waist of the opposite side. The raw flesh lay open to expose the bones beneath.

Niles, unable to restrain himself longer, broke under the stresses he had carried for so long. In a fury of savage rage, he shouted, "I told you to keep that pig-sticker of yours sheathed!" By instinct he wanted to leap at Brog, tear him limb from limb, choke, as if he were the enemy rather than the storm.

"It warn't me, Captain," Brog objected as he threw his saturated woolen coat aside to join Niles on the floor.

"Who then?" Niles demanded.
"Nobody. You know the matie---he wanted---"

“Wanted what?”

"We all know how you've been about drinkin' on board, Captain. Kleet here didn't think, seein's what's ahead now, it would make much difference one way or the other. None of the crew could sleep with the ship pitchin' us all over the place. So he got the idea to try to get a bottle or two from the hold. Mind you, we warn't meanin' to get soused or anything like that. Just a few drinks to pass around," he struggled to explain. "But hell man, we's goin' down. You can't deny a man a few drinks 'fore dyin'!"

Dire emergency at hand, Niles ignored the man's explanation and ordered, "Help me get him onto my bunk."

Brog continued his explanation as they carried the groaning mate. "We was headed back from the hold when the whole mainmast crashed down on us. He got pinned same as if he'd been pegged right to the deck. Wonder warn't killed on the spot. I been out there fightin' the storm while strainin' my guts to pry him free of the wreckage."

"We'll lie him face down so I can work on this," Niles instructed. They eased the injured man onto the bunk. "Victoria, get the roll of bandages and the big green bottle from Captain Leyden's closet. I need to clean this wound to assess the damages."

She stared immobilized, eyes wide, at the blood covered patient. Niles shouted with impatience. "MOVE! before this man bleeds to death." The sharp edge on his voice brought her into action. She ran to obey. Her hands quivered as she handed him the items.

Bent over the ugly wound, he speculated, "That explains the powerful noise we heard---mainmast going down."

Kleet squirmed upon sight of the sterilization concoction in the green bottle. "None of that!" he yelled. "Just wrap me up so's sharks don't smell blood when we go down."

"Shut up!" Niles snapped. His eyes darted in Victoria's direction. Already panic-stricken, the mention of sharks would only increase her fears.

He began to cleanse the wound. Kleet howled like a banshee under the painful sear and sting of the potent fluid. "Keep this up and you'll catch me," Niles casually remarked. He knew the mate understood what was meant by the comment without further elaboration in the presence of the lady. "Bring any with you Brog?"

"Any what?"

"Those bottles you went for."

"No sir, Captain. When the mate went down, I dropped 'em to dig him out."

"He'll need a bracer to deaden the pain. Break out a bottle of my Madeira," he motioned toward his closet. "And mix it strong. Shame I don't have any cursed Dill Devil like he usually swills down to burn his guts. After that poison, mine likely won't penetrate his brain."

He took care to be gentle while he swabbed the affected region, his initial anger by now calmed. Face lined with anticipatory concern, he paused to tip the wine to the mate's twisted lips. "Here, drink this. It may help ease the pain hen I pour the captains miracle cure directly into the open wound to prevent infection."

The first mate bellowed his objections and struggled to break free. "We're goin' down! Don't you understand? Why make me suffer that green fire? Let me get stinkin' drunk instead. Then I can at least die happy."

"Drink! We're not down yet. Victoria, bring more candles." Exasperated when she failed to respond, he barked, "What's the matter woman, never seen a shirtless man before? No different than when covered. Now get those candles!"

A stream of the green liquid flowed over the entire length of the wound; the harsh fluid seared deep into the utmost tender recesses of the laceration. Kleet's hands gripped hard on the edges of the bunk. Shrieks of pain escaped from deep within his throat.

"Brog, more Madeira. Victoria, get the small wooden box from the shelf over there. Drink up Kleet, you'll need it before we're done." More wine was shoved against the mate's lips. "Stand over here, Brog, and hold him down."

Victoria watched while Niles removed a slender silver needle from the box and threaded a fine strand of white silk thread through the eye. She felt the color drain from her face; the room began to spin before her eyes.

"Victoria, I need both hands to close the edges of flesh together. When I ask, hand me the shears or fresh bandage to sop blood."

He saw her reel at the suggestion and reach out a hand to grope the wall for support. Understanding, he allowed time for her to recover. "You all right?"

She nodded, stifled her qualms and lifted her head at a determined tilt. Thus assured of her stability, he forewarned, "When he starts to howl, which he will, close your ears. You can do it, if you set your mind. Ready?"

She turned her eyes from the shafts of light that reflected off the sharp needle.

Steeling herself, she forced her fingers to pick up the small shears and thick roll of white bandage cloth. Niles, braced to steady his balance, leaned over the lacerated back. Immediately Brog's strong hands closed on Kleet like iron circlets, securely pinning him onto the bunk.

Niles' body swayed and lurched with the violent pitches of the room. Any movements on his part would need be paced to take advantage of brief moments of respite from the storm. He drew a deep breath. The tedious process of careful stitching and tying began.

Sweat beads formed on the first mate's body.

They grew larger.

No longer able to retain their globular form, they ran in glistening rivulets to saturate coverlet and pillow. A barrage of oaths fit to singe the hardiest ear escaped from the tightly drawn lips. Each time the needle probed the flesh he bellowed a volley of threats accented by uncontrollable howls. Brog's hands held the man fast.

Niles reached for the shears. Tremors flowed through the metal from the lady's hand to his own. "Hold on, we've only a little farther to go," he encouraged. Her tension was understandable, unaccustomed as she was to the dangers of life at sea.

Perspiration formed dark patches on his own shirt in the cold room. He had never had occasion to work under such adverse conditions. His hands began to quiver from the strain the intense surgical procedure required.

He whipped a final knot into place and wiped his face with a sleeve. "Get a good hold, Brog, while I pour on more disinfectant." Kleet emitted one last crazed scream, his back arched, then he went limp.

"Too bad he didn't pass out sooner; he wouldn't have suffered as much," Niles said, and tore a long length of bandage. The wrap completed, he straightened, filled his lungs with air, and exhaled slowly.

"We'll cover and leave him right here." He replaced the wiped instruments to the box and turned to Brog. "It's much too dangerous out there to return to the crew quarters. Better you stay here with us."

The husky man shook his head and shrugged into his heavy coat. "Might be needed over there."

Niles did not offer an argument. He knew Brog would do as he deemed right; the door closed behind the man. Niles sank into his chair and laid his head against the backrest, totally drained both physically and mentally. His clothes were damp and clammy against his skin.

From behind closed lids he heard Victoria attempt to coax additional heat from the inadequate burner. He heard her footsteps cross to his side and felt a delicate hand move tentatively to rest over his. The touch, the warmth, was a comfort in his exhaustion. He waited to absorb the pleasure of her nearness before he spoke.

"I'm not asleep, you know." The hand immediately withdrew. He reached to restrain the movement, his face slowly turning to her. "It's all right. I am touchable."

"Sorry---it's only that---with Kleet, you were so different, so---"

"Human?"

"You can say that, yes. But it doesn't fully express what is on my mind. Always you are so firm, harsh. Tonight while I watched I learned you are a man capable of much compassion. It helped me understand why, with the life you live, that your surface reflection is a necessary element to survive." Contented to leave her hand within his, she continued. "I was very mistaken about everyone on the *Pearl*, about buccaneers---"

"Boucaners," he corrected, eyes at rest on her hand, while the fingers of his other hand idly traced its fragile lines.

"Yes, boucaners." She scanned the visible lines of fatigue on his face. "You're worn out. Lie down, at least for a while."

"A bit difficult, wouldn't you say?" One eyebrow lifted toward his bunk. "He won't revive until it's over. Maybe those two over there are the lucky ones."

"Then take my bed."

"No, you also had a very difficult night," he gently squeezed the soft hand. "Go to your bunk and I shall stay here. Best hurry though, while you can make it across before the floor starts to pitch again."

She moved closer and moved her head where it rested against his shoulder. "No, please, I beg you. Let me stay. I'm afraid to die alone."

"Will it help if I lie beside you for a while?" She stared agape, taken aback by his unexpected overture. "I'm a gentleman," he assured, and rose to place one strong arm about her tiny waist. Together, they crossed to her cubical, clinging to anything available to keep their balance.

Once inside, he felt her body tremble in the darkness against his own on her bunk. He shifted his position to cradle her in his arms on the narrow space. Grateful, she nestled closer, head at rest upon his chest. Her silken hair brushed his jaw and sent a sensation of excitement along his neck. Her hand sought and closed tightly about the jeweled medallion were it lay exposed at his open shirtfront.

"Do you mind?" she asked, with a voice that quivered with fright. He drew her nearer in answer. Her soft curvaceous endowments pressed close and he felt her heart against his chest pound in unison with his own---treasured each beat and found solace in her nearness on this night of trial.

The slight voice muffled against his skin whispered, "While the necklace is in my hand I will know I'm not alone."

"I will be here for you," he promised, voice husky with emotion. He ached to crush her close, overcome with desire in their plight. Longed to kiss the terror from her quivering lips, feel their bodies melt together in oneness.

Instead, he steeled himself to limit his satisfaction to the pleasure of her womanly warmth against his manliness. She trusts me to be a gentleman of upright morals, he told himself. I must not, in any manner, violate her child-like innocence. Above all, I must uphold the honor of my captaincy.

There followed a long silence. Just when he thought she was asleep, she stirred, soft as a kitten beside him, and whispered, "There is one question you never answered while we talked---the scarlet gown---is she---"

"Nicole?" he smiled sleepily in the darkness. "As beautiful and remarkable a lady as anyone could meet. She has attributes and capacities for love beyond comprehension. Someday, if we live, I shall tell you about her."

If Victoria posed any further questions he was unaware of them. The pitch and moan of the stricken vessel quickly faded into the background. The sweet depths of sleep overtook his physically and mentally spent body.

Somewhere in a far away dream he repeatedly heard his name, more as an echo out of the mists than a distinct voice. Amid the sound, he began to feel his body being spasmodically shaken. Slowly he recognized the echo in the gray dreamy fog as the voice of Captain Leyden. He jerked upright; sweat beads broke forth on his forehead. The sudden movement caused the necklace to bite into the flesh of his neck. Victoria, in slumber, still tightly clutched the medallion. Carefully he loosed the fingers from the jeweled piece and slipped his arm free. He turned, prepared for the worst of news. Captain Leyden stood beside the bed in the dim light.

"Listen!" the old man whispered, one ear cocked.

Niles heard nothing---not wind, not a creak nor moan, only a soft lap, lap. He leaped to his feet and dashed to fling open the door of the quarters. Before him a hazy pink dawn spread itself across the horizon of the eastern sky.

The ocean gently undulated as far as the eye could see. This can't be true, he told himself. We are sinking. I am drowning. A vision before death comes? I have heard such things happen before death. Captain Leyden's crutch thumped from behind.

"She made it, Son!" The crinkled gray eyes, misted with tears of joy, surveyed the debris covered deck. "Old girl's a shambles, but she brought us through!"

Niles stared about in disbelief while his mind made a slow return to reality. "Don't ask me how," he breathed. Awestricken, his vision took in the tangled lines. Pulleys, landing boats and broken rails lay in jumbled heaps across the decks. Ragged shreds of canvas overhead lightly stirred in the breeze. The broken mainmast, like a giant felled tree, rested atop the remains of the foremast, broken under the force of the mainmast's thunderous descent.

Victoria, awakened by voices, joined the two captains. A playful wind rippled through Niles' dark hair and fluttered the open shirtfront. Ecstatic, he encircled his arms around Victoria and Captain Leyden. Dawn and *The Sea Pearl* never looked so beautiful as at this moment of reprieve.

All salvageable materials had been stacked in neat piles by mid-afternoon. Unsalvageable debris were discarded over the side. The cleanup job progressed exceptionally well. The shattered masts and yards, however, lay a grim reminder of the perilous night.

Brog was temporarily promoted to first mate for the duration of Kleet's recuperation. He pushed the men like a whip-less slave driver. Captain Leyden, almost strong enough to walk without the crutch, watched the operations. Unable to assist, he was forced to basked in the first welcome sunshine in months. The men, however, secretly remained apprehensive of his chest condition. All hoped the warm sun would draw out the severe congestion. The Captain motioned Niles over, attention arrested by the labors of the crew.

"Looks mighty good, Son. She'll be seaworthy in no time."

"Lot to be done to make her even halfway seaworthy," Niles sighed, with a dubious shrug of one bare shoulder where beads of perspiration glistened. "Hardly a whole piece left on her."

The gray head responded with a wizened nod. “She had heart to survive, which is the important thing. Rest assured, she'll come alive again. I been thinking. If we can find that Bermudez island group we can anchor in to put her in sailable order." Niles opened his mouth to object, but was stopped by a gnarled hand. "Hear me out. Those islanders, for their vital needs, depend on ships that pass. In our condition, it would be good to lighten our load. There's another advantage to consider. They exchange products in payment. An ideal way to restock our food supply, I'd say." He watched to observe Niles' reaction to his idea. One inquisitive, shaggy brow lifted. "Still dead set on the American Colonies?"

"No choice."

"I dunno---" the elder rubbed his whiskers and feinted deep thought. "When I woke you this morning things looked mighty cozy in there. I could have sworn you'd changed your mind. You know that could very easily happen." The mischievous eyes behind the half closed lids held a playful twinkle, while a slow amused smile twitched at the corners of his mouth. The lips pursed to continue the taunt. "Searched the whole place before I noticed her open door. Didn't know if it be safe to peek or not."

"You can furl your imagination. Fact is, she was afraid to be alone."

"Was she now," the old man gave a subtle chuckle. "Curled close and comfy helped, I suppose? Next, you'll say you were sleepy." His eyes rolled skyward in thought as he reflected. "I'd likely taken advantage of the invitation myself if I was a young blooded buck like you. I doubt either of you got cold, that's for sure."

His tone took on a more serious note. "Truth is, sort of good to see you finally attracted to a woman. You sure took your time about it, I must say, when one considers how long we've been at sea---"

"Wait up right there," Niles cut in. "Enough of your tongue in cheek fun. It wasn't what it appeared. She's an English lady, remember?"

"So? And that makes me think---"
"In the wrong directions."

"No, no, not about that," he waved a hand to discount the subject. "Our men have worked all day like mice in a cheese factory to clear some of this mess. Suppose we call it a day and have us a party?"

"A party!"

The old man with emphasis slapped the coil of rope on which he sat. "Yes, a party. We're alive! That deserves a celebration. Blast it, Boy, we've a lot to be thankful for. Who knows, it might even give you the chance to see what's right under your blind nose."

"Meaning?"

The captain ignored the question. "Break out a keg of English grog, more if needed. It'll give all of us a chance to let off a little pent up steam." Enthusiasm roused, he began to elaborate with excited gestures. "Call out the music makers. When it turns dark hang lanterns on the decks. What we need is to kick up our heels like old times! Maybe share your little lady so's each man can dance a turn with her.

"She's not my lady to share," Niles corrected. "However, if a party is what you want I'll go make the arrangements." He took a step to leave, but felt the captain's restraining hand on his arm.

"She could be, Son, if you weren't so blasted stubborn and proud! All I ask is for you to think on it. Now go tell the crew to get scrubbed and put on their fancy trappings; that includes you and I. We'll make merry in the tradition of *The Sea Pearl.* After what she's brought us through I want to see her decks come alive again!"

"Yes Sir, Captain," Niles feigned a salute and left to seek Brog to give the order. Jubilant whoops and hollers erupted as the word was passed. There was an immediate rush among the men to strip their sweaty clothes in preparation to dive over the side.

"Avast there!" Niles shouted. "There's a lady on board. Get yourselves to the forward bow before you bare any backsides." With a flurry of discarded shirts, pants clutched by fists at the waist, they obediently scurried toward the bow. Niles followed to dive deep into the semi-tropical water. The aches from his tired muscles washed away in the coolness and left him refreshed. All tensions and frustrations accumulated throughout the weeks of trial began to clear within his brain.

Accustomed to life without vanity among men of his profession, he gave no thought to the lady when he stepped shirtless into his quarters until an audible gasp escaped from her. In his abstraction, he had failed to anticipate the affect his bared upper torso would have on someone uninitiated to life on the high seas.

Ugly body scars, undesired trophies of numerous hand to hand combats, went unnoticed among the crew. Each possessed marks of his own. Niles' body, crisscrossed by many savage mementos, did not present a pretty sight. To a land dweller, particularly a woman of refinement, the revelation proved quite a shock. Quickly he covered himself while he drew out fresh clothing.

Dusk was settling in when the men began to assemble on the main deck. Attired in the finest fabrics, spit shined cuffed boots, they stood with grog tankards held high. Improvised musical instruments appeared from pockets and sea chests. The owners' work stiffened fingers would limber after a few more trips to the keg. After a series of squeaks, squawks and zums emitting from strings, they readied themselves to blend with reasonable harmony.

Laughter on smooth shaven faces now took precedence over former despair. They danced and cavorted about, as though unable to constrain their feet, while they waited for the makeshift orchestra to synchronize.

Meanwhile, in the Captain's Quarters, a contented Victoria turned about to survey her appearance. She was a vision in a delicate pink gown chosen from the crates. Tiny ribbon rosebuds accented her wasp waist and seductive bust line. She smiled to herself with satisfaction.

A sound from behind brought her about. Her eyes widened. A hand flew to the crimson mouth to stifle a frightened cry. A rakish pirate, Captain Niles Brett of the renown *Sea Pearl,* in full regalia stood tall, assured, in full command. Rows of gold buttons gleamed down the front and cuffs of the flared maroon velvet coat. At his throat, fine ruffled lace adorned the immaculate white shirtfront. Thick ropes of gold were draped around his neck. The raven black cuffed boots reflected the light when he moved.

He looked her over with a nod of approval. Then placed her reluctant hand upon his sleeve. Her touch recalled to him the pleasure of her closeness of the night before as she clung to the medallion, now concealed against his chest. At the doorway he turned and called back to Kleet. "I'll send Toro to assist you to your quarters. I aim to retake possession of my own bunk tonight."

"Forget Toro. I'll be out for my share of the keg. Ol' Kleet never yet missed a chance to swill free grog."

"You're weak as a starved alley cat," Niles cautioned. "Try to stand and you'll fall on your face. He can bring you a tankard---only one, mind you. Get boozed up and you'll tear those stitches." An uncouth sea song rose from the men outside. He turned his attentions to the behaviorisms of the crew on deck.

"Avast there! Silence!" he shouted. Heads turned and voices trailed off. The lady stepped into their midst and they stared in awe at the transformation. Niles raised a hand. "Captain Leyden and I know you have more than earned the right to a lively shindig. However, let's show proper respect for our guest. That means batten down your language."

The old captain nodded agreement. Tankard raised, he addressed the musicians. "Shape up men. Play something respectable to set our toes atappin'. Let's hear *Off To The Sea*."

Work calloused fingers picked the strings with amazing flexibility. The men stirred into action. They whirled one another, or capered solo. High heeled boots clicked and stomped the deck to the beat of the music.

Final note struck, Captain Leyden again hailed the music makers. "This time, a slow number just for me, if you please. Isn't every day we have the pleasure of a lady to grace our festivities. Before the rest of you crowd me out, I shall park this crutch of mine. I aim to limp a turn or two around the deck with our lovely guest. I may be old," he winked, as a twinkle flashed from his merry eyes, "but not too old to enjoy twirling a beauty 'round the floor!"

From the sidelines, Niles watched the pair with warm pleasure. The elderly captain, with nary a hint of limp, glided around the cleared area with the grace of a sea gull. Victoria fell into step, a cloud of misty pink within the curve of his arm.

In Captain Leyden's younger days, too fleet of foot for an opponent's thrust, he was known to flit lightly as a bird among branches. Now the stately man, with the same agility used to insure his survival through years of hand to hand conflicts, exemplified fluid motion before the circle of revering crewmen. He dipped and turned, executing the intricate steps, in perfect time with the rhythm.

Niles watched and reflected on the past. When he was but a lad, the captain had recognized that like himself, Niles must be prepared. The day would come when he, too, would meet deadly encounters with assailants whom habituated the Main. He taught Niles with patience and practice to master these same lithe movements while the boy grew to manhood. Together the pair now fought side by side with equal dexterity of cutlass, saber, epee, and Spanish *Pistolas.* In this close manner they defended the name of The *Sea Pearl* and that which was their own.

Niles' pulses began to race as the couple drew near. The old captain glanced in his direction. The pair, to his disappointment, proceeded onward to stop before Cleve.

"Here, you ol' fish fryer. Seems you have the most cause to celebrate. You shall return home to meet your eighth."

Victoria looked at the two with a quizzical expression. "Eighth?"

"Didn't he tell you about his family?" Cleve's round ruddy face beamed with pride. "Cleve's wife waits with his latest. Likely another son, I'm guess'n, same as the other seven."

"Why Cleve, I had no idea you were married."

"Most of the men are," Captain Leyden ascertained. "Or at least have a woman they call their own in port. Take Weasel here, he needs a few turns to keep in practice. If his feet get too rusty, his wife will have his hide when we arrive."

"Weasel, married?" She turned to the sulky little man, normally the grubbiest, tonight meticulously scrubbed.

"Married? Why, he's got himself a woman wide and high as he's short and shriveled," the captain proclaimed. "She can steer him by the ear all over the place; yet he's the one most anxious to reunite. She's a match for his argumentative temperament."

His attention returned to the cook. "On your way, Cleve," he motioned an invitational arm to the center of the circle. "Never make a lady wait."

With an impish chuckle, he returned to Niles' side. "Thought I'd turn her over to you; but by danged, figured I'd make you stir up nerve to ask her yourself." His face sobered. "I'm tuckered after that exertion. Think I'll leave the rest of the night to you younger men while I turn in." As he moved away Niles noticed he breathed with an unfamiliar raspiness. This stirred fresh concern. Was it only the dancing? Or has his illness taken a turn for the worse? he wondered, and strolled to the grog keg for a refill.

The night deepened. Victoria graciously danced the entire evening with the lonely men. The hours all too quickly passed. Men dropped out, one by one, to fall upon their bunks. Fingers of musicians slowed their tempos to more nostalgic melodies: songs of home, of loves. Victoria stood in idle conversation among the stragglers that remained. Niles watched from where he lounged alone against a cannon carriage. The longer he watched the more envious and lonely he became. Finally, pride and stubborn resistance gave way. He stepped forward to offer a hand.

"Why Captain Brett, I thought perhaps you were offended with me," she cooed flirtatiously from within the curve of his arm.

Rather than admit the hours he spent consumed with jealousy, yet too restrained to bend, he evaded. "I thought it best to first permit the crew their turns." To himself he asked, why must I make excuses to her for my actions? I can do as I please. What do I care what she thinks?

"Tell me, do you ever stop being a captain?"

"Would I be a good captain if I did?" He guided her smoothly toward the far end of the deck. Isolated in this world of semi-darkness, he was amazed to find she felt light and delicate as an orchid petal in his arms. Here in the dim shadows, he was comforted by the fact that they could not be easily seen nor overheard by the others.

Thousands of stars twinkled overhead. Romantic music, carried on the soft breeze, coiled its way among the tarred ropes of the rigging. The pair glided and dipped as one to the rhythm. As they moved Niles became acutely aware of finally touching, holding, this beautiful woman, whose eyes first met and enchanted him in Mr. Silvas' office. It seemed so long ago. Her silken dark hair now tumbled in loose curls across creamy white shoulders. Occasionally a strand brushed against his jaw and sent his pulse racing.

They drifted in a dream state: caught in a magical world of warm trade wind breezes and silvery moonlight, alone in a world enhanced by the excitement of her closeness, conscious only of the gentle lap of waves that rippled along the hull. Their fluid movements blended sensuously in synchronism with the soft music. Long after the notes on deck ceased, their enthralled bodies continued to sway to a melody they alone heard.

He gently placed a forefinger to her chin and tilted her face to his. Starlight reflected from her uplifted eyes. Her flawless loveliness, bathed in the lunar glow, waited for his advance. Parted lips invited his to brush hungrily, yet tenderly, across hers. Moralistic inhibitions strained against masculine vulnerabilities that rippled along his jaw line. He fought against the fervent desire that overwhelmed all reservations. With a sense of urgency, he wanted to crush her exciting body to his; to savor the sweetness of her full lips. He wanted to feel again, as at the height of the storm, her heartbeat next to his.

His mind shouted---My position, I must not forget my position as captain. Duty drew him back with extreme effort. He steeled his will against nature's urges. With resolute determination, he released her from his arms and drew a ragged breath.

A stray lock of dark wavy hair fell across his forehead. He brushed it into place with a hand that shook. Then he turned away: gripped the rail, knuckles white, eyes lifted to stare into the endless galaxies overhead. The awesomeness of the universe only increased his sense of aloneness that gnawed within. The hushed rustle of her skirts as she approached escaped his notice until she spoke. Her voice stirred an awareness that although he removed himself physically, his heart had not followed.

Scarcely above a whisper, she asked, "Did I do, or say something to offend you, Niles?"

He continued to stare into the starlight while he braced his resolves. Even then he only half turned. He did not wish to meet her searching eyes. Most surely he would weaken, gather her into his arms again. "I am Captain Brett, Miss Silvas," he corrected, with what little firmness he could to muster.

If she reached out---he knew all his honorable resolves would crumble. He withdrew farther along the rail to place safety of distance between. I must remain apart, aloof, he reminded himself even as his entire being cried out---Forget my world, my position of command, my moral virtues! Why shouldn't I be like Kleet? Be the man her eyes plead for! Kleet would never hesitate to submit to her endowments. I had the opportunity to take her when I shared her bed in the storm . . . But, unlike the first mate, his mind staunchly refused to forsake honor.

"Miss Silvas---"

"Please Captain, I am Victoria, remember? Don't push me so far away as to address me as Miss Silvas. I thought after these many months at sea---the association we shared---I know you didn't like me when I first boarded. My presence, I realize, was an extreme inconvenience. I've tried very hard to learn and understand your ways, really I have. Moments ago while you held me, I gathered the impression former resentments had disappeared." Head bent, she added disconsolately, "Evidently, I was wrong."

"No, you were right. That's not the point."

"What can possibly be more to the point than how two people feel toward one another?"

His passions again began to rise rather than recede. For the sake of his passenger's virtue he knew the intoxication of night combined with closeness must somehow be quickly diverted. "Victoria, it's late," he began in desperation, with a voice that rang of a control he did not feel. "Let me say you adapted very well to life on a ship. I commend you. However, as I explained before, there are certain responsibilities to which I must adhere. Therefore, I suggest we forget what happened here tonight and retire to our respective bunks."

Tears misted the starlight in her lovely eyes. She stamped a slippered foot in a mixture of confusion, frustration and anger. "Oh yes, I almost forgot, you are the Untouchable Almighty Captain!"

He braced himself to reply, grateful for the shadows lest she detect the flush of guilt that crept across his profile. "Yes, and as such, I am responsible for the safety of my passengers, whomever they may be. That includes surveillance over the integrity of my crew and myself."

She lashed out in return, angered by his air of superiority. "Integrity? Am I to understand you are afraid you may taint your own honor, Captain?"

Caught by his own phrase he remained silent then sidestepped with an evasive reply. "What I meant was, it is time you went to your bed."

"That an order, Captain?"

"If you wish to classify it as such. At any rate, I expect it to be followed."

She remained. Her eyes followed his unseeing gaze across the expanse of calm water. "All right, Captain, if that is what you want. I hoped . . . never mind what I hoped." Slowly she turned and drifted, a pink cloud, across the now darkened deck. He watched her disappear among the shadows with regret.

More than anything he wanted to call out, reach to draw her back within the circle of his arms. He ached to touch her, hold her close again, feel the heat of her responsive lips pressed to his. But alas, he thought, I am captain of *The Sea Pearl.* I dare not sacrifice honor for personal desire.

He remained at the rail, shaken and with a tinge of guilt. The night breezes, like cool wings, fluttered across his fevered face. His eyes roved aimlessly over the moonlight splashed water. The familiar creak of lines reached his ears. All was serene. The ship swayed gently on the calm sea. The ship---always the ship. No room in his life for anything but the ship.

Overhead he observed the battered rigging silhouetted against the night sky; it made the *Pearl* appear as a ghost ship. She was a dark skeleton: tattered, splintered, its bared limbs draped in ragged clothes. His eyes lowered to the mainmast. It lay indomitably the length of the decks and extended beyond the stern. He gave a heavy sigh. To restore it to a state of temporary seaworthiness would present an almost insurmountable challenge. And yet somehow it must be raised if they were to limp into home port. Tomorrow ---tomorrow they would again bend their backs; this time to bind up and heal her scars.

He loosened the ruffles at his throat and unbuttoned the shirtfront. The cool sea air drifted across his bared chest. Moonlight reflected from the vibrant jewels of the medallion, where it lay against his tanned flesh. It seemed no longer to belong solely to him alone ever since she held it. Slowly he crossed to his quarters hoping she was already asleep. In his present frame of mind, should they have another encounter, he was too unsure of himself. Could I persevere against her seductive feminine entreaties? he wondered. Throughout our weeks of close cohabitation I managed to maintain a reserved stance. Now however, I have at last held her, thrilled to her nearness. During our brief moment of intimate contact we were transported into a new dimension. I can never again look upon her with the same noncommittal reserve. Each time she speaks, each time she draws near, each time our eyes perchance to meet I will feel a magnetic current span the space between.

He tossed restlessly in his bunk before finally dropping into a deep sleep. After what seemed only moments he felt a soft hand on his shoulder. Someone repeatedly called his name. From the depths of sleep he heard the tone of urgency in the voice.

"Captain Brett---Niles, wake up!"

He endeavored to part the webs of sleep from his brain. His face twisted into a dark scowl at being disturbed. "No, Victoria, what happened tonight is over and done."

"Captain Brett, I beg you, wake up!"

The desperation in her voice brought him up on one elbow. The flicker of her candle illuminated the room. He had slept much longer than imagined.

Face reflecting alarm, voice hushed, she urged, "It's Captain Leyden. You better take a look. Hurry, I fear he's in a bad way!"

The mere mention of the older man brought instant awareness to Niles. He pushed her aside and ordered, "Stay with him while I grab some clothes."

In his haste he arrived bootless and shirtless at the bedside. A glance revealed the cause of her anxiety. The old man gasped and fought for air: face vividly flushed with a bluish hue, mouth open. Gnarled fingers clawed with desperate jerky movements at the quilts. His entire body wrenched with violent spasms.

"Quick, hold his head," Niles ordered. "What will you do?"

"It's pneumonia. He's swallowed his tongue and blocked the air passage. Do as I say." Obediently, she took the gray head of the struggling man between her palms. "Firmer!" Niles ordered. He pinned the shaking form with his own body, thrust a forefinger into the open mouth and sought to move the obstruction. Precious time was passing. Beads of perspiration glistened on his forehead as he concentrated on this dire emergency.

The man needed air. He must clear the passageway before it was too late!

One more try.

The tongue must be moved or he would suffocate and die.

Just when it seemed all efforts would fail Niles quickly withdrew. Captain Leyden inhaled raspy gasps of air and ceased to struggle. "You can let go, Victoria. I've gotten it forward. Pray it doesn't happen again."

"He suffers a high fever."

"I know. We'll try some cold packs on his head. Then pile on more quilts to sweat the crisis out."

"Think he will be all right?"

Niles was knowledgeable of the critical prognosis they faced. He had witnessed many such cases. "If he makes it through the night the crisis point shall have passed. If not---"

Their eyes met. He saw fear and compassion within hers. She turned away to gently administer a cold wet cloth to the furrowed forehead. Each time her fingers touched the older man's skin Niles could feel them on his own. He forced himself to stroll across the cabin.

The cold floor against his bare feet gave cause to remember his half-clothed state. Attire, however, was the least of concerns for his worried mind. He reached for whatever was handy: the garments he wore for the celebration.

Before the darkened porthole, he buttoned the shirt, and stared blankly at the waning moon. The remainder of this night could prove a long vigil while they awaited the outcome. He lifted his face heavenward as Victoria had watched the older captain do at the peak of the storm. Niles' pleas, however, were for the life of the man nearest and dearest to him.

Victoria's frantic call brought him instantly around. "Niles, quick! He's not breathing!"

He took the room in long strides, to again struggle over the man. In the midst of his efforts he felt the form relax. Head bent, tears flooded his vision. When he next spoke it was a choked whisper. "Let go, Victoria."

"Is he all right?"

Slowly he rose and turned away to hide the unchecked tears of sorrow that streamed down his face. With a cracked voice that forced its way past the lump that swelled in his throat, he answered, "Yes, his suffering is over."

"Is there nothing more we can do?"

"Nothing," he shook his bowed head. "His illness worried me the entire voyage. That's why I tried everything I knew these past weeks. I'd hoped when we broke into warmer waters . . . no strength remained to fight what was meant to be."

He returned to the porthole unable to continue, jaws locked against the pain that twisted deep within his soul. Tears flowed unheeded onto the lace shirtfront as he gazed unseeing across the empty expanse of open sea. She reached to console his misery only to have him move away from her touch.

"I'm sorry. I didn't mean to be intrusive." To grant privacy in his deep sorrow she retreated.

A ragged disconsolate sigh ended his silence. "I'm sorry, too. I didn't mean to be rude. He was the only father I knew. I remember very little of my real parents. Through the years I admired and loved him as a son loves a father, perhaps more-so. He was an exceptional man in his own way."

Overcome by guilt she cried, "It's all my fault!"

"No, you must not think that way," he tried to ease the pain of her sobs.

"It's true," she wailed. "This cold voyage was made to save father and me. He wouldn't be---"

He cradled her in his arms and laid her head against his chest, former reservations cast aside. Her tears mingled with his. "No, no," he soothed and tipped his head to hers. "It's a mistake to blame yourself. Guilt is too heavy a burden for anyone to bear, least of all, you. He was an old man; older than most men's years." Wet cheek to hers, he added, "The captain would not wish us to grieve." Immersed in mutual sorrow, they drew strength from one another in the eerie silence of the small room.

The quarters, accustomed to the familiar raspy breathing, seemed strange and quiet. He clung to her, lifted his head and coughed to clear the tightness in his throat. "The crew must be told and arrangements made to commit the body."

"Yes, Captain Brett. Now that you are truly Captain Brett, sole captain of *The Sea Pearl,* my heart knows you will be the best captain to ever walk her decks."

"Not the best---the best lies over there. If I could be half the man he was---"

"Niles, you are! Captain Leyden told me you exceeded all his expectations. He said you are a far more accomplished captain then he ever was."

"I would like to believe he placed that much faith in me. I owed it to him."

"Believe me, he loved you as his own. Last night while we danced he told me---" she checked herself and her face lowered.

"Told you what?"

She answered with a negative shake of her head and her eyes begged him not to pursue the subject. "No, Niles. Captain Leyden would not wish me to say."

Arms about her, he gently wiped away the last wet tear from her upturned face. "You called me Niles again," he reminded softly, with a voice that lacked the severity of the night before.

"Forgive me. Captain Brett sounds so formidable and distant. After last night, you seem more like Niles to me."

“I must admit that during these past hours I have felt more like Niles than an austere, confident captain. As you saw, even captains experience their moments of weakness."

"No, not weakness---compassion," she murmured, relieved to discover he possessed this heretofore unseen quality.

He looked down into her soft misty eyes; his arm tightened on the trim waist. His lips bent to meet hers, lightly at first, then in a hard embrace that overflowed with emotion. Here was someone with whom he could share his pain and loss. All the agonizing months at sea: the worries, frustrations, helplessness as they struggled to save the crippled ship---and now the added grief of his dear mentor's passing flowed into his caresses. He drew her slender body to his and thrilled to feel her willing submissiveness.

He felt her arms reach up to slide about his neck, one hand pressing the back of his head to bring his lips to hers with responsive ardency. He crushed her unresisting form to his, for the moment erasing all worldly care from mind. Consumed with mutual passion, they found solace to ease the ache within their hearts.

Her hand pushed halfheartedly against his shoulder several minutes later. He withdrew with reluctance, laid a cheek to hers, while he continued to hold her close. Her round maidenly breasts against his chest aroused pleasurable sensations within him. He buried his face in the sweet smell of her dark flowing hair.

"Niles?"
"Um-h-m---"

"You are the captain, remember? The crew must be told." Yet she clung to him. The throaty quiver within her voice, however, belied the crew was not her main concern. A thrill passed through him with the knowledge she, too, did not trust their emotions if they remained in close contact any longer. She slipped from the circle of his arms to further quell temptation. "You best go to your men, Captain."

The crew, in an uneasy silence, received the news with sincere grief. Several shirtsleeves passed across watery eyes as the men quietly shuffled from the galley to begin work.

Toro, somber dark eyes misted, observed, "Sad to drop in sea, 'stead by 'is woman."

"Can't be helped," Niles gave a heavy sigh. "No one knows when we shall spot land, much-less arrive in home port." The thought that sharks may tear at the bundle as it sank brought a shudder. "We'll put him over the side at sunset. Be sure it's well weighted, Toro."

"Yes Suh, Cap'n. Toro see go straight to bottom. He like sharks no mor'n Toro."

Niles set to work with the men, not trusting himself to spend time alone in the quarters with Victoria. They struggled throughout the day with the broken remains of the ungainly heavy mainmast. Finally, they managed to reconstruct a temporary affair. It bore little promise to remain intact until they sighted land. Next pulleys and lines were rigged and readied. All that remained was to make an attempt to hoist its weight to point skyward.

Too soon dusk overcame the sweaty bodies of the tired workers and their battered vessel. The men ceased their efforts and with heavy feet headed for the galley. A shout suddenly broke from a lookout, interrupting their progress.

"Land to port!" All heads spun about. Anxious eyes scanned the horizon.

"Veer to!" Niles called to the helm, who had spent the day working on repairs of the steerage. Niles ran for his spyglass. Identification of the island may at least offer a thread of hope to pinpoint their location, or even possibly to anchor. Then again, Caribe Indians may inhabit it: cannibalistic Caribes, who fled their home islands ahead of foreign colonists. If so, it would be far too risky to drop anchor on its shore. Armed with the glass, he strained his eye across the watery expanse. Visibility was extremely difficult in the fading light of evening.

The muscular black, toughened feet bared, padded without a sound to his side. "Cap'n, it 'bout time," he reminded with reverent solemnity. "Toro be thinkin'---'spose could wait, see land, put in ground?"

Niles nodded without removing his eyes from the horizon. "Yes, Toro, hold off. A few hours won't make any difference. Somehow an unmarked grave doesn't seem right for him."

Even as he spoke, he detected the dark strip that jutted above the surface of the gray sea. It was much closer than he anticipated. With luck, provided the light held, they could safely maneuver the crippled *Pearl* into the safety of a cove. Joyful shouts erupted from the men as they, too, sighted the landmass. Each hoped for the opportunity to feel solid ground under his feet, if only briefly. Land! Although not home port, it was a symbol their survival may yet be a possibility.

CHAPTER NINE

"Swing her close for a look at the coastline," Niles called out to the helmsman. Hands cupped to mouth, he shouted up to the lookout. "Keep an eye peeled for signs of Caribes."

All idle hands crowded to the broken rail to peer through the dusk for submerged reefs, a cove, or signs of life. After weeks of struggle and near death at sea, their hearts ached to once again catch a glimpse of green grass, trees and land creatures.

Weasel gave a triumphant yell just as the last traces of light faded from the sky. He pointed a grubby forefinger. Niles swung his spyglass. The crew intently watched, with increased concentration, for obstructions that may jut from the sea floor. The very last thing they wanted now was to hear the *Pearl's* bottom being ripped or hear her grind aground on a sandy shoal. Suspense at being so close to land was at a height. A small secluded cove was sighted. Men ran to drop plumb lines off the bow to measure the water depth. To a man, they hoped to limp the sluggish ship into the sheltered cove.

No one knew whether the island was inhabited perhaps by dreaded Caribes. Since it would be wise to avoid detection as much as possible in case hostile eyes watched their approach, they would slip in under cover of darkness that preceded moonrise.

Any moment Niles expected to hear the rasp of rock grating against wood, followed by a shudder underfoot. They progressed deeper through the opening; his hopes lifted. It proved better than anticipated. The helmsman inched her as close to shore as was advisable under the circumstances. The capstan was slowly released at a signal from Brog. The anchor slipped without a splash into the water. Kleet, with the aid of silent hand motions, directed his men to furl the makeshift sails.

Ship secured, Niles approached the crew. "No man is to leave the ship until I give the order." A rumble of dissent rose from the assembled men. "Come daylight we'll see what is hidden over there in the brush before we stick our necks out. The place may crawl with bloody Caribes. Try to slip off and you may find yourself served up as a main course at their next meal. Brog, double the lookouts tonight. Everybody keep the noise down and candles snuffed."

Later he strolled alone about the deck, lighted only by the white glow of a quarter moon. Before him lay the silvered strip of sandy beach. Eerie sounds of nocturnal creatures drifted to his ears from somewhere within the black band of trees---lonely sounds that crept shivers up a man's spine. Mentally, he imagined noxious insects, slithering reptiles, piercing black eyes. He leaned on the rail and stared into the foreboding dark tangle of underbrush. His eyes and ears strained for signs of movement on or near the shoreline. Victoria, reveling in the balmy warmth of the night air after the miseries they had suffered, stepped to his side.

"It would be wise if you stayed within the safety of the cabin," he admonished, while his attention remained on the shoreline.

"Speak for yourself, Captain," she retorted. "If there were life over there would they attempt to board the *Pearl*?"

"Depends on who they are. Wild tribes on some of these islands can be extremely crafty and bloodthirsty. Even if we are among the Bermudez group, I prefer not to take any unnecessary risks."

"If there are Caribes, as you mentioned," she said with a flippant shrug, "they can't any more than kill us."

"No?" he lifted a skeptical eyebrow. "Guess again. They are known to dismember alive their victims and eat of the human flesh."

"How ghastly!" she shuddered.

"Personally, I've never witnessed it, or care to." He saw the color drain from her cheeks. It was time to change the conversation to a pleasanter subject. "Most of them are found in the Lesser Antilles group. I'm almost certain we didn't drift that far south. However, I have also heard of encounters along the Bermudez." He straightened and turned to find her lovely face bathed in silvery moonlight. Immediately, he was overwhelmed with desire---if only to touch the silky dark hair that tumbled loosely over her bared shoulders. Honor forced him to refrain from the impulse.

"I don't mean to be an alarmist. Get some sleep. The lookouts will let us know if anything stirs. Everything will look different come daylight."

"And if they do try to board?"

"Then we will have no choice but to stand and fight them off. For certain the ship is in no condition to make a run for it," he looked upward at the battered rigging. "It's sad to see

The Sea Pearl crippled like this."

"You speak of the ship almost as you would a human."

"She has a heartbeat of her own. Each time she takes a beating we can't wait to nurse her back to health again, so to speak. She's a wondrous vessel, with a soul as golden as the mermaid on her bow."

"Mermaid? Come now, Captain, there is no such thing."

"Don't be too sure. The *Pearl* has one, and a proud beauty she is."

"If that's so, I dare you to show me where the creature hides herself."

"Not hidden. She's mounted just below the bowsprit. One needs to disembark to see her and you have not been off the ship since you joined us." he explained. "Now, off to bed with you. Tomorrow could prove a long day."

"I'll retire when you do."

His fingers nervously curled and uncurled on the rail. Her body swayed with the gentle movements of the ship, as she waited for his answer. Face deliberately averted, he felt the warm distraction of her arm against his, imagined her deep blue eyes beckoning in the moonlight, her lips waiting in invitation. He fought with extreme difficulty the urge to turn to her, to take her into his arms again, as when they danced so close the night before, drifting in a world apart. He wanted to experience again the excitement of her crimson mouth pressed to his, as in the cabin only this morning.

His muscles tensed anticipatorily when she moved closer. He felt her hand slip with feline grace along his forearm and come to rest on his shoulder. He reached up, laid his over hers, hesitated, then forced himself to push her hand down to her side. A slow deep breath helped steady his voice. She must not know how much her presence, her touch, moved him.

"Victoria," he motioned toward the open water and back to the ship, mind searching how to best express himself within his confusion. "The sea, the ship---"

"I know. I, too, have learned to love it," she interrupted. Her almost inaudible whisper sent tendrils of desire to match his own.

"No," his forced tone came firm, "you must not. As soon as we make her seaworthy again we sail for the Colonies." Already unnerved, he wished she would not look at him with those large eyes behind dark lashes. "When you step ashore at Boston you shall forget all about the Pearl and any that sail on her."

"Be honest, is that what you want, Niles?---To forget everyone?"

To evade an answer he turned back to the rail. Evidently she was not to be put off so easily. The hand again slid softly along his arm and the touch again generated electric impulses across his shoulders. "What are you afraid of Niles, hurting, or being hurt?"

"Blast it, Victoria, stop!" he cried, voice strained. "I am only human. Go to the cabin."

"With or without you, Niles?"

"Without."

She hesitated a moment, then slowly retreated. He remained on deck late into the night. Events of their voyage churned over and over in his head: the charts, star locations overhead, sextant. He tried to disentangle their present location. His efforts at concentration only met with a confusion caused by distracting thoughts of Victoria swirling through his brain. Victoria: grubby deck hand, jeweled gown, pearls in her hair. He could still see the shocked expression to his proposal she wear masculine garb, feel the tremble of her hands as she passed bandages for Kleet's wounds. Mostly he saw her lovely upturned face as it met his caresses.

Torn between duty and her alluring aura, he crossed to enter the Captains Quarters. His eyes rested on the empty bunk across the small room, a tangible reminder that tomorrow, once assured it was safe to go ashore, his first sorrowful duty was to officiate the burial.

A soft tinge of pink slowly edged upwards across the eastern horizon. With the fingers of dawn, Niles reappeared on deck. First he checked on the night's activities with the lookouts, then scanned the empty shoreline, not only for movement thereon, but also to formulate a picture in his mind of the island. He needed to know the lay of the beach in conjunction with his charts. A point that ended in a shallow bar drew his attention.

After last night, he was not in a mood to confront Victoria, lest she again make advances. Yet curiosity over the sandy point and a sense of urgency overcame his evasiveness. After all, he told himself, it is my right to enter the quarters to survey the charts. This is my ship. She is only a passenger. I'll not allow her to influence my actions. It's high time I act like a captain, not a smitten, emotional, foolish youth. Besides, she's as unreachable to a man of my profession as the sun that rose over those swaying treetops of the island.

Upon entry, he found her impeccably dressed. Her long dark hair glistened from strokes of a brush. Her face glowed with the anticipation of a visit on land after the weeks at sea. One glance told him she resented his rejections to her overtures of the previous night. He chose to ignore her silent attitude and crossed directly to the charts, where he concentrated on a specific small island. If, when they went ashore, he could find a second sand bar beyond the first, he could be certain of the island's identity. This would pinpoint their location.

He returned on deck, impatient to explore this possibility. The crew had gathered around the mainmast area, feet shifting impatiently, waiting for permission to go over the side. They presented a ragged lot after the weeks of struggle against the ice storm. Their eyes stared from unshaven faces, tattered clothes, boots dried and cracked. Secretly he hoped no islanders would be there to greet them. They would make poor representatives of the proud *Sea Pearl*.

The telltale bulges of cheap wine bottles concealed in large pockets of their coats surprised him. He had surmised they long ago exhausted any originally smuggled on board. Behind him Victoria emerged from the cabin.

"Now hear me," he called out. "You,

you and you," he pointed, "will remain on board." Met by discontented scowls and surly grumbles, he added, "We can't leave the ship unguarded. First we'll investigate the island to see if it is a safe anchorage. If so, then everyone will have their chance to go ashore while we make repairs. Those going ashore, take care. If you see anything suspicious give the sign to alert the others." A movement caused him to turn. "Wait up there!" he grabbed Victoria's arm. "Where do you think you're going?"

"Ashore, naturally," she smartly quipped.

"Not until I go."

"If you don't mind, Captain," she jerked free and spoke with a sting, "I prefer the company of the crew."

The first mate, sufficiently recovered to move about, interceded. "It's all right, Cap'n. Ol' Kleet will look after the little lady."

She tipped her head in polite acceptance and turned on Niles. "You see, Captain, Kleet will oversee my safety. You need not concern yourself over my welfare. You said he was a dependable, capable man, did you not?"

The defiant stance and smolder in her eyes bore witness this was her strategy to get back at him for the previous night. His mind, divided between the forthcoming sad burial duty and the search for the questionable sand bar, made a careless mistake. The cocksure expression on Kleet's face should have warned him of trouble ahead. She would beg to return to the ship, Niles thought, once she discovered the island lacked comforts. He stepped back to allow her to pass.

Ashore on the island, Niles stood beside the shallow rectangular hole dug amid the profuse underbrush. Brog and Toro lowered the canvas wrapped bundle to rest beneath the canopy of trees. The crew gathered around, heads reverently bent.

"There isn't much I can say you all don't already know," Niles began. The words were difficult to speak through the tightness of his throat, yet speak he must. "Captain Leyden, being a man of the Book, always performed this duty far more eloquently than I can ever hope to do. Let us take comfort in the knowledge his trials on this earth are over. We know he is in the hands of our Maker." Consumed by grief, unable to continue, he quickly said, "I suggest we each bow our heads in silent prayer."

Rather than stand by and hear the sand drop with a note of finality onto the canvas, he turned away. With slow heavy steps he returned to the beach and silently stared at the severely impaired vessel listing at anchor. Her ragged sails and broken masts became a blur amid the mist of tears. His mind began to drift over the years spent with the older captain. Not until Toro spoke did he stir back to the present.

"You cel'brate wi' men, Cap'n?"

Slowly he shook his head and continued to gaze at the ship. "Maybe later. First I want to see what lies beyond the bar over there to our right."

The black's brows knitted together. "You leave lady wi' crew?"

Palms turned up in resignation, Niles sighed heavily. "She thinks Kleet will look after her."

"But Cap'n," the black persisted in alarm, "you know mate an' women. Not safe leave wi' him."

"You heard the lady. I don't have time to argue with her changeable temperaments."

"Cap'n---"

"All right, if you're so worried keep an eye on her yourself. As for me, I have a ship to run. That requires I take a look over there." He turned on a heel and strode off along the sandy beach.

A desire to savor the change of climate came over him after he had gone but a short distance. Stripped of shirt and boots, he opted to walk bare foot in the warm sand. The gold medallion caught the sun's rays and reflected multicolored fires from the profusion of inset jewels. He reached the bar and dropped onto the sand to lie, eyes closed, under the luxuriant warmth of the sub-tropic rays.

The distant whoops and hollers verified the crew had already generously tasted of their concealed liquors. Reminded of his purpose, he casually rose, rounded a small wooded point and discovered the second bar. Their location now confirmed, it seemed their location troubles were over. With a lot of luck and hard work, they could make the *Pearl* sufficiently seaworthy to proceed to the Colonies. Passenger delivered, they would point their bow homeward---Port Royal, Jamaica, in the clear blue waters of the Caribbean. His face took on a relaxed smile as his gaze drifted across the gentle waters of the cove.

"Ee---yah!" he gave an exultant shout, arms lifted to jubilantly shake fists skyward. The sudden burst of elation was a release from the heavy burdens of the past weeks. The *Pearl* had made it!

Suddenly, his euphoria was cut short by hands seizing him from behind! He struggled with all his might to break free of his captors. Flashes of brilliant color jostled against him, pinned his arms and legs---Spaniards!

His efforts to wrench from their holds were in vain. They spread-eagled him into submission by force of numbers. He cursed under his breath. How careless! Distracted by his discovery, caution had been forgotten. He should have known better. The uniformed men yanked him roughly to his feet and without speaking or an offer of explanation pushed him forward beyond the second bar.

Why did they not kill me? he wondered. Where are they taking me? Rounding another small point---he saw it---the giant galleon anchored in all its majesty. The same galleon that passed them in the night and later protected them from the English ships.

Allowed to pass unmolested on both occasions, he stared, puzzled, unable to understand this sudden reversal of intentions. Still his attackers said nothing. Perhaps in the belief he was English they assumed he could not understand their language? Stony faced, they rowed their captive out to the floating palace.

The landing boat slid alongside the hull of the magnificent structure. To Niles, it appeared even larger as it loomed above the small craft. They motioned him to board, then shoved him toward what he presumed was their Captains Quarters, but could not be certain. The entire vessel was so immense and elaborate by comparison to any he had boarded in the past that he did not trust himself to draw any conclusions.

One of the captors rapped sharply on the door. Within moments he was pushed into a room profuse with ornately carved woodwork and highly polished brass. There he found himself face to face with their captain, a young man, who stood very erect, resplendent in a gold trimmed uniform.

"That will be all," the officer said in native Spanish to the captors. "I do not anticipate any difficulty with our prisoner." Niles, familiar with the tongue from his many contacts with Spaniards along the *Main,* had no difficulty understanding the words.

The man relaxed, extended a hand of welcome, much as he would greet an old friend. "Niles Brett, captain of *The Sea Pearl.*"

Niles accepted, perplexed even more, not only at being recognized by name by an enemy, but the friendly approach, as well. A ruse this captain used to put his victim off guard? The Spaniard lifted an eyebrow and continued. "Do I detect confusion and distrust,

Captain Brett? Rest assured there is no need. You see, we are not strangers. Or perhaps you do not recognize me in this uniform? May I suggest you look closer; imagine me as a lad in ragged clothes."

Niles studied the slender man, so trim of physique and suave of manner, accented by the perfectly fitted uniform. He searched his mind, but found no answer. He watched a slow crafty smile creep across the smoothly shaven face of the glorified young captain.

"Do you remember a time when you accompanied Captain Leyden in an attack on a Spanish fort near Santa Marta? Ah, I see you do. And do you also recall what Captain Leyden said of a boy taken captive in the attack? To be explicit, 'the boy should not be killed along with his countrymen. He can not be blamed for what his elders do'?"

"Juan Ramolo!" Niles exclaimed on recognition. "As you say, the uniform ---this ship---" he motioned an arm to take in the overall grandeur of the quarters where they stood.

"Captain Ramolo now. You like this vessel?"

"Like it, it's magnificent! Largest I've ever seen."

"Indubitably," Juan agreed with obvious pride. "It is the largest on the *Main*."

Anxious to cut through to questions foremost on his mind, Niles implored, "I fail to understand---then it was you who passed us in the night---intercepted the English that we might escape---now ordered me brought before you. Why?"

"Sit down, Captain Brett," he indicated toward a richly upholstered chair beside his desk. “I know you have no problem to understand, or speak my native tongue. You speak it as fluently as your own. That makes it easier since I never fully mastered your English language," Ramolo excused himself in precise Spanish. "I shall strive to fill you in from the start so you have a clear picture of where we stand at present."

"A very good idea," Niles agreed, as he easily adopted the same language, desirous of answers to enlighten his consternation.

"As you will recall, your ship later released me near another Spanish settlement where you knew I would find safety among my own people. I was very grateful you spared my life. Captured by any other ship I fear I would not have been so fortunate."

Niles recalled the details very clearly. Juan, the same age as himself, had become a close boyhood friend while aboard the *Pearl.*

"Later I was shipped back to my homeland," Juan quickly spanned the years. "In time, they gave me command of this ship."

"Captain of so majestic a vessel must be quite an honor."

"Not exactly. True, she's a commendable piece of workmanship with extremely good speed in her sails. However, as a fellow captain, I am sure you noticed her enormous dimensions. Size alone creates problems of maneuverability. Rest assured my superiors did not do me any favors when they assigned me this command." Niles agreed he could comprehend the complications and felt grateful for the simplicity of the *Pearl.*

"Let us get down to business. I did not order you brought here to talk about my ship. You are now in full command of *The Sea Pearl*--"

Niles' eyes narrowed warily. "How do you know about Captain Leyden?"

"First things first," Juan lifted a hand. "I identified the *Pearl* when she entered the cove last night. Your golden mermaid was spotted by my lookouts long before you dropped anchor," Ramolo smiled. Considering her sad condition, you did a fine job bringing her in. I also know you stayed on deck until late. A beautiful woman joined you for a while. My information says it appeared she is more than a casual acquaintance, however, that is neither here nor there. The unexpected appearance of *The Sea Pearl* gave me the opportunity to make contact with the captain." Abruptly he turned, and changed the subject.

"As for Captain Leyden, I personally witnessed a burial this very morning. He was not beside you at the graveside, Captain Brett. That explained who lies in the grave. Please accept my condolences. The sea could use more men such as he."

"Amen," Niles nodded assent.

"Ah! Then you do not deny his body occupies the grave?"

"It is that of Captain Leyden."

"I remembered how he always insisted on honesty, particularly from you as a lad. Confronted, I felt quite certain you would admit to his death."

"Juan---Captain Ramolo, if I may venture to ask one question? How did your men know which man to bring before you?"

"You identified yourself when you removed your shirt," Ramolo's smile broadened, eyes on Niles' bared chest. "They were instructed to find the man with the medallion. No one else along the *Main* flaunts so priceless a fortune around his neck. Really, Captain Brett, sunlit rays reflected from such jewels makes you stand out like a beacon in a storm. Quite frankly, I am surprised someone has not chopped off your head to obtain it."

Niles' boots shifted impatiently on the floor. He hoped the captain would shortly explain the reason for his unannounced seizure. To his dismay, the man seemed in no hurry. Did he wish to gloat for a time over his prize before issuing an ultimatum?

"I arranged this meeting to clarify a few points. In case you have wondered, we did not fail to see your ship when we passed in the night. Sorry we came a bit too close. Visibility was extremely bad in the fog. You understand how difficult that can be, Captain." Niles nodded in agreement. "Not wanting to become engaged in confrontation, my men were ordered to stay out of sight.

"Later, in the English harbor, it was not difficult to detect your own countrymen pursued you. On both occasions we could have easily blown you to bits---"

"I agree," Niles nodded soberly. "Your guns were aimed right down our throats."

"It is good you did not risk a shot. If so, I would have been forced to return your fire.

The point is, twice we had the opportunity to destroy your ship and every man on board. Captain Leyden spared my life at the fort; in return I spared yours twofold. An eye for an eye in reverse, one might say. Now I feel the score is evened. Do you not agree I repaid my debt, Captain?"

"Yes, it seems so."

"I hope we never meet in battle, but if we do in the future, I want you to know I will not henceforth ignore, nor protect the *Pearl*. You will be quite helpless while you make repairs. I give my word not to attack while the *Pearl* is crippled. But let me give you a warning. You will be only another English ship to me once you leave this island."

Niles opened his mouth to speak. "One more thing, Captain Brett. The *Pearl* boasted a bell when I was aboard her. It is missing. If it were replaced Captain Leyden would rest easier. There happens to be one in our hold---much more beautiful, I might add. Accept it as a token to his memory. Then I shall feel my debt is indeed repaid in full measure."

"A most gracious gesture on your part, Captain Ramolo."

"It amazes me why you have not already confiscated a bell from another ship in an attack? But then, Captain Leyden always was a man of rare honesty. Loot was never the *Pearl's* style. Tomorrow, after we leave, your men will find it hidden in the brush of the point. It would be a pleasure to renew our association, Captain Brett. Alas, we cannot change the way leaders of the world feud among themselves. To conclude our short reunion, may I take your hand in farewell, Captain. I wish you God's protection."

"I understand your position, and mine also," Niles agreed, as he returned the warm handclasp. Other hand on Ramolo's shoulder, he looked directly into the Spaniard's eyes. "And God's grace go with you, Captain Ramolo. May we meet again when our two countries have settled their differences."

Ramolo sadly shook his head. "Their petty arguments may go on for years, perhaps centuries. You and I are of the present; neither knows what tomorrow may bring. We have shared our moment of peace today."

A strange melancholia crept across his face. Quickly, he turned away. When he again spoke the words were crisp. "You are free to leave now, Captain. My men will not detain you. It is better this conversation continues no longer."

Niles retraced his steps along the beach, retrieved his shirt and placed it over an arm. Slowly he followed the shoreline, mind on the conversation with Captain Ramolo.

The carousing of the men grew louder as he approached the *Pearl*. He was in no mood to join them in celebration after his unexpected reunion. Considering his present state of mind, he felt it better to row out to the ship. It had been a strange encounter. The discovery of the identity of the galleon captain made it even stranger. In a world so vast, with many lands as yet unexplored, for an instant time had stood still. On the ship he could be alone with his thoughts.

He signaled for the first group of men to return to the ship. They needed time to regain their equilibrium before repairs would begin in earnest at dawn. They must be prepared to work like mules: sweat and strain, to the last light each day. They would labor, with curses muffled by gritted teeth, until the ship was gone over from fore to aft; toil without complaint, until the *Sea Pearl* became seaworthy again. For, to a man, each felt it a part of himself.

A lonely emptiness swept over him on the moonlight washed deck. Victoria's absence left a haunting aura. This is foolishness, he told himself. I have stood alone at the rail like this hundreds of times in the past. After depositing her in the Colonies my life will go on as before. These months of her presence shall be but another memory among many.

Yet as his eyes drifted across the water he felt his heart pulled toward the shore and Victoria.

On land, he heard the drunken men staggered into landing boats moored on the beach. Four began to row with jerky uncoordinated motions. Others lolled off balance, legs over the side trailing in the water. Nice on the boots, Niles mused. The figure of the first mate swaying unsteadily in the craft caught his attention. Where is Victoria? Niles panicked! Fear for her safety was quickly replaced by anger. Anger at himself for inexcusable carelessness and negligence of his duties as captain. Enraged, he dashed for the Jacob's ladder to confront the mate. Before he had gone but a few steps he was suddenly grabbed from behind. He tried to shake loose, but two vise-like hands spun him around.

At sight of Toro's face, he demanded sharply, "Where's Victoria? You were to keep an eye on them!"

The black calmly gave a negative shake of his head. "You say I watch if want to," he corrected. "Toro watch. No to worry 'bout, Cap'n. Toro put Missy in cabin where belong. Keep Kleet away long 'fore you come. Toro warn Cap'n no good let Kleet take her."

Eyes narrowed, Niles' anger rose with heightened suspicion. "What happened?"

Toro drew himself up with pride. "Missy all right. Toro see to." The Negroid considered the matter closed and strode away. Niles stared after him, taken aback by this turn of events.

To verify Toro's statements, he crossed with long strides to the Captains Quarters. There he was met by a haughty toss of her head and a swift retreat into the privacy of her cubicle. Apparently, he judged, she did not intend to offer any explanations. Fine, he thought. Perhaps she learned a lesson. He definitely did not intend to pressure for dreaded answers---nor sure he wanted to hear them.

At first light Cleve, along with a crewman, rowed ashore. They pulled the landing craft onto the beach and set out in search of a fresh water source. Their eyes searched among the greenery as they made their way through the dense undergrowth, knowing any edible foodstuffs found on the island would be a welcome reinforcement for the ship's food supply.

The remainder of the crew fell to on the work at hand; their most urgent task being repairs to the mainmast. This presented no small challenge. With few materials available on the island this, at first, seemed impossible. But it was a task that somehow must be done. They could not remain stranded forever on this sandy bit of land surrounded by sea.

They climbed among the maze of tangled rigging with the dexterity of a colony of monkeys in a rope jungle. When night came they fell exhausted into their bunks and hammocks. So their days continued, with scarcely a break to wolf down a bite to eat.

At last they succeeded to again point a makeshift mast skyward. Ratlines, pulleys, and ropes began to take their proper places. Sail menders worked for hours, fingers calloused. Progress was slow, but each day brought the *Pearl* closer to her proud self again, albeit patched and mended. Of necessity many repairs were of a temporary nature until proper supplies could be obtained in a port. On the whole, everything progressed superbly well. Niles' world was at peace again ---with one exception.

Victoria, he noticed, repeatedly sought Kleet from among the workers to engage in flirtatious conversations. Often he watched the pair slip from their respective quarters under cover of night. He could hear them laugh and speak in low tones within the secluded shadows of the rigging. Each time it felt like a dagger pierced him through. The hidden glances that passed between the two when the men went ashore on rest breaks did not escape his notice. Nor later, when they removed themselves far down the beach to bask in the tropical sun, did they leave unseen by him.

Niles chafed each time he caught a glimpse of the pair together.

Why should I care? he asked himself. Kleet, too, is a man far below her social status. I warned her. Told her he's a dangerous man wholly without honor. If the warning frees me of further responsibility for her welfare, why do I feel guilty? Perhaps it's because I know it's the captain's obligation to assure the safety of a passenger. Yes, that must be it, he told himself. Still, his mind remained disturbed.

Early on, Kleet convinced her to discard her heavy clothing in the warm climate. At first the change was reasonably modest. Days passed, however, and her experimentation became more daring. Niles was not the only one to observe the change. After months at sea the eyes of the crew began to stray. Their attentions lingered longer as her mode of dress became increasingly obvious. The way she openly flaunted herself infuriated Niles. Her actions were an open invitation to trouble. His resentments toward the first mate, who encouraged her blatant behavior, deepened. Unable to stand this display any longer, he approached Kleet on the matter.

"Now Cap'n, why you crawlin' all over Kleet's back?" the mate sneered, the usual confident grin deepening the cleft of his chin. His feet shifted to an arrogant stance of challenge. "I doubt what the lady wears or does not wear is what scrubs you. Could it be you are a wee mite jealous? Wish it was you with her on the beach instead of me?"

Before Niles could feign denial the mate continued, smooth voice filled with mockery. "Perhaps if you weren't so concerned with our little toy over there," he motioned an arm to take in the ship, "she'd roll with you. As is, she's putty in ol' Kleet's hands!" Head tilted back to emit a derisive harsh laugh, he waited for Niles to take issue with him.

Niles recognized it as a deliberate attempt to provoke a confrontation; an opportunity for the mate to display his masculine prowess in front of the lady. Thereby he chose to maintain his composure rather than give him satisfaction. As for the mate, it was a foolish game. Although a very good contender, he was no match against Niles, and knew it. Some other scheme in mind? Niles wondered. Neither the disruption of the harmony of the ship, nor instigation of a bloody pirate duel for the sole purpose of the lady's entertainment was acceptable conduct. Instead, Niles chose to stare directly into the man's face. Minutes passed. Finally the mate's boots shifted nervously.

"That be all, Cap'n?"

The days wore on. Kleet and Victoria continued to take advantage of every opportunity to drift apart from the group. Another crewman, Niles noticed, also disappeared from sight on each such occasion. He pondered the synchronized actions. To his mind, it was doubtful that Toro would have made any arrangements with the first mate. The black never went along with any of Kleet's underhanded schemes. Yet, if that were not the case, then what was afoot?

The day came when Niles strolled the length of the decks. Eyes skyward, he made a critical survey of masts, rigging and sails. The men tested it against the wind. Everything held fast. With a nod of approval, he waved an all's well to the crew. *The Sea Pearl* was back to a semblance of herself again: spotless with fresh paint, scrubbed decks, and her brass polished to a mellow gleam.

"Everybody get cleaned up," he called out. "We'll celebrate with a party on shore tonight!" The announcement was met by a unified whoop from the various sections. Cleve scurried about to move his cook pots ashore. The men, stripped of clothing, hastened to dive over the side into the cleansing water below.

Niles was attending to a last minute check when he heard a commotion on the foredeck. He ascended the ladder to check it out. A group of half clothed men were clustered at the rail. He saw arms swinging and heard boisterous yells of encouragement to someone in the water. Kleet held the end of a rope and shouted taunts to someone below. Intermittently he playfully jerked the end of the rope, while, head thrown back, he roared with malevolent laughter. Pranks were common among the men in casual moments; Niles was about to shrug it off as unimportant. Then came the high pitched scream!

He spun about and leaped for the rope. Too late. The first mate, aware of his captain's intervention, released his hold to let the line immediately disappear over the side. Without hesitation, Niles dove and cut the water like a dagger. He rose to the surface. Victoria was nowhere in sight. She must be down, he thought. Quickly, he again submerged to search the dark depths below.

Then he saw her, arms moving feebly, as her body slowly descended downward into the murky shadows. Time was short. He sliced the water, scooped an arm about her waist and turned to swiftly ascend.

Breaking the surface with her limp body, he caught a glimpse of Toro and hoped the man would assist to get her aboard. With a surge of disappointment, he saw the black take powerful strokes around the bow to the opposite side of the ship. Voices overhead caught his attention. The glistening wet body of the black was at the rail. With a fierce scowl

Toro heaved Kleet aside and cast another rope downward. Niles watched the coil snake toward him.

As Niles reached to clutch the rope he saw Kleet spring at Toro like an angry panther. The black whirled about. A huge fist, a dull crack to the jaw and the first mate went down on the deck. Niles secured the line in place under Victoria's arms. On signal, Toro worked the rope hand over hand to raise the lifeless body to safety.

Weasel crowded to Toro’s side and squeaked down, "Grab the line to port." Now Niles understood why the black rounded the bow and how he boarded so quickly. He cut the water, scaled the side and raced to where Toro knelt beside the prone body.

Weasel was already at work over her. Niles' heart threatened to pound out of his chest both from exertion and anxiety.

"Gotta get the water pumped out of her," Weasel shouted, without interruption of his motions. "You want to take over, Captain?"

Niles, too shaken for the control necessary to carry on with the rhythmic rescue motions, declined. "Keep at it while I catch my breath." He turned to glare at the first mate. Kleet lay as he fell, out cold. Niles' throat constricted, not only from exertion, but from hate that welled up in him to the point were he could not speak.

Toro's eyes were on him. "No need worry 'bout him, Cap'n. He not move for while. Only thing worry, right here." He gave a nod toward Victoria's inert form. Small wrist in his large hand, he urgently sought a pulse beat. His brow deepened. Nearby the crew waited, each silenced with shared guilt.

Weasel continued the measured movements. Sweat dripped from his forehead and glistened along his shoulders. The lady failed to respond to his efforts; yet he refused to give up.

"Come on, Missy," Toro urged, as if to beg her back to life. "Come on." A slow smile crept across his wet face. "She back! She back wi' us, Cap'n. No strong yet, git better."

Niles watched the perspiration drip from Weasel's face and chin. He knew he should take control of his emotions and relieve the little man; but he was too wrapped up in anger. Anger at Kleet to instigate the near tragedy---anger at himself for allowing such a dire thing to happen---anger because he was too shaken to react responsibly. The latter unnerved him most of all.

What is wrong with me? he screamed to himself. In the past I took over in emergencies without any problem. Why is this incident any different?

In the battle between cool control and fury, he was seized by an insane desire to grab her still body, shake it back to life. Hot rage welled up within him; a rage liken to a savage animal, to lay hands on Kleet. He took a deep breath to steady himself and managed to say in a hoarse voice, "You're tired, Weasel. I'll take over for a while." The activity would give him the satisfaction he did everything he could for her.

Weasel continued a few more movements before he agreed to relinquish his position. "All right, Captain, get ready. Don't want to interrupt the rhythm." Niles knelt on the deck, hands firmly on her ribcage. Weasel straightened and stretched his aching back muscles. "Keep workin', Captain. She's gotta come around soon. Appears we got all the water pumped out of her."

Toro, face drawn in concentration on the pulse, nodded. "Get more strong. She gonna make it Cap'n." Niles could only pray and hope the pressure of his hands breathed life into her lungs. Suddenly he felt a slight cough. The cluster of men waited. Each listened intently for another sound from the unconscious figure.

"Think we got it, Cap'n," Toro exclaimed, a wide grin across his face, fingers as yet on the wrist. "She come 'round." Again

Niles felt the cough. The head moved ever so slightly. Her eyes fluttered open. "Best stop, Cap'n. She be back." Toro released the wrist. A shout rose from the assembled crew.

Gently Niles rolled her over to cradle her in his arms. She stared in bewilderment, coughed and gasped for air. "I'll take you to our cabin," he soothed. Passing Kleet, he looked down with disdain at the mate's sprawled form.

"Heave a bucket of water on the bastard to bring him around. I want every man on the quarterdeck immediately, him in particular. There better be some answers on how this got started!"

Inside the quarters he eased her onto the bunk. "Comfortable?" She nodded. Her lips parted to speak. "Don't talk now. You need rest and time to get your wind back. I'm going out on deck. If you like, Toro will stay with you." She gave a negative shake of her head and again made an attempt to speak. "Don't talk," he admonished.

"I must," she insisted in a hoarse whisper. "The meeting---I should be there."

"You're in no shape to be anywhere except right where you are," he insisted.

"Please, it was partly my fault," she

objected and struggled to raise herself on an elbow.

"You're weak as a beached porpoise. Lie down and leave the men to me." He eased her shoulders to meet the pillow.

"No! Let me have my say."

"Why? To defend that worthless Kleet?"

Her eyes flashed in defiance, but the voice was steady. "Yes, to defend Kleet."

"For what?" he snarled, an angry edge to his tongue. "To stand up for someone who deliberately tried to drown you?"

"He didn't intend to drown me."

"No? Well, for a man who did not intend, he very near did!"

"I can explain, Captain Brett," she lashed out his title with a sarcastic bite in her words, "Only you never want to listen!"

"You can't tell me anything I don't already know. There's a streak of the devil in his veins. I intend to get some damned good answers when I get out there on deck. If need be, I'll wring it out of them!" He strode out, face grim and menacing, to where a drenched first mate sagged against a cannon carriage.

"This incident was utterly inexcusable--"

A voice spoke from among the gathered men. "Kleet---"

Niles whirled with a sharp demand. "What about Kleet?" No answer came. "I can guess. His wild talk convinced all of you to go along with his game." Heads lowered in guilty assent before turning away in shame.

"We didn't think it would come to any harm. Just funnin'---"

"Did it look like fun when she lay there on the deck?" he shouted. "It was downright stupid to let him talk you into such a dangerous idea." He pointed a finger of accusation toward Kleet. "What's your excuse? None of your smooth talk this time. I want straight answers!"

"Aw, now Cap'n," the first mate resorted to his habitual slippery tongue. "We wasn't meanin' anything. It got a little out of hand, is all. Could happen to any of us---"

"Facts, Kleet. I want facts!" Niles shrieked and jabbed a forefinger soundly into Kleet's chest.

"I will give you facts," Victoria's weak voice spoke from the cabin doorway.

He turned on her and yelled, "I told you to stay put!"

"No!" her small foot stamped with determined emphasis.

Toro quickly stepped forward to assist the lady to a large coil of rope where she could sit. "It be all right, Cap'n. Best she say."

Toro's attitude astonished Niles. Had the black changed sides? If so, he fully expected Kleet, upon discovery of a new ally, to sneer in satisfaction. Instead, the man's eyes were downcast. His body shifted, like a mouse that squirmed to escape from under a cat's paw. The eyes tried to flash a warning to Victoria. The quick discreet glance that passed between the pair puzzled Niles. Tensions tightened between the first mate, the lady, and himself. He waited.

Victoria was first to break the silence. "I will tell you how it started. He declared it was a rule that everyone on board the ship must be an accomplished swimmer. Since I am not, he offered to teach me. I had no idea he would---"

"Throw you over the side---sink or swim?"

Her confidence melted under the truth of his blaze of anger. "Something like that."

He eyed the pair with distrust. "I think

there's more behind this."

"'Scuse, Cap'n," Toro interceded.
"Yes?"

"I---I think in respect for lady, it best if four continue talk in quarters."

"Four?" Niles asked, confused. A shocked expression of fear displaced all self-assurance from Kleet's stance.

"Yes Suh, four," the black repeated.

This new development gave Niles cause to wonder. How did Toro fit into the picture? "If that's the case, we'll retire to my quarters."

The first mate lingered behind. Niles called out sharply. "Kleet, get yourself in here!"

Toro took a stand inside the door, as if to prevent anyone to enter or leave. Victoria, like a disciplined child, seated herself, mouth tight. Kleet began to pace nervously about the small room. Exasperated by his restlessness, Niles ordered the man to sit.

Niles turned to the black. "What have you to say?"

"Beg lady's pardon," Toro began, and tipped his head apologetically in her direction.

"What Toro must say he think not good for crew hear."

"Such as?"

"Lady and Kleet keep together on island---"

"That is common knowledge, Toro. Get to the point." The mention of their association made him bristle with undesired thoughts---secretive laughter of the pair as they lay close together on the beach---stolen hours of privacy while they strolled arm in arm through the dense growth of trees. Afraid to hear the ugly truths the black man may expose, his jaw muscles tightened.

"Go trees, Toro follow, Toro watch."

With a fierce lunge, Kleet sprang at the big Negroid. "Why you black---"

Toro sidestepped. With one swift motion he wrapped a muscular arm around the man's neck and pinned him fast against his broad chest in a chokehold. With a heave, he threw the mate onto the chair. "Stay put, or Toro put sleep on deck again! Cap'n hear Toro first, then you talk."

Breathing heavily, face flushed with rage, Kleet's eyes smoldered. Niles waited for the black to resume.

"As say, Toro follow, watch. First nothing. Then each time go, Kleet try more. Last night tire of game, try force lady. She break loose, run. Toro catch, hide on ship. Kleet look, no find." He paused to stare at the man with loathing before turning back to Niles. "He mad she cheat him. Today he talk swim to her, then smooth talk men. They not know Kleet plan. He try get even. Almost did."

His eyes rolled toward the mate. "Kleet no want keep lady. Only use get back at Cap'n. Then throw away same as do other women. Toro no like, Cap'n." Finished, he retreated into silence beside the door. Victoria stared open mouthed at the mate, eyes wide with astonishment.

"That true, Kleet?" Niles demanded.

In defense the first mate snarled, "He's got no business sneakin' around spyin'---"

"And you have no business using your connivery at the expense of innocent people!" Niles cut in hotly. "Any more trouble from you and I vouch to put you ashore at the first port." While this ultimatum sank in he turned on the lady.

"As for you, Victoria, when you first boarded I warned you. These are a different breed than the English gentlemen your skirts enticed back in England. Here men play for keeps. Wave a lure, and you are liable to catch a fish too big to handle. Consider yourself lucky this time. You almost became dinner for the sharks. If so, Kleet would only laugh. His conscience, if the man has any, would not be bothered in the least."

Eyes downcast in shame, defiance drained from her face. Initial wrath subsiding, his voice softened. "If you wanted to learn to swim all you needed do was ask. I can designate someone to teach you the safe way. We cannot risk any more scares like today." Hand under her chin, he raised her face to meet his eyes and urged a feeble smile in return. "Kleet and you go on deck while I speak with Toro alone."

The first mate made haste to depart. Victoria rose more slowly to follow. Niles strolled across the room to stare evasively out the small porthole. He hesitated before asking his next question, unsure if he wanted to hear the answer. "All right, Toro, let's hear the rest of it."

"No rest, Cap'n. Toro tell all."

"Does that mean Kleet never---accomplished his endeavor?"

"No, Suh, never."

A relieved sigh escaped from Niles.

"One more question. Why did you choose to follow them?"

"Toro no trust," the black somberly shook his woolly head. "Mate got dark evil in blood. Toro see with Cap'n's woman---get mad---"

"With captain's woman? I have no woman."

"Cap'n have woman now."

"Ridiculous! Miss Silvas is a passenger."

The black head gave a mindful nod.

"Toro watch Cap'n's face, see Missy Victoria in heart. Cap'n on lady's face, too, but Cap'n too busy. No see her. She turn Kleet to make---how you people say?"

Jealous? Was that the word Toro searched for? Niles wondered. Absurd, he told himself. And yet---in the light of what the Negroid said, reality slowly took over. Yes, he admitted, jealousy motivated my attitudes of late. Maybe the man was right. Undeniably, from the first moment I saw her in the jeweled gown my emotions were stirred. I've fought desperately to keep my passions locked tightly as in a dark closet ever since. I wanted to protect myself from the pain when it came time to part at the Colonies.

The repairs were a distraction, an excuse. So many duties, throughout the entire voyage, served the same purpose, a convenient diversion, rather than succumb to intimacy. I knew it would prove extremely risky if I spent too much time in close proximity. Meanwhile, I burned with resentment, anger and distrust each time I witnessed the pair together. When all else failed, I reminded myself of my position as captain and she a passenger.

Toro's deep baritone interrupted the examination of his inner motivations. "Toro sad for Cap'n. Cap'n 'fraid to love." Niles' eyes remained averted to the peaceful undulation of the sea outside the porthole. "Cap'n best take lesson from my people. Live today, may not be tomorrow. Come morning, Cap'n best walk beside woman, teach swim. Then she no look at devil Kleet. Cap'n and lady be happy while can."

Preoccupied in thought, he did not hear the black soundlessly slip from the cabin. Incidents of the past months began to flow through his conscious mind. The bolt that locked his personal emotions slowly slipped away as he balanced the man's words, pros and cons. He ran his fingers through his hair and questioned his disconcerted emotions.

Once I submit to my love for her, can I

bear to leave her in the Colonies? Can I proceed to Port Royal and return to life as it was before? Can I easily forget how she felt in my arms? No, already it's too late to erase her from my heart. Her presence on the *Pearl*, the memory of her in this very room, will long remain.

Either way there's no winning. Perhaps Toro's people, in their somewhat crude uncivilized ways of accepting life as it comes are the wiser. Live each day, take of life while it is yet in their grasp. Tomorrows for island slaves often never come---equally so for men who sail the *Main*.

Then again, could Victoria accept my lifestyle without regard for tomorrow? If I continue to lock her from my heart will we not both be losers? Maintaining a reserved air while I yearn to reach out to her tears me apart. Already too often I have seen the pain of rejection in her eyes---rejection brought on by my own actions.

The frustration of their association, he concluded, could not continue on its present level. It was time for an intimate discussion with the lady and hear her views on the subject. His shoulders lifted. Relax. Listen to Toro's people. Let time choose the moment. Swimming lessons, he mused, and smiled. She's a strange one. Dignified, yet wants to swim, of all things.

He crossed to the doorway and called out. "Victoria?"

The lonely battle with truth ended when she cautiously entered, unsure of his temperament. "It's all right," he met her with an easy grin. "Do you still want to swim after today's experience? Under safer conditions, that is."

"Most definitely."

"Fine. Any teacher in particular you prefer?"

Embarrassed to mention the one foremost on her mind, she flushed deeply. "I---I shall let you chose which crewman."

"Crewman? How about me?"

In mock surprise, she spun around. "You, Captain?" she exclaimed, face aglow. "I watched you swim many times in the moonlight when you thought I was abed. You are magnificent in the water!"

"Please, flattery does not befit me," he laughed. "Shall we try in the morning?"

"On one condition," she countered, head at a wary tilt.

"Which is?"

"You don't drop the rope!"

"What rope? We shall begin in shallow water where you'll be perfectly safe."

She relaxed. "With you, I'm sure I will."

His expression turned serious.

"Victoria---"

"Yes, Captain?"

"Toro says---" he decided this not the proper time and aborted the issue for the moment. "Never mind. Perhaps you'll understand better at a later date."

"Captain, you again talk in circles."

"True. And since a circle is round, it's ends always meet. So there's nothing to worry about. For now," he changed the subject, "you get all prettied up. Wear a fancy gown to celebrate the *Pearl*'s readiness. I want to see a lady tonight not a deck hand."

"The red one?" she challenged, in an effort to pry the secret from him.

Before he answered, he strode away. "No. It's not your size."

"What you mean is, I'm not Nicole."

"Right, you are not Nicole. However, that is not the reason. Don't touch the red gown, ever." He watched her wordless retreat to her cubical and immediately regretted the sharpness of his tone.

CHAPTER TEN

They gorged themselves on Cleve's inventive culinary masterpieces ashore that evening. Fully sated, the crew lolled about on the sandy beach. On occasion one or another glanced with pride toward *The Sea Pearl*. She waited at anchor, scarred, but prepared to set back to sea.

The men's hearts soon warmed on cheap wine and grog. Their mood spilled over to outbursts of lusty songs, replete with lurid obscenities. Niles agreed they had earned the right to display excessive exuberance. This in mind, he did not have the heart to remind them of the lady's presence. Instead, he approached Victoria and suggested she join him in a walk along the shore. This allowed the men to indulge uninhibited in their own manner of pleasure.

The pair strolled in silence around a curve of the shoreline. "Kleet acts very sulky tonight," Victoria observed. "Several times I noticed his eyes on you. Do you think he plans to get even?"

"He knows better."

"After the way you berated him in front of the men today, he seethes with anger." Anxiety crept into her voice. "Intoxicated he could become quite vicious."

"Kleet is always vicious. A poisonous snake doesn't need bottled spirits to strike. He proved that to you today. He's fresh out of stitches, yet primed to fight a ferocious lion if given a chance. It never pays to turn one's back on a man of his caliber."

"Why do you keep him?"

"Why? Because he's one of the best around when you need the best. You see, the men who man the *Pearl* must be as bad as they are good."

"Yourself, also?"

"When necessary," he nodded in agreement. "The title of captain must be earned if he's to gain the respect of his crew. Ours is a life of the strong; the weak end up at the bottom of the sea. Does that answer your question?"

"Put that way," she said, scarcely

audible over the sound of gentle waves hissing against the sand. "I don't know whether to trust, or be afraid of you along with the others."

The farther they distanced themselves from the disorderly crew the more acutely aware he became of their aloneness. He turned to look down into her upturned face. "Trust me," he whispered with sincerity. Then he took the liberty to touch a hand to the loose soft waves of her hair that tumbled over bared white shoulders.

Beneath the full moon island sky, she was again a vision of loveliness. The fuchsia gown, profuse with sheer nile green lace, accented her skin's ivory whiteness. Her pristine beauty, the filmy gown and the moonlight combined to lend a mystic aura to her presence.

"I want to Niles," she breathed softly as the spell that surrounded the night. "I want to very much."

Aroused by the sensation that passed between, he longed to take her into his arms again, hold her as he never held a woman before. Caution bade him take a step back from temptation. "Victoria, there is a matter we must talk about."

"Now?"

"Yes," he nodded. With a motion of a hand, he invited her to sit on a small dune. She complied, spread her skirt neatly and looked up expectantly.

His boot tips nervously toed the sand. He searched for the right words to introduce what was foremost on his mind. Normally so assured, in this situation he felt completely incompetent and insecure. What if I only imagine she feels as I do? If so, I will appear as a fool before her. Will she be appalled at Toro's theory?

His mind raced and pushed with an unfamiliar urgency. It throbbed with a fear unlike any fear he had known before---yet he desperately needed her answer. The truth of their association must be confirmed before they sailed for the Colonies. It could not be put off any longer. Although it would be weeks before they docked at the settlements, time would quickly fly. They must not lose those precious moments together!

"Victoria---," he faltered and shifted his eyes from hers.

"Yes?" she prompted.

"I want to discuss the remainder of our voyage." He dropped onto the sand by her side and began to toy a scrap of driftwood idly between his fingers. "Due to our close quarters these past weeks---"

"Niles," she interrupted with impatience, "come to the point. Surely by now we can speak freely and less formal. Don't you agree?"

With a nod he continued to fidget with the stick, reluctant lest he speak too boldly. "Likely I shall always be a man of the sea. You will embark on a new life in the Colonies, whereas I shall continue onward to Port Royal."

"We discussed this before, Niles. Quite frankly, I'm a little scared of this new land among strangers and the necessity to adjust to different ways. After being at sea so long I feel at home on the *Pearl*. I wish," she mused, and delivered a sly glance in his direction, "I wish I could remain with you and the crew forever."

Surprised by this remark he felt, in all fairness, he must warn her of the facts. "Unlike other men who settle down, return home each evening and raise families, men of the sea do not lead a normal domestic life. True, some captains marry. Their wives remain behind in port. Others don't like the idea of being apart from a wife while he puts back to sea."

"And you?"

"Marriage is a very serious commitment. One enters into it only if they care deeply for each other."

"Marriage, yes. However, I heard pirate captains either carry wenches with them, or at least keep one in port," she teased.

"You forget. I'm not a pirate."

She shifted her position to look more directly at him, neat brows drawn in confusion. "Niles, I find it difficult to understand what you are trying to say."

Discomfited by the cowardly manner in which he was handling the conversation, he faced her with determination. The words began to spill forth completely out of control. "Victoria, I want these last few weeks to be closer---between us, I mean. I need to know if you feel the same as I. Granted, once we reach the Colonies, I can make no promises. If you don't feel the same I shall try to understand . . . I'm sorry, please forgive me. I'm acting too presumptuous and---and have asked the unthinkable." He started to rise, but she caught his arm with a musical laugh.

"Frankly, that's the best suggestion you've made since I came on board. But," a mischievous gleam entered her eyes, "what about Nicole?"

"Nicole is not who you imagine. True, a wonderful woman, who is very important to me. She's part of the scheme of things, even as the red gown. Let it go at that."

"Is she the one you return to in Port Royal?"

He nodded. "In a sense, yes."

"You are being evasive again."

"Trust me," his voice conveyed sincerity. "Forget about Nicole. We can never be close if you keep her between us. For security reasons I cannot tell you more."

"Now you sound mysterious." Her amusement faded. "Actually, I like what you propose. All through our voyage, you continued to push me away, close me out. Please, Niles," she pleaded and leaned forward, "don't shut me out anymore!"

"I'm sorry if I caused you pain," he took her small hand into his own. "At the time, it seemed necessary to respect your position as a passenger, my position as captain, and your departure at the Colonies. Even now we must ascertain whether you can accept in your heart to live for the present, treasure each moment together and meet tomorrow when it comes---in the manner of Toro's people."

"So that's what you meant before when you mentioned Toro."

With a nod, he explained the island slave attitude. When finished, he ended, "They laugh when there is pleasure, love while they can and take of life's few joys to carry them through the sorrows of tomorrow."

Gentle waves continued to lap softly against the sandy beach where they sat. Eyes upon the silvery sparkles of moonlight reflected on the water, she observed, "In many ways they make a lot of sense. If we don't take of these next weeks together, whatever pleasures we could have shared will be lost to us forever."

"Are you prepared to suffer the pain when it's time to part?"

"The shared memories we carry shall ease the pain. Even a memory is better than not to have loved at all."

Their reservations drained away like the bubbly ripples upon the sand. He reached a hand to slide slowly down the silken smoothness of her raven hair. And let it come to rest upon one bared shoulder. The warmth of her skin under his palm caused his blood to race and throat tighten. The wall he had built began to crumble, melt away, as barred gates opened. With it came a flood of released tension. "You can't imagine the many times I've wanted to touch you as I am now."

Perfume of tropical flowers wafted the air as she tipped her head against his. "I likewise, Niles."

The soft moonlit night, swish and hiss of water against sand, her presence, spun a mesmerizing web that captured his mind. With a hand under the delicate chin, he tilted her face to his. A lock of his long wavy hair slid forward and brushed against her temple. He bent to gaze deeply into her eyes---sapphire eyes that reflected the stars overhead. Against a backdrop of rhythmic sea, his mouth lowered to meet her parted lips. Hungry and responsive, they pressed to his as her arms drew him closer. If any traces of doubt remained they were washed away like the tiny seashells upon the beach.

The newly discovered lovers lay against the warm sand. Their ardent caresses strove to recapture time---precious time lost while they were preoccupied with the fight against the storm. Both were vividly remembering the weeks of loneliness---weeks spent within the same room, unable to reach out, muchless share tenderness. All of the wasted arduous days and nights flowed into their embraces. Yearnings long suppressed, agony and moments of savage desires unfulfilled now culminated. Softly as butterfly wings, island breezes brushed their faces. Inland night sounds drifted from dense foliage. Waves rippled along sand with a hushed murmur.

His hand slid across one inviting breast, lingered a moment before it progressed along the sensuous body: the body he had so often watched discreetly in their quarters. And when, on occasion, they perchanced to brush against one another in their close perimeters, he had reacted with a thrill of deep arousal that promised pleasure upon contact. He remembered how, when they lay through the final height of the storm, he dared not allow himself the liberty, other than to give verbal reassurance.

Now she was his. Her warm mouth pressed in response. Never had his soul stirred to a woman as at this moment. Overhead the very stars in the night sky seemed to send down a shower of heavenly sparkles around them.

At length, emotions spent, they released with reluctance, her head comfortably nestled in the hollow of his shoulder. He laid his cheek against her silken hair. A peace and serenity crept over the pair such as they had never experienced before. Contented, they remained within each other's arms, as they gazed unseeing across the expanse of dark moonlit water. He felt her hand gingerly move along his bared chest and her fingers close around the medallion.

The medallion! Engrossed with repairs and thoughts of Victoria, he had completely forgotten the medallion incident and Ramolo.

He rose and drew her to his side. "Come," he took her hand. "Let's explore a little farther down the shoreline."

"Now?" she asked, incredulous.

“Yes, now. I just remembered something.” He clung to her hand and hurried along the beach while he told of the unexpected session with Captain Ramolo.

"Weren't you frightened?" she gasped, struggling to keep pace with his long impatient strides.

"Out of my boots!"

Suddenly he halted. "This is the brushy point where they overpowered me." He turned, eyes searching the area where the grandiose ship was anchored. Only an empty expanse of sea lay before him. The galleon, silently as a departed ghost, had slipped away.

"Stay here while I look around in the trees." At the suggestion to remain alone on the deserted beach a little shiver transmitted from her against his arm.

Her eyes clouded with doubt as she glanced about the area. "I'd rather go with you."

"The underbrush will tear your gown. I'll be back in a few minutes. Either it's here, or not." Before she could voice further objections he disappeared. Within the tangled undergrowth it was dark, lighted only by streams of moonlight that filtered through the leafy canopy above. He peered about and found visibility extremely difficult. Ahead, unidentified night creatures skittered away at the sound of his approach. About to turn back, his eyes caught sight of an extraordinary bulky shadow.

His arms flailed at the tangle of vines and branches that blocked his way. The shadow, he found, was a crate much larger and heavier than he anticipated.
"If this is what he spoke of, it must really be some bell!" he voiced aloud. Consumed with curiosity he tried to loosen one of the boards with his bare hands to peer inside. It refused to budge. He cursed under his breath. If only he had some tools to pry it open.

Remembering Victoria alone and frightened on the shore, he abandoned the crate to rejoin her.

"It's there," he called out when he emerged. "But I'm not sure if the men can move it all the way to the Pearl."

"Then it seems to me, the only solution is to bring the ship to the bell."

"Right," he agreed. "That would also provide a good opportunity to test her mended sails before we weigh anchor for the Colonies."

Hand in hand, unhurried, they retraced their steps along the shoreline. A heady current that sufficed for words flowed between them. Ended were the strained emotions of the past tortuous weeks. Was she experiencing the same relaxation and warmth as he? he wondered. A shadow flitted across his inner happiness. Too soon they must part. In an effort to recapture the joy of her nearness, he slid an arm about her trim waist. Under the star filled sky the couple strolled in listless bliss along the water's edge.

"We're almost there. See the *Pearl's* lanterns," he pointed. Their steps slowed, and he again folded her within the circle of his arms. Her parted lips invited his mouth to join hers, and thrill to her quick response. Breathless they parted. His lips brushed along her satin smooth temple. Her head again nestled against the hollow of his shoulder. Voice husky, he stroked her long brunette hair. "Forget the party on shore. Let's take one of the landing boats and go directly to the ship where we can be alone."

"I wish we could stay as we are right

now," she whispered. "I wish this night would never end and there was no such place as the Colonies---"

"Sh-h-h. Let's not speak of them. The cloud that hangs over us won't be as dark if we pretend it's not there."

"Meantime, maybe we shall find a way---"

"No, Victoria," he shook his head slowly against hers, foreheads touching. "Don't tempt yourself with such thoughts. They will only make it harder when the time comes. Your father wanted you to live like a lady. My life is with the sea. A seaman's wife leads a lonely life while her man is gone. I love you too much to see you suffer that fate."

"But if I---"

He laid a finger gently to her lips. "Please don't, Victoria. If you looked into the eyes and faces of women whose men go to sea you would understand. Many once were beautiful like you, but time and---no, Victoria. We agreed to share our love in the present. Let's keep it within those bounds; it's the price we must pay for today. Now," he gave her a playful squeeze to break the tension, "you need rest for our swimming lesson in the morning." His eyes lifted toward the *Pearl* and his heart filled with gratitude. Except for her seaworthiness, they would not have been granted these precious moments of happiness.

On board they lingered among the lacy shadows cast by the rigging. Hands around her tiny waist, he gazed down into the eyes that beckoned. Her arms slid eagerly about his shoulders, and he felt the contours of her soft feminine body pressed to his. Their lips met in the hush of the night.

With reluctance, they withdrew, yet remained entwined together. He touched the silken gown and inhaled the perfumed scent of her hair and skin. The rise and fall of her firm bosom against his chest stirred fires deep within his soul---fires that warned. Steeled to temptation, he stepped back and guided her slowly to their quarters. She closed the door, turned, and whispered close to his ear. "One little detail we did not discuss on the beach---"

"I know," he answered, voice constricted. Relieved the room was in darkness, he chose the moment to clarify the matter. "It's best if we maintain our billet arrangements as in the past."

"Anything you wish, my darling."

"Victoria, when I suggested this relationship I didn't mean that you defile yourself. Far from it. I'm fully aware you are not mine to take. I shall respect your honor as a lady, even though it will not be easy."

"I must say, you are very blunt, Captain. However, it does answer my question clearly and completely and I appreciate your respect. I should have known the position you would take. Captain Brett, you are a very rare gentleman and I love you all the more for it." Her hand lingered, then slowly slipped from his, as she retreated into her tiny partitioned room.

Under the new anchorage off shore, Niles sent his crew to retrieve the huge crate. Victoria waited, clad in men's trousers and knitted shirt, plaited hair twined about her head in a tiara. When he entered the quarters, she caught his surprised expression. Piqued, she exclaimed, "I couldn't swim in skirts, could I?"

"With all those clothes you'll sink like a brick."

"B---but," she flushed crimson, "surely you can't expect me to strip like your crew!"

"Of course not," he laughed at her embarrassment. "Let's see---" he smoothed his slim, smartly trimmed mustache. Enjoying the rose of her cheeks, he deliberately delayed. Advancing, he drew an ominous blade from his belt.

Eyes wide with fear, she backed away.

"What is that for?"

"Stand still while I cut the pants up to knee length," he explained, and began to cut away the fabric. "There, that should help." His eyes followed her shapely legs upward, and came to rest on the reddened face. "No need to feel self-conscious. Down among the island---never mind about that. Let's get you acquainted with the water."

In a shallow secluded cove, an arm protectively about her waist, the instruction began. He soon discovered her a fast learner. The wet garments clung enticingly to the rounded curves of her lithe form. Almost immediately he began to wonder if the lesson was harder on him than it was on her.

“Let’s take a rest break,” he suggested. They ran, splashed ashore, and flung their wet bodies onto the warm sand. He lay beside her, appreciating her curvaceousness. Her rounded breasts beneath the close knit shirt rose and fell with the recent exertion. The sun shone along the graceful line of her hips and long, tapered legs.

"Niles?"

"Um-hum," he answered dreamily.

"You promised to show me the *Pearl's* mermaid. How about now?"

They leisurely rowed out to the ship and around the bow. The artistically shaped figurehead came into view overhead. Bright sunlight struck the golden metal of the cupped hands that extended out to sea. The half human, half fish figure reflected the golden sunbeams to dance in a golden sparkle on the water below. She gasped in astonishment.

"She's positively beautiful!" she cried. "Does she really hold a pearl in her hands?"

"The largest most perfect known." He smiled with pride as his eyes drank in the loveliness of the image.

"No wonder you revere it."

"Now you have truly met *The Sea Pearl*. It's time for us to go aboard, I hear the men approaching. They rigged a pontoon raft to float the bell out to the ship. I don't deem it advisable for them to see you dressed as you are."

He broke the first board loose as soon as the crate was safely on deck. A second and third were torn away to afford a quick look at the contents within. Catching sight of the treasure he released a low whistle of appreciation, then emitted a jubilant shout.

"She's a winner! Worth every drop of

sweat you men lost to get her aboard."

The men swarmed over the crate, iron claw hooks in hands. Soon the golden bell was completely exposed. Their eyes feasted on the superb piece of craftsmanship. Voices muffled in wonder, they surveyed its glow in the bright sunlight. It was an exquisite cast. Decorative etchings caught the sun's rays. Reflected flashes of gold shimmered from its mirror polished surface.

"She's enough to blind the eyes," Weasel exclaimed

Brog's finger slowly slid along a section of the smooth metal. Weasel leapt forward to grab his wrist. "Avast there. You're gonna get dirty fingerprints all over it!"

Victoria, now properly attired, spoke from among the group. "Look, there are words engraved around it." Her eyebrows drew together in bewilderment. Slowly she circled the object of attention. "I can't read it. Can you, Niles?"

"I don't wonder. It's Spanish. In English it translates, *'Part the fog and angry seas, and let her pass in the security of your hands, Almighty God'.*"

"Such a beautiful prayer!" she breathed, then turned. "I had no idea you could read Spanish."

"Along the Main one picks up on their language." His attention shifted to the men. "Let's get her mounted before the day is wasted.

The new bell was larger than the old. Before it could be mounted into place alterations had to be made. Securely installed, they stood back to admire the prized acquisition. Brog, usually the most silent, was first to speak.

"I'd say she makes a mighty good match for our mermaid." With a nod of satisfaction, he added, "Now the *Pearl* is ready to go to sea again."

"I say you're right," Niles agreed.

"Kleet, prepare to hoist anchor. There's one more thing I must do before we leave." Victoria turned to follow, only to be halted by Toro's firm grip on her shoulder.

"This time Cap'n need go alone." They watched Niles row to the deserted shore and disappear into the trees beyond.

With heavy heart he lingered beside the fresh grave of Captain Leyden. It was a time of farewell---a time to let go of the old man's guiding hand---time to set to sea on his own. The ship was his responsibility now. A last hand salute and he turned to retrace his steps to the beach.

Boots planted solidly upon the quarterdeck, he drew himself to full stature. Sole captain of *The Sea Pearl*, he surveyed the ship bow to stern. Satisfied all was well, he motioned to weigh anchor and ordered full sail. Pride swelled within his breast. He watched the canvases billow; felt the vessel shift underfoot. She slipped from the sheltered cove and again pointed her golden figurehead toward the open waters.

"Cap'n," the first mate spoke beside him. "What say you be first to ring the bell as a sort of initiation? We can call it a celebration of the *Pearl's* return to action."

"Fine idea. However, let's do it right and proper. We'll let the lady do the honors."

"The men would favor that extra touch. Sort of like a woman is blessing her. They've come to admire her grit."

"No. It's your ship," she responded to their proposition. "Yours and the crew's." They turned and called out for the crew's verification of approval.

"The lady!" they shouted almost in unison. "We've a lady on her bow, let a lady ring her bell!"

The crew stood back in a wide circle as she stepped forward. All waited for the first mellow peal. When it came, the purity of sound thundered about their ears. Spellbound, they stood frozen until the last tremor faded. The quality of tone that lingered on the air was soothing as balm to their souls. To a man, no one wished to break the moment. Without a word each reverently returned to work.

CHAPTER ELEVEN

The next weeks passed smoothly under fair skies and a calm sea. Niles and Victoria spent hours talking or laid on the decks to bask in warm sun. The bond between them deepened. To him the entire world held a rosy sunrise glow. Blissful as were their days, he remained haunted by one dreaded shadow---the hour when they must part. He watched her with concern. She too, must be disturbed by the same turmoil within. Often he was disturbed by misgivings. Had they erred? Was their interlude of shared happiness a mistake?

Each time he took her into his arms he loved her more. He reveled in the sound of her laughter, the glow of her eyes. Too soon they would be as two lonely pieces of driftwood afloat on separate tides. The very thought brought a dull ache to his heart. The northwesterly course brought a chill to the air, an invisible sign the end of their association drew closer with each day.

The second week of May, in the pre-dawn grayness, his dreams were suddenly invaded by a familiar voice. Cleve's hand clutched his shoulder with urgency. Long habit brought Niles instantly alert. He sprang from his bunk and raced to the quarterdeck.

The lookout shouted the alarm. The cook pointed across the dark water. Niles squinted to peer into the semi-darkness. The shadowy figure of a nearby ship came into his vision.

The giant galleon! It loomed like a huge monster posed for prey. Captain Ramolo's words of warning blazed through his mind. He shouted orders to the steerage. *The Sea Pearl* rolled in the sudden turn. Her decks came alive in response to the call. Dark figures ran to their stations.

Cannons appeared from under concealment covers. Balls were stacked, as if by magic, beside the canon carriages. Grim faces scurried about to layer down the decks with wet sawdust as fire protection.

Victoria appeared in the quarters' doorway, awakened by the sound of boots astir. Her eyes registered confused surprise. She no longer recognized the friendly crew she had come to know; these wore barbarous faces. All manner of weapons were strapped or tucked in readiness about their waists.

Razor sharp blades threw vicious gleams that spoke of death. Heavy pistols protruded from sturdy belts. The men moved quickly, coordinated, without need of orders. Eyes mirroring fierce determination darted and flashed. Neither grumble nor word of dissent was heard.

The lookout shouted down a second alarm.

Niles spun about.

Another galleon, slightly smaller, was about to close in.

The first mate stared across the distance. "I'd venture that one 'pears mighty like ol' Doubleface, himself."

"Precisely," Niles agreed. "His water line shows he's running empty. That means he's out on a prowl for booty."

"Do you 'spose he's set up with the big one over there?"

"No, Ramolo doesn't need Doubleface. I am inclined to believe Doubleface wants to take advantage of the fact Ramolo has us blocked on the opposite side. If the pair get us in crossfire, the odds certainly aren't in our favor. Means either outrun them, or stand and fight."

Kleet dubiously scrubbed his chin. "Doubleface runnin' empty could edge in fast. The big one on our to our other side carries so much sail it's likely fast, too."

"You forget. Doubleface has a disadvantage. He doesn't run a unified crew. Ramolo, with all his crew and sail, lacks maneuverability. Those drawbacks may give us the advantage we need. We got any more sail?"

"She's been under full since the first alarm. That's it, Captain, unless we all start flappin' our shirttails to the wind. They're gaining on us, but not very fast."

"Enough to eventually overtake, unless we use evasive action."

Toro slipped silently from behind. "You know who out there?"

"We know," Niles nodded. "Kleet, have the men hold their fire. We don't want to bite off more than we can chew."

"He be after Missy Victoria," the black muttered, face twisted in angry hate. "Toro know what Doubleface do wi' women."

"We're close to the American coastline---" Niles calculated aloud to himself. "Could run at an angle, maybe hide in a secluded cove---

no, they'd see where we pulled in. We would be trapped. Better hold to a southerly course. God willing, they'll give up the chase."

"Not Doubleface," Toro disavowed. "He want lady. Big one not attack Doubleface, 'cause he empty. Spanish only attack for cargo. They's both good reason no give up. We got woman and cargo."

Throughout the day, Niles maintained his vigil. Darkness deepened and he retired to grab a bit of rest. Victoria looked up expectantly when he entered his quarters. What could he say? She was in danger of becoming the prize Doubleface desired? Far better she did not know.

In the days that followed, the two ships on either side inched closer, narrowing the distance considerably. The crew of the *Pearl* expected a volley from one of the pursuers any moment. The time arrived to make a decision--fight, or flight. Neither alternative offered promise of survival for *The Sea Pearl.*

Niles, determined set to his jaw, studied his charts. His mind weighed the dire prospects of what may lie ahead. Decision made, he turned to face Victoria and drank in her beauty. He spoke with calm yet solemn urgency. "Victoria, they are about to close in. You have a right to know I plan to change our course. This decision may not prove very pleasant."

Her eyes went wide with fear and apprehension for his safety. "You cannot fight both of them and win!"

"No, it would be suicide against such odds. I shall order a run for the *Sea Of Lost Ships*. Doubleface is superstitious and may not follow. As for Ramolo, I hope to lose him in the fog I hear hovers in the region." Hand on her shoulder, he warned, "You may never reach the Colonies."

"I'm glad," she said, and laid her head to his shoulder. "That means, my love, we will be together longer."

"Don't take this news lightly, Victoria. Have you heard about the *Sea of Lost Ships*?"

"No, nor do I care. All I want is to be with you."

Cherishing the moment, he held her close, stroked her silken hair and regretted what he felt must be said. "We may not come out of it, my dearest---ever. Many ships who enter are never heard from again, thus its name."

"Where do they go?"

"No one knows. They either disappear,

or if found, are adrift with no one on board."

Aware of what the ship meant to him, her head lifted in surprise. "You will risk losing the *Pearl*?"

"If we elect to stand and fight the *Pearl* will be lost anyway. And---" he held her tight, before adding in a resolute tone, "I will not let Doubleface lay hands on you. Better you were at the bottom of the sea, than taken captive. You would be nothing more than another one of his playthings, a slave to his lusts."

"But the *Pearl*! I will not let you lose her on my account!"

"You wouldn't say that if you knew Doubleface. There's no greater hell on the Main than what a woman suffers as his captive. No, Victoria. We'll take our chances in the *Sea of Lost Ships*. Pray the tales aren't true. If we make it, we'll head for Port Royal. It's closer than the Colonies."

"This captain, who is he?"

"The name, Doubleface, evolved because one side of this face he was born with, whereas someone once recarved the opposite side with a wicked cutlass. Let's say it's best not to look at it. He's regarded as one of the most treacherous, devious privateers to prowl the *Spanish Main*."

Her face paled. "His prisoners, what does he do to them?" Nile evaded the question by tipping her trembling lips to meet his and held her tightly, then quickly left.

A low murmur, accompanied by a nervous shifting of feet, spread across the decks. Anxious eyes faced the direction of the turn with misgivings. Brog and Kleet approached.

"You meanin' to enter the Dead Ships area, Captain?" Brog exploded in disbelief.

"I am."

"You gone plumb daft?" Kleet objected. "You can't take the *Pearl* in there!"

"I can and I will. That is, unless any of you have a better idea." The two fell into sullen silence. "Look, they run parallel to us. A volley from either can land any minute. We don't stand a chance in a crossfire. Face it, this is our only hope of escape."

The first mate shook his head. "We're goners either way."

Niles jerked a thumb toward the galleons. "Rather face their crossfire?"

Kleet cocked his head to the side. His

face broke into a wry grin, mouth twisted toward one ear. "Since you put it that way, Captain, I do believe I'm inclined to agree. Heaven help us. Come on, Brog, we best spread the word to the crew."

Evening deepened and, as Niles hoped, Doubleface's smaller ship veered from its pursuit course. Romolo, however, continued to bear onward. Perhaps, Niles thought to himself, he's confident his ship can defy the strange mysteries that surround the region ahead. If so, he may find himself greatly mistaken.

Dark of night settled over the decks and the nervous stir of the crew increased. The sound of Kleet's boots, muffled by wet sawdust, came to stand beside Niles. The mate shifted a cheap cigar with his tongue to the opposite corner of his mouth. When he spoke his hushed tones matched the tension of the night. "Any orders to change course?"

"No," Niles shook his head. "Keep her so'easterly. We'll cut close to the islands ahead. Make it appear we are bound for Hispaniola. With luck, we can shake them there, cut through Windward Pass and cross to Jamaica. Once we are under the coastline cannons leading to Port Royal, we'll be safe." Head laid back, he scanned the black sky above the soft creak and groan of the rigging. "Strange. Not a cloud nor fog in sight. Yet neither stars nor moon are visible up there."

"I noticed, likewise the crew. No need to tell you they're a might skittish about this idea."

Niles released a heavy sigh. His shoulders sagged with exhaustion, the result of hours of anxiety. "Post the night watches. I'm going to try to get some rest. Have the men do the same. If anything happens I don't want a tired crew."

"Aye, Captain."

In the privacy of his quarters he answered Victoria's questions without elaboration. "You are tired. Lie down," she soothed and brushed a cool hand across his forehead. He allowed his tall cuffed boots to be removed without any objections. Nor did he disapprove when she loosened his clothes. But when she gingerly touched the heavy Spanish *pistole*s, his hand shot out. "You cannot rest decently with---" Seeing it was useless to argue, she relented. "I shall place them on the floor beside you."

Vaguely he felt the weapons and cutlass clear the belt and likewise secreted knives. What difference, he thought disconsolately. If the tales are true, neither pistoles nor cutlass will provide any defense against the unknown phenomena that waits.

Briefly he roused and pulled her down onto the bunk. "Lie with me again," he urged and cradled her in his arms. Unhurried, he loosed the front of her bodice and drew her body close to his own. His lips brushed across her smooth forehead. The clean fragrance of her brought pleasure to his senses. "You wanted to know about the *Sea of Lost Ships*---" he began softly.

"You're tired. Wait until morning."

"No," he objected, close to her ear. "Morning may be too late. The men know and have every right to be afraid."

"Afraid of what?"

"Sh-h-h," he silenced. "Let me finish. Every man who sails the *Spanish Main* knows the stories that surround the area. Sometimes they refer to it as the home of the devil or Devil Sea. Some believe evil spirits live in this region, or a mystic creature floats across the waters---a phantom one can neither see nor fight---an invisible monster that rises from the deep.

"The few who have entered and lived to return tell all manner of tales about what they saw and heard while there. Some people declare they have lost their minds, perhaps they have. I never imagined *The Sea Pearl* to fall prey to it---nor us."

"What can we do?" she whispered in the darkness, body tense beside him.

"Do?" He fell silent a long moment. "Pray the inscription on Romolo's bell is seen by whatever power guides the fates of men."

An awesome silence crept over the room. No movement of the ship could be detected. The two lovers felt as though they were suspended in time, removed from the world, aware only of their closeness on the narrow bunk.

Her hand closed around the jeweled medallion and an almost inaudible whisper escaped from her. "Part the fog and angry seas---" His voice joined hers with equal reverence. "And let her pass in the safety of your hand, Oh Mighty God." Silence. Her head cradled in the hollow of his shoulder, his face buried against the tumbling waves of her hair, they drifted into deep sleep.

Hours later Victoria called out in a voice muted by terror. Her hand clawed at the fabric of his sleeve. "Niles, something is wrong! Niles, I'm cold!"

"You can't be. We're back in semi-tropical waters where the nights are warm." Then he became conscious of his own body temperature. "That's strange. I also feel it." He stirred and became aware of the dim quality of light that permeated the room. The hand on his sleeve tightened.

"The porthole! Niles, look at the color!"

"That is odd," he observed. "Let's take a look outside." He jerked on his boots and jabbed weapons into place. At the same time, she threw a wrap about her shoulders to ward off the chill. He stopped at the door, grinned down at her, and carefully buttoned the open front of her bodice while she blushed modestly at her forgetfulness. "Whatever may be out there, be it spirit or devil," he teased, "I would not want to tempt it with any ideas about my cargo."

Through her embarrassment, she cried, "Niles, this isn't funny!"

"I wasn't being funny. I meant it."

They stepped outside. What they saw caused him to instinctively extend an arm to protect her. The entire ship was enveloped in an eerie greenish haze of neither fog nor mist. The masts disappeared into the murky green overhead. Everywhere green, the color of slime . . . the sea, the decks, the sails. Even the silent faces of the stupefied crew that stood nearby reflected the sickish iridescent shade of green.

The air, though warm, bore a penetrating chill; a dampness unlike any he experienced off a northern sea. It sent a course of shivers through their bodies. Oxygen starved air made breathing difficult, constricted.

Sails hung limp. The ship stood motionless. He peered through the green gloom and recognized the first mate. "Kleet," he called out. His voice sounded overly loud in the eerie silence. "Where are the lookouts?"

"Don't know, Captain," he shook his head, as if in half trance.

Niles remembered the tales of vanished crews. His anxiety increased. "Everyone spread out. Search bow to stern. Toro, take a couple men and check the hold. I want them found!" The men shifted, then drifted in the various directions on unsteady legs.

Kleet passed nearby and intoned almost imperceptibly, "Maybe they're not here, Captain. Maybe it's done got 'em."

The muscles along Niles' jaw tensed to the possibility. He would not make conclusions until certain a thorough search turned up nothing.

Victoria, huddled at his side, ventured a

frightened whisper. "You did say crews disappear---"

"In those cases every man was gone. We are here. Only the lookouts are missing. They must be here somewhere, even if dead."

In the steerage the helmsman stared idly into the blanket haze that obliterated the expanse of sea. His hands lay lax on the tiller.

"Sorry, Captain, there's no way I can steer her." With one hand he shoved the arm of the tiller. It swung freely as if disconnected from the rudder. "I get the feeling she's controlled by another hand. A hand that's got us locked helpless in this green pocket. Now I know how a fly feels when caught in a spider's web."

In the face of their hopeless situation Niles issued a heavy sigh, unsure what to do next. "Stay at your post in case something breaks. Meantime, I'll try to make some sense of all this."

This indiscernible thing was beyond his comprehension. Whatever it was, it seized its prey without benefit of any man created weapon: a phenomena that lived within the air. It held the power to need only touch its victim to make human or ship disappear into eternal nothingness.

A stir of voices from the main deck brought him around. Two crewmen assisted one of the lookouts toward a large coil of rope. They eased the man down and leaned him against a cannon carriage.

Niles crossed with long strides to the men. The wild terrified stare in the eyes of the lookout revealed all was not well. "Thank God, he's alive!"

"Not much mor'n that, Captain," one of the men observed in hushed tones. "Found him crouched over by the anchor sorta like he was hidin'. I'd say, by the look of him, he's seen something wot's cracked his mind."

Niles began a careful examination. "Let's not jump to any rash conclusions. I don't want to upset the whole crew until we have a closer look." He lifted one of the lookout's hands, released it and watched it drop limply to the man's side. The sightless eyes neither blinked, nor shifted when Niles moved his own hand back and forth before them. Niles closed the lax jaw only to see it drop open again.

"Acts like he's dead, Captain," the other crewman observed. "Even cold when I touch him, yet he not be dead, heart still workin'"

"I'd say more like shocked into insensibility by something," Niles speculated.

He stood back to analyze the unfamiliar symptoms. "I hate to get rough with a man in his pathetic condition. Still, we need to try something to bring him out of this state." He stepped forward to smartly slap the face with an open palm. The man's head rolled to one side.

"Niles!" Victoria screamed and reached out to protest. "How can you do such a thing?"

"Stand back, Victoria!" he pushed her aside. "I don't relish striking a helpless man either." He then proceeded to slap first one side and then the other.

Upon detection of a slight hint of resistance, he immediately stopped. "I do think there's a response. Quick, massage his arms and legs to stimulate feeling back into him."

A voice spoke from behind. "Captain, here's the other one."

"Put him down over by the capstan while I finish on this one."

"He's coming around," a man nearby muttered, "but will his brains have any sense when he does? I heard it said---"

"Shut up!" Niles barked, to avert alarm

among the crew gathered around. "That remains to be seen."

He watched the head lift, mouth close, eyes move, and lips try to formulate speech. Upon this sign of life the men swarmed around to ply the patient with questions.

"Leave him alone!" Niles shouted. "He'll talk when he's ready. For now, help him to his bunk to rest."

He turned to the second lookout. Again he applied the same harsh treatment until he saw movement. The emergency under control, he leaned back, tired and shaken.

"I am sorry," Victoria touched his shoulder. "I shouldn't question your judgment or methods. Apparently you knew best, even if it did appear cruel."

"All I knew was I must try something," was his honest reply. "It worked, thank God. That's what counts. All we can do now is wait to see if they've gone mad."

The water, like a sheet of flawless glass, held not a movement to be seen through the murkiness. He moved to the rail and looked down, puzzled. The water surface is completely stilled, he observed. The ship is stilled; even so, I can detect turbulence in the depths. How can this be? Nothing, he shook his head as if to clear it, makes any sense: not the greenish quality that blankets everything, the currents, nor the tiller that swings free and useless or us. As if that isn't enough, I feel that unexplainable chill penetrating air that by all reason should be warm.

The canvases hang limp, there's not a movement of ship or sail. Not a ripple in her wake. Yet I'm filled with a strange sensation we're moving. It's as if we are being drawn by some unseen, magnetic force. If this is true, drawn toward what? I must find a logical explanation. It's bad enough for my men to succumb to superstitions and weird sea tales. I must not allow myself to do likewise.

The men drifted aimlessly about the decks all through the day. One could almost see them slowly slip into trance states. Even their habitual surliness reverted into listless silence. At times he, too, feared he might drift into the same strange melancholy.

A soft green layer closed over at evening. It encompassed the men in comatose sleep wherever they perchanced to be on the decks. Bodies collapsed into limp heaps, like grog soaked riffraff that habituated the wharf areas of ports.

Roused in lethargic depression by a murky dawn, they staggered up on unsteady feet. Niles, own mind clouded, struggled to take the initiative as their captain. Somehow, he must draw the sullen men back from their stupor. They were like ragged shreds of humanity. Whatever power controlled these waters had drugged them into total submission. Their minds, Niles insisted, must be stirred to fight back at this creeping unseen enemy. They must rise in defiance against the empty void they are being steadily pulled toward. THEY MUST! But, he asked himself, what manner of means do I, a mere human, have at my disposal to fight so overpowering a presence? One thing he noticed---his ears heard no sounds to disturb the profound ethereal silence and illusion of utter peace. The very essence of it gave him an idea.

"Kleet," he called out, surprised by the weakness of his own voice. He felt it sap his strength even as he spoke. Too tired to lift his boots, he scuffed the sawdust with a heavy gait until he reached where Kleet leaned against a carriage. "Sounds!" he pulled up short. "Sounds! Kleet!" he nudged the mate. The mate only stared across the green murk that obscured the water. His mind, perhaps, already lost to another entity.

In desperation, Niles grasped the man's forearms. With what little strength he could muster he savagely shook the man. "Kleet! Listen to me. You're the first mate, remember? I need your help. Take a look at the men---at you and I. Can't you see what's happened to us all? We must convince the men to fight back!"

The mate grunted a response. "Aye, Cap'n. Fight what? If you can see it, then you fight it!"

"You don't understand," he shook him again. "It wants us to silently drift into its hands. We need noise! We need to wake up, sing, dance, work---anything to make noise, lots of noise and movement!"

The mate's clouded face began to clear. "Go kick them up," Niles pressured. "Drag them by the scruff of their necks if need be. Gather them together here on the quarterdeck where, hopefully, we can talk some fire into them. Go man, go," he persisted, as faith in his strategy gained strength.

While waiting, he searched for ideas to make his plan work. Meanwhile, the men slowly dragged themselves into a cluster at the center of the ship. When all were accounted for he stepped forward with forced confidence and elevated himself to a stance of command by leaping upon a large coil of thick rope. When he looked down the uplifted faces displayed only a small degree of cognizance.

"How many think we are doomed?" he forced a shout he did not feel. A ragged rumble of assent rose from the assemblage. "Then I assume you are convinced the voyage is over for us, and for the *Pearl*. Therefore, as your captain, I beg one last favor. Listen closely. Then think hard on what I say.

"The Sea Pearl is like a second home to most of you. She provided a livelihood and, on occasion, helped us strike at the bloody Spaniards. You walked her decks proudly through good and bad times." He allowed time for his remarks to sink in, then continued. "Now our beloved *Sea Pearl* is in trouble. Deeper trouble than ever before. She needs the help of each and every one of us. She can't talk, so I shall plead for her---" A voice interrupted from the rear.

"Ya, you talk. How can we help her now? Can you reach out, Captain, take hold of whatever lurks here? If so, string its neck on a yard! Go ahead, Captain, fire that *pistola* you got in your belt. See if it does any good!"

"This time I do not suggest a fight," Niles countered calmly, almost humbly. "If a fight were the answer, you would have already done so. No," he shook his head, "this time all I ask is for you to give thought to *The Sea Pearl*. She's a proud ship. If, as you say, this is her time, we owe her a proud departure.

"I propose we pitch in, clean and shine her from bowsprit to stern. Clear the sawdust from her decks, polish the salt air scum from her brass and rub down her rails. Let us scrub 'til the skin is scoured off our elbows!

"Whether our energies feel up to it or not, I want to hear us sing." Warming to the subject, he motioned his arms to instill enthusiasm. "Laugh and dance your feet. Let this enemy know what kind of ship he chose this time. How about it, men, are you with me?"

The crew, with no signs of movement, remained silent. His heart sank. The last futile hope had run aground. He began to turn away, defeated. Then, to his astonishment, a face advanced forward.

"Where you be wantin' us to start, Captain?"

Hope renewed, he detailed the men to various sections of the ship, then turned to Victoria. "You will clean the Captains Quarters top to bottom, wall to wall. Shake and air the bed covers, clean every storage and drawer, polish everything in sight. That done, do whatever else you can find to keep busy."

Next he pointed a finger at Cleve. "Provide an abundance of food for the men. Also, I want every dish, tankard, pot, table---everything in the galley scrubbed down and put into place. We'll show the *Pearl* how much she means to us!"

As the group dispersed, Kleet bellowed,

"All right, you cussed deck swabbers, it's time we wash our backsides with a little honest sweat!"

So far so good, Niles thought to himself with satisfaction. Now if only the seed I planted takes root and grows.

He joined Victoria in his quarters. "Don't disturb anything on my desk. I want those things where I can't find them in a hurry."

"My dear Captain," she challenged, "considering our plight, what might you need in a hurry?"

"Never can tell," he smiled secretively. "Something unexpected may happen."

"Please, don't be ridiculous! It would take a miracle to pop us out from this insufferable green vacuum."

"Who's to say miracles aren't possible?"

"Listen to the great optimist! I'm afraid I fail to share your groundless hopes."

"Come, my good lady, we cannot afford a pessimist on board. Get into the swing of things. Smile!" he gave her waist a playful squeeze. "Live for today. Tomorrow may be too late, as they say." Abruptly his mood turned serious.

"I mean that Victoria. We don't know what tomorrow may bring, or even today. For your own good, live while there is yet time. Live, treasure, enjoy and make every minute golden. Work, sing, laugh---anything. Drink of every moment you are granted as if it is your last." With another squeeze of reassurance he stepped back. "To work, wench. There's no time to indulge in dreams of personal pleasures behind closed doors. We have a ship to save."

"Save? You said---"

"Never mind," he grinned, and began to work noisily at his desk. Charts rustled, drawers and cabinets opened and closed with deliberate loudness. Sound, there must be lots of sound.

Throughout the day he strolled the decks, boot heels intentionally made to strike sharp against the deck surface. Along the way, he inconspicuously touched everything that held the potential for noise. A rattle of chain here, a shake of rigging there, as if to test tension. Mid-afternoon found him in the galley. He called out to Cleve. "Come on, let's hear those pots rattle all the way to my quarters. If not, I shall assume you are lazing on your backside."

At nightfall he ordered the work to cease and the men to bathe and get cleaned up. Although thereby refreshed, the men were bone tired. Hunched over their hot evening meal, they indulged in little conversation.

The table in the Captains Quarters was laid in the finest tradition of *The Sea Pearl*. Silver gleamed and reflected the flicker of candles in their ornate silver holders. Victoria sat across from Niles. Her regal low cut English gown befitted the atmosphere of the room. Her hair, brushed to a heightened sheen, flowed over one bared white shoulder. Suddenly she looked up and spoke with unexpected candor.

"Niles, why all this absurd pretense? You admit the *Pearl* is going down, or at least that none of us shall survive---"

"I beg to correct, my little lady. I only agreed there was a possibility we may not make it through. Strange things happen out here. To be precise, I said something on the order of, 'If the *Pearl* is to be lost, we should let her go proudly.' That did not mean I thought all was lost, nor a signal to give up. When a person gives up he has lost before allowing himself a chance. One must continue to fight if he hopes to win on anything worth while."

"Be that as it may, you are being unreasonable to work the men as hard as today. If that isn't enough, you've demanded all this fuss and fancy."

"Not unreasonable at all. Quite the contrary. A bath and clean clothing uplifts the spirit. Admit it, don't you feel better now?" Then added with a smile, "And I must say, your hair is lovely by candlelight tonight."

"Oh, you are positively disgusting!"

Her irritation, he sensed, came from something deeper.

He leaned forward. "Care to share your problem with me?"

Discomfited on being confronted so candidly, she toyed with her fork before she confessed. "Very well, so it's not only the ship. It's this pretense between us; your rigid stance of honor that keeps us apart. Answer me, what good is honor now?"

With pursed lips he gave her remarks his undivided attention. "Victoria, I thought we cleared all this up on the beach."

"Everything is changed now."

"Nothing is changed, really."

Her face tightened. "What do you mean, nothing? The Colonies are no longer in my future. Now it's only you and I, if we ever get out of here, which I doubt."

"You may draw that conclusion, I do not. I don't intend to give up. I plan to bring this ship through!"

Her shoulders sagged in resignation. "Be reasonable. There's not a thing you can do! Look out there," her hand shot toward the porthole. "What do you see? Where is the hope you cling to?"

"The mere fact we are still afloat is encouragement enough for me. The men show signs of recovery. If you lack faith, Victoria, at least leave me mine. I will not give up. That is final!"

"All right, so be stubborn," she rose and turned a rigid back to him. "That doesn't alter the facts. Even if we do break out, all indications are we shall sail for Port Royal. That means there'll be no parting at the Colonies and I see no logical reason for this impasse. To quote your very own words, why can't we 'live for today'?"

He approached from behind, placed his arms about her and drew her close. Her hands trembled in his and he nuzzled his face against her silken dark hair. "Victoria, believe me, I would like nothing more than to fantasize with you. I wish we could sail out of this gloom to the sunlit shores of Port Royal and be there together into eternity." He began to rock her in his arms. "Lovely as the illusion may be, we must accept it as only a beautiful dream. Nothing more. Eventually all idle dreams end. When that happens all that remains for us both is the pain of loss."

She turned, buried her face on his chest, clung to him and sobbed. "Niles, can't you see? You are the only force that keeps us apart. How can I believe you love me if you continually refuse me? Or is it because you desire me only until we reach the Colonies, then return to Nicole?"

He tipped her face to his and looked down into her misty eyes. "Victoria, trust me. She has nothing to do with us. True, if we survive, we shall head for Port Royal. But Royal will not be forever. Once proper repairs are made we shall return up the coastline to deliver you at the Colonies."

His head bent to kiss a tear upon her cheek. "I promised to respect your honor. That promise is as difficult for me as it is for you."

"Then why keep it?" she cried, and pounded her fists in desperation upon his broad chest. "Why can't I stay with you now we have found each other?"

"No," his head shook sadly. "I gave your father my word and I'm not one to break my word."

"My father is dead!" she broke away. "Why must you insist to keep a promise to a dead man?"

He gazed down at her a long moment before he dropped his hands and strolled over to the porthole. There he stood, jaw set, face to the green night. Tense ripples played along his cheek. Long moments passed before he broke the silence.

"One thing I do know, Victoria, you father would not want you married to a pirate."

She whirled on him. "Pirate?" Hot tears gathered in her darkened sapphire eyes. "Who's a pirate? I speak of you, Captain Niles Brett, not a pirate!"

"In the eyes of the world I will always be regarded as a buccaneer. It makes no difference to them whether we fight for good or bad. They group us all together, hunt and accuse equally." He released a heavy sigh. "I'm branded a murderous pirate. You are an English lady of respectability. The two can never mix. Sure," he nodded sadly, "we can love in our beautiful dream while it lasts, but one day it will end."

She cupped his lean face in her slender hands, looked up, and murmured softly, "What if I don't wish to be a respectable

English lady, as you label me?"

"Please, my love, don't make it any more difficult for me than your nearness already has." He held her close and spoke in a choked voice near her ear. "I've seen women left behind too many times. If something happened to me while at sea the waterfront riffraff would descend on you like sharks. No, Love, I cannot bear to think---" He struggled for voice control. "Enough talk. Let's see if I can stir the men to play some music. Perhaps it will serve to buoy everybody's moral."

Music, of itself, was not what he had in mind. True, music would soothe, cheer and mellow the tired crew that lounged about the decks. Music was also another source to call upon for the creation of noise.

Dawn penetrated the blanket of green murk that enveloped the isolated ship. At first light, the scrubbing and polishing resumed with decidedly more vigor than the previous day. The minds of the men focused more on the ship than the eerie world that surrounded them. Absorbed in the tasks at hand they began to ignore its presence.

Weasel was ordered to keep salt scum polished from the golden bell. This held a twofold purpose. The inscription presented a visible challenge to whatever sinister phantom lurked and conveyed hope to each man as he passed by.

Niles and Kleet circulated among them. Own qualms concealed behind a mask of cheerfulness, they encouraged one and all to join in boisterous rowdy sea songs as they labored. The experiment soon became contagious; before long the entire crew rubbed and scrubbed to the tempo. Tensions started to fall away in carefree, if off-key, harmony. Not only did it provide a release for taut nerves but also, and more importantly, it generated sound.

The ship was soon trim under the restored activity. It gleamed with cleanliness fore to aft. Five men lowered themselves on ropes cast over the bow to carefully polish the golden figurehead; her hands extended seaward as if offering her giant pearl to the Gods for deliverance.

The increased energies of the past days succeeded to revive the men and improve the condition of the ship. Now Niles faced a new dilemma. What next? If the men were to remain motivated and the noise continue, a new idea was needed; else the crew would most surely slip back into their former lethargy.

Worried, he paced the decks, own hopes beginning to falter. No ship, after so lengthy a time, was known to return from *The Sea of Lost*

Ships. It seemed his scheme had only forestalled their eventual disaster. One thing was certain. Whatever lurked within and over these waters, it would not be easily cheated of its prey.

His hands clenched and unclenched on the freshly polished rail. Envisioning no hope, no future, he felt the depths of defeat. Although he tried to bolster his spirits his heart sank lower. He stared at the ivory white knuckles that gripped the wood. The men must not witness his heightened anxiety. It was imperative he exude an air of confidence, be it justified or not. He climbed to the foredeck, face seaward and spent a long time in deep thought, asking himself what Captain Leyden would have done in the same situation. Abruptly he turned to survey the men below. In a rash move he called for their attention.

"What say we hold a real celebration after our evening meal? We'll kick up our heels in our grandest finery. We'll have music, grog and rum. Whatever you want from the hold is yours!"

One of the men, baffled by this sudden outburst, looked up and scratched his head. "What be we celebratin', Captain?"

"Anything! Maybe our treasured mermaid, may she ever shine as brightly as today," he said in an effort to instill enthusiasm. "We'll celebrate in honor of her beauty and toast her golden loveliness!"

"Good enough excuse for me!" another voice rose from the rear. The group nodded in anticipatory pleasure. Several licked lips, prematurely tasting liquors on their tongues.

They scurried off to bathe, spit shine boots and don their finest attire. Meanwhile, Victoria debated over which beautiful gown to wear for the impromptu occasion. Wedgwood blue, buttercup yellow, or should it be the lilac colored one? Unable to decide, she turned to Niles for his opinion.

Face averted, he walked away. "Tonight you can wear the red, if you like."

"The red gown?" she exclaimed, perplexed by this sudden change of attitude. "You strictly forbade me to so much as touch it before. Why now?"

"Because it doesn't matter anymore," he answered in a toneless voice, feeling her eyes stare into his back.

"I must confess," her tone softened, "I can't wear it even if I want to. It's not my size. No, I think the yellow. It will be a contrast against the green of whatever is out there."

Niles, not in a conversational mood, offered no further comment. Motions slowed by own state of depression, he took a last swipe across his dress boots. He shrugged into a maroon velvet coat and fluffed the gathered silk lace visible at the throat and cuffs. Satisfied with his appearance, he unlocked the weapons cabinet.

From within their black velvet lined box he selected a fine brace of Spanish *pistoles*; a matched pair reserved for the most impressive occasions, never for warfare. Remarkable pieces of precision craftsmanship, he mused to himself. One hand slid along the etched silver inlaid handles adorned with costly jewels; their colorful fires flashed in the candlelight.

"Yes," he whispered. "If ever there is an occasion to appear in full captain dress tonight is such a time."

He laid them momentarily aside while his attention turned to the etched silver trims of a long leather sheath. The hilt that extended above the sheath was encrusted by an array of matched flawless pearls, faceted green emeralds, blood-red rubies and fire opals. At its end waited a keen, custom designed blade, half sword, half cutlass. Weapons securely buckled at his waist he stood tall, impressive, fully attired in honor of the *Pearl's* surrender to the sea.

"How grand you are!" Victoria's awed voice spoke from behind. "Turn around and let me look at you." Hesitant, he shifted to face her. She recoiled, stark terror mirrored in her startled eyes. "I---I've never seen you quite like this before!" Her fingers lightly slid along the rich fabric of the velvet coat, rows of natural pearls down its front, matched by rows of additional pearls along the wide sleeve cuffs.

Niles delivered a careless shrug. "So, what are a few pearls? In Port Royal they are passed by the basketsful over counters in lieu of money."

Attention riveted on the array of ominous, though beautiful jeweled weapons, she shuddered with revulsion. "It---it's not only the pearls. Seeing you now makes me realize the man I thought I loved doesn't exist. You really are Captain Brett, a dangerous formidable stranger!" She whirled about and fled out the door onto the main deck.

Unlike Victoria, the crew, accustomed to their captain's appearance in full dress, paid no attention when he emerged. Particularly since the men, even when at work, often wore a sizable fortune in gems that flashed from fingers, wrists, shirtfronts and throats. To see captains richly adorned head to toe, therefore, was not unusual along the Main.

Musical instruments appeared and owner's fingers warmed with the help of nearby wooden kegs tipped on their sides.

Tankards bumped and sloshed as toast after toast was offered. Toasts to the golden mermaid, *The Sea Pearl,* and Miss Victoria. A refill was validated by whatever excuse they could conjure up.

Victoria joined the music and revelry. She danced with all the men and laughed in reckless abandon. The first mate plied his charms on the lady with the utmost expertise, and it was apparent she had no objections. His advances did not go unnoticed by Niles, who stood at the sideline. What manner of underhanded trickery does he have in mind this time? he wondered. Regardless, he will not have long to implement any schemes. Time is fast running out.

Someone shoved an overfilled tankard into his hand as an invitation to join the group in yet another toast, his first of the evening.

Grog, rum, and wine flowed like streams of plenty from the kegs. When one ran dry it was, with ribald laughter, hoisted over the side. While it bobbed away on the surface of the dark green sea, a fresh barrel was already being tapped. Niles placed no limitations on the number of kegs brought up from the hold.

Cleve staggered to and from the galley. A slopping tankard in one hand, a precariously balanced tray of food on the other. The party rapidly progressed into one such as *The Sea*

Pearl had not seen on board for many months.

Now and then, Niles caught a momentary glimpse of the filmy yellow gown swirling like a misty sunbeam amid the noisy assemblage. Emotionally drained, he paid it no mind. Victoria, *The Sea Pearl*, or any dreams they may have harbored were now over. This night was the end of their voyage---the end for all aboard. He dismissed the cavortings from mind, let each man pass what scant time remained in his own way. Their lives would end soon enough.

The hour grew late. To his ears, the music, shouts of inebriated men and stomp of boots, grew to a cacophony of advancing destruction. He stifled an overwhelming desire to retreat to his quarters, close out the sound of the inevitable. Instead, as captain, he steeled himself to remain with his men.

Gradually the heady spirits, frizzled intellects and thickened tongues ceased. Bodies sank into drunken heaps wherever they perchanced to fall when all consciousness deserted them. So much so, that one needed to take care lest they trip over a crumpled form.

A limited few still managed to maneuver about the kegs. And while the more seasoned musicians continued to play, the tempo slowed. Kleet maintained his lavish attention on Victoria. Niles wandered off and climbed to the foredeck. There he stood alone at the rail and gazed in submission into the green-black night. Silently he shouted in defiance to the unknown specter that held them fast. I'm here, take me, take *The Sea Pearl,* take all of us. I shall no longer fight you. You have won!

With no comprehension on how long he remained concealed from his men, shoulders no longer squared, all pretense abandoned, he clenched and unclenched the rail. A lock of dark wavy hair dropped over his forehead unnoticed.

A hand lightly touched his shoulder. He heard Victoria's soft voice as from a distance of unreality.

"Captain Brett?" The cloud of yellow, dimly visible in the moonless night, tugged at his semi-consciousness. His depressed mind refused to answer. He had no answers. The dire thoughts he kept hidden were best left unsaid.

"Captain Brett, do you hear me?" The voice took on a tone of anxiety. She grasped his elegant sleeve. "Is something wrong?"

He answered, but did not lift his head. "I'm all right. Go back to the party."

"I came to ask---should Toro close the kegs? You never permit the crew to get into such a state."

"Far better they enjoy themselves. If their senses are deadened with spirits they will not know, nor feel, anything when it comes."

Fearful premonition crept into her words. "What are you talking about?"

He motioned an arm toward the blackness beyond. "Take a look out there. It's over. There's no hope for *The Sea Pearl* or *us.* Before morning---"

She grabbed his shoulders and spun him about to face her. "Niles Brett, you listen to me!" She shook him in desperation. "You cannot give up. Not you! Don't you understand? If you quit there truly is no hope."

"Victoria, it's over. This thing, spirit, phantom, or whatever it is, hovers and plays games with us. We are its toy, dangled at will. It will be tired of play before this night is over. It's poised to take us the same way it took its past victims."

She remained silent. Her eyes searched his face in the darkness. Slowly her brows knitted together. "You really believe what you say, don't you?"

"I not only believe, I'm convinced. The saddest part lies in the knowledge it is not only the end for the *Pearl*. It's the end also for you and I," he whispered hoarsely. His hands slid along her arms. They touched the dark, silken hair that tumbled in thick waves over her shoulders. Image etched in his mind, he could clearly visualize each detail of her face in the darkness. Eyes closed, he buried his head against her softness.

He clung to her, striving to remember each precious sensation of the moment. The rise and fall of her rounded breasts against his chest---the nearness and feeling of oneness together---the way she melted into his arms---her warmth. So little time to store up memories; make each treasured second count. This may well be the last time he would be granted the pleasure and thrill of her feminine contours so near to him.

Lips close to his ear, she pleaded, "If, as you say, this is our last night, grant me one favor, Niles---"

"Anything. Anything you wish." Voice husky with emotion against her throat, he asked, "What happened to Captain Niles Brett of earlier this evening?"

"You stood so proud, so removed and distant in the bright light of the cabin. I can't see your fine clothes, priceless jewels, or weapons here in the darkness. I see only Niles---my Niles. We are two people caught up in our own world again."

He held her, absorbed the pleasure and regretted the need to break the spell. "You asked a favor. It's yours, my dearest." With a forced laugh he did not feel, added, "Within limitations, that is."

"It may sound like silly romanticism. Especially when everything around us appears doomed. But if we must die, I want to carry the memory of dancing together one more time here in the darkness."

"That be the case, there's nothing I'd rather do than share your silly romanticism."

Arm about her trim waist, they glided in a dream state among the rigging---two lovers, alone in the semi-darkness, drifted in rhythm to the musical strains in the background. His muted jewels flashed an occasional subdued fire toward the deck lanterns below. The buttercup yellow gown floated ghost like among the shadows.

Her head lifted from his shoulder with a contented sigh. "Words can't begin to express how happy I am at this moment. I must admit one thing though. I'm very tired after dancing all evening with the men while I waited for you."

"Come sit by the rail, lean back, and relax. I'm sorry, I haven't been very good company tonight."

"It's not that," she corrected, as she carefully arranged the fullness of her skirts on the scrubbed deck. "It's turned chilly," she shivered. "I should have brought a wrap."

"Here," he seated himself and cradled her close within the warmth of the velvet coat. Lowering her head to rest against his lace shirtfront, he asked, "That better?"

"Much," she smiled in gratification, hand on the medallion beneath the shirt.

An ethereal sensation of utter peace descended over the two lovers. Unseen currents of intimate closeness flowed between their warm bodies. Within the flutter of an eyelash, they drifted into the soft cottony folds of slumber.

CHAPTER 12

Shortly before dawn Victoria stirred and sat up with a start. Her eyes darted about their surroundings. She clutched his arm, urgency in her tone.

"Niles, wake up! It's gone!"

He squinted against the early lavender glow of a clear sky. The sun, just under the horizon, began to send shades of rose and yellow across the eastern sky.

Overjoyed, he crushed her in his arms. "We made it! *The Sea Pearl* came through!" A tremble of excitement passed through them. They clung to each other, thrilled with the knowledge some mysterious hand of grace had granted them a second chance to remain together.

He shouted, voice quivering with emotion, "Come, let's wake the crew and tell them the *Pearl* lives again!"

They stopped beside the golden bell on

the main deck. Hand reverently placed on the glistening surface, he repeated in a solemn choked whisper the prayer inscribed thereon. "Part the fog and angry seas and let her pass in the safety of your hand, Oh Mighty God."

Turning, he shouted to a groggy helmsman collapsed beside a cannon carriage. "Wake up man! Lay to the rudder and put her on course!"

A gentle breeze rippled through his hair. He looked up at the formerly limp unfurled sails and watched them begin to billow. Inhaling a deep breath of crystal air, he prodded the fleshy bulk of the cook with a boot toe. "Off to your galley, Cleve! You have men to feed."

Victoria in tow, he made a triumphal round of the decks. Man after man was roused from intoxicated stupor. The pair watched with amusement as one by one each snapped to, saw the azure sky overhead, and stood mouth agape in astonishment. Fingers of morning sunlight touched the uplifted faces and bewilderment quickly changed to joy.

Mid-morning Victoria, Brog and Toro joined Niles and Kleet where they leaned, backs against the rail. "Whatever that monster was," the first mate remarked, as he chewed vigorously on the stub of a foul cigar, "I don't care to go back to find out."

"Me neither," Brog growled. "I want to see what's tryin' to kill me so's I can at least fight back."

Niles listened to his men compare tales they had heard previous to this first-hand experience. "Now that it's over," he ventured, "I'm convinced nothing was out there."

"You gone crazy, Man?" Kleet whirled to cast an askance glare of doubt. "That inhuman thing held the *Pearl* in a death grip and near killed us all!"

Niles shook his head. "No, I've given it a lot of deep thought. I think it was only an illusion. Convinced on the validity of the tales that surround *The Sea of Lost Ships*, our imaginations tricked us to act in the manner of the tales."

"Oh, yeah? What about all that green stuff?" Brog challenged.

"An' the lookouts goin' crazy and rest of us one by one droppin' drifty in the head?" Kleet interjected.

"Exactly what I mean. Don't those tales mention everything being green, men gone crazy, windless seas and ships that disappear?"

"Well, sure, Cap'n," Brog agreed with

reluctance. "We've all heard it said."

"So there you are. Imagination overpowered our sensibilities."

"I don't know, Captain," Kleet hedged. "All I can say is it sure seemed mighty real to me. If it was imagination, as you say, then why did it go away last night?"

"Maybe it didn't."

"An' maybe you're still daft in the head. For instance, if that's so, then why isn't it green out there now?"

"Look at it this way, if it was never there in the first place there would not be anything to go away, now would there?"

"You ain't makin' any sense," the first mate muttered in disgust and tossed the ragged soggy cigar butt over the side. "We all saw it, felt it clean through our bones. Imagination being the case, explain why we don't imagine anymore, if you can."

"Simple. When we started to polish and clean, our minds were diverted to something other than the tales. With the help of last night's liquors your mind never had a chance to revert back to the tales. Those forgotten, we returned to reality. Our imaginations were longer in control of our minds."

"I dunno," Brog took a deep breath and emitted it slowly. "You must be right, since there's no other explanation."

"Unless, that is," Kleet voiced with uncertainty, "it decided on its own to leave."

"The main point is, it's behind us. We have a ship to run and Port Royal waits. Someday you'll be able to tell your grandchildren all about it."

"Grandchildren!" the mate scoffed. "Cap'n that green muck really addled your brain! This bloke has far too much fun entertaining by the dozens than to settle down married to any one woman. Nay, when ol' Kleet looks into any little faces and calls 'em grandchildren it will be a long day in hell!"

Niles pursed his mouth in a secretive smile. "I think what you mean to say is that you refuse to claim any little faces."

"You have something there, Cap'n," Kleet emitted a boastful laugh. "See that?" he pointed to the deep cleft of his chin. "Just might be quite a few grubby little faces in a dozen or so ports sportin' same! What's more, git me into port again and, with a little help from grog and Dill Devil, there's liable to be a heap more of 'em." A sudden cry of alarm from the lookout interrupted their playful jest.

"Ship to port! Ship to port!"

All heads whipped about to scan the water. Moments ago only gently undulating waves of open sea and gulls were seen. Now, seemingly out of nowhere, the giant Spanish galleon had mystically emerged.

"Ramolo!" Niles exclaimed. Muscles tensed, he made swift mental calculations. The *Pearl* would never stand a chance against the firepower of their opponent. The galleon was already closer than necessary to inflict disastrous damage.

Why didn't the lookouts spot it sooner? Yet Brog, Kleet, Toro, and even himself were all faced in the same general direction yet failed to notice it. "We must be blind!" he swore under his breath. A quick analysis of their situation and he opted to allow his men to go down with a fight, pride intact. He spun around, waved an arm and shouted the crew to their stations.

They sprang into action. Hatch grates lifted. Men descended into the hold. Kegs of powder, ball and sawdust were passed to hands that waited above. Meanwhile, the incomprehensible advance of Spanish craftsmanship held Niles' attention. Gradually he noticed something very strange about their oppressive opponent. He scanned her broadside bow to stern. Unsure of his suspicions with the naked eye, he motioned urgently for Kleet to bring his spyglass. Eyepiece focused on Ramolo's decks his observations were confirmed. Nowhere was there a sign of human activity.

"What you plannin' to do, Cap'n?" the mate inquired.

"Keep a close eye until we get a clue on what he's up to," Niles answered. He explained the lack of movement and handed over the glass. "Here, take a look for yourself."

"Personally, I'm for high tailin' out o' here, movement or not."

"Ordinarily I'd agree," Niles frowned, perplexed. "But something over there isn't right. Call it satisfaction of my curiosity, or whatever, I want to stick around a while---follow my hunches."

"I sure hope it's your hunches that get butchered, not our bloody necks, that's all I can say."

"Instruct the helm and lower sail."

They waited.

The hot sun passed its zenith and moved into mid-afternoon heat. Niles lowered the glass and turned to Kleet. "Pass the word for the helm to bring her in close. Prepare to lower a landing craft. I'm going to board her."

Kleet exploded in alarm. "Captain, you gone daft? Only a downright fool would go near that thing!"

"Then call me a fool," Niles calmly replied. "Because I'm going to try. Give the order." The mate barked to his men. "I shall take Toro and you with me---"

"Not me, you're not!" Kleet sputtered with emphasis. "Go ahead. Let those bloody Spaniards slit your throat from ear to ear. Ol' Kleet here isn't ready to commit suicide yet!"

Victoria, who by now joined the pair, spoke. "Kleet's right. This could prove very dangerous. Send a couple of the men instead," she pleaded, praying that he change his mind.

He looked down at her in disdain. "Do you think I'd consider sending my men where I felt it too dangerous to go myself?"

She searched for a logical argument to thwart his intentions. "I beg you, please. If something goes wrong, as you have often said, the *Pearl* will be left without a captain on board."

The memory still burned in his mind of her responses to the mate's flirtations of the past. "Kleet is perfectly capable to take my place, if need be." He did not fail to catch the mate's sly glance in Victoria's direction at the mention of this possibility.

"And what is that supposed to mean?"

"Figure it out yourself, Victoria"

Her eyes flashed with scorn to the first mate. "If he considers himself man enough to be captain, let's see if he's man enough to go in your stead."

"Woman," Kleet held up a defensive hand, "that doesn't take a man, it takes an idiot!"

"Look at him," she jeered, desperate to deter Niles from the venture. "He's too coward to so much as accompany you and you want to leave the *Pearl* in his hands?"

"If Kleet doesn't want to risk his precious neck, Toro and Brog will do just as well." With a practiced eye he measured the distance between the two vessels. "Give the order to lower the landing craft."

"Niles!" Victoria screamed, fearful for his safety.

He silenced her with a steely glare. Wheeling on a heel, he tightened the weapons about his belt and swung over the side. Hand over hand he lowered to the boat. Toro and Brog followed immediately behind.

The hull of the galleon towered overhead as they drew their small craft alongside. Grapple hooks quickly snaked through the air and landed on the main deck overhead. Tested to insure the sharp iron claws held fast, they scaled the ship's side. At the top they leaped over the rail, weapons drawn in readiness for whatever awaited topside. Every muscle tensed, ears alert, their eyes darted about for warnings of movement.

Rigging groaned and creaked with a familiar sound. The repetitious slap, slap of waves lapping against the hull gave no obvious signs of danger. Slowly the trio edged forward. Nervous fingers twitched on weapons. Tension mounted as they searched the entire ship without any encounter of resistance. Niles signaled toward the Captain's Quarters. He darted to flatten himself beside the door, kicked it open and spun inside.

Silence.

Upon Captain Ramolo's ornately carved desk stood an open jug of expensive Spanish wine. Beside the jug waited a partially empty goblet. A glance at the open logbook revealed nothing. The last entry ended in mid-sentence. Perhaps the writer interrupted by an emergency? Toro's eyes rolled about the room; Niles shared the black's uneasiness.

"Toro don't like, Cap'n. Don't like at all. She be spooked. Feel *El Diablo* himself be watchin' our every move. Raise hair on a man's back."

"Forget your people's beliefs in ghosts and spirits. We have a hold to check." Brog and Toro, with no desire to be separated from the other, followed close at his heels. "Watch yourselves, they may wait there to entrap us," he cautioned.

They arrived at the hatch opening and Niles read reluctance on the faces of his two partners. Their hesitation was understandable. The area below the opening was pitch dark. Almost anything may be down there, man or beast. Someone must be first to descend. As their leader, he volunteered. With each successive step down the ladder he fully expected someone, or some thing, to roughly seize him; if not grabbed, at least be the recipient of a blow to smash him into unconsciousness.

Relieved, he felt a boot touch solid surface. Quickly he drew a candle from his coat and lighted the wick. Its flicker cast an eerie glow on the surroundings. Joined by Brog and Toro, they inched forward, candle in hand.

The stench that met their advance constricted their nostrils until they felt they must surely suffocate. Stomachs turned nauseous after the elaborate elegance of topside. Toro sidled close to Niles. Beads of sweat glistened on the black face in the candle glow. Eyes wild with apprehension, he reached out and laid a hard grip on Niles' arm.

"Cap'n, you no want go more," he rasped in a whisper. "There be things ahead no man want see, 'cept maybe Spaniard."

Niles halted in step. "What sort of things, Toro?"

"Toro think be slave ship, Cap'n. Toro be on one 'fore. No good see. We go back now?"

"Not until we're certain there's no one here."

"Cap'n be sorry. No one here. Be ghost ship, like we hear tell. We leave 'fore it git us, too."

"If anything was here it's gone now, so there's nothing to fear."

"That's what you say," Brog spoke quietly from behind. "Anything as unnatural as this, nothing would surprise me."

"Don't you get spooked and freeze up on me, too. Come on, let's see what they've got down here."

Senses attuned for instant action, they cautiously crept forward. At first they passed stacks of kegs, crates and bales. These soon gave way to slatted wooden racks built closely together in tiers. The candle flame began to sputter as if it coughed for oxygen. Here the foulness increased in intensity. Repulsively putrid, it stimulated uncontrollable retching among the three intruders. Somewhat recovered they probed onward.

Attached to head and foot of each narrow slatted space they found heavy chains attached to iron shackles securely locked in a closed position. Niles moved the candle closer and touched one of the restraints. The iron band revealed fresh wet blood. Human flesh had recently wrested here in an agonized struggle for freedom. At sight of the blood on his hand, his insides boiled and churned. Again he doubled over in a seizure of retching until his stomach contracted in misery.

A sound reached his ear. He whirled about, weapons drawn in readiness, only to see a large rat scurry from where it had been feeding on a pair of shackles. His hands went limp. They no longer possessed the strength to hold his weapons. Toro's hand laid a firm grip on Niles' shoulder. "You go now, Cap'n. Toro warn not good see." A short distance away Brog also succumbed to the wretchedness.

Operations of the galleon verified, the trio retraced their steps and ascended to the clean air of topside. They leaned weakly against cannon carriages and rail. No one spoke. There were no words to express how each man felt. Strength regained, they oared back to the *Pearl.*

A shout rose upon their safe arrival. The crew, anxious to hear what they found, clustered around.

"Well?" Kleet pressed, as he nervously danced from one foot to the other. "What happened?"

"Not a thing," Niles muttered. Head lowered, he turned away. "As Toro surmised, she's a ghost ship. No one on board"

Activated by greed, the first mate glowed with excitement. Here was a prospect to confiscate booty and enrich his purse. He clawed at Niles' arm to detain him. "We gotta transfer her cargo. A ship that regal must have a wealth in her hold. Maybe gold!" Niles shook the hand away with an icy glare of contempt.

Kleet, bewildered by the action, temper

on the rise, demanded, "You mean to say we leave it untouched? It's our chance to get rich!" Niles did not reply. Flustered by his stance, the mate sputtered, "The Gods have handed us this treasure on a silver platter. Only a fool would pass it up!"

Hesitating in stride, Niles turned on the mate. "We leave it to the Gods, or whatever. Do I make myself clear?"

"You're crazy!" Kleet ranted and stomped the deck. "The crew wants their share of the take!"

"What you mean is, you want your share," Niles coldly eyed him. "No one is to board her. You want to act like a thieving pirate? Then sign on with a different ship when we reach port. Now give the order to unfurl sail and get under way."

"I say---"

"The subject is closed!" Niles wheeled to enter his quarters.

To his own mind, his clothing reeked of exposure to the stench. He washed and scrubbed until his skin was red and nearly raw, yet his flesh felt like it was covered with crawling vermin. It seemed the putrid filth could never be cleansed away. The odiferous foulness could still be felt burning in his nostrils. Nausea accompanied the vile taste in his mouth. Contemptible contamination permeated the very depth of his physical being. Deep in his soul he knew no amount of soap and water would ever purge the repulsive memory from his brain. This experience was something he would carry with him forever.

He cast away the exposed clothes and pulled on fresh ones. Profoundly shaken by the entire ordeal he drew out a bottle of Madeira. About to tip a large goblet to his lips he heard Victoria's soft rap and saw the expectant face.

"I don't want to talk about it---now or ever. He downed the glass, poured another and turned from her. Normally he sipped wine slowly, savored the flavor. Today he drank of it quickly and returned to the deck. Clean sea air struck him full face. He took a deep inhalation in an attempt to expel the dormant rankness that still remained in his lungs.

Mind cleared, he sought the galleon. It had vanished as mystically as it first appeared. Relieved, he took another deep breath. No desire remained to see either Ramolo or the majestic galleon again.

The gentle undulation of waves held his attention while he cogitated on the incomprehensible revelation of the past hours. How could his boyhood friend, commander of so magnificent a vessel, condescend to such depths? Why stoop so low as to be involved in the inhumane commerce of the slave trade?

Standing before the confident Ramolo, so grand, so superior, he was envious. Now he felt only pity for the man's soul. Ramolo sailed under the flag of Spain, he reminded himself. Perhaps they left him no choice other than to obey his superior. That consideration in mind, Niles somewhat forgave the man he once regarded as a friend. So much for Ramolo, he told himself, it's time to focus my attention on *The Sea Pearl* and her safe arrival at Port Royal, Jamaica.

CHAPTER THIRTEEN

The crew of the *Sea Pearl* was in high spirits. Bathed in warm sunshine, the ship skimmed smoothly through the water. They neared the Windward Passage, where many small islands could be seen. Already the lookouts sighted several ships headed toward Hispaniola. Their presence raised no cause for alarm. Flags of many countries, friends and foes, flew atop the masts of vessels that frequented these waters. The Spanish, for the most part, went to great lengths in their efforts to dominate the entire Main region. *The Sea Pearl,* interested neither in attacking nor being attacked, prudently maneuvered a course to avoid direct encounters.

Having survived the many perils of this voyage, the familiar sub-tropical climate warmed the hearts of the men who manned her. However, within a few days it became insufferably hot. Their only recourse from the scorching sun and stifling humidity was a shady spot. Scantily clad, bodies wet with perspiration, they relished the relief brought by any cool air wafting in from the sea.

For the present, it was springtime, beautiful and exhilarating to the soul. They sang as they worked. Splashed in the crystal blue waters alongside the slow moving ship. Or stretched themselves on the decks. There they lay basking in the sun, soaking up its vigor restoring warmth.

Between duties as captain, Niles, joined by Victoria, lolled sleepily under the clear skies. On these occasions, he shared with her the names of islands they passed. And in answer to her many questions, ventured bits of information with regard to the inhabitants, and colorful histories. The scream of gulls, warmth, and gentle monotony of the rhythmic roll of the deck often lulled them into blissful slumber. Each found inner peace within the presence of the other, and their intimate closeness.

Victoria's interest in this new world heightened. She was filled with child-like wonder and enthusiasm. Day by day, she begged him to tell more about this area, his world since childhood.

"Excuse me," she interrupted his historical summarization. "A moment ago you said something I don't quite understand. Aside from slave labor, the island of Jamaica is progressive and peaceful under English rule. Why then do they tolerate boucaners and pirate ships in their ports?"

Aware of her previous strong belief in the integrity of her native England, this question evoked a rueful laugh from Niles. England, as with many other countries, did not always approach matters from a right and wrong perspective. Would she take offense to his answer? Surely not after the tales she heard the crew tell throughout the voyage. In recent days the sight of foreign ships and exotic ports brought excitement to her eyes. The *Pearl* was past Hispaniola, and already her mind raced ahead to Port Royal.

"The answer is rather long and complicated," he began. I'll try to explain without going into complete detail. Basically, English defenses were weak when they first took over the island. They were quick to recognize well armed boucan and privateer ships in their harbors proved an advantage. The ships provided a barrier of protection against retaliation by the Spaniards.

"Landowners wisely view them as a free Navy. Therefore, they chose to be tolerant. They cater to their raucous whims in exchange for this security. Call it a mutual agreement for the benefit of all, if you like. The English need additional defense; the ships need a port of safety."

Not content, she pressured him to elaborate on the present operation of the island defenses. "England has provided six strong forts ringed around Port Royal. Between them, they share a total of over 300 cannon," he assured. "The forts are staffed with several hundred troops. In addition, there's a reinforcement of 2,200 militiamen.

"You must understand, at least 8,000 people, of mixed descent, regard Jamaica as their home. The majority is English, but we also have Scots, Jews, Irish, and even a few Spaniards. Also, there are over 3,000 slaves spread throughout the plantations. And that's not counting the constant flow of visitors. Their numbers, determined by the season and activity at the time, range between 500 to 2,000."

Victoria stretched in the sunlight. "After all the stories I heard, I was more than a little apprehensive about my safety in your port. I'm glad you put some of those worries to rest. One more question. If it's so heavily populated now, why do they still tolerate pirates?"

"Make no mistake, even in the present, Port Royal can be a very dangerous place," he warned. "The tolerance part is difficult to explain clearly. This is 1692. Under their new laws the courts have begun to impose sentences of hanging or extradition. This brings about some reduction of piracy activity. But a number of buccaneers remain advantageous to the island. Therefore, the authorities have no desire to bar them entirely."

Her brow furrowed in concentration while she tried to understand. "If they, as you say, have their own forts and cannon, how can pirates be an advantage?"

A slow smile of amusement crept across his face. "It's a bit of a ruse and a rather clever one at that. The officials came up with the idea to classify the pirate ships as part of their Unofficial Navy. As such, they issued them Letters of Marque. They're papers to clarify they have received permission to attack enemy ships, principally those of Spain.

"Since then, the practice has been disbanded; but it served to start legalized attacks. The pirates bring their plunder into Port Royal. Shopkeepers and English merchants are quick to fatten their pockets off this enterprise. Also, bear in mind, the pirates spend their share of the booty while in port. So the establishments profit twofold. Does that explain why they are welcomed?" Victoria nodded, fascinated, as he continued.

"Always fast to grasp the opportunity of easy money, taverners began to finance the purchase of ships. They turned the operation of those ships over to the pirates. While pirates suffer the bodily risks, owners simply sit back and rake in profits from the booty. On top of that, his investment is secured by the indebtedness of the pirates. By the time the pirates set sail again, they need to win an attack to pay off their port debts. The cycle, once set in motion, feeds upon itself. Quite a shrewd, comical scheme on the part of the English, wouldn't you say?

"That's not the only manner in which the English profit. The King's Officers are first to board each ship as it comes in. The captain presents a cargo list. The Officers collect ten percent of the cargo value for the Treasury. Creditors come next in line to strip their due from the crew. Only then are buyers allowed on board.

"After the remaining cargo sale the money is divided between the men. They rush ashore and spend their moneys directly back into the hands of the buyers." Victoria laughed, amused by this circuitous operation.

Niles did not mind answering her many questions. But as they drew nearer to Port Royal he became increasingly disturbed by her ecstatic anticipation. The subdued, poised lady displayed a flippant, venturous attitude. She was consumed with excitement to see for herself the many things of which she heard. This was a new fire that must be quenched before they reached port. If not, her innocence would immediately be recognized by unsavory waterfront rabble. Caught alone, without a man to protect her honor, could prove very disastrous.

He tried to disillusion her fantasies, only to be met by renewed rainbows in her eyes. As captain, he would be busy when they first entered port. There would be no time for him to concentrate on her security. Toro, who up to now kept a watchful eye, was also needed to handle the cargo auction.

Farther south they entered heavier ship traffic. The lookouts were increased. They had orders to give the alarm if any ships approached in a suspicious manner. The remainder of the crew was placed on alert. With so many vessels in close proximity there would be little time for preparation if an enemy suddenly turned hostile.

The increased heat and humidity added to already tensed nerves. After such an extended treacherous voyage the men were irritated by impatience. Everyone aboard was eager to get home. Tempers were ready to flare over the slightest inconsequential incident. This presented a dangerous atmosphere. To move about the decks was like treading on a powder keg with a short fuse.

Two days out of port the first gray signs

of restlessness stirred within Niles. He stopped to look up at the billow of the canvases. Strange, he thought, not even the sea breezes seemed to blow in a normal fashion.

One day out of port, he stepped onto the main deck. The sound of Victoria's laughter drifted to him. At the far end she listened in rapt attention to Kleet's animated revelations. Feigning checking a ratline near the couple, Niles watched and turned an ear to their conversation. The first mate, in his own suave characteristic manner, held her attention by extolling the wonders and virtues of Port Royal. As usual, he was preoccupied with spinning a web with his flamboyant tongue, dangling a string of false promises before the lady. Her visible excitement revealed the facts all too clearly. His questionable intentions were succeeding in penetrating her innocence.

Irritated, Niles tore the sweaty shirt from his sun-bronzed torso. It landed across a coil of thick rope beside his feet. The morning sun fired the jewels of the exposed medallion as he brushed a damp lock from his forehead. With a chunk of boot heels to announce his approach he intentionally, yet casually, advanced. Kleet glanced briefly in his direction, then quickly excused himself from the lady and slithered away. Niles leaned against the rail a short distance from Victoria. The intrusion brought a flash of hostility to her eyes.

"Enjoy Kleet's wild tales?" he inquired.

With an indignant toss of her head, she retorted, "I'd have you know I find everything he says very interesting."

"It is," he nodded, "except he doesn't tell the whole truth."

"I swear, Captain Brett, I cannot understand your constant objections to Kleet. As for me, I can't wait to see all the wonders he's spoken of. Not only things he has said, but also what the entire crew, right down to you, have talked about."

"Fine, but there's something else you must bear in mind. Port Royal is home to us. Occasionally we get a little carried away in our enthusiasm. After all, the familiar is nostalgic for us. To some it means a return to home and family. At such times people tend to speak of the good. They forget to mention the ugly."

"I fail to see how any place that flows with all the riches of the world: precious jewels, pearls and gold in pockets can be regarded as ugly."

"True, true," he continued to nod with calm patience. "Except, that is only half the picture."

"Do you imply, Captain, you were lying?"

"No, it's true. You'll see pearls like you never imagined. They're bartered across the board by the basketsful; and jewels of which dreams are made. Put those together with gold, silver, carved ivory, and many other commodities of priceless value. However, there's also a sordid side. Riches and greed draw ugliness like a magnet. The more beautiful and priceless, the more ugliness and greed surrounds it."

"Nothing can be both beautiful and ugly at the same time," she sniffed. "As for me, I'll be more than glad to escape the confinement of this horrible ship. Soon as I'm free of it I want to take off on my own and explore this fantastic place. Blast you and your silly cautions. Once we hit port, Captain, you no longer have anything to say about what I do!"

"You are still my passenger."
"Not in port."
"If we reach port, that is."

She whirled and glared. "What is that remark supposed to mean?"

Calmly he tilted his head back to face up to the sails. They had begun to go limp in the dying wind. "Take a look for yourself. Normally this early in the season there is ample wind to carry us in with no problem. It's too still, too humid, too hot, too everything for this time of year. This is strange, highly unusual. I don't like it. I don't like it one bit." He watched a moment longer, then added hopefully, "If we keep her like she is we'll make it. Inasmuch as if that wind subsides any more it might be days or weeks."

"Weeks!" she cried out in despair. "You said we'd dock tomorrow."

He gave a careless shrug of one bare shoulder. "I only control a ship; God controls winds."

With a toss of her head she spun on a heel to retreat, slamming the door of the cabin behind her. Within its stifling confines she remained pouting until late in the day. Not a single cloud drifted across the sky. No promise of rain to lend momentary relief to earth and sea below. The sails appeared to gasp for air, along with the shirtless crew that toiled below. Heat sapped their energies. They moved slowly as they performed the necessary preparations for the auction.

Finally Niles looked at the heat exhausted crew and called out. "It's too unseasonably hot. We'll stop and resume after the sun drops over the horizon. No use to sweat blood."

The men worked late into the night aided by the thin light cast by the ship's lanterns. Darkness brought small respite. The air remained heavy and hot, bodies dripped sweat, tempers rasped.

The men grumbled under their breaths on how they had never seen such heat so early in the year. Niles expressed the possibility they only noticed it more after their experience in cold northern waters, but he knew better. They all retired after a swim in the moonlight to wash away the grime. All except Kleet, that is. Niles combed his hair neatly into place and entered his quarters, only to meet Victoria as she prepared to leave. "And where are you going in such a hurry?" he asked.

"Ashore with Kleet."
"No, you are not."

"You have no more control of me and from now on I can do as I please,"
She spat back as she passed through the doorway.

"You'll be sorry!"

"Let me be the judge of that," she called back over her shoulder.

He turned away rather than watch her court disaster. Nicole---if only he could contact

Nicole. News traveled fast as a barracuda along the waterfront, but Nicole was accustomed to the sound of *The Sea Pearl*'s old familiar bell. She would doubt the authenticity of the rumors if anyone said the *Pearl* was in port.

Nor could she possibly know about Victoria unless Kleet, belly filled with rotgut, started to spill his mouth. That in itself might evoke more trouble.

Niles' hope lay in Nicole, shrewd woman that she was. Perhaps she would grasp the situation. Send one of her messengers? No, her operations and movements commanded too much attention in port. She dared not risk reckless chances on her emissary being seen and thereby reveal a connection with *The Sea Pearl.*

Neither could Niles go ashore at this time. His appearance could arouse suspicion among her jealous competitors. They would like nothing better than to discover her methods of retaining wealth and power. He paced the floor while minutes became hours. Imaginary visions began to race through his disturbed thoughts.

He stepped out onto the deck to escape the mental torture. Nighttime shadows wound their fingers through the rigging. A mixture of yellow lamplight and ochre-gray dust could be seen to port. The trample of feet, rumble of carts and general confusion of the overly crowded waterfront hung in the stagnant unshifting air. He was all too familiar with the dust, filth and odors that accompanied the throng. A repulsive mass of humanity shoved and staggered over there in the night. The Port Royal waterfront was always a chorus of shouts, curses, carousing, fights---a bawdy cauldron of evils.

Niles was never attracted to the decadence, scum and corruption of the place. He was filled with revulsion by the very things that exhilarated other seamen and pirates. It brought on a choking, smothering sensation, which always compelled him to break free to breathe the open air of sea or backlands. He saw beneath the gaudy facade, resented the greed of people who filled their pockets at the expense of the ignorant or less fortunate. The skullduggery, cruelty, and plotting rubbed against his own honorable principles.

To others Nicole seemed no better than the rest. In her establishment patrons were kept occupied and happy with games of sin and immorality. She fleeced their pockets, given the opportunity, to the last gold piece. Niles, however, knew a side of her other than the surface veneer; her perceptions on life flowed much deeper than visible to a stranger. This was the private person Niles respected and loved.

With the exception of Captain Leyden and himself, few others were allowed into her chambers. She was not one to drop her pearls before every pig that drooled pretty words and promises at her feet. She needed none of their selfish advances.

From his vantage point on the ship he watched the street slowly come alive with night people who crawled from their holes to shuffle and jostle among the pandemonium, each in seek of their own vices.

Beggars pleaded for pittances with hands that shook, eager for coins to buy another swallow of Dill Devil for their already burned out insides.

Whores coiled their venomous serpentine charms about their victims. The young, half naked as yet sensually gifted bodies, curled themselves around sex starved men fresh from the sea. Their feminine curves and eyes signaled, follow me, follow me.

Middle-aged female solicitors, oppressed and diseased, waited in pretentious rags and paint; women who, to survive, accepted the rejected leavings of their younger sisters of sin. Men, for lack of sustenance, frequented garbage laden alleys and shadows.

He did not need to see beyond the open

lighted doorways to imagine the activities within. His nostrils knew all too well the smell of smoke and stench of closely packed sweaty unbathed bodies. Liquors passed, slopped and tossed, cast their bittersweet scent to his olfactory senses. The clamor reached his ears interlaced with indiscernible music, scarcely heard above the stomp of boots. To the left he heard the sick mushy sound of a fist strike against flesh, an action taken to settle a drunken disagreement or simply for satisfaction.

Somewhere the tinkle of fine glass was drowned by a loud thud of heavy pewter tankard slammed for emphasis upon a heavy plank table or bar. In the shadows a knife flashed, warm red blood flowed unchecked, a body slowly slumped downward, come morning it would be hauled away unmourned. Life came cheap in the richest pirate port in the world.

Niles knew Kleet was in one of those taverns, or staggered an errant route somewhere in the shadows. Niles' heart pounded with concern for Victoria's safety, abandoned and alone amid that savagery. Kleet, mind on his share of the auction, would head straight for the nearest alehouse. Standing there, Niles could visualize the scene. Kleet, to impress Victoria, would first gallantly order the finest Madeira wine and relish its rich flavor as it trickled down his throat. Up to this point she was safe, except Kleet's interest always changed. To stretch his purse he invariably switched to cheaper rum punch, one day destined to die of its lethal poisons as so many others before him. After searing his brain with Dill Devil Victoria would only become something for his envious counterparts to feast their eyes on, while he took drunken pleasure in gloating over their discomforts.

Before long, blood heated to a fever by the rotten Dill Devil, he always disappeared in the nearest cheap brothel of disease, there to wallow among a bevy of jaded whores. And what of Victoria? Was she at this very moment being accosted, propositioned, attacked over there among the throng that overflowed the cobblestone roadways and dark recesses?

It was common knowledge any woman who entered those streets unaccompanied after dark, could be bought for a price. Where could she turn, abandoned, innocent of waterfront survival?

With a low groan Niles forced himself to turn away and return to the isolation of his quarters. He waited through the agonized hours, reminding himself over and over it was her own choice. He tried to warn her. No amount of rationalization, however, served to ease his tormented mind.

The small cabin became like a cell, the

ship a dungeon. Pride restricted him from rushing to throw himself between her and the lechers. Bottle of Madeira in hand, he wanted to curse the *Pearl,* curse himself, curse the heavy responsibility of being a captain. He sank into his chair and sipped the liquor amid the profound stillness of the room, where the very walls radiated her absence.

His mind began to race into the future. He imagined casting off from the Colonies, never again to see or know her presence. Could his heart turn back to sea with the same contentment he knew before she entered his life? Throat constricted, he poured another drink. Caught up within his own misery, his mind ignored noises on the main deck. He stared into the crystal goblet and as he lifted it to his lips the door to his quarters suddenly opened.

His hand arrested midway, the crystal goblet slipped from his fingers and with a shout he leaped toward the disheveled figure.

"Victoria!"

Her captors half shoved, half carried her into the room. Tears streaked down her dusty face as she struggled to break free. Her hair was in matted tangles, the elegant coral organdy and lace gown torn and soiled. At the sound of his voice her terrified eyes sought him out.

"Niles!" she wailed, additional tears forming rivulets through the grime on her cheeks. She threw herself forward to fiercely cling to him.

"It's all right, my love," he soothed, protective arms about her trembling body.

"These men---they grabbed me---" she wildly stammered. "Help me, Niles! They're animals, same as all those others in the street. Please, Niles, help me!"

He held her close, stroked the disheveled hair and signaled with a nod to the two men. "You're safe now, Victoria. No one here will harm you."

A brown hooded head shook sadly beside Toro. "Poor child," the slight built, brown cowl robed man spoke softly. "She's been frightened out of her sense by the vermin over there. Come, let's help her to lie down."

"No!" she shrilly screamed. "Keep them away; don't let them touch me!"

"Victoria, listen to me. They are friends. Why else did they bring you to me?" Niles reasoned. He lifted her in his arms, laid her on the bed, and gently rested her head against the pillow. Her hands clawed at his shirt, pulled him to her, refusing to let go.

The compassionate face within the hooded threadbare robe wisely remained beside Toro. Niles tried to calm her hysteria. "Victoria, don't be frightened. You are safe. I want you to look at these men---"

"No!" she cried in terror, and buried her head deeper against his chest. "Make those horrible brutes go away!"

"Victoria, you were too frightened to recognize him in the dark on deck. Look at him here in the light. Then you won't be afraid anymore, I promise." Chin in hand, he forced the reluctant head to face the men.

Victoria gasped. "Toro! I'm sorry---I didn't know---"

"It be all right, Missy," the woolly head tipped in acknowledgment. "You was fightin' Padre when he bring. Toro no make you hear name. He only think to get you to captain. Sorry, Missy, if Toro little rough---"

"Oh no, Toro," she breathed in relief. "You---you are beautiful."

The black chuckled, white teeth gleaming in the ebony face.

"Missy so scared she not know she talk 'bout. Ain't nobody call Toro beautiful 'fore."

Her eyes moved to the sleazy faded brown robe and placid silent face of the man alongside. "Who---who is he?"

"That admirable man," Niles smiled up at his friend, "is Padre Jose. Some say the angels direct his feet to those in trouble. Angels or not, he has a way of always being there to hold out a hand of help."

Confusion crossed her face. "But if he wears the collar, how could he strike the man who attempted to violate me---I mean---a priest doesn't hit people---do they?"

"Let's say Padre Jose is a slightly unconventional priest," Niles answered, with an ironic lift to one eyebrow. "Sometimes he finds the Good Book needs a little assistance in persuasion."

"In the darkness I thought him another of those---those awful beasts attacking me." To the padre, she added, "I truly am grateful. So sorry---I didn't know---"

The hooded head nodded and the voice that came from it was soft and gentle. "I understand, Child."

Toro entered with a pan of water and offered a wet cloth to Niles. He touched it carefully against her scratched forehead. "I'm a mess," she wailed and again began to sob. "Niles, why did you let me go to such a vile place?"

"I had no power to stop you, remember?"

"Still, you can't deny the crew and even you, deceived me with your tales. You all claimed this was such a wonderful island. It---it's horrible! Lies, all lies! I hate you for that, Captain Brett!"

"Here, better give me the basin, Niles," Padre Jose intervened. "Leave me to speak a while with the lady. Meanwhile, you sit down, light your pipe and relax. This night has been a bad experience. She didn't mean what she said. Everything will be all right in the morning. Dawn always paints a fresh face on this ugly world. Shoo, go along with you now." He motioned Niles and Toro out and quietly closed the door of the small cubicle.

Niles drew another goblet, poured the measured mixture of water and Madeira and offered it to Toro. The big black smiled broadly at the rare prospect. The two waited, seated in the massive chairs. Padre Jose's voice could be heard murmuring indiscernible words on the other side of the thin wall until late into the night.

Niles touched a lucifer to the tip of an expensive cigar and offered one to the black. "Didn't you tell me you once had a woman in port?"

"Aye, Cap'n," the black sadly nodded. "She not have Padre to help when need. No have anyone. My master sent me to fields. I back too late to protect."

Niles, familiar with the life forced upon island slaves, needed no further explanations. Nor did he care to put the man through the torment of remembrance.

"It all right," Toro said, after a long reflective silence. "We have our time." He continued, large eyes distant in thought. "Like I tell before, Cap'n. There be rewards when take life, live while have before too late. My woman, me, we did that. No regret. Now you, Missy Victoria---"

Padre Jose tiptoed from the cubicle, silently closed the door and motioned the men to remain seated. "She'll sleep now. A bit restless, perhaps, if nightmares choose to cross her eyes, but," he nodded in satisfaction, she will sleep. That's the best thing for her right now."

"Madeira, Padre?" Niles offered.

"Don't mind if I do," the priest replied with a tired smile. "No, no, don't get up. I shall help myself. I know where the glasses are. When Captain Leyden was yet with us, many's the time we shared a nip in this room."

"You heard?"

"Yes, rest his soul. He was a good man," padre nodded and mixed his wine. "News, as you well know, travels fast through the waterfront. One hears everything almost before it happens, if they sit quiet, ears open." He took a sip of the drink and smacked his lips.

"Your arrival is much later than we expected. When Doubleface dropped anchor he boasted you'd gone down in the Lost Ships area. We'd about given up hope, let me tell you. Mighty relieved when I heard you'd been sighted in the harbor."

He helped himself to a cigar from the wooden box, leaned back in one of the chairs and watched with pleasure as the grey-blue smoke rose in the air. "You'll be interested in the devilry astir in Doubleface's brain."

"Which is?"

Padre shook his head, pushed the cowl hood farther back and revealed his thin drawn face. "Only little dribbles here and there to make these ears wiggle for more. I have nothing positive to relay to you right now. Nicole may know more. It's been too risky to contact her with so many adrift in port lately. I do know you best be on the watch."

He blew a couple of smoke rings, amused himself as they rose in the air and withdrew into deep thought. "I'm amazed you were able to limp into port. Been weeks since any vessel captured sufficient wind to carry her in or out to sea. And it's hot." He wiped across his brow with one loosely fitted sleeve. "Positively insufferable. Has everyone on edge. The entire island is shrouded in an eerie, ominous atmosphere. Downright spooky. You'll see what I mean when you come ashore."

"All this information, as usual, is important to me, however, Victoria is foremost on my mind. I sense you're avoiding the subject on what happened tonight."

"First, Niles, let me ask a question. What does this young lady mean to you?"

"She's a passenger bound for the Colonies."

The priest pursed his lips a long moment. "I think more. Be that as it may, there's not a thing to worry about, my son. She will be all right; a trifle roughed up, but no real harm done."

He paused to refill the glass and proceeded to explain. "Found her hemmed in and knocked down by some---well, you know the sort I mean. I immediately recognized her as a woman of class and knew something was amiss. She cried out your name and I put two and two together."

"See anything of Kleet?"

"No," the thin mouth spread into a slow ironic smile. "I'm rarely invited into the places he frequents this time of night." He turned to focus his attention on Toro and chortled. "Well, Boy, by the looks of that glass and the fat cigar in your hands, your new captain must surely beat you to death."

Niles rose to stare idly out the small porthole. "She's going to hate me after tonight," he muttered in a half whisper, more to himself than the other occupants of the room.

"Hate you? Of course not," Padre discounted his fears. "Maybe someday, my lad, but not for what happened over there. If she hates your stubborn hide for another reason---but that's conversation for another day," he craftily closed the subject.

"It's time I get back ashore to help my sheep. I may be on time to reach some poor soul, robbed of purse, slumped in shadow, victim of another dagger. The least I can do is bend over him and offer consolation to his last breaths: remind him of the promise of our loving God; convince him angels watch over us, then watch the lifeblood flow from his body to seep between the cobblestones."

The robed figure stared sadly at the floor and emitted a heavy sigh. "I've lived to see too many suffer. Each time I beg the Master to call me home in their stead."

Abruptly he stirred. "Well, I must be on my way. No," he motioned, "no need to see me off in my leaky little rowboat. I can find my own way over the side. See you again on shore, Niles."

In the doorway he paused, turned and added, "Take care of our little lady. She's one jewel worth keeping, Niles. As for tonight, don't blame her too harshly. She only defied you in an attempt to gain your attention. It wasn't Kleet's company she craved." With a knowing wink he silently disappeared into the darkness of the main deck.

Toro strode off to the crew quarters. Niles, too restless to relax, eased the door to the cubicle with a sense of guilt. This was not meant as an invasion of her privacy; it was an act of genuine concern for her welfare. To his surprise he found her in peaceful slumber. Her face, shoulders and arms were bathed clean. The freshly brushed hair flowed across the white pillow. He shook his head and smiled.

Padre always managed to perform miracles with soft words and gentle hands. Satisfied she slept like an innocent child he stretched out on his own bunk.

CHAPTER FOURTEEN

Victoria emerged, voice meek. "I'll take morning meal with you, Captain, if you don't mind."

"Mind?" he glanced up briefly from his bowl. "Of course not. Good to have you back."

"Not only am I back, what's more, I intend to stay right here until we sail again. Wild horses couldn't drag me to set foot on that vile piece of ground again! There are no fit words to express my opinion of the despicable place."

"You can't judge the entire island by what you saw last night."

"If you don't mind, I prefer not to discuss it."

"Bear in mind," Niles replied, voice calm, "you saw Kleet's view of the island---"

"I said, I don't want to discuss it!"

"Calm down, Victoria. You will hear me out, like it or not. What happened was of your own undoing---"

"Oh, spare me the lecture, Captain," she snapped, a sarcastic twist to her lovely mouth. "It's not necessary to say, 'I told you so'. After what I saw they are all filthy animals!"

"Granted. But one cannot look at a few pebbles and judge an entire island. Later in the day, when I go ashore, you are going with me."

"Never!"

"You will," he ordered. "Either bound up in a canvas bag or as a dignified lady on a captain's arm; take your choice." He shoved back his chair and stomped out the door.

The first shift straggled back to *The Sea Pearl* after the sun ascended to its zenith. Niles buttoned his shirt woven of the finest silk available along the Main; its gathered sleeves billowed to end in gathered lace at the wrist. At the partially open front the jeweled medallion lay exposed against the tanned chest. The rustle of Victoria's full skirts brought him around.

Her eyes rested on the weapons at his

sides. Not the same as worn for the Lost Ships party, but equal in quality and command of respect. Slender daggers, blades honed to deadly perfection, quivered with anticipation as he breathed. A matched brace of Spanish *pistolas* jutted from a thick leather belt, its etched gold buckle gleaming above loose pants that extended into mirror shined cuffed boots. Wide gold bands incrusted with perfectly matched jewels encircled his wrists, their facets playing with the light as he advanced toward her.

He observed her high necked puritanical attire and shook his head in disapproval. "Too hot," he frowned. Discarding the concealing shawl, he loosened the neckline of the gown and draped it to bare her shoulders. "Add a pretty hat with a wide brim, top it off with one of the sun parasols I bought for you and you'll be more comfortable."

"I dare not go ashore like this!" she sputtered. "Last night---"

"Last night you were with Kleet," he admonished, hands on the bared shoulders to hold her undivided attention. "Today it is I who shall escort you. There's a difference, as you shall see." Under his steady gaze the eyes that lowered again stirred him with desire to take her into his arms. No, he told himself, not until her resentment has mellowed. Better to wait until she makes the first move. "Are you ready?" She nodded assent.

He stopped to open his closet door and her face registered surprise. The space formerly occupied by the forbidden red gown was now empty. While she speculated on this, she saw him retrieve a tiny box from the shelf and withdraw a gold locket. Her heart leaped with the prospect of the glittery trinket. Curiosity, however, met with disappointment when he let it slide into his pocket without an explanation.

"I'm starved," he exclaimed, when they alighted on the shore. "Therefore, I suggest we indulge in a change from Cleve's culinary arts. We'll stop for lunch before going any farther." He took her hand and smiled when she cringed with apprehension. "Come, you'll enjoy it," he coaxed. They walked along the shoreline where pens extended from the sandy beach into the water. Suddenly he heard a gasp and felt her tug against his arm.

"What are those horrible things wallowing around out there?"

He laughed. "Your dinner, Princess."
"Not mine!"

"You are about to partake a feast like you have never eaten before. You see, they keep the giant sea turtles in the water until time for slaughter. That way the meat is always fresh for the tables."

"Ugh!" she grimaced. "You expect me to eat those?"

Seated in the cool shade of a small dining room that overlooked the sea, he expressed their desires to an impeccable waiter. Almost immediately the man returned with platters heaped high. Niles watched as his guest gingerly tasted a small bite.

"Delicious, but what is it?" she asked.

"This main platter features sea turtle, parrot, lobster, crab, and fish bits. The food in this establishment is prepared to perfection. The chefs use the finest herbs and spices found along the Main."

"I must admit, everything is very tasty." Her eyes roved over the picturesque interior with appreciation. "And the atmosphere is so dignified. I never imagined such places existed here."

"There are many respectable businesses on the island. It was your misfortune to see only the bad ones last night."

"That's what Padre Jose said."

"What else did he say?" he asked, curious what the murmurs were of the night before.

"Whatever one discusses with a priest is confidential," she evaded and changed the subject. "I do believe I would like a little more wine."

Prepared to leave he tossed a small pouch to a short rotund man, who deftly caught it in one hand while he mopped his forehead with an oversized handkerchief. Immaculate in white linen shirt he smiled broadly in recognition and clasped Niles' hand with enthusiasm.

"Great to see you made it safely home! I must say though, with the heat like its been you were better off at sea." He paused to mop the fleshy brow again and continued. "Never seen anything like it. All winter nary a drop of rain. Then all of a sudden in May all heaven opened up. Like to have flooded us all right out into the drink. Now the heat is so stifling night and day one can hardly breathe."

Warmed to his subject he waved his arms. The heavy jowls quivered as he added with disgust, "The rain brought out the danged bugs. They've spread malaria and fevers all over the place. As you well know, the so-called physicians here are nothing but fakes, like everything else here on the spit. Quacks, every last one.

"As for the port, it hasn't changed while you've been gone. Still overflows with the same rabble scum. Moreso since many can't get back out to sea until we get some wind." Irritation vented from his system he sobered, voice lowered in sadness. "Sorry to hear about Captain Leyden. He was a right good man. One of the best on the Main."

"That he was," Niles agreed. "You may like to know he died in peace."

"That's good," the proprietor sympathized, jowls shaking.

Niles diverted the topic of discussion. "Aren't you going to check whether my pouch covers our meal?"

"No need," the proprietor shook his head. "Captain Leyden nor you ever cheated me yet; I'm sure you'll not start now." He gripped Niles' hand firmly between his own sweaty fat ones. "Let me offer my best wishes to the new captain. I know you'll handle *The Sea Pearl* as honorably as he did. She couldn't have passed into better hands, Captain Brett." Tears of sincerity glistened in his round eyes. "If God wills, I'll see you again before you leave port."

Out on the street Niles bartered with a passing owner for the rental of a carriage. After he assisted Victoria onto the seat, he took the reins. "Now, my fair lady, I'll show you what our island is really like. First though, we must stop at the King's Warehouse. All passengers must sign in or be subject to immediate arrest. Count yourself lucky. It's a wonder you weren't tossed into the Birdwell women's prison last night. That would have meant an appearance before the magistrate for judgment this morning." Her face paled.

Registry completed, they proceeded through the narrow cobblestone streets. Enroute they passed gaudy colored shops that fairly clamored over one another competing for space. Each strained to reach into the street to lure the pockets of incoming seamen through their doors.

They saw fishermen at work on small boats off the western end of the cay, fishermen who also stole eggs from the seasonal sea turtle layings, given the opportunity. Along Fishers Row venders bartered their many varieties of fresh fish, lobsters, crab, turtles, sweet manatee flesh and highly prized delicacy of parrot. The prices were exorbitant, as was everything sold in Port Royal.

Entering a busy thoroughfare their carriage was soon surrounded by a surging throng. Merchants, smugglers and pirates pushed shoulder to shoulder. Each was intent on a quick ruse to fill his purse or to exchange booty garnered from points along the Main.

All manner of merchandise acquired from Tortuga, Santa Marta, Curacao and down the coastline of South America was readily available.

From the west came rare treasures acquired through raids deep into Central America and southward to Puerto Ballo and Columbia. Bars and cakes of gold, wedges and pigs of pure silver, wrought stolen plate, precious gems, natural pearls by the basketful and gold dust changed hands. Here was found an amassed conglomeration of the rare, the beautiful and the valuable; most of which had been ravaged through the bloodshed of less fortunate victims of the oppressors.

Gold coins and treasures flowed like rich red wine overflowing the cup. The populace panted and shoved, faces flushed, eyes bright with inner greed. Here beat and pulsated the heart of the renown richest port on earth. To the fascinated Victoria it was like being surrounded by a world only imagined in fairy tales.

Niles guided the carriage past noisy boisterous gaming houses, whose crafty proprietors gleaned a wealth by false assurances of a win with the turn of a hand, which seldom occurred.

Taverns spewed forth drunken customers who reeked of foul odors as they staggered onto the streets: eyes and brains glazed and fired by the rotten Dill Devil, their bodies burning with fevers wrought by the devil's potion.

Brothels, closed doors stimulating imaginations of mysteries beyond, beckoned. Some bore balconies where harlots in paint and scanty garments enticed male minds with promises of joy for a price. Kleet lies behind one of those doors, Niles mused to himself, and snapped the reins to hasten the horse.

Their carriage entered the square where a slave auction was in progress. The blacks, stripped to the minimum coverage, waited in chains for their turn on the block. Prospective buyers inspected the muscular builds for breeding purposes or hard labor. In the midst the auctioneer continued his monotonous chant. His job was to drive for a higher bid on each subjective Negroid being offered up for servitude.

Victoria pointed a finger toward a sturdy post in the middle of the square. "What are they doing over there?"

A handsomely built, whip scared black, hands bound, waited beside it. He was being prepared for the lash at the hands of a muscular white man of mixed descent. The flogger laughed with obvious glee at the prospect. Clutched in his fist was a vicious leather whip. A cat-o-nines quivered from its tip.

"That's where I met Toro," Niles answered, mouth set in a grim line. "Care to watch them carry out the sentence?"

Her face blanched. "No! Take me where I won't even hear it. Now I understand Toro's blind devotion to you. How can anyone be so inhumane!" Niles gave a sharp snap to the reins and sent the carriage swiftly onward.

They jogged past more markets. Their nostrils picked up assorted pleasing aromas of smoked and pickled meats, lumber, tar, molasses, rum, foodstuffs and tangy spices. Farther along prominent structures of the island became visible. Niles used this opportunity to point out the palatial Governor's Mansion, the Audiencia, the Exchange and the magnificent Saint Paul's Catholic Church.

They crossed the dry moat that connected the overcrowded cay to the main body of the island. Inland they headed into the area of plantations and smaller farms. Niles inhaled deeply of the clear air of the countryside. Relaxed against the seat the pair passed orderly citrus groves, mansions and mud and wattle houses. Slaves in cotton fields glistened with sweat, where they labored under the surveillance of foremen, whips in hand.

Niles paused intermittently to glean news from acquaintances along the road. The islanders' main concern, he learned, was fears of an invasion by sea from the French. Gunners at the forts were on twenty-four hour alerts. The Governor had dispersed his men throughout the island to ferret out spies. The islanders feared the entire island might turn into a bloody powder keg overnight. Niles' uneasiness increased.

Much as he hated the intrigue and dishonesty of the waterfront, if trouble broke he knew it would be wise to be near the *Pearl* come nightfall. Therefore, he chose to turn the carriage and return across the moat. He looked back and was possessed by a strange premonition he would never return. An omen the French would soon overtake Jamaica? Although he tried to dismiss the thought the depressing possibility persisted.

Returning to the port area they passed a variety of shops where craftsmen plied their trades. When night took over the sandspit the panorama changed. Soon a nocturnal throng of revelers threatened to overflow the waterfront beyond its capacity. Streets became a glutinous sea of humanity. Each inhabitant's sole intent was to indulge to the fullest of the profusion of vices available. Niles inched the horse through the shifting throng and tossed the reins to the owner.

Victoria clung to Niles' arm as they

pushed their way on foot past a nondescript assortment of sleazy peddlers who grasped and clawed for their attention. Among them, Niles noticed an exceptional increase in the number of self-made prophets. They shouted warnings of perdition, waved their arms, pleaded for each soul to repent before all damnation descended upon them. Seers were not unusual in the port. Several, who proclaimed they possessed powers of visions, always inhabited the streets. Their voices repeatedly foretold dire things of the future, which rarely came true.

Ordinarily, Niles ignored these fanatics. Tonight his ears refused to close them out. Somehow their terrible omens of destruction seemed to echo from the very cracks of the buildings. Irritated by the discomfiture created by their prophetic shouts, he shoved Victoria into a quaint eatery. Here they could escape the clamor, if only for a short while.
At a sound by the doorway, Niles glanced up from the delicacies set before them. Padre Jose entered, homespun robe wet with perspiration, dust of the streets covered its damp threads. Uninvited he took a chair at their table and sighed. "I see a long night ahead."

"By the sounds of it," Niles motioned toward the street prophets, "you have quite a bit of competition out there."

"Oh, those," he motioned a hand of

dismissal. "Their idle claims and howls don't bother me. I must say though, I find them quite interesting."

"Interesting? You, Padre?" Niles lifted a skeptical eyebrow.

"Yes, interesting," the padre nodded assurance. "It always amazes me how many versions they can invent to explain their powers of perception. But then---" he waved the idea aside, "I suppose when silver is passed across the hand it isn't hard. Money stimulates the imagination to keep the jingle alive."

"They get money for saying those things?" Victoria asked in disbelief.

"Of course, Child," he nodded. "It seems some people like to hear of their own damnation in advance; others pay because they look upon it as a service to the community, or to forestall a bad omen."

Niles changed the subject. "Tell me, what's all this talk about the French?"

The slight man leaned back as if to sort his thoughts and stared idly into space. Returning, he leaned forward to answer in a low whisper. "I'd say bad, my friend. If you can catch a breath of air in the *Pearl*'s sails, leave this place while there is time. Port Royal is not a good place these days. Many factions are astir, more than you know."

"Then suppose you bring me up on things."

"The entire island is a witch's pot about to boil over. In short: stagnant pools left by the floods unleashed an epidemic of fevers and malaria. Sickness swept the entire island like a run away fire. These quack doctors stir together worthless concoctions that only deceive the sick. More often than not, it kills the patient before the fever has a chance to take them. But," he held up an assured finger, "not, mind you, before the quacks receive their fat compensation for those fake medicinals."

His lined face, aged before its time, reflected deep sadness. "I attended more bedsides and burials in the back regions this week than I normally do in a year, too many the results of quacks." He helped himself to a tidbit from the tray in the center of the table. "And now the drought has turned our economy upside down, the French are ready to attack and we're infiltrated with spies."

Niles signaled and a waiter appeared. "Bring another plate for Padre, if you please."

Padre's hand shot up to motion the suggestion aside. "No, no, Lad. I must be on my way."

"You also must eat to sustain yourself. Fill your innards while you bring me up on the news. After all," he chuckled, "if the prophets are right, this may be our last meal."

"Miseries to those dreamers!" Padre scoffed. "If I believed their hopeless predictions I'd given up on mankind long ago." He heaped a plate high, grateful for the sumptuous free meal to fill his shrunken stomach.

"However," he reflected between mouthfuls, "they aren't entirely wrong. Who can say my day, or even your day, will not end tomorrow? When I walk out of here someone might sink a knife in my back. And you, Niles, may not cheat the heavens of your presence many more times." He paused to laugh in jest, but the eyes reflected no humor. Cautiously he glanced about, then leaned closer. "Tell me what happened out there in the *Sea of Lost Ships*?"

He listened to the details of the escape from Doubleface and Ramolo and nodded. "That confirms Ramolo is no longer a matter of consideration. Doubleface remains. One thing I do know, he has not given up. You have beaten and outwitted him; he is not one to take it lightly. To save face he must try again. This time he'll insure his success one way or another."

"I have no cargo on board. What can he hope to gain, aside of the ship, itself?"

Padre threw a meaningful look toward Victoria. "It's a matter of principle. *The Sea Pearl* always presented a challenge. His foolish ego feeds on reputation and prestige. He feels a need to add you to his list of conquered. As for cargo," the eyes beneath the lowered lids again slid in the lady's direction, "it takes many forms. One piece, which we will not discuss at this time, was not sold at the auction."

The priest mopped a faded sleeve across his forehead and motioned toward the street. "Take a look out there. The people pant like animals running in a pack. Their rabid brains are crazed with passionate fevers, wild and threatening. It's as if an evil specter hovers over the port; a specter that lusts for an eruption of such magnitude as to ravage the entire harbor; an evil that will leave nothing but death and destruction in its wake---"

"Now you sound like those insane soothsayers," Niles chided, himself disturbed by his friend's worried countenance.

"Who can say the works of the mind, Lad? They get paid to instill fear. I offer comfort for free. Yet however we work, we both serve the Master." Suddenly he stirred and brightened. "Blamed if my head doesn't sound like it's down with the fevers along with the rest of them. It's time I am on my way."

He rose from the chair with an effort. "Somewhere out there in that reeking, stumbling, cavorting street of the devil a desperate soul may need me." They watched the brown robe disappear through the doorway. A shudder passed through Niles, much as when he looked back at the moat.

"The Cathedral you pointed out today," Victoria drew his attention, "is it Padre Jose's church?"

Niles laughed. At the moment it seemed a hilarious, ironic joke.

"What's so funny?" she asked, confused by his reaction to her simple question.

"Nothing," he sobered. "You see, they excommunicated him long ago from the priesthood. They don't agree with his methods and beliefs. Padre Jose doesn't have a church of brick or stone. His is more magnificent than any constructed by man."

"I don't understand."

"Since his expulsion from the fold he has devoted his life to all classes of mankind. He gives his services to everyone: from the pitiful creature in the gutter, to the mighty in their mansions. All are equal in his heart. No one even knows his priestly name. Everyone calls him Padre Jose, because it's easy to remember.

"He suffers mockery, is beaten, cursed and condemned; yet he doggedly continues on his way to spread comfort wherever he's needed."

"It must be a very hard life for an old man."

"Old? He's only two years older than I am!"

"But he looks---"

Niles turned serious with remembrances of the past. "Like he says, he's seen too much suffering in his years." Suddenly he rose and added with agitation, "I've eaten enough. Let's get out of this waterfront hellhole. We'll return to the ship as soon as I make one more stop."

Outside an old hag, shriveled by time, crouched in a protective niche where two buildings butted together. Her twisted arthritic fingers reached out to clutch at Victoria's skirts. "Your future, my lady---cross my hand with silver," she cackled in a cracked voice. "I tell of riches, fortunes that await you!"

Niles struck the hand free of the fabric and scowled at the insolence shown by this remnant of street scum. "Who are you, beggar, to lay your filthy hand on this lady!"

"Wait, Niles," Victoria tugged at his arm. "Please, I would like to hear what she says."

"Victoria," he shouted above the calamitous street din, "I'm surprised to see you fooled by such fraudulence. Fakes like her only fabricate deceptive presages to get their hands on your money." He looked down and saw the anticipation that danced in her face and relented. "I must admit, a prophetess who uses fire presents a new twist to an old game."

Multicolored flames licked upward from a clay bowl set before the hunched figure. The decrepit woman bent closer to peer intently at the pair before her. The dark eyes glittered with greed as she appraised the flawless pearls Niles dropped into her outstretched hand. The shriveled face cracked in a grin of satisfaction that displayed an irregular row of stained and rotten teeth. The hand quickly flew to secret the treasure somewhere within the mysterious folds of her tattered garments.

"Now, my lady," she descended upon her prey with glee. "A coin, press a coin to your lips and make a wish. That's right. Drop the coin into the magic bowl. The fire Gods shall reveal your future to me."

Victoria dropped the coin, heard it strike the bottom of the bowl. With surprising agility the old prophetess flicked mystical powders from a small vial onto the flames. Instantly the miniature inferno leaped with a roar into the air. Victoria quickly stepped back to avoid the flames.

With a wild wave of arms the hag began to mutter and wail to draw the unseen spirits. Then she settled down to stare into the conflagration, oblivious to the couple before her. Niles began to think his pearls, safely in her possession, the forgetfulness was deliberate. He was about to press onward when the dry lips began to move. The hands lifted to points at either side of the flames.

"I see a lovely dark haired lady---very unhappy---mind troubled." Suddenly, as if touched by the flames, the hands flicked and the beady eyes brightened. "Aha," she exclaimed and almost pounced upon the imaginary fire encircled vision. "I see another lady---a rival?" She paused to glance up momentarily toward Victoria. Her attention, as if called, immediately returned to the flame. A furrow deepened across the creased brow. "She is rich, a schemer surrounded by much mystery. Do not fear, she desires something more." Immobile, she stared intently into the yellow-blue flame. The piercing eyes sought the heart and soul of the fire a long moment.

"I see a tall dark man. A red coat with many jewels---jewels upon his chest---he stands between two women. A cloud of secrecy flows between him and one of the ladies---he is worried."

Again she retreated into silence and stared. "Your wish will come true ---I see you in the arms of---" Victoria trembled with excitement.

"I hear noise---" the hag cocked an ear to the flames and listened. "A strange swirl. A dark angry swirl like I never saw before---he shelters you in his arms---the noise," she pressed her hands over her ears and cringed with intense agony. "The noise is deafening me!"

Suddenly the eyes flew wide with horror.

"No!" she screeched, and sprang to attack Victoria. "Go away! Leave! Remove your evil from this place!"

Niles responded swiftly. He jerked the woman back and threw her against the building before she could inflict injury to Victoria. The bowl rolled on the ground, spewing a trail of fire. Huddled in her crouched position by the wall, the hag retrieved the pearls. With all the force her aged body could muster, she flung them at Victoria.

"Take your seeds of Satan. Woe to me that touched them!" She grabbed the hot bowl from the ground and ran through the crowd as if the devil himself snapped at her heels.

Trembling, Victoria clung to Niles. To dispel her fears, he soothed, "Didn't I tell you? They're all a little mad."

"Niles, I'm scared. What did she see that frightened her so?"

"Forget it. She's old and well practiced in her art. Competition is strong here; it takes a good act to draw attention. Come along, we still have the other call to make."

They moved on and entered the most exclusive establishment in all Jamaica. Victoria's fears quickly dissipated. She stared in awe at the elegance of this oasis of vice and pleasure. Niles watched her face with amusement. Her eyes danced with excitement upon seeing for herself the flow of jewels, gold, and silver exchanged across the gaming tables and counters. An intoxicating flush rose to her cheeks amid the noise, music, color and riches. Two crystal goblets filled with the finest Madeira of the house immediately appeared at their table. If she were perplexed because no payment was made, it was soon forgotten.

Young brown skinned prostitutes of mixed bloodlines, faces painted, plied their trade among boisterous customers. They slinked their slim tantalizingly attired sensuous bodies against first one man then another. Red rouged lips bespoke of honey that waited to be tasted. Full firm breasts that rose and fell begged for the touch of a man. Slender hips swayed and beckoned for the caress of any hand capable of the exorbitant price. The nymphs signaled silent promises of ecstasies and retreated to secluded rooms with their prey.

An exquisite serpentine form, sensuously endowed with divine features and slinky movements, extricated herself from sweaty hands to slither alongside Niles. Her pungent sweet perfume permeated the air about the table. Victoria watched the familiar advances being made toward him by this enviable creature. She squirmed, discomfited with jealousy. If this is Nicole, she thought, is it any wonder she has captured his heart?

The intruder melted onto his lap, entwined an arm around his neck, her rosy lips brushed his, coaxing, coaxing. A jeweled hand slid teasingly along his face, feline fingers slithered into his hair. One hand, brazenly suggestive, roved along his thigh. She purred with a liquid tongue too soft for anyone except

Niles and Victoria to hear.

"What lovely bauble have you brought me this time, my brave captain?"

Niles' heart went out to the flushed Victoria, obviously embarrassed by this display of seduction. He could do nothing about her discomfort---not until the game was over, the message conveyed.

Suddenly the temptress sprang like a cat and hissed in rebuke. The crowded room, assuming he had been rejected, roared with amusement. The seductress, with a haughty lift of one shoulder, melted among the revelers amid jeers and lewd comments.

A bulky hulk of a man leaped with surprising agility atop a stool to command attention. He thrust a slopping tankard at arm's length above the heads. His voice boomed through the haze of the smoke filled room.

"A toast to Captain Niles Brett, captain of *The Sea Pearl*! Second best captain on the Main, the best being ME!" The exaggerated laugh which followed held an edge of sarcasm that belied his boisterous statement.

"Who's that?" Victoria inquired of Niles.

"That," he replied with forewarned emphasis, "is Doubleface, himself."

"I don't understand. You said he---"

"Wait until he turns his head," he cautioned, amid the tinkle of crystal and thunk of heavy tankards in response to the call.

Doubleface leaped down to forcibly elbow his bulk through the sea of bodies. When the scarred twisted face came into full view Victoria visibly recoiled. Tankard lifted, he bellowed, "Now for the rest of my toast. May your guts rot in the gutter fires of hell, Captain Brett!"

He leaned forward with bleary eyes that bulged and rolled in their sockets. A huge grimy fist reached out to where Victoria cringed. "And what be this little wench you hide?"

Niles rose to intercede, ice shattered from his words. "Lay a filthy hand on her and I'll see you lose it!"

They faced each other: eye to eye, tensed legs spread in readiness. The space between crackled with animosity.
Every head turned.

Scarcely a breath was drawn.

Dead silence covered the room.

All movement stopped. The witnesses waited for the outcome of this long anticipated confrontation between the renown rivals.

Doubleface weighed his odds through heavy slitted lids, while his fingers nervously twitched near his weapons. The air released from his lungs. The broad shoulders relaxed and he reverted to a nonchalant pretense to save face.

"No hurry," he shrugged. "Doubleface will take her at his will in due time." One curled fist scrubbed against his tangled beard while a finger of the other hand waggled toward Niles. The scarred lips curled. "The Lost Ships area saved your hide this time, Captain." he sneered. "We'll see how your luck holds under different circumstances. Mark my word, *The Sea Pearl* will soon be MINE!" He shot an ominous look to Victoria. "And her cargo as well!" Tossing a last warning over his shoulder, he melted back into the revelers.

"What a repugnant crude man!" Victoria grimaced.

Niles, repulsed by the atmosphere and clientele urged, "Come, let's get back to the ship where it's quiet."

As they picked their way to the shoreline, she asked, "Are you worried? About Doubleface, I mean."

"Not especially. He's tried to take the *Pearl* before. I reckon he'll keep on until one or both of us are killed." She shuddered with the thought.

"At present, I have more urgent matters on my mind. Now that we have circulated and been seen on shore, we'll go aboard, change into dark clothing and return to keep our other appointment."

After changing and concealing his weapons about his person, he surveyed Victoria. "The jewelry must go," he said. "The slightest reflection would draw attention to our movements in the darkness."

"You sound so mysterious. This must be a very unusual appointment."

"No more so than any other time we anchor in Port Royal," he answered, as he guided her through the door.

"May I ask whom we are to meet at this secret rendezvous?"

He bent to kiss her parted lips in the moonlight, caressed her long hair and felt its silken texture flow beneath his fingertips. Gazing deep into her eyes he whispered,

"Nicole."

Her heart stopped; a smothered gasp escaped her mouth. She struggled to withdraw. "Victoria, don't pull away," he tightened the arm about her. "She has been a dark spot on your mind the entire voyage. I didn't feel it necessary, under the circumstances, to explain. You wouldn't have believed me anyway. Now it's time to show you the truth." He traced the lines of doubt within her face with a forefinger and added with a smile, "I think you will meet with her approval."

"B---but Niles," she continued to struggle, powerless against his strong arms. "Surely, you can't expect me---"

"Not only expect, but insist. I want you to see her and learn what she means to me."

"I have a very good idea," she responded with petulant resignation. "The disappointment is my own fault. I should have realized from the moment we met you would return to your personal life."

"Half true," he agreed. "Tonight we shall put this misunderstanding to rest."

"Is she pretty?" her eyes lowered, embarrassed by her own precociousness.

"To me, the most beautiful lady in the world."

"And rich, I suppose?"

"Very," he assured with a nod. "Her wealth is the envy of everyone on the island. However, personal values do not hinge on whether one has or has not. Take Padre Jose. He's penniless, yet one of her closest, dearest friends. In a sense, they feed each other to exist."

"You sound mysterious again."

"Come. You shall understand it all before this night is out."

"No," she shook her head and stepped back. "You were right all along. I am only a passenger and should know my place. It was foolish of me to think otherwise. I cannot compete with her beauty or her wealth. I have no funds to my name. Go to her. When we sail, I shall step out of your life at the Colonies---"

"Maybe. Right now you will accompany me to her place. As for you," he held her close and buried his face in the softness of her hair, "I need you more than ever." Desire welled from the depth of his being. When he spoke her tresses muffled the hoarseness that crept into his voice. "We must hurry if we are to take advantage of darkness before the moon rises."

CHAPTER FIFTEEN

On shore, he assisted her to alight from the small landing craft and, taking her hand, began to snake through the dark alleys and between buildings until he reached a narrow opening behind Nicole's establishment.

Quickly he darted into it, Victoria in tow. A short distance away, he entered the building through an unimpressive door. Inside waited a long hall with several doors. Without hesitation he headed for the one at the far end. Stopping before it, he tapped out a signal. A female voice called out from within. Victoria drew back, hesitant, as he took her arm and ushered her inside.

A flash of scarlet rushed forward. "Niles!" Outstretched arms enfolded him in a crushing embrace. "I'm so relieved you are safely home!" She gripped his shoulders and held him at arms length. "We almost gave you up for lost." His hand in hers, she led him into the room. "I must say, I was really worried when Doubleface arrived and reported your disappearance in the Devil's Sea."

He glanced with amusement at Victoria's shocked expression. She had not expected to see a poised, regally erect, middle-aged woman wearing the very gown which was the object of her jealous torment.

"You said we were to meet Nicole---" she whispered. He nudged her into silence.

"I heard an unfamiliar bell enter the harbor," Nicole continued. "Since I didn't know about your new acquisition, I didn't associate it with your arrival. What a lovely quality of tone! Almost as if it spoke from the very depths of the sea itself." Victoria continued to stare, bewildered.

To her astonishment the stately lady stepped forward, took Victoria's hands into her own and smiled. "Please forgive me for being so ungracious and rude to a guest. I am Nicole. Welcome to Port Royal, my dear, such as it is." She motioned jeweled fingers toward the heavily draped windows that muffled the street noise. "Oh yes, I have heard about you. There isn't much I don't hear, as Niles can attest." She paused to cast an impish eye in his direction and added, "And that includes a few things even he doesn't seem to know as yet."

Niles could see the well-proportioned

lady impressed Victoria. The trim figure, endowed with the fullness of youth, retained a beauty that defied the lines of age. Although capable of stirring the emotions and imaginations of seamen, her desirous sensuous body was never for sale at any price.

The past she kept shrouded in mystery. Niles knew somewhere in years gone there was a man, one man. To him she gave her heart and soul. What happened no one knew. Nor did she allow anyone to take his place in her heart.

All anyone could say for certain was that one day she appeared in port and started a business from scratch. Her aim was to supply the finest quality girls, food, and spirits to fulfill every desire of lust hungry men in from the sea. Diligent and shrewd, she built herself an empire on the small sandspit. Here she ruled with the hand of a queen, for queen she was, to those who knew and loved her; a knowledgeable and powerful enemy to those who chose to oppose her.

Her hired spies, planted throughout the sand spit, were her ears and eyes. Nothing stirred in the port that escaped her knowledge. Her operation was so tightly guarded no one knew Captain Leyden, Niles, nor Padre made any contact with her.

"Oh yes, and I also heard about Ramolo.

A pity. I watched you both grow to manhood. But then," she shrugged, "it doesn't surprise me he went over to the Spanish. He was different from the rest of us. Important people and position always impressed him too much." For a long moment she fell silent while she indulged in the luxury of meditating on the past.

Niles, too, remembered. He was a young boy when Nicole extended a motherly wing. With love she not only helped rear him, but nutured him with a set of morals as well. After Captain Leyden took over *The Sea Pearl*, she showed as much interest in its successful operation as anyone did---with good reasons.

Nicole, along with Captain Leyden and Mr. Silvas, put up the money to purchase the *Pearl*. This made her equal in ownership. She also held a genuine interest and affection for her partners. Her own profits depended on the success of the venture as a whole.

Although she no longer maintained any share of ownership, the secrecy of their meetings continued. It was insurance for the safety of the ship and all those who sailed on her. Now, even as she once did for Niles, she was spreading protective wings toward Victoria. His attention was drawn back from its reverie when she quickly returned to her usual vibrancy.

"Come, we have much to discuss and time is short." She guided Victoria into a room furnished in the height of luxury. The red gown rustled with her graceful movements. Over a shoulder, she called out, "Padre, pour us a drink."

If anyone else viewed the scene, it held all the elements of a happy reunion among old friends. The crispness of her words, however, indicated to Niles there were more serious matters on her mind.

She lifted her crystal goblet in salute. "A toast to our Captain Brett and *The Sea Pearl*! May the lovely tones of her recently acquired bell forever echo through the harbor of Port Royal!" She sipped of the wine, then reverted to more urgent matters.

"It's time we get down to business. First, before I forget," she drew the gold locket from the low cut bosom of the vivid red gown and handed it to Niles. A baffled expression crossed Victoria's face. "Surprised?" Nicole asked. "No need. The girl in the tavern is one of mine. Very good at deception. It's very simple, really. Niles puts a message inside the locket. In this case, when to expect him. He slips it to her and she, in turn, brings it to me.

Victoria eyed them dubiously. "B---but I didn't see it change hands."

"Of course not. Nor did anyone else with prying eyes." She turned to Niles. "I see you remembered my penchant for red, as usual. Bless you for the lovely gown. Although in no way are you obligated to always bring me gifts from far away ports. I must say, your Toro certainly enjoys knowing you trust him to make the delivery." With brisk step she seated herself with a congenial smile behind a massive desk, a clear signal she was about to express her mind. Niles leaned forward.

"My people are busy as ants in a honey pot. Even so, I still don't have all the details for you. Perhaps because the parties involved haven't decided on concrete details themselves. The drought, rains, fevers and now so many stranded in port has made things difficult. This place is a regular hornet's nest to move about in. Very risky, dangerous. Hard to sort rumors from facts without arousing suspicions."

"So I've heard," Niles nodded.

"This much I do know. Doubleface, you want to watch close, very close," she said, and delivered a meaningful look to Niles. "As you know, he's wanted the *Pearl* for so long it's an obsession." She paused for a discreet glance toward Victoria. "Now another fire is added to his coals."

"He knows in a fight he doesn't have a crew capable to take over the *Pearl,*" Niles interjected.

"True," she agreed. "Not by himself, that is. My informants tell me he conspires with Captain Donnergut of the *Silver Cross*. Wants to join forces. Between them, Niles, *The Sea Pearl* stands in grave danger. Your men, greatly outnumbered, would not have a chance."

She paused for another sip of wine. "Quite frankly, as many times as he failed in the past, I'm amazed he didn't come up with this strategy long ago. Then again," she shrugged, "he's not very bright. Nor is it easy to find anyone gullible enough to throw in with him. Other captains know he cannot be trusted to stick to any agreement. Donnergut is new to the game. He's unfamiliar with the many malicious conspiracies that surround this port. He could be easily swayed by Doubleface's talk of power.

"If I know Doubleface, he will use him and give nothing in return. Or, his twisted mind may think once the *Pearl* is taken there is nothing to stop him from taking over the *Silver Cross*, as well.

"One thing you must never forget," she raised a jeweled finger in warning, "you are from the bucaner faction. Doubleface and

Donnergut are privateers, pirates in every sense of the word. Their minds think differently. Among boucaners there is honor. No such thing exists among privateers.

"From what I gather, you could use a little less honor. However, that is another matter and has nothing to do with the discussion at hand." Niles wondered what she meant by this insinuation but elected, for the moment, not to question.

"Meanwhile, Doubleface sounds too confident for comfort," she continued. "He openly boasts his intentions. Some people along the waterfront have already laid wagers on the battle."

"He mentioned his ambitions in the tavern today," Niles volunteered. "But didn't implicate Donnergut. I, too, got the impression he sounded more assured than in threats of the past."

"Confident, he is," Nicole nodded emphatically. "Why not? How can they lose? He has a sure thing and knows it."

"The soldiers and volunteer militia are out in full force in anticipation of the French," Niles calculated, brow furrowed in thought. "Thereby, under the cannon of the forts, if they attack in the harbor they'd cut their own throats. With no wind, we can't set to sea.

This buys us some time---"

"Time for what?" Nicole pressed. "To work up a strategy to counteract their numbers?"

"I don't know---" his voice trailed off. "As you always told me, tomorrow is another day. A lot of things could happen between now and then. For the present, dire as it may seem, I say take one day at a time."

"Too bad you haven't listened closer to what I told you," Nicole grinned, tongue in cheek. Niles, confused by the unexpected statement, was unable to grasp her implication.

"Before we move on to a new subject would you bring an aging lady another drink, Niles? I see Padre slipped away to the streets again. Perhaps he'll hear more information for us."

With a sigh she leaned back in her padded chair. "I often wonder whatever I would have done over the years without that quiet man. I can always count on him to relay the secret undercurrents of the port to me. He's simply invaluable to my operation."

"The door swung both ways, didn't it?" Niles reminded. "In exchange for his consistent gleanings of information you provided a safe haven for him."

"Let's not forget to mention his service as my intermediary with *The Sea Pearl,*" she insisted. "If the opposition ever discovers our association we all have a lot to lose."

"If I may," Niles interrupted, "what did you mean about listening to myself?"

Nicole stared absently across the room with rouged mouth pursed. She debated how best to answer the question. Finally she looked directly at him. "I am a blunt person, Niles. I see no use to tiptoe around on this matter any more than any other subject. In the short time while Ramolo was with us,until Captain Leyden deposited him where he could return to his people, the Captain and I tried to guide and instill in both of you boys honorable traits to live by. You never disappointed either of us. This time I feel you are wrong, very wrong.

"Granted, honor is a precious attribute. If we possess it, we take pride in ourselves. However, the value diminishes when personal honor affects or hurts another. Sometimes pride in self clouds our hearts. When that happens honor becomes as a tarnished coin; the rich gleam is lost."

Niles shook his head. "I fail to understand what this has to do with the *Pearl*---"

"Nothing. I'm not speaking of the ship, Niles. Tomorrow there may not be a ship. I speak of your personal life. Answer me something. Padre informs me you insist on setting sail for the Colonies. Why?"

"Because I gave my word to Victoria's father and---"

"Niles," she stirred with impatience, "remember when you were a young lad? More than anything you wanted to be at Captain Leyden's side when he put out to sea. He wanted you to stay ashore and learn a safe, respectable profession. Heartbroken, you begged, pleaded with me to talk to him, make him understand how you felt. I intervened. Convinced him to change his mind." She leaned forward whilst her eyes sought and held his.

"How would you have felt to watch him sail away while you remained behind? Think deeply, Niles. Remember the torment and despair you felt? How profoundly you hurt? How unloved? The sense of utter rejection and betrayal? Agony cried out from the very depths of your young soul."

Niles shifted in discomfort and stared down at his boots. "Yes, I remember very well."

"Then pray tell me, why this stubborn insistence on the Colonies?"

"I gave my word to---"

"Gave your word to a dying man!" she cut in with exasperation. "Kleet told me the whole story. Oh yes, don't look so surprised. I have my ways to learn what's going on. Has it occurred to you the dying man was expressing his wish for the future happiness of his daughter? At the time, that happiness to him seemed to lie in a new life in the Colonies. While you dwell on honor aren't you missing the point of his request? Might he have said, 'Take my daughter where she can find freedom and happiness'?"

Stirred by anger, she rose to pace the floor. "How can you even think to put this lady ashore in the Colonies? Left there to fend for herself she'll have only painful memories to sustain her. Is your word worth the price you force upon her?"

With practiced discipline and a ragged sigh she returned to the chair. Voice lowered she began to tell the secret she carried within in her own heart. "Once I was left safely on a shore. Each day I waited and watched the empty sea. His ship never returned. Time forced me to pick up the pieces of what remained of my empty life. It happened a long time ago, but the ache remains with me."

She fell silent taking a few minutes to compose herself. Misty eyed with the memory, she asked, "And what of you, Niles? Can you bear to sail away, leave your heart behind?" Niles' hand sought Victoria's. Nicole gave a knowing nod. "A woman of my experience can see you love her. I can look in her eyes and tell where her heart and happiness lies. Please, don't throw away the most precious thing in your lives, your love for each other. Believe me, once you have loved another, life can be very lonely alone." Again she retreated into silence to visit her memories.

"I'm sorry," she stirred. "But it galls me when men can't see beyond the wind in their sails. I don't want you to make a regrettable mistake. Think it over very carefully, Niles. Don't waste too much time, either. One never knows what turn life may take tomorrow or the next day. All we can do is drink of it while we live."

She rose, smoothed the folds of the gown and touched her fingers to the meticulously groomed hair. "It's late. If we are away from the public eye too long people will become suspicious of our whereabouts."

As the young couple prepared to leave Nicole suddenly rushed forward. She clasped their hands in hers, gripped firmly, face sober, without words, as if to convey a message through touch. Almost, Niles thought, like a last farewell blessing. Why?

Niles and Victoria furtively retraced their steps through the night darkened streets. Nicole's words kept echoing in his mind, rang in his ears, followed him each step. 'How can you put this lady ashore to fend for herself---your word worth the price
---can you leave your heart behind---very lonely alone---what turn life may take---drink while we can---'. His eyes traced the outline of Victoria's shadowy figure ahead. In the darkness he was struck by an unexpected revelation.

No longer did he view her as an insignificant person, a passenger. She became part of his being. Someone who belonged with him and him only. A precious life to be loved, treasured and protected. Never before had he experienced this unique sense of oneness with any woman.

Nicole's stern words hit him full face. Hiding behind honor he had denied the truth from himself. The moment Victoria floated into her father's office he had lost his heart. Thinking of Nicole's words, he envisioned Victoria in the Colonies waiting beside an empty sea. He shook his head to dissipate the unpleasant sorrowful vision.

At the second pier something ahead

jarred him back to awareness of danger. His arm shot out to stop Victoria's advance. Daggar in hand, silver blade glistening menacingly deadly in the moonlight, he stood tensed, ready to spring, voice cold as the steel in his hand. "Who's there?" he demanded.

The dark shape huddled in their small craft stirred. "Niles? Padre." The air released from Niles and he replaced the weapon. "Come, sit a while," Padre motioned. "I waited for you. Nicole's session lasted longer then usual."

"What happened?" Niles asked in jest. "Run out of poor souls to save over there?" Padre did not laugh.

Instead, he waited until the pair was seated before speaking in measured words. "Something bothers me." His position shifted to look out across the harbor. Moonlight reflected a deceptive illusion of peace over the constant undulation of the slow waves. As if from far away he continued, ignoring the other occupants.

"It's not good over there," he observed with a nod to indicate the waterfront filled with revelers. "Can't put my finger on it. I've a strange feeling, a very heavy feeling in here," he crushed a fist to his chest. "Something ominous beyond all comprehension hangs in the air."

Niles, concerned for his friend, speculated, "Could be you are upset over Doubleface's---" Padre raised a calm hand for silence.

"No, this is more, much more." The eyes squinted in deep concentration. He stared seaward as if trying to see something beyond his vision across the water. "The length of this waterfront is a crawling bloody nest of the Devil. Mark my word, Son, it will see its day of reckoning by God's hand, even as did Sodom. I fear the time draws very near."

"Now you really do sound like the street prophets back there," Niles chided.

"Bah!" the man motioned with impatience. "Such fools have prophesied doomsday for centuries. No, this ache is entirely within myself. Each day it grows stronger. Tonight I can scarcely live with the torment. The very air that surrounds us forebodes, warns, like a giant hand is about to descend upon us. I feel suffocated by it."

"It's the heat, stillness and humidity. Everyone is on edge."

"This is much greater. It waits out there, just waits." For a long while he remained silent, face turned to the sea, before he again spoke. "Run, Niles. Escape as fast as you can on *The Sea Pearl*. Take your lady and flee this horrible den of iniquity!"

"A bit difficult," Niles admonished, "with no wind to catch her sails."

Padre turned a haggard face. "If so much as a breath comes grab it and run. You must go before it's too late."

Niles peered closely at the agitated Padre Jose. He could see the man believed very strongly in what he said.

Abruptly the priest shifted and tore his attention from the eternal sea to face the pair. "It's you two I'm most worried about." Niles opened his mouth to object, but was silenced by the raised hand. "No. Allow me to speak my mind now. I may not see you again before you leave. This notion of the Colonies is a tragic mistake you'll both regret for the rest of your lives. Instead, take each other as one." He leaned forward and pleaded, "Accept the greatest gift of God---love. Everything else on His earth is unimportant." With gentle hands he clutched theirs with urgency. "Marry. Treasure each precious moment together while there is yet time. Draw comfort, hope, life and happiness from each other."

"Who will perform the marriage, you Padre?" Niles' voice sounded loud and harsh against the night after Padre's soft hushed reverent tones.

"Please, I beg you to listen to what I say, dear friend. Life is so very short, share your love while you yet live. No," he hung his head in sadness, "I no longer have authority in the sight of man to perform marriage rites. But," his palms turned upward in submission, "what is this ceremony created by mortal men and decreed by law? Nothing more than names written on paper, a means to keep a record of the populace. Babbled words nor paper are marriage in His sight. Only the bond, man and woman as one, seal the union in His eyes. Do you understand what I say?"

The intense eyes burned somberly into those of his two friends. "Go now to *The Sea Pearl.* I shall pray for wind to carry you out to sea. Think deeply on what I've said. Search your souls. Recognize truth, and deny your love no longer."

He waited until his passion cooled, then added with warm sincerity, "And may God bless you both. Now, I must bid you farewell and return to the streets and gutters." He lingered a moment, firmly gripped their hands, then disappeared among the shadowy haunts of the raucous waterfront.

Aboard the *Pearl* Niles looked down at the unusually still water of the harbor. His mind recalled the angry sea that crashed over their decks at the height of the icy voyage from

England; remembered their death struggle against the elements and Victoria's presence. And Nicole, what of her soul searching question? How would he feel after leaving Victoria at the Colonies? In his heart he already knew wherever he looked on *The Sea Pearl* he would see and feel the ghost of her presence. Her nearness would haunt him: the empty cabin, awakening from a dream only to find her no longer at his side. His imagination saw her suffering equal torment on that far away shore and his heart wrenched with the thought.

His preoccupation was interrupted by her voice at his side. "What are you thinking?"

"Several things: Nicole, Doubleface, Donnergut and Padre. Like him, I felt an eerie premonition the moment we made port. I tried to tell myself my apprehensions were caused by the threat of so many ships in close proximity. Later, when I heard of Doubleface's scheme, I laid it to that. Now you heard Padre' words. Like him, I still can't put my anchor on what it is. All I know is that something almost mystical waits out there," he said, and motioned a hand across the water.

"I don't imagine the old woman with her fire helped quell your uneasiness, either."

Niles sighed. "Who knows, maybe she did see something."

"Surely you don't believe that! You said yourself those street beggars only dream up sensational ideas to get money."

"True, I never believed anything they said in the past. This time, there are too many things which cannot be explained away. For instance, I'm certain she was genuinely frightened. It was no act. And Nicole---she hasn't talked to me like that since I was a young boy in need of a reprimand. When we left, did you notice she spoke as if she didn't expect to see us again? Now Padre Jose, normally a calm person who lends assurance to others, suddenly revealed his innermost anxieties and fears. It's enough to convince me my own intuitions have not been groundless."

"Like you said to Padre, it's this unbearable heat," she said and loosened the gown from her shoulders. "You can stand out here and meditate in the moonlight if you like. As for me, I'm going inside to put on something loose and comfortable."

"You'll suffocate in there."

"No more so than here. There's no air astir in either place."

"You're right," he nodded and turned to her. "We'll both go inside."

In the quarters he stripped the

perspiration soaked shirt and, bared to the waist with the exception of the ever present medallion, reclined onto his chair. Through the flame of a lucifer touched to the tip of a cigar, he watched Victoria. A loose airy robe accented the slender curves of the sensuous body. Head tilted back, she fluffed her dark wavy hair with slender tapered fingers and reached to light a candle.

"Don't," he stopped her movements in the dimness. "Darkness lends an impression of coolness. Let's talk a while."

"All right," she complied. "What shall we talk about?"

"Us," he answered and rose to stride to the small porthole. "I think Nicole and Padre are right. I never thought about our relationship quite the same as they expressed it tonight. Since then, I've searched my heart and agree with them."

The room remained silent before Victoria ventured, "If, as you say, you are convinced, why tell it to the window? Why not to me?"

Embarrassed by his cowardice in the face of a woman he turned. "I've never felt a love like ours before. It's very difficult to put into words what I want to convey." He returned to the chair, drew her down, and cradled her in his arms. The long silky hair he had grown to love cascaded across his bare shoulder and down one arm. With a hand he gently brushed the damp wisps from her forehead.

"Like she said, if you go ashore at the Colonies and I put back to sea, we'll both be miserable. I fought against loving you, but I must confess this is one battle I lost." He was glad she had not lighted the candle. It was easier to express himself in the semi-darkness.

"I closed my heart the entire voyage, refused to accept the truth. Now I find myself totally committed. I cannot imagine life without you beside me. From the very first moment I saw you, it's been liken to music in my life. I told myself I was only infatuated with your beauty; when the time to part came you would pass out of my life as easily as you entered. I know now I don't want to let you go."

His lips brushed hers and came to rest tenderly against a cheek. "I love you so much, my dearest. All that remains between us is for you to 'search your soul', to quote Padre." He kissed her gently and drew her close.

"I completed my soul search a long time ago," she breathed. "I tried to tell you, countless times throughout the voyage, how I felt. My happiness is here with you on the

Pearl. I would be only half a person in the Colonies, the other half far out to sea. I could never bear to watch you leave, never to return to me. Your face, your touch, everything about you would forever haunt me. I'd be an empty unfulfilled shell. Please, Niles, no matter what happens, let us stay together forever."

Her pleading eyes glistened moist in the shaft of moonlight that entered the porthole. His fingers slid slowly along her cheek as his head bent to embrace. An arm slid around his neck, hand on the back of his head, pressing his lips to hers in a hungry caress. At length, with reluctance, he withdrew and spoke slowly with a voice hoarse with desire.

"Time. Padre must surely have implied the speed of a lifetime. Nicole made me realize how misplaced was my blind stubborn insistence on manly honor. Already we've lost so many precious moments because of my error. For the first time I feel as if I'm really free to hold you, kiss you, give of my heart without reservations. Can you understand what I am trying to say?"

"Does this mean," she asked hesitantly, "you are not going to force me to go to the Colonies?"

"The Colonies can live without you, I can't."

"Niles," she relaxed and buried her head against his shoulder, "I've waited so long to hear you say that."

Head bent, he met her parted lips, crushed her to his bared chest. In the darkness he was aware only of the warmth that flowed through their embrace, pleasant touch of her skin and the heady dizzy sense of virile exhilaration.

"How shall we be wed?" she whispered close to his neck.

"I never did put much stock in fancy churches or their formalities. A seaman carries his church in his heart, as you saw with Captain Leyden. If, as they say, our God is great and powerful, I'm sure He is present without benefit of man made churches. Nor does He need formal words on legal papers."

"Do you suppose that's what Padre Jose tried to tell us tonight?"

"Beyond a doubt." His hand slid slowly down her back. It brought a shiver of anticipation through her body pressed close to his. They caressed passionately, hungry for fulfillment.

She withdrew and whispered, "Niles, to say I don't want you at this moment would be a lie. Even so, before we allow our passions to cloud our sensibilities let's be certain. We don't want any regrets to arise later to tarnish our love. Pour us each a Madeira. We'll take it out on deck, where we can calm our emotions and think with clear heads."

"Very sensible idea. As for me, I'm already sure, but what's a few minutes or hours, when we have an entire lifetime before us?"

At last for him it was no longer a matter of convictions. His entire outlook had undergone a change within the past few hours. Even so, he could use some time to adjust: time to admit his heart was lost now and forever to this enchanting woman; time for the last traces of walls between to crumble and disappear forever.

He passed a goblet to her and their fingers made contact for an instant. Then he slid an arm about the tiny waist and they strolled onto the main deck. Each swathed in own thoughts, neither spoke as they moved side by side among the shadows of the rigging.

Memories drifted across his mind: the icy deck and guide rope; the thunder of the main mast crashing in the height of the storm; Victoria's hands as they held bandages; the comfort he drew from her presence through the heart-wrenching burial of Captain Leyden.

He tasted again the passionate kisses that sealed their temporary relationship agreement on the beach. But most recurrent among all these memories was their closeness while they danced on the foredeck, isolated from the crew. He could still smell the clean fragrance of her, see silvery moonlight illuminate her face, even as it was doing now. His ears heard the distant music as the warmth of her body swayed together with his.

His emotions once again stirred within the intoxicating web of moonlight and shadows. It was difficult to resist the temptation to take her into his arms as he did then. Instead, he chose to stand, arm about her and gaze in dreamy silence toward the lights of port. With love by one's side silence, too, held its rewards of pleasure.

Silhouetted in the moonlight he felt an aura of peace settle over the *Pearl* like being enveloped in soft fog, isolated from turmoil, wrapped in a world of their own; a place where their very nearness transmitted more than words could ever say. He drew her close amid the tranquility, bent to meet her willing mouth, her arms responded in eagerness.

With a blissful sigh she whispered, "This doesn't help to clear our heads for serious thought."

He looked deep into her uplifted eyes.

"Any doubts?"

"None. And you?"

"None whatsoever."

"Our glasses are long since emptied," she stirred. "I'll take them to the cabin."

His grip tightened. "Don't leave," he begged, and enfolded her again. "After the torment we've been through I want to remain together like this to eternity."

"Do you know what I'd like tonight?"
"Name it, it's yours."

"Remember when you laid with me, comforted me through the storm?" He nodded. "As I see it, the storm between us ended this night and we've come through to a calm sea. Would you lie with me again, hold me, as you did then?"

"Since we've both confessed our love I can't see any reason to refrain. Tonight will be for all our lives, for all the days and nights we'll share forever."

Her head rested in the hollow of his shoulder. He lay beside her and thought on how well she expressed their tumultuous relationship. The storm of frustration he grappled with the entire voyage was now ended. His mind was at peace, her body warm against his. He caressed her closed eyelids. "You'll have no regrets?"

She nestled closer. "Mankind may judge us sinners, but if a love like ours is sinful, then I---"

Their parted lips met. He crushed her nude curvaceous body to his. Hearts closed against the world, they submitted to the ecstasy of sealing their love. Their passions soared as one, unrestricted among the heavenly galaxies overhead.

CHAPTER SIXTEEN

Niles awakened to a morning of steamy oppressive heat. Beside him Victoria remained asleep. He gazed at her dark hair swirled across the whiteness of the pillow. Her face in relaxed contentment, to his admiring eyes, was even lovelier than before. Taking care not to disturb her, he slipped from the narrow bed and drew on his clothes.

Out on the main deck the fiery sun greeted him with the promise of another day heavy with insufferable humidity. Not a breath of air stirred over the glassy sea. He stripped and plunged into the water to refresh himself. Ashore the port activity was more sluggish than usual; the energies of the inhabitants sapped by the constant days of discomfort.

Under the searing sun people drifted listlessly in and out of taverns and grog houses, each searching for a place of shade and the promise of something bracing to drink.

Victoria emerged, blouse draped carelessly off her shoulders in an effort to catch a breath of cool air. Together at the rail he slid an arm about her. "Regrets?"

"Not a single one," she replied, and nestled her head against him.

Toro approached the pair from behind. "Will you be going ashore, Cap'n?"

"No, Toro. Everything I want is right here." His eyes met Victoria's. "And Toro, notify the crew we have another captain sailing with us."

"Another cap'n, Sir?" the black face twisted in bewilderment.

"Or perhaps we shall address her as Missy Captain Brett. The Captain married us at sea last night."

The dark face broke into a broad pleased grin. "Yes Suh, Cap'n Brett! Toro know you be very happy. I go now, tell others." He backed away, bowed slightly, then broke into a joyful run.

"You know what that means, my love?" Niles teased. "If *The Sea Pearl* goes down, as joint captain it will be your duty to go down with me."

"I wouldn't want it any other way, Captain Brett," she snuggled closer. He hugged her to his side and thoroughly enjoyed their closeness.

"Today is June seventh, 1692. The first day to share our lives as one," he declared. He cocked an eye skyward. "And right about now the sun says it is 11:40 a.m. Cleve will spread our lunch soon."

"I'm not hungry," she murmured in contentment.

"As they say, you can't live on love," he urged. "I'll not have a co-captain who says she's too love stricken to eat proper."

"Yes, Master," she condescended, with a mirthful laugh.

Filled with contentment and happiness the pair leisurely strolled toward their quarters.

Suddenly Niles stopped.

He whirled around to face the shoreline.

His brow furrowed in question and apprehension.

All along the waterfront people were running in and out of establishments. Screams of panic and fear reached his ears. Pandemonium rapidly broke loose the entire length of the sandspit.

Victoria's eyes grew wide as she exclaimed, "What's happened?"

"I'm not sure. If it were an attack by the French the forts would retaliate. Wait---hear that rumble? It's---it's an earthquake! I should have expected it. They often suffer quakes after hot spells such as this."

The tremor ceased.

On shore the populace, believing the danger over, began to drift back to their various diversions. Assured it was only a minor alarm of no consequence, calm returned.

Removed from the noises of the port, however, Niles heard the ominous rumble return. Low at first, it quickly gained in volume. The convulsions of the earth's crust drew nearer. The water surface blackened and began to churn in anger. In the next instant it burst into violent waves that heaved and crested throughout the length of the harbor. The crew aboard *The Sea Pearl,* to avert being tossed overboard, clutched tightly to any means of support available.

Awestricken they watched the fast impending destruction.

The island, overtaken by the immense power of the upheaval, began to buckle and shift. Strata split apart with a deafening crack and roar. Long jagged chasms cut across the land surface, then like lethal jaws closed with a thunderous slam. Whatsoever fell into the deadly tomb, be it material or human, was forever buried.

Massive billows of ocher-gray sand dust spewed high into the air. They belched upward like clouds of swirling steam coughed from the very core of the earth. Within the dense roil of haze came the horrified screams and cries of stricken inhabitants.

Surge after surge the quake shook and tore at the very foundations of the island. A giant specter, it fought to wrench the port free of its roots, toss it aside, destroy it forevermore!

Caught within the catastrophic upheaval the people were left with no place to flee for safety. Like undermined sandcastles, prominent buildings crumbled before the onslaught. Below, panic-stricken people were buried alive beneath the rubble of dislodged bricks that tumbled down upon them.

Deep rents of the land surface brought a

roar to split the eardrums.

Whole streets and buildings were swallowed within the yawning chasms. Each successive upheaval added thunder, more destruction and more death. Thick wall sections plummeted downward crushing the victims below on impact. Erupting cobblestones, moments ago roadways, became eternal cemeteries. The dust and debris within the cloud increased in density. No longer could the sandspit be seen from the decks of the ships in the harbor.

The *Pearl* thrashed wildly and tore at her anchor. With a scream, Victoria clapped her hands over her ears, but the cries and shrieks of the dying could not be closed out. Again and again, long fissures split, closed, reopened, and crashed shut with whiplash swiftness. Huge chunks of landmass tore away and slid forever into the sea. A revengeful God had struck with a vengeance. The richest, wickedest port on earth was to be no more.

An eerie unfamiliar shudder passed through the timbers of the *Pearl*. It pitched wildly upon waves that had lost all direction. Most of the other ships, already wrenched free from their moorings, bobbed and tossed amid the froth and foam like so many discarded corks flung from bottles of Dill Devil. Many were thrown to crash against one another. The harbor became a cacophony of splitting wood and mass demolition.

As vessels sank, pirates and merchantmen alike jumped for their lives. Left to struggle for survival, their hands clutched onto any debris in an effort to remain afloat. Sadly, soon they too, were swallowed by the roll of foam topped waves. The anchor chain of the *Pearl* strained mightily against the twist and churn of the turbulent sea.

Niles caught a brief glimpse of Doubleface's ship being rammed by another. Under the powerful impact timbers crashed and caved. A huge gap appeared in her side. Water rushed in. She quickly listed and was claimed, along with so many others, never to rise again, by the gnashing dark waters. Wave after wave heaved and rolled to deluge the decks of the helpless *Pearl*. Niles wrapped one arm around the rail to increase his grip, the other tightened about Victoria to keep her from being swept overboard into the frothy turbulence. Victoria screamed in terror. "Help me, Niles. Help me!"

"Hang on!" he yelled.

She clung to him.

It was impossible to maneuver her to the safety of the cabin. Caught in their present situation any such attempt would prove futile.

Preoccupied with the struggle to save their lives, there was no time to give further attention to what was happening to Port Royal.

Amid all the death and destruction, he strained to maintain his hold on both the rail and Victoria. He gasped for breath, looked seaward and stared in horror!

A mammoth wall of water bore down with a force of consummation. Overwhelmed by the power of nature, he hunched his shoulders against the inescapable oncoming disaster. Desperate to shield her from harm with his body he flung his arms about his beloved. Towering high overhead the catastrophic tidal wave crashed over *The Sea Pearl*. In an instant it was swept into oblivion somewhere at the bottom of the Caribbean Sea.

THE END

EPILOGUE

Port Royal, Jamaica was once called Cagua Cay by its original inhabitants, the Arwak Indians. Under English rule it grew to become known as the richest wickedest port on earth. Ninety percent of the cay, along the base of a v-shaped limestone ridge, was formed of sand and silt. A cataclysmic series of earthquakes struck Port Royal at 11:43 a.m. the fateful morning of June seventh, 1692. The tidal wave that accompanied the quakes swept the sand and silt mass from the main body of the island, carrying everything thereon into the depths of the Caribbean Sea. Only approximately ten acres of mountainous area prevails today of a port that once overflowed with wealth.

Although over 2,000 souls perished in the disaster, many of the bodies were never recovered. Port Royal was never rebuilt.

Recent historical researchers have become involved in scientific charting and salvage operations in the area. They search for clues on the life and times of an era long buried in the seabed. But the sea is a jealous sea, it gives forth few of its treasures.

Only haunting memories and legends of

the thriving port and its people remain. These, too, are being lost to the sea with successive generations.

Once there was a legend that claimed on still nights when the sea is calm, a mellow resonance of a bell calls out from the depths. Some say it is the golden bell of *The Sea Pearl.* Others believe it is the bell of St. Paul's Cathedral, also swept away.

It has also been said that when mists are across the waters a phantom ship can be seen, mermaid on its bow, sails unfurled. Upon its deck stand a young man and his lady in passionate embrace.

ABOUT THE AUTHOR

Eileen Thennis spent her formative years on a South Dakota farm established by her German immigrant grandparents, who were among the first homesteaders in Dakota. At the age of fourteen she was left to fend for herself. She worked her way through high school working as a waitress, hotel cleaning girl, housecleaner and baby sitter.

After her marriage the couple spent ten years in northwest Florida along the shores of the Gulf of Mexico. With their two daughter and two sons they moved to Colorado where they lived for the next twenty-four years. They now reside in Texas.

Eileen has always been attracted to the

old sailing ships and her hobby is researching United States Indian and frontier history.

After her latest writing of her novels, ***Swing Low Silver Chariot***, and ***The Sea Pearl***, she is presently drafting yet another, tentatively titled, ***Carla.***

She has been published in a variety of genre in assorted magazines for thirty-seven years.

www.ingramcontent.com/pod-product-compliance
Lightning Source LLC
Chambersburg PA
CBHW020920020726
47495CB00002B/270